Eric Wilder

Black Magic Woman

Gondwana Press

Edmond, Oklahoma

Other books by Eric Wilder

Ghost of a Chance
Murder Etouffee
Name of the Game
A Gathering of Diamonds
Over the Rainbow
Big Easy
Just East of Eden
Lily's Little Cajun Cookbook
Of Love and Magic
City of Spirits
Primal Creatures

Gondwana Press LLC
1800 Canyon Park Cir. Ste 401
Edmond, OK 73013
gondwanapress@gmail.com

For information on books by Eric Wilder
www.ericwilder.com
www.gondwanapress.com

Front Cover by Higgins & Ross Photography/Design

ISBN: 978-0-9791165-7-5

Acknowledgments

I would like to thank Donald Yaw for helping me edit the book, and providing valuable input involving timeline and character development. Thanks to Higgins and Ross for their great cover, and Jovon Tucker for creating a memorable book trailer.

For Marilyn

Black Magic Woman

A novel by
Eric Wilder

Chapter I

There are more ghosts in New Orleans than just about any place on earth. I realized as much when I awoke with a start from a vivid dream. Something I couldn't quite remember left me disturbed even as the final dreamy image faded from my memory.

My cat was licking my chin, and I realized why. Early evening according to the clock by the bed, I'd been in a state of fitful sleep for more hours than I cared to count. After giving her a long stroke, I dragged out of bed and plodded toward the shower.

"Sorry, Miss Kisses," I said when I fed her on the balcony overlooking Chartres Street. "I know you're hungry."

A nip of winter chilled the back of my neck as I scraped the last of the cat food into her bowl. Noisy tourists, some already inebriated, passed on the sidewalk below. I tried to remember the purpose of the festivities as I returned inside to finish dressing.

Late December, football fans had already begun arriving in town for the upcoming Sugar Bowl at the Superdome. Mardi

Gras in the Big Easy is the world's largest block party. New Year's Eve runs a close second. A lifelong resident of the city, I usually stayed home and out of trouble. Sometimes I even succeeded.

Late afternoon sun shined through the window when I came down from my room above Bertram's bar, not immediately remembering what all the fuss was about. As I grabbed an empty stool, Bertram saw me and winked.

He was polishing a glass as he held court with a half dozen football fans. Breaking away from the noisy argument about who had the best team, he ambled over with a mile-wide grin. He poured a glass of lemonade for me from a pitcher he kept beneath the counter.

"Where you been all day?"

"Working," I said.

"Good, cause your rent's past due."

"Front me some more time. Business is a little slow right now."

"Yeah, yeah," he said. "Pay me when you can. I know where to find you."

"Your business is booming. Who's playing this year?"

"Who gives a damn? Ain't no better customer than someone whose football team's coming' off a ten game winning season. I guarantee I'll run out of beer before the night's over."

Lady, Bertram's collie, was also enjoying herself, tail drumming against oiled hardwood when I reached over the bar and gave her head a rub. Bertram poured himself a shot of Cuervo and quickly drained it. Forty-something, he had the dark eyes and complexion of a French Acadian. I was so used to seeing him gesture like a lunatic when he spoke, I'd forgotten to wonder if he could still talk if his hands were tied.

When one of the tables began calling the hogs, I thought a riot was going to break out. Bertram raked the trapper's hat off thinning hair, mopping his brow with a bar rag. His little mustache twitched as he rolled his eyes and started pouring three pitchers of Dixie.

"Right back," he said. "Gotta fan the flames."

Bertram returned with two empty pitchers, a handful of cash, and an even larger smile than before.

"The party never ends," I said.

"Amen to that, bro. You seen Mama Mulate since she got back from her cruise?"

I shook my head. Mama Mulate taught English at Tulane. She was also an authentic voodoo mambo. Some time ago, I had called on her when a potential client developed a problem he thought only the right spirits could explain. He was right. Mama had the answers to his questions, and the experiment had become an on-again, off-again partnership. She'd spent her summer vacation working as a rent-a-mambo on a cruise ship sailing out of New Orleans.

"She went to South Carolina to visit family when she returned from Jamaica. I haven't seen her in six months."

"She was here last night and banged on your door. You musta been someplace else."

"Guess so," I said, not admitting I'd been asleep and hadn't heard her knocking.

"You hear about Carla's mama?"

Carla Manetti was my sometimes girlfriend I hadn't dated in more than a year. Her mother was probably the best Italian cook in New Orleans. Carla had repeatedly accused me of liking her mother's lasagna better than I liked her. Though it wasn't true, I'd never had another girlfriend whose mom could cook like Mama Manetti.

"Something the matter?"

"Heart attack, I heard. They got her over in Oschner."

"Severe?"

"Hell, bro, there ain't no such thing as a good heart attack."

"When did this happen?"

"I just found out. You going to see her?"

"I'd already be there if you'd told me sooner," I said as I headed for the door.

The sun had set as my cab passed the old Metairie Cemetery; I barely saw the towering crypts and magnificent statuary. It wasn't the only cemetery in town, just the most impressive. Lights of the French Quarter behind me beckoned as the cabbie let me off at the main entrance to the hospital.

A tired woman at the information desk provided directions to Mama Manetti's room. I found the door ajar and entered without knocking. Distant neon flashing through open curtains briefly illuminated the dismal scene.

A widow, Carla was Mama Manetti's only child. I paused in the doorway, watching as she held her mom's hand. She'd changed little during our separation, her dark hair longer than before. She jumped when I touched her shoulder.

"Wyatt..."

"I came soon as I heard. How's Mom?"

Carla hugged me, burying her head against my shoulder.

"Asleep. We've had a long day. She finally passed out from exhaustion."

"Then you must be beat. When did you get here?"

"Last night."

Mama Manetti's soft snores melded with the hum of medical equipment and told me she was fast asleep.

"You look beat. Let's get coffee."

"But what if Mom wakes up?"

"She'll be fine till we get back."

Apparently having made the same observation, and needing a shot of caffeine, she didn't argue. After telling the duty nurse where we were going, we took the elevator to the cafeteria. Carla remained at the table while I went through the line. She tore into the chicken and rice I brought her as if she were starving.

"I wasn't expecting to see you," she said, nibbling on a piece of bread. "How you been?"

"Tolerable. You?"

When she smiled, I remembered how bright her teeth were, and that her eyes were a brilliant shade of green. Always thick and curly, her dark hair now sported a permanent. It somehow made her look younger than I'd remembered. Though not quite pretty, she had striking features that had immediately attracted me, and still did.

"You're such a liar, Wyatt Thomas."

"What?"

"I heard about your ex-wife dying, and your romance with the runway model. Sorry it ended so sadly for you."

4

"I'm fine. Same old Wyatt."

"You sure?"

"Battling a little depression, maybe."

Carla grinned. "What's new? You're the moodiest person I've ever met. You aren't drinking again, are you?"

"I fell off the wagon awhile back, but not for long. I'm onboard again. I'll be okay."

"Wyatt, you could keep a team of psychiatrists busy for a decade."

"Maybe I just need a pretty woman's hand to hold."

My words brought another smile to her face. "How many failed relationships have you had now? A thousand?"

I grabbed her hand and squeezed. "You know there's never been anyone else but you."

"Such a liar," she said, though without snatching her hand away.

"What about you? Seeing anyone new?"

"Jim Watts. Every now and then, at least."

"Who's he?"

"A chemistry professor at U.N.O.," she said.

Carla was the head librarian at U.N.O., the city's university near Lake Pontchartrain. I couldn't account for the momentary pang of jealousy her words invoked.

"Serious?"

"We're sleeping together if that's what you mean."

"That wasn't what I meant."

"Then what?"

"Nothing, really. What have the doctors said about your mom?"

"They don't know much yet. Aunt Beth is on her way from New Jersey."

"Aunt Beth?"

"Mom's sister. She married and moved away years ago."

Seeing her cup was empty, I got up from the table. "I'll get more coffee."

I returned with a large carafe and kept pouring until we'd drank every drop of the dark coffee.

"Thanks for coming," she said as we returned to the hospital room. "Mom still loves you, you know."

5

"No, I didn't."

"You liar."

I gave her no chance to settle back into the chair by the bed.

"Go home and get some rest. I'll stay with Melissa."

"You don't have to."

"I don't have to do anything. I'll be here when you get back."

Too exhausted to pass on my offer, she hugged me, and then disappeared into the hallway.

It wasn't just dim in the room anymore. Someone had turned out all the lights while we were gone, only the green glint of pulsating medical devices illuminating the room. I sat in a comfortable chair next to the bed, digital beeps, and steady drip of an I.V. soon lulling me to sleep. When a clammy hand touched my face, my eyes opened. It wasn't so much touch as a mild surprise that sent a chill shuddering up the back of my neck. When soft light flashed in my eyes, I wasn't sure if I were awake, or still dreaming.

A shimmering image stood at the foot of Mama Manetti's bed, lighting the dark room with a dull, blue glow. It was something not quite real. When I blinked, it didn't disappear. I tried to say something, but words clumped in my throat.

"Who are you?" I finally said.

"Someone who needs your help," the ghostly image replied.

The back of my neck and hands had become damp from the chill filling the room. The pale specter was dressed in clothes from an era long passed.

"Are you..."

"A spirit," the flickering image replied.

"What do you want from me?"

"Redemption."

"I don't understand."

"Yes you do. You cursed me. Now I am doomed to follow you forever. Unless..."

"Unless what?"

"Unless you lift the curse."

"What curse?"

6

"The one you had the voodoo man place on me."

He nodded when I said, "That's not possible."

"Oh, you cannot imagine how I wish that it were not."

"Who are you?"

The wraith reached toward me as his face began fading away into the darkness of Mama Manetti's hospital room.

"Zacharie Patenaude," he said, his words a dying whisper. "Have mercy on my soul."

Sometime later, I awoke holding Mama Manetti's hand. Morning sun had begun lighting a gray sky outside the hospital window. Melissa Manetti was sobbing, her face flushed as tears dampened her face. The door was still cracked, and someone shuffled past in the hallway outside the door.

"Melissa, why are you crying?"

"Wyatt, what are you doing here?"

"Carla was exhausted. I sent her home for some sleep and to change her clothes."

Melissa glanced at the I.V. and wiped her tears with the sleeve of her hospital gown.

"How long have I been here?"

"Going on two days. You apparently had a heart attack."

"I thought a mule had kicked me."

"Pretty much what happened. Carla will be back soon, and your sister Beth is on her way from New Jersey."

"Oh my God! I don't like causing trouble."

"No trouble. Now tell me why you're crying."

"I can't," she said, shaking her head.

"It's all right. You're in capable hands. You're going to be okay."

"That's not why I'm crying," she said. "I'm glad to see you. No one around lately to appreciate my lasagna."

"Carla said she's seeing a professor."

"Poof! That one's got no blood in his veins. He don't eat Italian food. Says it's too fattening, him."

I squeezed her hand. "Then he must be crazy. At least Carla likes him."

"That girl, she don't know what she wants. One thing I do know. She liked you."

"I like her too. Maybe it's why I kept running from her."

"She doesn't think you do."

I smiled. "Maybe not quite as much as your lasagna."

"You two," she said. "Dumb kids."

"You're pale," I said, changing the subject. "Maybe I better call a nurse to check your vitals."

"No, no! I'm okay. Papa was here for a visit, and I'm still shaking."

I didn't know Melissa's age but guessed she was at least in her mid-seventies. Her father would be pushing a hundred if he were still alive.

"You must be on some heavy drugs. Sure it wasn't just a morphine hallucination?"

"He was here."

"Your father is alive? Carla has never mentioned him."

"Whatever they're giving me is making my head spin. Doesn't matter because what I saw was no dream. It was Papa, sitting right where you are now, holding my hand, just like you're doing."

I could see by her expression that whatever happened had profoundly affected her. Having seen my own spirit I understood. Green lights on the instruments monitoring her vitals continued to flash as she stared at me. The red neon sign I'd seen through the window advertised a distant restaurant and had faded in morning's light.

"What did he say?"

"He wanted to explain something to me."

"Like idle chitchat?"

"No. Something I've never told Carla."

"Tell me."

Melissa's eyes became dreamy, looking first at the ceiling and then at the green lights of her monitor.

"IO ero solo un bambino quando papà è morto."

"Please, Melissa. I don't speak Italian."

"I was only a child when Papa died. Mama raised Beth and me. I barely remember how he looked."

"Are you sure it was him? How do you know?"

"I just know. It was Papa, and he was so sad."

"Why?"

"Because of something he told me."

"Tell me."

"Mama and Papa were married in Italy. They were so young when they arrived here in New Orleans. Mama was pregnant with Beth."

"They were very brave to come all the way to the New World alone."

"My grandfather was already in this country. He sent money."

"That must have been..."

"Before the turn of the century. He was doing well, making a decent living. Grandmother had died in Verona. She never made it to America."

Melissa started crying again, when I asked my next question.

"What did your grandfather do?"

"Assassin," she finally said.

"Pardon me?"

"He'd fallen in with the Black Hand."

"Mafia?"

She nodded. "They were preying on grocers at the time, taking a portion of their profits. Grandpapa got Papa work with the same people. Poor Papa didn't know what he was going into."

"What was he getting into?"

"Murder," she said, her voice cracking.

"Your dad was also an assassin?"

"No. They hung him for a murder he did not commit. That is why he was here tonight. He asked me to help him clear his name. Wyatt, what can I do?"

She grimaced, clutching her chest before I could answer. When her instruments turned red, three nurses and a doctor descended on the room. The young doctor pumped her chest until her vitals responded favorably, and then one of the nurses gave her a shot of morphine.

After watching them leave without saying a word, I stood backed against the wall, Melissa's eyes closed, my heart racing as I pondered her near-death experience, her ghost story, and my own.

Chapter 2

Like Melissa Manetti, I was asleep when Carla returned. When she shook my shoulder, I opened my eyes. Unlike Carla, the older woman with her wasn't smiling.

"You saved my life," Carla said.

"No problem. You owe me."

Ignoring my blatant hint, she said, "Wyatt, this is Aunt Beth."

Beth looked like a slightly older version of Carla's mom, with the posture of a West Point cadet, her hair inhumanly black through the miracle of some talented salon worker. Unlike Carla's eyes, Beth and Melissa's were obsidian. She finally smiled when I shook her hand.

"Thank you for staying with my sister."

"No problem."

"I have some things to discuss with her, so, please excuse us."

"Of course," I said, backing out of the room.

Carla followed me into the hallway.

"Aunt Beth can be a little rude at times."

"No problem. I'm glad I could help."

"She booted me, too. Told me not to return until she calls. Can I give you a ride somewhere?"

"You sure?"

"I offered, didn't I?"

It was her turn to smile when I said, "You haven't seen my apartment lately."

Not bothering to comment on my proposal, she led me downstairs to her old Volvo. We were soon driving on Veteran's Boulevard toward the French Quarter.

"I love this part of town," I said as we passed the Metairie Cemetery. "You're the local historian. What's the story on all the ornate graves?"

"You kidding me? You genuinely don't know?"

"I wouldn't have asked if I did."

"The cemetery was the site of the Metairie Race Track. Horses from all over the world raced here, and most of the local elite belonged to the Metairie Jockey Club. Very exclusive."

"What happened?"

Carla's eyes rolled, as if she were dealing with an idiot. We'd passed the cemetery, the tall buildings of downtown New Orleans beckoning us, and cars passing on the nearby freeway.

"Charles T. Howard, the person that started the first Louisiana lottery, applied for membership to the club and was denied."

"Why?"

"You live here. You know why, and you know what I mean when I say he wasn't from 'old money.' No matter how much wealth he possessed, the members weren't going to let him into their club."

"Not much has changed."

"Mr. Howard took it personally and promised he'd live to see the race track turned into a cemetery. No one knows how, but that's what eventually happened."

"Quite a story."

"Look at an aerial photo of the cemetery, and you'll see it's in the exact shape of the old race track. Mr. Howard has a prominent crypt, and a controversial statue."

"How so?"

"The statue of a man has its finger to its lips as if something nefarious might have happened."

"Did it?"

"Tell me. You're an investigator. I'm just a historian."

"A gorgeous one at that," I said.

"You need to stop coming on to me, Wyatt Thomas."

11

"Why?"

"Because you have no intention of being faithful to any woman."

"I never played around on you."

"You're such a liar."

"Then I guess it's no use asking you to come home with me tonight."

Carla laughed aloud. "By dark, I'll probably hate you again."

"You never hated me."

"Don't get me started."

"We were quite a couple. Things like that don't often occur."

"I have a new boyfriend. Remember?"

"Your mother said he has no blood in his veins."

"So that's what this is all about. You're jealous because someone else likes me."

"Not true. I remember all the incredible times we had."

"Uh huh! Your little ragdoll until someone prettier and sexier came along. Well, there are men out there that like me for who I am. Someday you'll recognize as much."

"That's the problem with you," I said.

"What problem?"

"You're smarter than I am and never let me win an argument. I was always on the defensive."

Carla shook her head, but her smile remained. "You never give up, do you?"

"Okay," I said. "I'll change the subject. At least for a few minutes. Tell me what you know about the hospital your mother is in."

"Oschner?"

"Yeah."

"It's public information."

"When it comes to N.O., no one knows more than you."

"There you go again," she said.

"I'm serious. How long has Oschner been at its current location?"

"Since the forties."

"This century?"

"What are you angling at?"

"Nothing, really," I said, not wanting to expound about the spirit I'd seen. "I've heard you talk about your paternal grandparents, not your mom's parents. Why is that?"

"It's personal."

She glanced away from the road and glared at me when I said, "Because your grandfather was hung for murder?"

Carla slammed on the brakes, slowing so rapidly a passing car stood on his horn and waved a fist at us.

"Where did you hear that?"

"Don't get us killed."

Carla continued to glare, but her gaze refocused on the highway.

"Who told you that?"

"Your mom."

"Impossible. Aunt Beth had to tell me."

Traffic had increased, and Carla yanked the wheel to avoid an oncoming car crowding our lane. Her eyes suddenly wide, she locked her gaze back onto Veteran's Blvd.

"I didn't intend to distress you. Want me to drive?"

"That's a hoot. You don't even have a license."

"Didn't say I do, and it was your mom that told me a story about your grandfather."

"No way. She wouldn't tell you and not me."

"She thought she saw the ghost of your grandfather last night. Maybe the drugs. It's not relevant because it was still frightfully real to her, and apparently painful."

"What did she tell you?"

"First, keep your eyes on the road before you pile into the back of that truck."

Carla popped her neck, and then took a deep breath. "Okay, I'm concentrating. Now tell me about this ghost Mom saw."

"She said your grandfather spoke to her. He told her he wasn't guilty of murder."

"No trial," Carla said. "A mob hung him. He never had a chance."

"Mob?"

"He wasn't the only one. There was much political and

social corruption at the time, the cops and local politicians bought and paid for. The citizens finally took matters into their own hands."

"And your grandfather was a victim."

Carla had slowed to a creep, another driver behind us laying on his horn. With a screech of rubber and a neck-wrenching yank, she pulled off the road into a shopping center parking lot.

"What am I supposed to do?"

Before I answered, my cell phone rang. It was Bertram.

"How's Carla's mom?"

"Stable but still in the hospital. Carla's bringing me to the city and is dropping me off."

"You kiddin' me! You bring her in to see me, you hear?"

Carla was staring at me as I stuffed the phone in my coat pocket.

"You have a cell phone? I thought you were a technophobe."

"Someone gave it to me during my last case. I kind of got attached."

"I see. Then you are driving now."

"Nope! I still prefer public transportation, but I do have a laptop."

Carla glanced skyward, shaking her head. "Oh my god! The world is coming to an end."

"Say, Carla, what was your grandfather's name?"

"Vincento Pedretti. What difference does it make?"

"Just wondering."

Forgetting about her grandfather, she eased back into the flow of traffic. We exited the off-ramp near the Superdome, soon tooling through the French Quarter toward Bertram's.

"You're not going to leave without saying hi to Bertram, are you? He wants to see you."

"You know I have to get back to the hospital."

"No, you don't. Not until Aunt Beth calls you. You told me so. Remember?"

"Well..."

"Bertram will kill me if he knows you were outside his place and didn't take the time to drop in and say hi."

"You're such a talker," she said. "No wonder I'm not a virgin anymore."

"Stop it. I wasn't the one that took your virginity."

Carla nodded. "Yes you did."

"No way."

"As God is my witness, Wyatt Thomas."

"Stop it!" Are you coming in, or not?"

Without answering, she found a parking spot instead. We walked the short distance to Bertram's, already crowded with rowdy football fans even though still early in the day. It didn't stop Bertram from sprawling across the counter top and giving Carla a hug when he saw her.

"I thought you told me you'd never be caught dead with this one again," he said, pointing at me.

"A moment of weakness. How you doing, Bertram?"

"Like a gator in a chicken coop," he said. "How's Mama?"

"She scared the crap out of me. I hope she'll be okay."

It was then I noticed someone sitting at the bar, smiling as he listened to our exchange. When he pivoted on the stool, waiting for an introduction, Bertram obliged him. It was my old pal Eddie Toledo.

"Glad to hear about your mama. You know this person?"

"No, I don't," she said.

"I'm Eddie," he said, flashing a Pepsodent smile and grabbing her hand. "Why waste your time with this loser?"

"Wyatt and I are just friends," Carla said.

"Best news I've had all day," Eddie said. "Bertram bring this lovely woman something alcoholic."

Eddie held a prominent government job, though his hair was a tad too long for the position he occupied. It didn't seem to matter. His youthful looks and upbeat personality had propelled him through the ranks at a rapid pace.

"I can't," she said. "I have to return to the hospital."

"I hope she's okay," he said.

Eddie continued to hold Carla's hand. After glancing to see if I'd noticed, she gently pulled it away.

"The doctors said we'll know more tomorrow, but one of the nurses assured me she'll be fine."

"There you go, then," Eddie said. "Nurses are always a

day or two ahead of the doctors."

"Hope you're right about that."

"Eddie's the Assistant Federal D.A. here in the city. Don't worry, though. I won't tell him about all the heinous crimes you've committed."

Carla gave me a dirty look that turned into a smile following Eddie's comeback.

"She's guilty of being beautiful. I see that much. At least have breakfast with me. There's a little cafe down the street that does excellent French toast."

"I don't know," Carla said. "Wyatt?"

"The loser can come along," Eddie said. "I'll buy."

"With that offer, we better go," I said. "He owes me at least three lunches, not to mention a Saints ticket, or two."

"Don't listen to him, pretty lady. I'm the most generous person in town."

When Carla glanced at Bertram, he gave her another hug. "Go on," he said. "We can catch up later."

We were soon out the door, a cold nip in the air, exacerbated by a chill breeze blowing down Chartres Street. It didn't matter because it wasn't far from Bertram's to a little cafe near Jackson Square.

Business was apparently dead, a man standing on the street in front hustling customers. Only five tables occupied the slate floor of the cafe housed in a row of old French Quarter buildings. They were all empty when the man seated us near the door. A trickle of tourists passed slowly on the sidewalk outside.

"Something to drink? Mimosa?"

"Coffee for me," Carla said. "With lots of milk."

"Make that two," I said. "But black for me."

"Kir Royale," Eddie said.

"What's that?" Carla asked.

"Chambord and champagne. Try one, you'll like it."

"Better stick with coffee," she said.

They were both as hungry as I was, and we were soon feasting on eggs and cornbread hash. Eddie was working on his second Kir Royale, finally succeeding in getting Carla to take a sip.

"Carla's a fourth generation Italian," I said. "Her mother is the best Italian cook in New Orleans, maybe the world."

"You kidding me? I'm from New Jersey. I grew up on Italian food," Eddie said.

Carla turned in her seat until their knees touched.

"You like lasagna?"

"Not just like, I lust for it. No one cooks Italian like my mama."

"Mine does," Carla said.

"I think I want to meet your mother. I'm off today, and that's why I'm slumming in the Quarter. Can I take you to the hospital after breakfast?"

"No, but if you're serious, you can come with me."

Eddie held up his credit card. We were quickly tabbed out, Carla and Eddie on their way to Oschner as I opened the door to Bertram's bar.

"Where's Carla?" he asked.

"With Eddie."

"You kidding me. You okay with that?"

"We broke up over a year ago."

"That Eddie's a mover, him."

"They call him Fast Eddie for a reason. I'm going upstairs," I said, yawning as I gave him a backhanded wave.

Chapter 3

Lost in a dream, I wrestled with a monster intent on killing me when the phone by the bed woke me. With temples still throbbing, my eyes popped open as I grabbed the receiver.

"Wyatt, it is Mama. Are you busy?"

"Mama? How are you? Bertram and I were just talking about you."

"You sound groggy. Did I wake you?"

"Just a nap," I said.

"I came by last night and knocked on your door."

"Sorry about that."

"On a date?"

"Probably sitting on the balcony and didn't hear you."

Mama Mulate didn't question my little white lie. "What are you doing right now?"

"Nothing; why?"

"Let's go for a jog in the park. I didn't get in much running time on the boat this summer and feel as if I've grown fat and lazy. My body needs exercise."

Mama Mulate had attended the University of South Carolina on a track scholarship. She'd continued running daily after graduation, her jogs more like lung-bursting sprints. She'd never be fat and was anything but lazy. Our runs typically turned into contests that she usually won.

"I've put on a little weight."

"Oh? How much weight?"

"A pound or two."

"You haven't gained a pound since I've known you. No one your age is in better shape. Get your togs on. I'll be there in an hour."

She hung up the phone before I could argue. It didn't matter because I needed exercise more than she thought she did.

"Guess I need a new pair," I said when my big toe protruded through the orange mesh of the lightweight shoe.

I was pulling on a sweatshirt when Mama Mulate knocked on the door.

She was resplendent in her pink jogging jacket and pants. Bouffant hair draped to her shoulders in curly waves. It didn't hide her gold hoop earrings that seemed out of place for a run in the park. Her shoes were also pink. Her choice of clothing color seemed to paint her as a want-to-be athlete. I knew better. Once her fancy sweats came off, she left fashion behind, along with anyone trying to keep up with her.

We were soon pulling into City Park. When the weather was warm, Mama Mulate liked to drop the soft-top of her old Bugeye Sprite. Even on sunny, fifty-degree days, it made for a chilly ride. The cold breeze whistling over the windshield made me glad I'd worn sweatshirt and sweatpants.

Cool weather didn't worry Mama. Nearly six feet tall, she was in excellent condition and had the svelte and toned body of an Olympic athlete. She doffed her pink sweats as soon as she'd parked the Sprite. Dressed only in a small racing singlet and sports bra that revealed her firm stomach, she was already eliciting admiring glances from passing walkers and joggers.

City Park is thirteen hundred acres of towering sculptures, picturesque bridges that span ponds, and bayous filled with ducks, geese, swans, and flowering lily pads. Massive live oaks had somehow managed to survive ages of Gulf winds and severe weather. Their limbs, draping with Spanish moss and resurrection fern, bordered miles of paths and trails through beautifully landscaped surroundings. It would have made a British gardener jealous. We started slowly, but Mama Mulate quickly increased the pace.

Mama was a competitor and hated to lose. Something she rarely had to worry about from me. Today was different. Three miles into our run, she stopped to tie a shoelace. I didn't wait for her to finish, tearing away instead at a lung-bursting clip. Mama responded to the challenge, racing after me.

Though not aware why, I was up to the task. I could hear her footsteps behind me. Though not turning to look, I sensed she was running faster than I was. With two miles to go, I drew on every ounce of strength I had. It wasn't enough.

The last mile, we ran flat out, side-by-side, crossing our imaginary finish line together. Mama was laughing when she hugged me.

"That was so much fun. What got into you?"

My heart continued to race, breathing coming in short bursts. Before I could answer her, the clouds opened up with an impromptu rain that sent us sprinting for her Sprite. We quickly raised the soft-top before getting thoroughly drenched. Neither of us spoke as she motored toward the Quarter, both of us grinning and reflecting on our run as rain beat down on the car's soft-top. She finally glanced at her watch.

"We covered that last mile in five minutes flat. You are a pretty good distance runner."

"I ran cross-country and 1500 meters at L.S.U.," I said.

"You never told me that."

"You never asked."

Mama reached across the stick shift and gave me a kiss on the mouth.

"You're so damn secretive," she said. "Maybe that's what I like about you. What are your plans for the day?"

"Don't have any."

"No hot date?"

"I told you, I'm not seeing anyone."

She stared at me a long moment. "You always have at least one woman waiting on your beck and call; usually two."

"It's different now."

Mama put her palm to my forehead. "I don't think you're lying. Are you feeling all right?"

"I'm fine."

"No, you're not. You're still depressed about Kimi and Desire."

My ex-wife Kimi had recently succumbed to breast cancer.

Desire was a beautiful runway model I'd met shortly thereafter. Our relationship had turned disastrous. I realized it was part of what was causing my depression.

"How do you know about Desire? You were on your cruise."

"Bertram told me. He's an old gossip, you know."

"No kidding," I said.

"I'm off work for today. Come home with me. I have gumbo simmering on the stove."

"I'm wringing wet from sweat and rain and don't have a change of clothes."

"I have a closet filled with castoffs from ex-boyfriends. You can shower in my spare bathroom. I won't even peek in on you."

"Maybe I'd like it better if you did. Just old clothes and a bowl of gumbo, huh?"

"What else did you think I meant?"

"Don't know. You just got me to thinking."

"Oh?"

"That maybe it's time our business partnership took on a more personal side."

Mama shook her head. "You're not as depressed as I thought. Maybe I better drop you at Bertram's."

"Just kidding," I said. "I'll settle for a shower, clean clothes, and that bowl of gumbo."

"And a little talk about your depression," she said.

It doesn't just rain in New Orleans. As often as not, it comes down in bucket loads. That's what it was doing as Mama headed down Elysian Fields toward the Central Business District. Her two-story house was in an old neighborhood not far from the river. Since she didn't have a garage, we had to make a mad dash for her covered porch. We may as well have strolled because we were both drenched as she fumbled to open the front door.

"You take the bathroom at the end of the hall," she said, pointing as she ran up the stairs to her bedroom.

I was standing naked by the shower, waiting for the water to warm up, when Mama opened the door without knocking and threw me a towel.

21

"There's a bathrobe hanging on the door hook. I'll see you in the kitchen after your shower," she said, shutting the door behind her.

I tried not to think about Mama's impromptu visit as I stood beneath the shower's steamy water. She was sitting at her white enamel kitchen table when I joined her. Her white terrycloth robe matched the one I was wearing, her hair still damp. The smell of strong, Creole coffee wafted from the pot on the stove.

"Why are you grinning?" I said as she poured me a cup.

"Nice tush," she said.

"Never knew you liked peeking."

"I wasn't peeking; I was ogling."

"I see. I thought this was only about clean clothes and a bowl of gumbo."

"You don't have to buy everything you look at in a store window."

"Not even a test drive?"

She let my comment pass. "The run was what I needed. Are you feeling better?"

"Much better, and this is the best coffee I've ever tasted."

"Wait till you try my gumbo."

"If I know you, it'll be the best I've ever had."

"Maybe not that good, but I think you'll like it."

Mama stood on her tiptoes, reaching for bowls in her cabinet.

"Nice tush," I said.

Although she didn't turn around, I could tell she was smiling.

"One of these nights we should get it on, but not tonight. After we eat, I want you to tell Mama all about what's troubling you."

"It's not that serious."

"I think it is."

"How would you know?"

"Maybe I can read minds."

"If you could do that, you'd slap my face."

She slapped my face anyway, though playfully. "Why Mr. Butler, you are no gentleman."

22

"And you, Scarlett are no lady," I said.

"You got me a job, I guess you know," Mama said, once again changing the subject.

"Oh?"

"The movie producer you worked for while I was on my cruise."

I'd recently investigated a series of bizarre deaths at a monastery south of New Orleans. The man that had hired me produced movies in Louisiana.

"Quinlan Moore?"

Mama nodded. "He wrote a book when he was in college. He's hired a writer to adapt it into a screenplay that takes place in New Orleans."

"Now I remember. He wanted to jazz up the script by adding elements of voodoo. I gave him your name," I said.

"He's hired me as a consultant. We are meeting at Bertram's tomorrow, and I think he wants to hire you as well."

"He hasn't called me."

"He said he'd already talked with you about it."

"Maybe," I said. "With this business of ghosts, my memory is a little hazy."

"Ghosts?"

"Long story," I said.

"Then eat your gumbo. We'll see if we can solve your spirit problem when our stomachs are full."

We devoured the delicious gumbo, Mama giving me a second helping without asking, or taking no for an answer. After topping up our coffee, we listened to the storm, still roaring outside.

"Where are your cats?" I finally asked.

"Oh shit!" she said, hurrying to the back door. "I left them on the porch. With all this rain, they must be ready to kill me."

When Mama opened the back door, her three cats, Cliffy, Bushy, and Ninja came running in. Cliffy was an orange tabby, Bushy a white Persian, and Ninja solid black. When my first cat died, I'd rescued Ninja from the pound, and Mama had fallen in love the moment she saw him. When Bertram gave me Kisses, a clone of my deceased cat Bob, I'd given her Ninja.

The little black cat remembered me and hopped into my lap.

"Maybe I shouldn't have taken him from you," she said.

"He loves you and is perfectly happy here."

Rain continued falling, though now even harder than before, sharp drops peppering the roof and windows. When thunder shook the old house, all the lights went out. Nonplussed, Mama lit a candle on the kitchen table.

"Damn generator for this neighborhood! Lightning zaps it at least three times every year. Good thing I have lots of candles."

We sat in darkness lighted only by the glow of a flickering candle. The rain on Mama's roof began sounding more frightening than soothing. Ninja had fallen asleep in my lap, Bushy and Cliffy having disappeared somewhere into the recesses of Mama's large house.

"What now?" I said.

"Not me; you. Tell me what's troubling you."

"I'm not sure."

"Yes you are. Tell me."

She was right, and I only hesitated a moment before beginning my story.

"I must be getting old. Nothing used to upset me. Now everything does. My blood pressure's through the roof."

"Have you seen a doctor?"

"I don't have one."

"Let's check it. I have a meter."

Mama soon had the instrument strapped to my wrist and grinned when she checked the results.

"You no more have high blood pressure than a man in the moon."

"Maybe not, but I feel as if I do."

"You're becoming a hypochondriac," she said.

Mama went to the stove and started a teakettle to boiling.

"Let this simmer awhile and then drink it when it cools," she said.

"What is it?"

"Flor de Jamaica. Known here as hibiscus tea. It lowers blood pressure when you drink three or four cups a day."

"You just told me I don't have high blood pressure."

"You don't, but a hot cup of hibiscus tea sounds good on such a stormy night."

"Pretty tasty," I said, taking a sip.

"And it doesn't have the sugar calories from all the lemonade you drink."

"It hasn't hurt me yet."

"Have you had your blood sugar tested?"

"I'm okay. High blood pressure and sugar aren't my problems."

"Then what is?"

"I've had a case of the nerves for a while now, and last night I saw a ghost."

" Real ghost, or were you dreaming?"

"Not sure. I was at Oschner visiting Carla's mom. She had a heart attack. I stayed with her so that Carla could go home and get some sleep."

"Seeing Carla again?"

"No," I said, shaking my head. "Just friends."

When wind rattled the windows, the candle flickered. Mama poured water for my tea.

"Tell me about this ghost you saw."

Without opening his eyes, Ninja changed positions in my lap. I rubbed his shoulders and sipped the tea. The storm and dimly lit kitchen caused me to remember with vivid recall the moment I'd seen the specter.

"I was asleep by Melissa's bed when something that felt like a damp sponge touched my cheek. I opened my eyes to something flickering in front of me."

"Are you sure you weren't just dreaming?"

"I was awake."

"What was it?"

"A man."

"Did you recognize him?"

"No. Someone in his thirties, dressed in what appeared to be a period costume. Like an actor playing the part in a movie about old New Orleans."

"Did he speak to you?"

"He said I'd placed a curse on him, and he was doomed to follow me for eternity, unless I lifted the curse."

"And you didn't recognize him? Was the encounter so short that perhaps you don't quite remember what he looked like?"

"I remember. His eyes and hair were coal black, his nose prominent, though more regal than grotesque. His clothes looked well made, probably expensive. He had the hands of someone that had never worked a day in his life."

"Did he tell you his name?"

"Zacharie Patenaude."

"What else?"

"That's all, but not the strangest part of the story."

"Then what is?"

"He was speaking French, and I understood every word he said."

"What's so strange about that?"

"I know a little Cajun French, but that's about it. The apparition was speaking traditional French; not Cajun."

"How do you know?"

"I just do. I know this is all confusing because it makes no sense. The ghost seemed familiar, as if I'd known him from someplace. Though I've searched my mind, I can't remember from where, or if I ever actually did."

"His clothes were from a different era?"

"Pre-Civil War, I'd say."

When lightning flashed through the window, I saw the unbelieving look on Mama Mulate's face. Ninja shifted in my lap again. Opening his eyes, he stretched, and then jumped to the floor.

"You're right. This all sounds strange."

"And it got even stranger next morning when I talked to Melissa."

"Stranger than what you just told me?"

"She was crying and had also seen a ghost."

"Your ghost?"

"The ghost of her father. Her grandfather brought her parents over from Italy and had gotten his son work with the Black Hand."

"What's that?"

"Same as the Mafia now. A mob broke her father out of

26

jail and hung him because they thought he was a killer. She said her father's ghost was begging her to help clear his name."

"You do have problems," she said. "Now I'm almost sorry I offered to help."

"It's okay. This is my problem. There's nothing you can do."

The storm continued, wind, and rain pounding the windows and thunder shaking the frame house with increasing intensity.

"Maybe there is. Have you ever experienced an induced trance?"

Chapter 4

After lighting another candle, Mama left me alone at the table. She returned with a jar, a necklace, and ornate box, Thunder, lightning, and pounding rain continued outside the house as mist swirled from our teacups.

"Hold out your palm," she said.

When I extended my hand across the table, she tapped something into it from the antique jar.

"What is it?"

"Mushroom."

"Like in magic mushroom?"

"Yes."

"Dangerous?"

"As long as I'm with you it isn't. I'm a practitioner. Remember?"

"I trust you."

"Good. I'm giving you just enough to help induce a trance so I can channel the spirit that visited you in the hospital. Chew the mushroom. Swallow it, and then wash it down with tea."

Thunder rocked the ceiling as she pushed the box toward the center of the table. Wax had begun dripping down the sides of the candle and drying on the tabletop. Mama didn't seem to notice, or to care. In the flickering light, I saw the box was constructed of polished wood with intricate markings carved into it.

"What is it?"

"Magic. A music box made by monks in the Early Middle

Ages. Christianity was in its infancy and still a mixture of folk religion and paganism. This music box produces a sublime melody and was used to create trances."

"For what purpose?"

"To ward off demons, curses, and the evil eye."

"You have to be kidding me!"

"I don't kid about things such as this."

"It must be extremely valuable. Where did you get it?"

"Don't ask," she said. "Is the mushroom working yet?"

"How will I know?"

"You'll know. Put this around your neck and drink your tea."

She handed me a necklace bearing a stone pendant, black as the sky outside the house. Gusting wind had set the chimes on the back porch sounding a discordant blend of percussive music. Something heavy slammed against the wall. I held the stone in my hand, rubbing its polished surface.

"What is this?"

"Psilomelane; a mineral with unique properties. It'll help us induce the trance."

"This isn't going to hurt, is it?"

"Stop kidding. I promise you this is serious. Take it that way."

"Sorry," I said.

Mama wound the music box, and then opened its carved lid. Centuries had not dulled the instrument's dulcet tones. A repetitive theme began filling the kitchen with metallic-inflected sound. As it continued, the plucked notes began to probe my psyche.

"Breathe in," she said. "Breathe out. Close your eyes and become one with the tones. Focus only on the melody."

The tune was enchanting, the pleasant pitch of metallic pins as poignant as a full orchestra. Noise of the storm died as the mushroom began working, the far wall rippling and changing colors from vibrant yellows and reds to ghostly white through my slitted eyes. I felt weightless as if I'd somehow risen out of the chair and was floating, not touching anything. When I glanced at the candle, wax pouring down its sides had turned to blood. It was the last thing I remembered for a while.

29

Wyatt's eyes had closed, his head tilted, chin almost touching his chest. He didn't see the shimmering cloud that had suddenly appeared behind him, or the apparition staring at Mama with steely resolve. It was the essence of a young man, his dark hair and distinctive clothes cut in the style of a different era. Though an aquiline nose dominated his face, it somehow made him appear regally handsome. He wasn't smiling.

"Who are you?" she asked.

"Zacharie Patenaude," he said. "Who are you?"

"A friend of Wyatt's. I summoned you for answers."

"Ask the man you call Wyatt."

"If that's not his name, then what is it?"

"Time and death bring changes."

"What is that supposed to mean?"

"Only that there are no answers. In the end, only questions."

As Mama stared at the flickering apparition, a python appeared around his shoulders. The eyes of the angry reptile glowed red as it jutted its neck toward her, Its mouth open with malicious intent. When Mama put her arm up as pentacles, pentagrams, and hexagrams began flying toward her. The melody from the music box had become suddenly and relentlessly loud, and she had to shout.

"You are the cursed one! Why have you attached yourself to Wyatt?"

"Although not his intention, it was he that attached himself to me."

"For what reason?"

"Revenge is a double-edged sword," the ghost said.

"Revenge for what? Tell me."

"Ask the man you call Wyatt."

"He doesn't know."

"The answer may be locked deep within his soul, but he knows."

"You make no sense. Why would he place a curse that would have such a deleterious effect on him?"

"I told you, he was seeking revenge."

"Someone else has cursed you. A facilitator of the Devil. Not Wyatt. You must have done something terrible to cause him to seek revenge."

"Elise," the spirit said.

"A woman? He cursed you because of a woman?"

"What does it matter? We are locked together for eternity," he said, his image growing dimmer.

"How can he lift the curse?"

"I am only a spirit. I have no answer to your question."

The music had become earsplitting, Mama's eyes rolling to the back of her head as she tried to muffle the music with her hands.

"Wait. Tell me his name," she shouted.

The spirit's words were barely discernible as his image began to fade. He held out his hand to her as he disappeared into a wisp of vapor. Mama continued shielding her face as the serpent, and flying Devil signs went with it.

When they were gone, she poured a straight shot of whiskey and then slugged it down in one gulp. After her second shot, the music box grew quiet. Thunder shook the roof, and the candle in the center of the table flickered and died.

❧⚶❧

I awoke the next morning on Mama's living room couch, an old Afghan pulled around my neck. The room was quiet, last night's storm no longer raging. Mama was shaking my shoulder.

"How's your head?"

"Like someone's inside with a sledgehammer, trying to break out."

With a grin, she handed me two pills and a glass of water.

"Take these. They'll make you feel better."

"More mushrooms?"

"A couple of aspirins. You had enough magic mushroom last night to last awhile. I put some fresh clothes in the bathroom for you. When you finish dressing, join me in the kitchen. After you eat my three-egg hangover omelet, you'll feel better in no time."

Several minutes passed before I could collect myself

enough to get off the couch, the robe and nothing else wrapped loosely around my waist. The red flannel shirt and bell bottom trousers Mama had left for me in the bathroom were old and didn't match. At least they fitted me and were clean. I followed the delicious aroma wafting through the house. Mama was sitting at the kitchen table, grinning when I finally joined her.

"What are you laughing at?"

"The last person I saw in those clothes was my ex-husband."

"I didn't know you have an ex."

"Doesn't everyone?"

"Must have been a while back. I don't think they make pants like this anymore."

"James was much older than I, and he never threw anything away."

"What happened to him?"

"He liked young women and ran off with one younger than me. Can't say as I was surprised."

"I didn't realize you like older men."

She didn't answer, pushing a cup of hot coffee toward me instead.

"Drink this. It'll make you feel better."

Rain from the previous night had ended, sunlight beaming through the windows. My head hurt, though not like the hangovers I'd experienced during my alcoholic years. After taking the first sip of coffee, I started feeling better. Mama was smiling when she opened the door to the back porch and let her three cats go outside.

Her hangover omelet consisted of onions, potatoes, and green peppers sauteed with a deseeded, finely chopped jalapeno pepper. That, along with a salty glass of tomato juice liberally dosed with lemon, was what I needed. By the time I'd finished eating, my mouth was on fire, but my head had stopped pounding.

"That was great," I said. "Though not quite the voodoo remedy I expected. What happened last night?"

"Your spirit visited me shortly after you closed your eyes."

"And?"

"Seems he's attached to you permanently."

"What are you talking about?"

"He's been with you longer than you've been alive."

"Are you implying I've had a past life?"

"Remember when you met Madam Aja? She called you a Traveler."

Mama and I within the past year had visited Madam Aja, a very old, New Orleans voodoo woman, to ask what she knew about the haunting of a French Quarter house. She'd called me a Traveler—a person that has lived many lives.

"So this spirit from a former life latched on to me because he thought I cursed him?"

"He said you were seeking revenge."

"This is all confusing. Why would I purposely attach him to myself, and why haven't I sensed his presence before now?"

"Kimi's death and your doomed love affair with Desire happening in the same month weakened your subconscious resolve. I promise you the spirit has been with you for decades, maybe centuries. You just didn't realize it until now."

Though I didn't know if I believed what Mama was saying, her words disturbed me.

"Who is this ghost that's haunting me?"

"Like you said, his name is Zacharie Patenaude. Are you sure you have no idea whom he might be?"

"Not a clue."

"You were apparently acquaintances during another lifetime. The spirit is a Frenchman. Though he didn't say when he was alive, I guess by his clothes it was before the Civil War."

Mama's cats were scratching at the door, wanting back inside. When she obliged, Bushy jumped into her arms. After giving the regal beast a full body stroke, she returned him to the floor. From a container of treats on her kitchen counter, she sprinkled some of the tasty tidbits in front of them, soon having all three cats dancing. Smiling as they bounded into the other room, she rejoined me at the table.

"The spirit told me your name."

"Not Wyatt?"

"He called you Matthieu Courtmanche."

Chapter 5

My visit to Mama's left me wanting answers, who was Matthieu Courtmanche the question plaguing me most. Hoping to learn what I needed, I'd spent the day at the Notarial Archives.

The founders of New Orleans were sticklers when it came to keeping records. Every marriage, land plat, birth and death, sale of land or slaves was recorded and stored in the Notarial Archives. The address and direction of this informational treasure trove changed shortly before Hurricane Katrina. It was still the first place to visit for someone seeking enlightenment about the complex social politics of New Orleans.

Morning had dragged into afternoon with nothing useful completed. The answers to my questions were there. I just couldn't find them. Finally deciding I was wasting my time, I went to visit someone more familiar with the archives than any living soul.

Madam Toulouse Joubert had worked at the Notarial Archives for years and had probably thumbed through every document at least once. She and Armand, her constant companion, knew more about the history of early New Orleans than anyone I knew. Leaving the archives, I set out to see them and find out about my ghost.

With a winter breeze blowing down my neck, I pulled up my collar and hurried across Canal, the widest street on earth. Tourists swarmed the Quarter, window shopping art and antiques on Royal Street while waiting for the nightly street party on Bourbon to begin. Trying to avoid being bumped off the sidewalk, I headed for an eclectic bar most tourists had never heard of.

There is no sign over Allemands' door. It didn't need one. Regulars sitting at the counter all knew how to get there and were never sociable when a chance tourist popped in off the street. Luckily I knew everyone and waved at Claude the bartender as I went to a booth in the rear of the dimly-lit establishment.

The booth was the office of Madam Toulouse Joubert and Armand. You'd normally find them there, Madam Toulouse sipping a Hurricane through a straw the same color as her puffy lips, and Armand drinking Johnnie Walker Red, neat, from a large glass.

Madam Toulouse had shoulders bigger than a Saints linebacker, and gave me a bone-crushing hug when I slid in beside her. Her leather miniskirt and bright red blouse matched her lipstick color though clashed with the purple shadow daubed over her eyes. She looked like living pop art with her bouffant hairstyle that pointed toward the ceiling.

Unlike Madam Toulouse, the only color Armand wore was black. Black pants, shoes, and turtleneck sweater melded seamlessly with his oiled hair, mustache and goatee. He was smoking, the joint's pungent odor produced by something other than tobacco. None of the patrons seemed to notice.

"My man," he said, reaching to shake my hand. "Long time no see. You don't like us no more?"

"If I didn't like you, I wouldn't have brought you this," I said, pulling a bottle out of a paper bag I was carrying.

"Eighteen year old single malt Laphroaig. Who's throat do I have to cut?"

Armand quickly downed his drink, replacing it with expensive Scotch from the bottle I'd given him. I barely heard his sigh of pure joy over the jukebox blaring a zydeco waltz. Madam Toulouse was looking over his shoulder when I handed her a box.

"I didn't forget you."

The little box contained a gold necklace with a ruby pendant. Madam Toulouse held it in her hand, her mouth open in disbelief.

"I can't accept this. It's an antique and must be worth a fortune."

"It was my mother's. She didn't tolerate cheap jewelry. I've had it on my dresser for more years than I know. Someone needs to wear it and give life to the stone."

"It's beautiful."

"It made me think of you. Mom would have wanted you to have it. It's the least I can do for all you have provided me over the years."

Armand clasped the necklace around her neck, a beautiful ruby gleaming from reflections of the flashing neon beer sign over the bar.

"Guess we're going to have to take back those mean things we accused you of," Armand said.

"Don't get carried away just yet. There's a little problem you can help me with."

"Little problem, or a big one?" Madam Toulouse asked.

"I was at the archives most of the day, looking for something. I came up empty, but was coming by for a visit anyway, even if I'd gotten my answers."

"What were you looking for?" she asked.

"I've had a problem with a ghost. Seems it's been with me for quite a while now."

Armand and Madam Toulouse were permanent residents of New Orleans. Like most locals, they'd both probably seen their own ghosts, or else knew someone that had.

"Go on," Armand said.

"I was staying with Carla's mom at the hospital a few nights ago when something absolutely eerie happened."

Madam Toulouse and Armand exchanged a knowing glance. "You're back with Carla again?" she asked.

"Not exactly. Her mom had a heart attack. I sat with her while Carla got a little rest."

"And you saw a ghost," Armand said.

"Yes."

"Not so strange," Madam Toulouse said. "Considering the trauma and death that occurs in hospitals, especially hospitals in Louisiana."

"This ghost doesn't haunt the hospital. It haunts me. Mama Mulate channeled the spirit when I told her about what had happened. Seems I knew this particular person in another life. Something I apparently did is causing him to stay with me forever."

"Doesn't sound very logical to me," Armand said. "Why would you have done that?"

"No idea. I know is the name of the spirit, and the name I went by in my past life. I was hoping to learn about the two at the archives. I came up empty."

A jazz funeral was passing outside on the street, horns and drums sounding a mournful dirge. When Armand crossed himself, Madam Toulouse gave him a peck on the cheek.

"Come to our apartment," she said. "My laptop is there, and perhaps we can help."

The winter sky was growing dark as we left Allemands and headed toward Madam Toulouse and Armand's apartment in the Upper Pontalba Building. Revelers had already filled the French Quarter, searching for strong drink and debauchery. Before the night ended, most of them would find all they could handle. Fireworks lit the sky over the Fairgrounds as we made our way toward Jackson Square.

The Upper and Lower Pontalba apartments, along with St. Louis Cathedral, the Cabildo and the Presbytère, border the old square. The lower levels house shops and restaurants. The upper levels are apartments. Every tourist visiting New Orleans sees them from the outside. Few visitors ever see them from the inside.

I'd visited friends that lived in the Upper Pontalba, but had never been to the apartment of Armand and Madam Toulouse. It was quite impressive as I had expected. The two dealt in fine art with a New Orleans' flair. It showed. The floors were gleaming hardwood. The baseboards, crown moldings, and granite countertops spoke renovation. Armand led me to the balcony overlooking the square.

"Best address in Nawlins," he drawled.

"And the best view," I said. "Some people would kill to live here."

"Don't we know it," Madam Toulouse said. "We waited a

year to get this place, and then only after calling in every political chit we possessed."

The city of New Orleans owned the Upper, the State of Louisiana the Lower Pontalba apartments. There was a long waiting list. Unless you were connected, it didn't help to be lucky. Armand and Madam Toulouse knew all the City's politicians and influential people, though many of them would have denied it.

"You two go outside. I'll get drinks," Armand said.

There was room for six on the spacious balcony. Madam Toulouse relaxed in the antique wicker loveseat, and I relaxed in a padded rocker. Armand soon rejoined us with a Hurricane for Madam Toulouse and a frosty glass of lemonade for me. He was working on more Laphroaig and enjoying every minute of it. Below us, tourists milled on the brick walkway as a passing tug in the nearby river sounded its mournful horn.

"Now tell us about your ghost," Madam Toulouse said.

"He looked quite young, probably in his thirties, his clothes and hair from a different century. He had a Gallic nose though it didn't detract from his looks. Not as much as the prominent scar on his cheek."

"A duelling scar?"

"Don't know."

More fireworks exploded over by the Fairgrounds, as crowd noise, and the melancholy rift of a tenor sax wafted up from Bourbon Street. Armand and Madam Toulouse were holding hands on the loveseat like infatuated teenagers.

"Baby, can you get my laptop?" she asked.

"You bet, Madam," Armand said with a bow.

He soon returned with a tray bearing a blender half-filled with Madam Toulouse's Hurricane mix, and a pitcher of lemonade for me. After topping our glasses, he handed her the laptop. She quickly fired it up.

"You said the spirit told you his name. What was it?"

"Zacharie Patenaude," I said.

I waited for her to start searching some database on the computer. She closed it and stared at me instead.

"And who did he say you were?"

"Matthieu Courtmanche."

Armand was grinning and shaking his head. "Hell, Wyatt, you could have told us all that at Allemand's. We don't need no damn computer to tell you who those two were."

"Then don't keep me in suspense," I said.

"Zacharie Patenaude was a cotton trader in New Orleans," Madam Toulouse said. "The eldest son of Leocadie Patenaude."

"Just about the most powerful family in Nawlins around 1840," Armand said.

"1840? My spirit was alive then?"

Armand laughed. "Hell, Cowboy, spirits can go back lots further than that," he said.

"Who was Matthieu Courtmanche?"

"His parents owned the Courtmanche cotton plantation. Up River Road, not far from here. It was the biggest and most successful cotton operation of the time."

"He owned slaves?"

"Lots of them," Madam Toulouse said.

"Then he couldn't have been me. I'm not a racist."

"Neither was he. That's how things were back then," Armand said. "We're talking more than one hundred fifty years ago."

"If I were rich and owned a plantation, then why am I broke now?"

Armand smiled and sipped his Scotch. "You ain't broke, man."

"Maybe not, but I'm not rich, and I don't own any property."

"Your family did. Everyone knows you was raised by one of the most prosperous and influential families in Louisiana."

"It didn't make much difference in the end," I said.

"Your grandpa ruled Louisiana. When your daddy got into politics, trying to be just like the old man, he found out pretty damn quick he was out of his league. Hell man, calling a Louisiana politician crooked is like calling a gator reptilian. Your old man wasn't much of a businessman either."

My father had lost the family fortune trying to follow in my famous grandfather's footsteps. His ensuing suicide still weighed heavily on my mind, as it had my mom's. After his death, she drank herself into an early grave.

"If we keep talking about my family, I'm going to have to have a nip of that Scotch, and I don't even like Scotch."

"Baby, you just drink your lemonade, and me and Armand will shut our mouths about your family," Madam Toulouse said. "Sounds like you got enough spirits to worry about."

Below us, a group of singers started clapping and singing an upbeat hymn as they paraded single file past Andy Jackson's statue. Their words echoed off the Cabildo and St. Louis Cathedral momentarily drowning out music and crowd noise coming from Bourbon Street.

"Tell me what you know about Patenaude and Courtmanche," I said.

Madam Toulouse patted my shoulder. "They duelled; just around the corner from where we are now."

"Duels were fought all the time but rarely resulted in death. At least until the Americans began taking over," Armand said.

"Courtmanche gave Patenaude the scar on his cheek and probably would have killed him if the seconds hadn't intervened," Madam Toulouse said.

"Why did they duel?"

Armand poured himself another shot of Laphroaig. "Don't know. Rumor has it a woman was involved, and maybe a little hoodoo."

"Hoodoo and not voodoo?"

Madam Toulouse laughed. "Hoodoo is what was left when African Vodoun got all mixed up with Catholicism, West Indies animism, and superstitious beliefs. Everyone's heard of Marie Laveau, but there were dozens of others such as African Rosalie, Sanite Dede, and Madam Popaleuse."

"And the gris gris men," Armand said. "Bras Coupe, the zombi maker; Doctor Cracker, a white, half Jewish, half gypsy magician, and of course Doctor John himself."

"Revenge was involved. For what perceived or actual offense we do not know," Madam Toulouse said.

"Doctor John performed the payback, ostensibly for Patenaude. At least we know that much."

"Doctor John?"

Madam Toulouse topped up my glass of lemonade as someone on the street below us popped a firecracker.

"Damn kids!" Armand said. "Now what were you asking?"

"Are you talking about Doctor John the singer?"

"The hoodoo man. A Senegalese prince, captured and transported to Cuba where his master gave him his freedom."

"He had ceremonial scars that marked him as a prince. His skin, they say, was darker than black. He kept snakes and scorpions, and it's said he often practiced black magic," Madam Toulouse said.

"And Patenaude hired him to curse Courtmanche for the purpose of revenge?"

Armand nodded. "That's the word on the street, so to speak."

"Then how is it the curse backfired?" I asked.

"Who knows? The answer is lost somewhere in the annals of time," Madam Toulouse said.

"What happened to Zacharie Patenaude and Matthieu Courtmanche?"

"That we know. Patenaude died of yellow fever during the plague of 1851," she said.

"And Courtmanche?"

Armand had left the loveseat to do something in the kitchen. His back was turned when he answered my question.

"It's possible he committed suicide."

Chapter 6

My brief escape from depression hadn't lasted long, the visit with Armand and Madam Toulouse returning me to that fragile state of mind I'd spent my life trying to cope with. I was thinking about sneaking behind Bertram's ancient countertop and pouring a tall glass of Black Jack when I got a surprise.

Someone I hadn't seen in six months spotted me coming through the door. Pushing through the crowded room, she smiled and waved, smothering me in a warm hug when I opened my arms.

"Wyatt. You're looking good," she said.

It was Lilly Bliss, someone I'd met while working a murder investigation at a secluded monastery south of New Orleans. Lilly's black hair matched the frames of her thick glasses that usually perched on top of her head. She had green, Irish eyes and a pretty face that barely reached my shoulders. Her height, or lack thereof, didn't keep her from standing on her tiptoes and planting a sultry kiss on my lips.

"Lilly, I'd forgotten you were meeting Mama Mulate here tonight."

"What an incredible woman. I love her already."

Lilly pointed to a table where Mama Mulate was sitting alone, sipping a colorful drink through an equally bright straw. She smiled and waved. Lilly wrapped her arm through mine and led me to the table.

"We were starting to think you had stood us up," Mama said as I took a seat between them.

"Just finished a meeting. Not too late, am I?"

"We both just got here and were getting acquainted," Mama said. "I didn't realize whom I was meeting. Lilly is my favorite writer."

"You're just saying that to be nice," Lilly said.

"No way. I've read all twenty of your books, and I'm waiting patiently for the next."

"Flattery will get you everywhere," Lilly said. "What are you drinking, Wyatt?"

"Lemonade, though I've taken a liking to Mama's Jamaican tea."

Bertram arrived with drinks for Mama and Lilly, and an icy glass of lemonade for me.

"You're mighty popular tonight, Cowboy. Sittin' between two good lookin' women."

"Did you meet Lilly?"

"Mama introduced us. If she hadn't, I'd have done it myself."

"Bertram's my bud," Lilly said.

"Watch him," I said. "He's everybody's bud, and he's been married more times than I can count."

"Don't be tellin' all my secrets," he said.

"It's all right," Lilly said. "I have a couple of exes myself."

The noise in the bar had already reached a fevered pitch, half the group calling the hogs, the other half showing them the hook 'em horns sign. When glass shattered on oiled wood, Bertram's smile disappeared.

"Gotta go tend to them wild animals. Be back later with more drinks. They's on the house tonight, by the way."

"I really like him," Lilly said as Bertram hurried away through the raucous crowd.

"And he must like you," I said. "I can't recall him ever giving anyone free drinks. He even adds the cost of my lemonade to my rent each month."

Mama reached across the table and grasped Lilly's wrist. "We're all here now. Why don't you explain how you want us to help you?"

"I met Wyatt at Goose Island, the resort and health spa south of here. He was working for Quinlan Moore, the movie producer. Quinlan wrote a book in college called *Blood Horror* and hired me to adapt it into a screenplay. He wants to shoot it in New Orleans and mix in a little local flavor. That's where you two come in."

"Baby, I'm kind of expensive. For lots less money, you can get the same thing from a local tour guide."

Mama's comment brought a smile to Lilly's pixie face. "They wouldn't have the insider knowledge of voodoo and perspective of local history like you have. Besides, with Quinlan money is no object. He wants this film to be his *Star Wars*."

"If you say so," Mama said.

"I promise you'll both be well compensated."

Mama broke into a smile of her own. "That's what I like to hear. Where do we start?"

"I'd like a primer on the City's past voodoo queens and gris gris men. You know, like Marie Laveau and Doctor John."

Mention of the two caught me by surprise, and I tipped over my glass of lemonade, hurriedly trying to absorb the spill with a woefully inadequate napkin. Seeing the ruckus, Bertram came running with a bar towel. After frowning at me, he winked at Lilly before leaving the table.

"Wyatt, you're white as a sheet," Lilly said. "What's the problem?"

"Sorry. I'm having an issue with a ghost. I found out tonight that a hoodoo man is part of my problem. I was a little unnerved when you mentioned his name."

Lilly clenched her fist, leaning her chin against it. "A ghost? Your home is haunted?"

"Not quite that simple," I said.

"What, then?"

"Wyatt's haunted," Mama said. "A spirit from the past is with him all the time. Even now."

Lilly glanced first at Mama and then at me. "You're making this up, right?"

"Unfortunately not. Mama channeled the ghost for me. It even told her his name."

Lilly turned her disbelieving gaze to Mama and then slowly back to me. She didn't even flinch when another glass bounced three times across the floor before exploding into a hundred shards. There was so much noise, no one else in the crowded barroom seemed to notice. Bertram shook his head as he waded through the crowd with a broom and dustpan.

"You can channel ghosts? For real?"

"Can't everybody?" Mama said, smiling and winking at me.

"You two are pulling my chain," Lilly said.

"We're not. I've apparently had this spirit with me all my life."

"And you're just finding out about it?"

"Stress," Mama said. "Though Wyatt's a mentally healthy person, he's had a tough year. Enough so he fell off the wagon for a while."

"What were you doing when you saw this ghost?"

"Sitting with a friend's mother in the hospital. The room was dark. I was asleep in a chair beside her bed when I felt something cold and moist touch my cheek. It was a ghost."

"You were dreaming," Lilly said.

"I saw what I saw. What's downright weird is the next morning, the woman I was staying with told me she'd also seen a ghost, but a different one."

Lilly shook her head as she massaged her chin. "You think the hospital is haunted?"

"Aren't they all?" Mama said.

"God, I hope not," Lilly said. "You two are creeping me out."

The noise level didn't stop me from hearing a voice I recognized. I glanced toward the bar just in time to see Carla Manetti speaking to Bertram. My favorite Cajun bartender immediately pointed to our table. When Carla turned toward the front door, I jumped up to catch her.

"Carla. Where are you going?" I said, grabbing her arm.

"I didn't know you were busy."

"It's just Mama Mulate and an old friend. Please join us."

"I don't want to interrupt."

I pulled her back through the crowd. "You're not leaving until you meet Lilly."

"Wyatt…"

45

"I won't take no for an answer."

Bertram almost beat us to the table with fresh drinks for everyone and a Hurricane for Carla. He winked at me when I mouthed him a silent thank you.

"Carla Manetti, this is Lilly Bliss," I said.

Looking like a lost puppy, Carla shook Lilly's hand. Recognizing the look in her eyes, Lilly let go and gave her a hug. When Carla began to weep, Lilly kept squeezing."

"What's wrong, honey?" she asked.

Before Carla could answer, Mama joined in the hug. "Baby, tell us what's the matter?"

By now, Carla was crying and couldn't talk. She finally got out a single word.

"Eddie..."

"What did that son-of-a-bitch do to you?" I said.

Carla's head was sagging, but she shook it and waved her hand. "Nothing I didn't allow."

"Are you talking about Eddie Toledo?" Mama asked.

Carla nodded. "He led me on, but I let him. It's all my fault. Still..."

"I know all about Eddie Toledo," Mama said. "I had a brief affair with him myself. Believe me, his karma will catch up with him one of these days."

"But I trusted him," Carla said, blubbering.

Mama held the Hurricane to Carla's lips until she'd drank a healthy swig. "Take a deep breath," she said.

"I'll kick his New Jersey butt," I said, joining in their group hug.

My comment made Mama smile and shake her head. "I don't think so. You're the most non-violent person I've ever met."

"It's okay," Carla said, pushing me away and taking the glass. "I needed someone to talk to."

"Baby, we're here for you," Mama said.

"Who is this asshole?" Lilly asked.

" Close friend of Wyatt's," Mama said, glaring at me.

"Hey, don't blame me for this. I didn't force either one of you to go out with him."

"Other than being good in bed, that's about all I can say

positive about him," Mama said.

Even Carla couldn't suppress a smile when Lilly said, "Maybe I should meet Eddie."

"He's attractive and intelligent. He held my mama's hand; even kissed it. He ambushed me," she said.

I motioned Bertram for more drinks but needn't have bothered as he was already on his way.

"Never trust a damn Yankee," he said, giving Carla's shoulder a tap.

"Thanks for being here for me. I'm okay now," Carla said. "Sorry for being such a pain in the ass."

"Men are the pains in the ass," Mama said, glowering at me.

"Don't look at me like that. You know I don't fit the mold of a predatory male."

No one at the table remarked on my comment, but all three women either rolled their eyes or else made disbelieving faces.

"It's all right, Wyatt," Lilly finally said. "We like you anyway."

I tried to change the subject. "Lilly's a writer. She's working on a screenplay with elements of the supernatural. Mama and I are introducing her to a little local culture with emphasis on ghosts, goblins, and things that go bump in the night."

"Tell me your last name again," Carla said.

"Bliss."

"The real Lilly Bliss?" Carla said.

"Afraid so," Lilly said.

"You have to be kidding me. I love all your books."

"Oh my! I'm turning red," Lilly said.

"I'm so happy to meet you," Carla said, shaking her hand.

"Thanks, but I'm just a normal person with a vivid imagination."

"That's a fact," I said.

"Like Wyatt said, he and Mama are helping me put a New Orleans' spin on my screenplay. Sounds like the first place we want to see is the hospital where Wyatt saw the ghost."

"It was Carla's mom that I was staying with when we both

saw a ghost."

"Oschner is not that old," Carla said. "If you want to visit the spookiest hospital on earth, you should check out Charity Hospital."

"Of course," Mama said. "What a brilliant idea."

"Carla's chief librarian at U.N.O. and knows more about local history than almost anyone," I said.

"What's the deal with Charity?" Lilly asked.

"The second oldest continuously operated hospital in America, the original location founded in the seventeen-hundreds. It was enormous, most of the patients were indigents."

"Was?"

"Flooded during Katrina, evacuated and never reopened," Carla said. "You must have seen it. Seems like every station showed the same clips over and over."

"Of course I did. Most of the patients had no insurance," Lilly said.

"The facilities weren't luxurious, but it was the only hospital homeless people had available to them," Mama said.

The three women stared at me when I said, "Three hots and a cot."

"Really, Wyatt," Carla said. "Have a little more compassion."

"I didn't create the saying. People understood what they were getting into when they went to Charity," I said.

"Charity had the second best Level I Trauma Center in the U.S., it's emergency room the busiest."

"New Orleans is a violent and dangerous city," Lilly said. "Katrina pointed out the fact to the rest of the world."

"I'll bet you're right, Carla. There are probably more ghosts in that deserted building than just about anyplace in the city," Mama said.

Carla agreed. "Maybe the world. I wouldn't be surprised."

"Then we need to check it out," Lilly said. "How do we go about it?"

Carla raised her hand. "The Louisiana State University System owns the property. My friend at U.N.O. is on the board. He'll get us into the hospital."

"When?" Lilly asked.

"I'll talk to him tomorrow and find out."

"Great!" Lilly said. "But we're not doing this unless you're a part of it. With your knowledge, I want you on my team, along with Mama and Wyatt."

Mama grabbed her purse. "I have to visit the lady's room and freshen up. You girls want to come along?"

I was soon sitting by myself at the table, listening to dozens of football fans as they grew ever louder. Eddie Toledo didn't see me when he entered the door and made his way to the bar. Mama, Lilly, and Carla didn't see him, laughing when they returned from the ladies room.

"We're going down the street for more drinks, and then visit a little blues club I just adore."

"Great," I said. "I'll clear our tab with Bertram."

"Just us girls," Mama said. "You're not invited, but you can still be a dear and clear the tab for us."

"Thanks," I said as they walked away without me.

Bertram was waiting behind the bar for me, check in hand. "I thought you said the drinks were on the house."

"And they would have been if Miss Lilly had tried to pay. Since she didn't, it goes on your tab."

I glanced at the slip. "Fine. Pile it on."

"Don't I always? Eddie's on the other side of the bar."

"I saw him come in. Good thing the girls didn't."

"Why, is he in hot water?"

"You kidding? That's how he stays when it comes to women."

"Ain't it the truth. I'll bring you a lemonade soon as I take another pitcher of beer to that table of drunk Arkies."

Eddie began smiling and waving the moment he saw me. "Pull up a stool, Cowboy. I don't like drinking alone and was hoping you'd be here."

"It's impossible to be alone in the French Quarter this time of year."

"That's a fact. What's up?"

"Your ass, thirty minutes earlier."

"Why, was..."

"That's right. I was drinking with two of your

49

ex-girlfriends."

"Just two? I was at a party once when three girlfriends showed up. Though they weren't exes at the time, they all were when I went home alone."

"I don't know if I should feel sorry for, or envy you," I said.

"Oh, knock it off. You're no saint when it comes to women."

"Tell me about it. All my exes have."

Bertram showed up with lemonade for me and another Chivas and soda for Eddie. He didn't have time to hang around for small talk. Eddie clicked my glass.

"Here's to our exes. May they long stay that way. Which of my past girlfriends were you drinking with?"

"Mama Mulate and Carla Manetti."

"Carla, huh? That didn't take long."

"Your ears must have been burning."

"You can hardly call her ex. We had breakfast, and then visited her mother in the hospital. That's about it."

"Apparently not. It took two Hurricanes to calm her down. I'm surprised she can still walk."

"New Orleans' girls can hold their liquor."

"You're still in trouble," I said.

"Not my fault. Carla's aunt was sitting with her mother. We left to eat but never made it any further than my apartment. She was like a wild woman."

"If it were her idea then why is she so mad at you?"

"I made a tactical error not long ago and gave another woman the key to my apartment. She came in without knocking. To say there was a row would be an understatement. At least she threw the key at me as she and Carla were storming out the door."

"Thank heaven for small favors," I said.

"I love Carla a lot. Smart woman, very attractive, and a tiger in bed. I think you know that already."

"I kick myself every time I think of it."

"And I was looking forward to her mom's Italian cooking."

"Give her a few days. Maybe she'll forgive you."

"Doubt it. I might get a date with her mom, though. She liked me. I could tell."

"If Mama Manetti liked you, then you still have a chance. She has Carla's attention."

"Maybe I should send her flowers."

"She might appreciate something else even more."

"Like what?"

Something you might be able to help with because of your job. She told me a story at the hospital when I sat with her."

"Don't keep me in suspense."

"Her great grandfather worked for the Black Hand when he came over from Italy. He got his son a job with the gang, and it turned out badly."

"Carla's grandfather was part of the Black Hand?"

"Great grandfather, yes. Though her grandfather claimed he never actually worked for them, he was accused of murder and hung by a mob. Since the prime suspect was dead, the investigation never went any further. The whole affair is still a stigma to the family name."

"How can I help?" Eddie asked.

"Find the real murderer and absolve Carla's grandfather of the crime."

Eddie grinned and sipped his Scotch. "You kidding? Talk about a cold case. How long's it been since they hung him?"

"Eighty years, I imagine."

"I'm good, Cowboy, but I ain't that good," he said.

"Maybe the facts don't have to be a hundred percent."

"Are you saying I could fake the evidence?"

"Why not? You're a Fed."

"I don't think I like that remark," he said.

"Comes with the territory."

"Even if I faked it, who would believe me?"

"Mama Manetti, for one."

"Hell, Wyatt, it would likely upset the victim's family if the presumed killer were ever exonerated."

"Even after eighty years?"

"You kidding me? The relatives of Jim Thorpe are trying to dig up his remains in Pennsylvania for reburial in Oklahoma. He's been dead for sixty years. Relatives don't give up. You're asking me to open a potential can of worms."

"Then you won't help?"

"Didn't say that. With all the historical data we have downtown, I could solve the case if anyone can."

"Great. Where do you start?"

"Not me, Cowboy, us. All this talk about Mama Manetti's lasagna has whetted my appetite. You hungry for a little Italian cooking?"

Chapter 7

We were soon on our way to Metairie in Eddie's commonplace Ford sedan, the lights of New Orleans disappearing in the mirror as we motored west on I-10. The unincorporated suburb lies between New Orleans and the Armstrong International Airport in Keener, and is home to nearly half a million people.

"No one cooks Italian like my own dear mother, but Via Vittorio Veneto is the best replacement I've found between visits back home. Ever eaten there?"

"Never heard of it."

"Lots of Italians live in Metairie, especially in Old Metairie. I was drunk one night and wandered into this place. I've been going back ever since, though I haven't visited in awhile."

"What's stopped you?"

"The owner's daughter. She has the hots for me."

"And?"

"She's the hostess and likes her family's cooking a little too much."

"She's fat?"

"A pound or so over two-hundred, I'd say. Too bad because she has the face of an angel."

"Is she a good person?"

"Great personality and wonderful to be around."

"Then maybe you shouldn't be so picky," I said.

"I have my standards."

"Yeah, like Mama said, your karma's going to catch you

one of these days."

"Mama Mulate said that?"

"Among other things I won't repeat."

"Don't worry about my karma. You're not entirely flawless yourself, you know."

"Maybe that's why we get along so well."

"I'll drink to that," he said. "Soon as we're seated at Via Vittorio Veneto. There could be a wait. It's quite popular with the locals."

Via Vittorio Veneto wasn't as expensive as its name sounded. The classic wooden building could have passed as an uninteresting box of a building, except for the neon sign in front advertising its existence.

"Relax," Eddie said. "It looks great on the inside."

"And the food?"

"You won't be disappointed, I guarantee."

I knew Eddie wasn't hyping me the moment he opened the door to the dim room, light supplied primarily by flickering candles and pulsating neon. An absolutely stunning brunette beamed when she saw us.

"Eddie," she said, rushing around the lectern for a hug. "Where you been?"

The young woman swept a hand through her long hair, dark eyes flashing in the cozy area's pale light.

"Toni, is that you?"

"It's me," she said, pirouetting to show her body. "How do I look?"

"Like a million dollars," he said.

He wasn't lying. Toni's low-cut blouse exposed lots of cleavage, pink lips causing a curvy body to seem even more abundant. Though maybe weighing one hundred thirty, she was nowhere near two hundred pounds. She spoke with a distinct Metairie accent.

"Who's your handsome friend?" she asked.

"Toni Bergamo meet Wyatt Thomas."

When I offered my hand, she pushed it away and gave me a hug. "If you're a friend of Eddie's, you already family to me."

"Then my thoughts are incestuous."

"You making me blush," she said, giving me another

54

quick hug.

"Hey, what about me?" Eddie said.

Toni pecked his lips. "Mama come see who finally came back to see us."

An attractive woman in a flowing black dress hurried out of the kitchen. She could have passed for Toni's older sister and began smiling the moment she saw Eddie.

"You no good," she said, hugging him. "Where you been?"

The diners in the small restaurant watched as Eddie twirled the woman around, hugging her when he finally returned her feet to the floor.

"Dreaming of your lasagna, Adele."

She slapped Eddie playfully. "You liar! You got some woman chasing after you and got no time to come see Toni and me."

"Not true. This is my friend Wyatt."

Unlike her daughter, Adele shook my hand. "Happy to meet you, Wyatt. I hope you're not as bad as this one," she said, cocking her head toward Eddie.

She also spoke with an accent, maybe Italian-flavored Metairie though it was hard to tell. People from every suburb in the metropolitan area had their own distinct speech characteristics, Adele probably born and raised in Metairie.

"Worse," Eddie said. "Wyatt's the person I ask when I need advice about women."

Adele shook her head. "Then come into this place. You are both welcome here no matter how bad you are."

The theme from *The Godfather* was playing as she led us to a table, complete with a red-checkered tablecloth, in a corner of the restaurant. Toni kissed Eddie again after handing us red, leather-bound menus. When she disappeared into the kitchen, leaving me alone with Eddie, I glanced at him with a grin.

"If you think she's fat, I'm going to have your eyes examined. She's a knockout."

"She's lost weight. That's all I can say."

We had little time to discuss Toni's body before Adele and an older man returned from the kitchen. Adele was carrying a bottle of chianti, the man two wine glasses. She poured each of us a glass before I could say something. Eddie didn't notice. He was on his feet, embracing the little man.

"You're looking good, Pancho. Don't you ever age?"

"Clean living," the person named Pancho said, his smile highlighting a set of white teeth.

"Pancho Bergamo, this is Wyatt Thomas."

Pancho had a firm grip for such a small man. Flour dusted his black pants and his checkered shirt rivaled the tablecloth on our table. His shoes were worn, but polished, his socks white. Like his pants, his dark flattop was peppered with grey, as was his bushy mustache. His smile never seemed to disappear.

"Glad to meet you, Pancho. Eddie's raved about this place so long, I finally made him take me here."

"And you won't be sorry," he said, patting me on the back before returning to the kitchen.

"No need for this," Eddie said, handing his menu to Adele. "You know what I want."

"I'll have the same," I said when Adele glanced at me.

As she hurried away to the kitchen, Eddie filled me in on their family history.

"Pancho's Adele's papa, Toni's grandpapa. Adele's a widow. Her husband was a roughneck on an offshore drilling rig, killed in a natural gas explosion."

"Dangerous work," I said.

"Adele's a terrific looking woman. Hard to believe she's been unattached so long."

"Maybe she likes it that way. It's easy to see where Toni gets her looks from."

Eddie nodded. "I've thought about asking her out."

"What stopped you?"

"Probably wouldn't be a good idea."

"You're probably right," I said.

"Pancho's lived here forever. Not much has happened in Metairie he doesn't know about. After dinner, we can ask him about Carla's granddad."

"Sure we won't be stirring up a bucket of worms?"

"Nah, he likes to gossip more than an old woman. He also likes to sample the house wine, if you know what I mean. His tongue will be loosed by the time we finish our cannolis."

56

"Got to hand it to you, Eddie."

"How's that?"

"You boys at the Justice Department employ all sorts of sophisticated investigative techniques. I'm impressed."

"Yeah, well the old methods still work best."

Music had segued into a Sinatra torch song, the ambiance and pleasant aroma wafting from the kitchen whetting my appetite. Other diners came and went as we waited for our meal, Toni smiling and working diligently as they did. Adele soon appeared, pushing a cart bearing two steaming entrees.

"You're not drinking your wine," she said.

"One sauce I have to avoid," I said. "The water you brought is all I need."

"Not to worry," Eddie said. "I'll drink what he doesn't."

"Good for you, Wyatt. My husband, may God rest his soul, had a problem with the bottle. I had to knock him out with a baseball bat one night he got so mean."

"Whoa!" I said. "I was lots of nasty things when I drank. Mean wasn't one of them."

"Then you just like Grandpapa. He drinks till he falls asleep on the old recliner in the kitchen, and then with a smile on his face. Half the time he don't even make it home."

"I've never seen him frown," Eddie said.

"Oh, I made him lose his smile a time or two when I was young."

"I'll bet you did," I said. "Your lasagna smells wonderful."

"Then eat," she said, backing away from the table.

"I think she likes you," Eddie said.

"I like her too," I said as she disappeared into the kitchen. "She's kind of sexy, in a mature sort of way,"

"Toni didn't get her good looks from Pancho."

"Maybe his positive personality though," I said.

As the last customer left the little restaurant, Pancho locked the door behind them and flipped a lightswitch to tell everyone the restaurant was closed for the night. He returned to our table with a fresh bottle of Chianti. Adele and Toni joined us when they finished straightening up, Toni sipping cola through a straw, Adele working on a gin martini.

"The only place I can get Italian food as good as this is at my mom's, and she lives in New Jersey."

"Bring her in," Pancho said. "We'd like to meet her."

"I'll do that. She's coming to see me next month, and it'll be her first visit to New Orleans."

"You kidding me?" Pancho said. "What about your dad? He coming too?"

"Dad passed when I was in high school."

"So sorry," Pancho said. "I know he musta been a fine man."

"Thanks, Pancho."

Eddie finished the last of his Chianti and Pancho topped up his glass, Sinatra still singing in the background. When Toni burped and grabbed her mouth, everyone laughed.

"How old's your mom?" Pancho asked.

"Pushing seventy," Eddie said. "Why? Need a date?"

"Sure. Maybe we can compare Italian recipes," Pancho said.

"She'd like that," Eddie said. "I'll bring her in."

Adele wasn't paying much attention to Eddie and her dad. She'd inched her chair closer to mine, finally grabbing my hand.

"And you, Wyatt? What do you do?"

"Ex lawyer," Eddie answered for me. "Now he's just a private dick and glorified tour guide."

"Ex?" Adele said.

"Long story. I'd like to tell you about it someday if you have the time."

Still holding my hand, she squeezed it.

"I'd like that."

Toni was watching her mother's hand and didn't seem too happy where it was placed. Bending over her lap, she grinned and gave me a glimpse of her ample breasts. Adele pushed her away, smiling when Toni gave her a dirty look. Eddie had a dirty look of his own, feeling slighted for attention.

"Tour guide?" Toni said.

"Wyatt's partner is a voodoo mambo named Mama Mulate. Local rich folks hire them when they need a spell cast on someone," Eddie said.

Toni's dark eyes grew wide. "Really?"

"Eddie exaggerates," I said.

"Then what do you do, Wyatt Thomas?" Adele asked.

"This and that. I work for myself. People hire me when they have a problem and think I can help them."

Like her dad, Adele's drink wasn't her first of the night. She wasn't soused but was feeling no pain. Her voice had grown huskier as we'd sat there. Toni wasn't smiling.

"I got a little problem," Adele said. "How much do you charge?"

"Moth-er!" Toni said. "You starting to embarrass me."

Grabbing her arm, she yanked her up from the chair.

"What?" Adele said.

"I want to talk to you. Alone," she said, pulling her away from the table and into the kitchen.

"Those two," Pancho said, topping up his and Eddie's glasses. "You'd think they were sisters the way they carry on."

Eddie was apparently not happy with the attention Adele was paying me. When he glared across the table, I shrugged. He soon forgot about Toni and Adele, remembering the reason, other than the food, we were there in the first place.

"Say, Pancho, you know about everything there is to know about Metairie."

Pancho nodded. "Lived here all my life. Why?"

"Wyatt and I were wondering about something and thought we'd ask you about it."

"Ask away," Pancho said.

"You're Italian. What do you know about the local mob?"

Pancho's smile disappeared, and he quickly crossed his arms tightly across his chest.

"Nothing," he said.

"Oh, come on," Eddie said. "I'll bet you know more than you're letting on."

"I said I don't know nothing. You got a problem with that?"

Eddie apparently failed to detect the faint rattle of Pancho's warning, persisting with his line of questioning.

"Everyone in town knows one thing or another. We have a question, and I bet you can answer it."

Pancho pushed away from the table and turned to go. He

wheeled around when I touched his arm.

"Pancho, we're sorry. Eddie misspoke. He's not suggesting you know anything about organized crime in Metairie," I said.

"He's an idiot. Get him out of my restaurant and don't ever bring him back. Now!"

I grabbed Eddie's arm, pulling him to his feet, and then dragged him to the door, Pancho right behind us. By now, Adele and Toni had stuck their heads out of the kitchen to see what all the fuss was about. Pancho pushed us out the front door, closing it with a not-so-subtle slam. Eddie stepped back and kicked the door so hard it rattled in its frame.

"Why that old bastard..."

"Let's go before he calls the cops," I said, grabbing his arm again and yanking him off the porch.

I had to push him across the parking lot to the car. Adele and Toni were waiting for us, and both were crying. When Adele grabbed Eddie and hugged him, his anger quickly diffused.

"What did you say to Grandpapa to make him so angry?" Toni said.

"I'm sorry. I'm going to apologize."

"No, Eddie. Papa don't listen to nobody when he flips out like this. He'll have his gun by now. He'll kill you."

"Why is he so upset?"

"What did you say to him?" Toni asked.

"Nothing. We wanted to see if he knew something that happened when he was younger."

"Like what?"

"The grandfather of a friend of ours was lynched by a Metairie mob because they assumed he was a hitman for the Black Hand. I thought your father might know something about it. He gave us no chance to ask."

Still hugging him, Adele shook her head. "Papa never talks about the mob."

"Your father worked for them?"

"Please, Eddie. You don't understand."

"I think I'm beginning to. Get in the car, Wyatt," he said, pulling away from her grasp.

A truck raced past on the street, horn blaring when the driver noticed the two women. Toni was crying, trying to pull her mother away from the car. Adele wrenched her arm loose and banged on the car window until Eddie lowered it.

"There's an old man that works in the kitchen at the Havana Club. His name is Paco. I don't know his last name. He's a friend of Papa's and knows about the hanging. Some say he was there when it happened."

"How do you know this?" Eddie asked.

"Just trust me," she said.

Eddie's anger faded again. Taking her hand, he kissed it.

"I'm so sorry about tonight, but I swear I'll make amends with your dad."

Toni cried as she wrestled her mother from the car.

"Don't bother, you bastard!" she said. "I hate you."

Eddie raised the window and raced off across the shell and gravel parking lot, spinning his wheels and not slowing until we were on the main road through town.

Chapter 8

"University of Virginia law school valedictorian, huh?" I said as Eddie narrowly avoided sideswiping a parked car.

"Shut up, smart ass. I didn't get any contributions from you."

My smirk was all the answer he needed. Wheeling into the parking lot of an all-night convenience store, he slid to a stop, slamming the door behind him as he hurried inside. He returned with a tallboy for him and a lemon drink he tossed to me.

"Thanks," I said.

Popping the top, he drank until beer dribbled down his shirt collar. After a moment, his frown had disappeared.

"Now what?" he said.

"The Havana Club. I'm game if you are."

Eddie threw the empty can out the window and cranked the engine.

"You serious?"

"As a heart attack."

"Might be risky. The Havana Club's the biggest mob hangout around. Half the customers are criminals, the other half wannabes."

"You afraid someone might recognize you?"

"Do I look worried to you?"

"Hell, Eddie, I don't think you'd worry if you were facing down a dozen screaming ninjas. Where is this place, anyway?"

"Fat City," he said.

"Then lead on, brother."

I hadn't been to Fat City, Metairie's response to Bourbon Street in years. It was once home to many lounges, Vegas-style nightclubs, strip joints, and happy hour bars. I'd heard some of the establishments had fallen out of favor, and that the area had started going downhill. I wasn't prepared for what we saw upon reaching the Havana Club's parking lot.

Pink and blue rotating lights flooded the entrance. A stretch limo was unloading passengers at the front door. Two doormen dressed in fancy uniforms smiled as they catered to the group of already well-oiled customers pouring out of the vehicle. They frowned when Eddie parked his own car, and we walked toward the throng of activity.

"You got reservations?"

"No, but I have a hundred dollar bill," Eddie said, waving it in the man's face.

His frown became a smile as he took the money and led us through the main door.

"Forty bucks cover charge," the doorman in a festive red sports coat said.

Eddie gave him three twenties. "Keep the change."

"Delores will take you to your table," he said.

When our hostess appeared through the door, loud music and crowd noise poured out behind her. Delores was a stunner, dressed in a short, low-cut red dress that accentuated long legs and other physical assets. Eddie couldn't stop grinning, and Delores didn't seem to mind.

"Where have you been all my life," he said as she led us into the club.

Her response was lost in a blare of trumpets and saxophones, and the combined cacophony of loud club patrons. We followed her to a booth not far from a large stage, Eddie giving her a twenty for her efforts.

"What are you gentlemen drinking tonight?"

"Blue martini for me and lemonade for my teetotaling friend."

"I didn't know the Justice Department paid so well," I said when Delores left the table.

"Lots of things you don't know," he said.

The stage was elevated into tiers, a showband in the midst of a number. Eight horn players formed a dancing row, a hot guitarist and energetic drummer helping heat things up. The big band sound had everyone captivated, though the musicians weren't all they were watching.

"Check those dancing babes," Eddie said. "They look like Vegas showgirls."

"Hell yes!" I said. "This place is perfect. I can't believe I've never heard about it."

"Like I said. Lots of things you don't know."

Delores appeared through the animated audience with our drinks. She winked again, and blew Eddie a kiss when he gave her another twenty.

"I know we'll both be broke before we get out of here if you don't stop passing out money like that," I said.

"Stop worrying. I got a wad tonight, and there's method to my madness."

"You got the madness part right. I don't know about your method."

"Shut up, loser," he said.

Lighting in the club had dimmed even further to focus on the show onstage. It took a while for my eyes to adjust. When they did, I realized many of the patrons weren't couples. Not far from us, the waitstaff had pulled three tables together for a dozen or more men.

"You see what I see?"

"If they aren't mob members, they're missing a bet," Eddie said. "I haven't seen that many gold chains, diamond rings, and pomaded hair since the last Mafia movie I saw."

"I'll bet every one of them is packing something beneath the fancy suits and sports coats they're wearing."

"Got that right," he said.

Everyone at the table was drinking hard liquor, no beer cans or wine glasses in sight. They were all having a terrific time, yelling, slapping each other's backs, and fondling the waitresses that had formed an endless procession to and from the tables. From the money changing hands, I could see why. They grew louder, along with the band, no one in the audience protesting.

"Check the saxophone player."

I'd already noticed. The woman had blonde hair and wore a short, black skirt. Like the rest of the horn players, she was dancing as she played, kicking her boots in the air.

"I think I know her," I said.

"You're shitting me!"

"We graduated from high school together. We were in band together for four years. At least I think it's her."

"You were in a band? What instrument did you play?"

"Sax, just like her. We used to hold hands when we went on bus trips."

"What else did you hold?"

"We had fun and did lots of things. Screwing wasn't one of them. She wanted to keep her virginity until she married."

"How shallow of her," Eddie said. "What's her name?"

"Jeneen Presley."

"As in Elvis?"

"Yeah, but I don't think they're related. I could be wrong, though."

"I hope you're not be making this up," he said.

"Why?"

"Cause I'm going to introduce myself and bring her over here when they take a break."

"No way."

"I'm checking out your story, buddy. If you're lying, you're dying."

"It's been a while. She might not be the person I think she is."

"You waffling on me?"

"Just saying..."

"Stow it, loser. If you're going to lie, at least stick to your story."

Before I could defend myself, Delores appeared with more drinks. This time, Eddie gave her his credit card. It seemed he'd forgotten why we were here in the first place.

"What are we going to do about Paco?"

"Nothing we can do. He's probably gone home already. Now that we know where to find him, we can question him later."

"Then are you ready to go?"

"Why hell no! I still have to meet Miss Jeneen, if that's what her name actually is."

The band was only into its first set, and we had a long wait before the break. When the last song ended, spotlights began flooding center stage. An emcee with greasy hair and sweaty brow appeared from behind the curtains.

"Brass & Sass, ladies and gentlemen. Now, the one you've all been waiting for. Straight from Las Vegas for one night only, let's give a whopping round of applause for New Orleans' own Creole angel, Latitia Boiset."

The crowd went wild as the emcee rushed offstage, and the band fired up a hot number in preparation for the appearance of the star of the show. We weren't disappointed.

White smoke blew up from center stage, a young woman appearing through it dressed in an outfit even more revealing than the ones the backup dancers wore. They quickly joined her in an energetic dance that left the audience in awe. When they finished the number, the lights dimmed again, finally brightening to reveal Latitia Boiset standing behind a microphone.

The band started playing a slow melody, backing the young woman as she belted out a show-stopper.

"What a set of pipes," I said.

"And a bod to match," Eddie said. "Now I'm really in lust."

After another number, the emcee returned amid thunderous applause.

"Miss Boiset will be back after a short intermission. Don't you dare go."

"What an act," Eddie said. "I can't believe I've never heard of her."

"With a voice like that, it won't be long before everyone knows her name."

"I'll be back."

"Where are you going?"

"I told you, to see if you really know the sax player."

"Don't embarrass us, Eddie."

"You only have yourself to worry about, loser."

I hadn't seen Jeneen in years. During high school, she'd been a brunette. I was beginning to think Eddie was right when he appeared through the crowded club, holding the woman's hand. Her smile grew when she saw me.

"Wyatt, oh my God! What are you doing here?"

"Slumming, Jeneen," I said. "Just like old times."

She scooted in beside me, hugging and kissing me, and then not letting go. Eddie slid in beside her.

"You can't imagine how many times I've thought of you," she said. "Last I heard, you were away at L.S.U. and had gotten married."

"Things change. I'm single again. What about you? I had no idea you were playing in a show band."

"A guitar player got in my pants shortly after we graduated high school. I followed him to Nashville. He turned out to be a sorry prick. We split, but not before he got me a gig as a studio musician. Been working there and making lots of money ever since, until my best friend Latitia talked me into joining the show band that travels with her when she's on tour."

"The singer is your best friend?" Eddie said.

"Want to meet her?"

"You kidding me? You bet we do. I can't believe Wyatt never told me about you. You can really play that horn. I was blown away."

"Why thank you, Eddie. Most of the customers are only interested in T. and A. You ought to see the pinch marks on my ass."

"I'd love to," he said. "Buy you a drink?"

"Rum and Coke," she said. "I'll get Latitia."

"What a babe," Eddie said.

"I don't remember her being that hot in high school."

"Then you're an idiot."

"I never said I was a rocket scientist."

"Got that right. Doesn't matter because I think I'm in love."

"Forgetting about Carla already?"

"Someone else is on my radar screen."

"Eddie, you're an idiot. You're in lust, not love."

"Stop telling me what I already know. When she comes

back, please, don't get in the way. Promise?"

"You're a freak. You know it?"

We watched Jeneen navigate past the mobster's table. She gave them a wide berth, her hands shielding her ass as she hurried past. It didn't stop a horde of wolf whistles and lude comments. When she returned with Latitia Boiset, my heart did a surprising somersault.

"Wyatt and Eddie meet the one and only Latitia Boiset."

The lighting in the large room had increased, everyone suddenly staring at our table. Jeneen slid in beside Eddie, Latitia beside me. She was more striking than I'd originally thought.

Black, curly hair draped to her bare shoulders, her pouty lips and obsidian eyes needing no makeup to keep one's gaze transfixed. Gold hoops hung from earlobes to shoulders, her ankles and wrists also awash in gold.

"What's the matter?" she asked.

"I have a strange sensation I know you."

"I've heard that line before."

It wasn't a line, my heart racing almost out of control. She winked when I grabbed her hand and squeezed.

"You have the voice of an angel."

"Trite," she said. "But I still enjoy hearing it. You okay?"

"I wasn't kidding. I feel I've known you all my life. Can I buy you a drink?"

"Janeen already has one, and Delores is bringing us something extra. We don't have much time before the next set starts."

Delores appeared through the crowded room with more drinks for Eddie and me, and shots for Jeneen and Latitia.

"Salud," Eddie said.

"Where you from, Latitia?" I asked.

"New Orleans. Grandmother called me Titia, and that's how all my friends know me."

"Then I hope you don't mind if that's what I call you."

We were still holding hands, and Titia didn't seem to mind. She had, in fact, scooted so close to me that not even the air-conditioned atmosphere of the Havana Club could chill the heat radiating from my body. Her frilly dress was a little-bit-of-nothing, and I could see goosebumps on her shapely thighs. Maybe it was why she was cuddling ever closer.

"And you?" she said.

"My parents had a plantation on River Road. We moved to the city when I was young. I don't even remember living there."

"You've never gone back?"

"No."

"Why not?"

"I don't have an answer."

"If you lived on a plantation, then you must be very rich."

"Would you still like me if you knew I wasn't?"

Titia's response was a passionate kiss. "I like you a lot, and feel you have many other good qualities."

"ESP?"

"My mother, bless her soul, could see things. Passed along in the family genes, she used to say. Though she's no longer with me, I sometimes think I'm just like her."

"Then she must have been a beautiful and extraordinary woman."

"Oh, she was," Titia said.

Lights were dimming, except for the dancing floods focused on center stage. A solo violin player was warming up the crowd for what was to follow. Delores brought more shots for Jeneen and Titia, and they quickly drained them.

"Gotta go," Titia said. "Will you still be here when we finish the set?"

"I'm not going anywhere."

"Promise?"

"I promise, unless an army arrives and yanks me out kicking and screaming."

Eddie grabbed Jeneen's arm before they could leave the table.

"Does your band work here a lot?"

"Whenever we're in town," she said.

"You seem to know everything about the place. Is there an old man that works in the kitchen named Paco?"

"You mean Crazy Paco?"

"Why do you call him that?"

"Because he is. He tells everyone he was once a hitman for

the Mafia."

"No one believes him?"

"You think the goons that frequent this place would let someone get away with saying that if it were true?"

"Guess not. Why do so many of the boys hang out here?"

"Because their boss owns the place. He owns more entertainment venues than anyone in south Louisiana."

"And who would that be?" Eddie asked.

Jeneen cupped her hands and whispered in his ear. "Frankie Castalano."

Chapter 9

The entire showband was soon onstage again, the lead guitarist, backed by horns and a half-dozen dancing girls, playing a wild riff. Mesmerized by music and dancing lights, the audience watched with rapt attention.

"Gotta go to the men's room. I'll be back," Eddie said.

Instead of the men's room, he made his way through the dimly lit hallway toward the door where he'd seen waiters entering and exiting. The kitchen area was awash in light and sound. When a woman dressed in a white smock walked past, he grabbed her elbow.

"Is Paco working tonight?"

"Who wants to know?" she said, revealing a missing front tooth.

"Paco's my uncle. I need to talk to him a second."

"Back that way," she said.

Too busy with the work at hand, no one noticed the man with longish hair and stylish sports coat meandering through the kitchen area. They kept pointing him toward a room in the back. Eddie opened the door to find an old man sitting on a low stool, a cigarette that was mostly ash protruding from his lips. He was working on a tub of potatoes with a shiny peeler.

"Paco, it's Eddie," he said, pulling up a stool beside him.

"I know you?"

"Course you do. You're my uncle. Remember?"

"If you say so."

Paco continued peeling potatoes.

71

"Last time I was here, you were telling me about your days as a hitman for the mob."

"Better not let my son hear you say that. He wouldn't like it much."

"You don't tell him and I sure won't."

Paco glanced at the door. "It's a long story."

"We have time. Remember when an angry mob lynched some Black Hand members?"

Someone outside the door peeked in, her load of dirty dishes rattling. When a cup crashed on the concrete floor, she kicked the shards against the wall and hurried away.

"You are talking a long time ago. I was just a kid then."

"But you know about it?"

"Oh yeah."

"Can you tell me?"

"Like I said. Frankie wouldn't like it."

"Frankie who?"

"My son, Frankie Castalano."

"You kidding me!" Eddie said. "What the hell are you doing peeling potatoes in this joint. Your son owns this place."

"Guess I talk too much. Frankie tells everyone I'm crazy cause he don't want to have to whack me."

"But you're not crazy."

Paco gave Eddie a puzzled glance. "Who you say you was?"

"Eddie. Can you tell me about the lynch mob?"

The door opened again before Paco could answer. Two well-dressed men, obviously packing heat beneath their expensive jackets, stopped in front of Eddie's stool.

"What are you doing back here?"

"Visiting from New Jersey," Eddie said. "My uncle left home when he was just a boy. Mom heard he settled in Metairie. His name was Paco. I thought this man might be him. I was mistaken."

The two men glared at Eddie, and then glanced at each other.

"New Jersey?"

"Yeah. Sorry, if I caused a stir."

Both men had little moustaches. One of them poked his

finger into Eddie's breastbone.

"The kitchen's off limits to guests. Next time get permission before you start rummaging around. Now get the hell outa here."

"Yes sir. Sorry, sir," Eddie said as he backed out the door.

The two goons didn't follow him. When he was safe in the dim light of the club, he headed to the men's room before returning to the booth.

❧

"Where've you been?" I asked. "You missed the last act. Jeneen and Titia are on their way back to the table."

"Tell you later, Cowboy," he said.

Their last set of the night completed, the two young women returned dressed casually, in jean shorts, Saint's tee shirts, and low-cut cowboy boots. They had light jackets over their arms as if they were ready to leave.

"Let's go have some real fun," Jeneen said.

"It's kind of nippy out there for shorts."

Jeneen and Latitia grinned. "You worry about your pants. We'll worry about ours," Jeneen said.

Duly chastised, Eddie flagged down a passing waitress, calling for our tab and paying it when Delores reached the table. No one seemed to recognize the two women as we walked through the club and exited the front door. We weren't so lucky when we reached Eddie's car, three goons waiting for us, propped against the Ford.

"I think you boys have a few questions to answer."

"Who are you?"

"Johnny Boy. I watch things around here."

"What did we do?" Eddie asked. "We paid our tab."

Johnny Boy's expensive shoes and gaudy sports coat flashed in the light of a nearby streetlamp. Dark hair, slicked-back with a tad too much styling gel, framed his face in the club's flashing neon. His attempt at achieving a chic look failed miserably, partly because of a gold tooth.

"We ain't seen you in here before, have we, Ray?"

Ray was six inches taller than Johnny Boy and as deep through the chest as a professional wrestler. His steely eyes were unnerving.

"I ain't ever seen 'em," he said.

"You, Petey?"

Petey looked enough like Johnny Boy to be his brother, except younger and taller. His gold earring glinted as he lit a cigarette with a cheap lighter.

"Not me," he said.

"First time here," Eddie said. "Is there a problem?"

"Don't know. Is there?"

"No problem at all. Now, if you'll excuse us."

The two men closed in beside him. Though their coats and shoes weren't as expensive as Johnny Boy's, the bulges in their jackets were just as menacing.

"Not so fast. We want to see some identification."

Eddie opened his wallet, flashing his badge. "I'm the D.A., dumbass."

As if embarrassed, Johnny Boy smiled, slapped his forehead with the palm of his hand and stepped backwards.

"Whoa, why didn't you say something? We weren't expecting you till tomorrow night."

"Sorry about that. Now, if you don't mind," Eddie said.

The three men backed away from the car, letting Eddie unlock the door. Titia and I crawled into the backseat as Eddie walked Jeneen around and opened the door for her.

"Sorry, pal. I'll tell the boss you came early."

"You do that," Eddie said as he put his foot on the gas and wheeled out of the parking lot.

"You're the D.A.?" Jeneen asked.

"Off duty, and Metairie is a little out of my jurisdiction."

"Hey, I love authority," she said, scooting across the bench seat toward him.

They were soon acting like a couple of horny teenagers on their first unchaperoned date.

"Would anyone like to take a moonlight drive around the lake?" he asked.

"Sounds romantic," Jeneen said. "I'm in."

Titia had also slid closer to me in the back seat. "Something I haven't done since high school. Sounds like fun."

"I wonder who those goons mistook you for," I said.

"Don't know," Eddie said. "Whoever it is, he's obviously not looking out for his constituent's best interest."

We were soon heading north to Lakeshore Drive, clouds over the lake masking the light of a partially full moon. By now, Titia was in my arms and cuddling even closer as we smelled the lake's salty air.

"No matter where I've been, I love returning to New Orleans," she said. "There's no lake on earth like Pontchartrain."

"You three call it a lake," Eddie said. "For me, it's an inland sea. Way too vast to be a mere lake."

"There's a beach up ahead where my parents used to take us swimming when I was a little girl," Jeneen said. "Stop, Eddie. I want to go wading."

"You kidding me? It's December."

"It's not that cold. Besides, we're just going wading. Not swimming."

"Yeah, Eddie," Titia said. "Don't be a party-pooper. Wyatt and I want to go wading. Don't we, Wyatt?"

"Anywhere with you, babe," I said, though I wasn't relishing the thought of treading into cold water in my bare feet.

"Who's a party pooper?" Eddie said. "Why settle for a wade? Let's go skinny dipping."

Eddie wheeled into the sandy area that was once a beach, open to swimmers. Parking the large Ford, he pulled Jeneen out of the front seat. She quickly removed her boots and socks and ran toward the water lapping against the shore. Eddie followed, doffing all his clothes, and then hitting the water with a splash.

"Oh my God!" he said. "It's freezing. Throw me a towel."

Titia and I were in the throes of laughter. Since there was no towel, Jeneen waded out to him, cradling him in her arms. When I called to him, my words echoed across the lake.

"You okay?"

"Getting warmer by the second," he said.

Titia and I didn't wait for them to come out of the shallow water. Holding my hand, she directed me along the shoreline until we found a stone wall to sit on. We were soon in the throes of our own unbridled emotions.

"Wyatt, what's the matter?" she finally said.

"Nothing. I'm in heaven."

"But you're so quiet."

I squeezed her hand. "I have the strangest feeling I've known you forever."

Titia kissed me. "You've already used that line. You know what I feel like eating?"

"I'm afraid to ask."

"A dozen oysters."

"If I ate a dozen oysters right now, I'd explode from lust."

Titia laughed. "Then maybe what we need is coffee and beignets."

"I'm all in. The wind whipping off the lake is cutting right through my sports coat. I'll bet Eddie's turned into a chunk of ice by now."

"If I know Jeneen, there's no chance. I'll bet they're getting it on in the front seat of that old ladies car he drives."

"You think?"

She giggled. "Let's peek. They are probably doing it."

Eddie had his clothes back on when we reached the car. He and Jeneen weren't humping in the front seat but were not far from it. They both jumped when we opened the back door and climbed in.

"Hell, now I owe Wyatt a hundred dollars," Titia said.

"What?" they chimed as one.

"I bet him you'd be doing it in the front seat."

"Another fifteen minutes and you'd have won the bet," Jeneen said.

"Well, since you two have all your clothes on, let's go to the Quarter and get coffee and beignets."

I had to snicker at Eddie's next statement. "You two know how to ruin a good mood," he said.

"Hey, the night's still young," Jeneen said. "Strong coffee and sugary bennies sound pretty good, and we'll still have time for other things later."

"That's all I needed to hear," Eddie said, cranking the engine.

Even at three in the morning, Cafe du Monde was still crowded. We found an empty table on the patio across the street from Jackson Square and were soon drinking strong coffee and eating the best sugary confection on earth. With the horse's hooves clomping against cobblestone and echoing against the Cabildo and St. Louis Cathedral, a carriage passed on the street. A tugboat on the river behind us blew its horn.

Eddie and Jeneen were clutched in an amorous embrace, making even the half-inebriated customers around us uncomfortable. They finally managed to pull away.

"Get a room," a man at the next table said.

"It's a long way back to my apartment," Eddie said. "Anybody going with me?"

"Me," Jeneen said. "Can we drop you off, Titia?"

When she glanced at me, I squeezed her hand. "My place is just down the street. Come with me?"

Chapter 10

Tony Nicosia backed his convertible Mustang out of the garage of his small, New Orleans home. The weather chilly, though not cold, he had the top down. Pulling into the driveway, he saw his wife Lil waiting on the front porch. She wasn't smiling.

"You take that dog of yours more places than you do me," she said.

Tony gave her a quick kiss as he hurried into the house, a little white dog with a black patch around his eye hot on his heels.

"Did you forget about date tonight? Dinner and a movie, just like old times."

"Don't change the subject."

"Sorry. I was actually thinking about what we might do afterwards," he said with a wink.

"You're hopeless," she said. "Where are you going?"

"Taking Patch to the vet for his booster shots. I forgot my wallet. Seen it?"

"Lord help us!" she said, handing him the wallet. "You left it on the kitchen table. I was bringing it to you."

Tony kissed her again. "Don't know what I'd do without you."

"Yes you do."

Their marriage had lasted more years than he remembered. After marrying right out of high school, they'd had five children in quick succession. Now, their kids were all grown, Tony and Lil living alone, except for Patch. Tortured tires of a vehicle on a nearby street screeched the noise ending with a sickening thud of tortured metal. Tony grabbed Lil's hand, not reacting to the nearby fender bender.

"If you're lonely, we can work on number six tonight."

"In your dreams," she said.

"Think about it," he said, rushing out the door. "I'm in the mood already."

"You were born in the mood. When are you coming back?"

"Shouldn't take long," he said as he backed out of the driveway, onto the street.

The N.O.P.D. had recently canned Tony after twenty-five years of service, unsubstantiated allegations of misconduct the reason. The entire unit had come under scrutiny of the U.S. Justice Department. Anything but corrupt, Tony had been the proverbial baby thrown out with the bathwater following a post-Katrina purge.

A crackerjack lawyer had saved his pension. Now, he was making more money as a private dick than he ever had as a homicide detective. Still, he'd loved every minute of his days on the force, and thought of his new role as interim work until the N.O.P.D. saw the light and rehired him.

Traffic was scattered on Terpsichore, and he had no problem making it to the vet's office in time. The reception area was crowded with dogs, cats, and caring owners. Though most of the dogs were squirming or barking, Patch was a dream, never moving out of his lap.

Tony had rescued Patch from an abusive situation during the last storm that had threatened New Orleans. He was batching it at the time as Lil had left him because of his affair with a younger woman. He'd left the woman, and Lil had finally forgiven the discretion, but not his adoption of the dog. Having never had a pet, Tony stood his ground. They had made amends, and now, he and the dog were inseparable. His cell phone rang as he pulled out of the parking lot.

"Tony here," he said.

"Tony, it's Frankie Castalano. Remember me?"

Tony's heart skipped a beat. He knew only one person named Frankie Castalano. It wasn't a person he'd admit knowing.

"I ain't with the N.O.P.D. anymore, Mr. Castalano."

"I know that, and you can call me Frankie."

Frankie Castalano was the highest Mafia boss in the southeastern United States. Tony had met him only once, and not on friendly terms. Suddenly in the throes of an anxiety attack, he was determined not to let Castalano know it.

"What's up, Frankie?"

"I got a little problem. I hear you're a private dick now."

"Yes sir. That's a fact."

"I was impressed with you when we had our little involvement. You came across to me as a man with integrity—someone I can trust."

"I try to shoot straight, though my wife would tell you I'm not a perfect person," Tony said.

Castalano chuckled. "Lord knows I'm not casting stones. What are you doing right now?"

"Right this minute?"

"That's right."

"Leaving the vet with my dog and on my way home."

"I got a job for you," Castalano said.

"Great. I got nothing going right now."

"Then be here in twenty minutes."

"I got to take the dog to the house first."

"Not necessary. You know where I live, don't you?"

Everyone in New Orleans knew where Frankie Castalano lived. Every teenager in the city had driven his girlfriend past the gated complex bordering Lake Pontchartrain. Castalano owned half the restaurants and clubs in the parish. He was famous, and not in a good way. Tony quickly realized he wasn't kidding.

"Yes sir. What about my dog?"

"Bring him with you. I like dogs."

Castalano hung up before Tony could answer. He was soon tooling down Pontchartrain Boulevard, the lake on one side of the road, expensive homes on the other. Castalano's was the only house on a spit of land jutting into the lake. He drove around the estate surrounded by a twelve-foot brick and cast-iron fence for five minutes before finally arriving at the front gate. Pulling to a stop, he punched the call button on an electronic keypad.

"Hello," a tinny voice answered.

"I'm here to see Mr. Castalano."

"And who may I tell him it is?" the voice said.

"Tony Nicosia."

After half a minute, the gate creaked as it slowly opened. Patch started barking when they drove into acres of manicured lawn fronting scenic Lake Pontchartrain.

"Bet you'd like this yard to run around in," Tony said, rubbing his head.

They followed the road to a house resembling a Scottish castle he'd seen pictures of in a magazine. When he drove around the circle driveway and parked in front, a valet appeared from nowhere, opening his door.

"Mr. Castalano is expecting you," he said.

"And my dog?"

"He's also expecting your dog."

A butler in a black tuxedo met them at the front door, leading them down a long hallway that seemed to extend forever. They stopped at a uniformed security man standing beside a metal detector. He was young, skinny and had a full head of curly hair. He also had a pleasant smile. Tony emptied his pockets into a container before walking through the detector.

"Hope you don't mind, Lieutenant, but I gotta pat you down," the security man dressed in blue said.

He raised his arms and allowed the young man to check him. When he finished, Tony tapped his shoulder.

"Nice job. They could use you at the N.O.P.D."

"That's where I work, Lieutenant. This is just a part time job I got to help make ends meet."

"Do I know you?" Tony asked.

"Jim Steele. I broke in a year ago. Everyone on the force talks about what an awesome cop you were."

"Thanks, Jim," Tony said.

As he followed the butler down the hallway, he wondered about the N.O.P.D. cop working part time for the mob, hoping the personable young man wasn't already on the take. He decided not to worry about it. The butler opened the door to a covered veranda overlooking the lake and acres of manicured grounds. Frankie Castalano was sitting at a table, waiting for them.

"Join me," he said.

"Sorry about the dog," Tony said.

"Stop it. I told you I like dogs."

Castalano looked nothing like the dapper Mafia don Tony had confronted several years before in district court. Instead of pinstripe suit, he wore red, white, and blue Bermuda shorts, a Saint's sweatshirt, and well-worn flip-flops. Even with his salt and pepper hair, he looked about fifty. Tony placed him at least ten years older. When Patch jumped into his lap and licked his face, he grinned and hugged the dog as if he'd expected as much.

"Patch," Tony said. "Come here, now!"

"It's okay," Castalano said. "I had a mutt that looked just like this one when I was younger. Wouldn't want to sell him to me, would you?"

"Sorry, Mr. Castalano. Patch is my baby. Don't know what I'd do without him."

"Glad to hear that. If you'd have said yes, one of my men would be showing you the door about now."

"You said you got a job for me," Tony said, changing the subject.

"You like jazz, Tony?"

"Sure, don't everyone?"

"Good answer. You listen to music much?"

"Mostly sports radio."

"Pull up a chair. I don't like looking up at the person I'm talking to."

When Tony took the seat beside Castalano, he saw for the first time the view through the window. St. Augustine grass covered the hundred yards to the lake, its blue-green hue contrasting with gray clouds floating above it in the December sky. A boat in full sail on the horizon caused the panorama to look like a watercolor scene painted by some famous French artist. Castalano saw him staring.

"I know. It's beautiful here."

82

"Got that right. You sail?"

Castalano smiled. "Can't even swim and I'm scared to death of the water. See my pool?" he said, pointing. "Never been in it. My daughter and grandson love it, though, and I love watching them have fun."

A young woman and a boy frolicked in the large pool situated just outside the window. As Castalano had said, they were both having fun.

"Is that them?"

"Yes. Josie and Jojo."

"Is your wife..."

"Lung cancer. Been single now for six years. You got children, Tony?"

"Five, all grown and moved on with their lives. My wife has empty nest syndrome."

"Josie is my one and only. I'm like you and your dog. I couldn't live without her, or grandson Jojo."

"Nice looking kid," Tony said.

"He's part of the reason I called you."

"Oh?"

"Jazz, Tony. Most people in this town love their music. It's the birthplace of jazz, you know."

"Yes sir."

"Frankie, call me Frankie."

"Sure, Frankie. You got a problem for me to solve for you concerning jazz."

"Yes. Locate something missing for more than forty years. Come with me and I'll show you what I'm talking about."

As Tony followed Frankie Castalano down another marbled hall, he realized that not only was the man shorter than him, he was also bowlegged. He'd seemed much taller in the courtroom. Lifts, he decided as Castalano punched in a code on the keypad on the wall. He wasn't prepared for what he saw when the mob boss opened the door.

"The finest jazz museum in New Orleans. Be thankful, Tony. You're one of a select few to see this place."

Castalano didn't have to flip a switch as sensors filled the open area with just the right amount and intensity of ambient light. Jazz posters and old black and white photos of early artists playing their instruments covered the walls. Scratchy music of a brass band recorded with equipment from a different era started playing from hidden speakers. The voice of a woman singing with the band was just as primitive though evocative as any current sound recorded in ultra-high fidelity.

"You must have spent lots of time and money putting this place together," Tony said.

"You wouldn't believe," Frankie said. "This piano came from the Tuxedo in Storyville. Buddy Christian was the last pianist to play it. The owner didn't want to part with it, and I had to convince him."

"It's gorgeous," Tony said, wondering but not asking what he'd done to convince the piano's former owner to sell it.

"This cornet belonged to Freddie Keppard. Jelly Roll Morton called him the greatest hot trumpeter in existence. If you touch it, I'll have to kill you."

Frankie was smiling, but Tony taking no chances.

"Just looking."

"I'm kidding," he said, handing it to Tony. "You play?"

"I played the tuba in high school. I was pretty pathetic, but I enjoyed marching behind the pretty majorettes in Mardi Gras parades."

"Man after my own heart. Pop a few notes."

Tony managed a few bars of *Way Down Yonder in New Orleans*. When he finished, Frankie applauded.

"Not bad," he said. "I like a man with a good lip."

"You play?" Tony said.

Frankie took the horn. "Thought you'd never ask."

Lifting the cornet, he began to blow, the room suddenly filled with an old jazz favorite, Tony wondering if what he heard was a recording. He quickly decided the mob boss was an excellent cornet player.

"Frankie, you're as good as anyone in town."

"Thanks. For most of my young life, that's all I wanted to do. It's also the reason I need your help."

"I'm here for you."

Tony followed him to a mahogany conference table.

"Sit," Frankie said. From a Manila folder, he removed an eight-by-ten black and white photo of an old cornet. "This horn is the reason I need your help. Notice anything unusual about the photo?"

"The word King engraved on the bell?"

"You're good."

He pushed a large book, opened to an old picture of a black man with a horn, across the table for Tony to see.

"You know who it is?" he asked.

"The caption says Joseph Oliver."

"The cornet player who gave Louis Armstrong one of his first significant gigs. He earned the nickname King when he played in Storyville. During his days, he was a rock star."

"You got a magnifying glass?"

"Thought you'd never ask," Frankie said, pulling one from a drawer and sliding it toward him.

When the jazz playing in the background stopped, Frankie tapped a button on the wall, a scratchy trumpet solo quickly filling the room.

"I'd say the horn on King Oliver's knee is the same as the one in the picture you just showed me. I can even see a few letters of the name 'King' on the bell."

Frankie reached across the table and whacked Tony's shoulder.

"I knew I was picking the right person when I called you. In my mind, the horn in the picture belonged to Joe 'King' Oliver."

"I'm not an antique expert, but I'd say you're right on target," Tony said.

"I'm jumping the gun because I haven't told you the rest of the story."

"Then please continue."

"King Oliver mentored Louis Armstrong. Armstrong worshipped him. He used to deliver firewood to some of the joints in Storyville. When he was delivering next door to where King played, he'd put his ear to the wall and listen. If it hadn't been for Oliver, Satchmo might never have gotten his chance to shine."

"And?"

"And he gave me his horn. At least someone did. I'm sure of it."

"Someone other than Oliver?"

"I got the instrument in '59. Oliver died in 1938."

"How did you get it?"

"It was a Sunday, at a school recital. I played a solo and got a standing ovation. After the performance, my band teacher gave me a leather case containing the horn. A man in the audience had given it to him for me."

"And he didn't know who it was?"

"Oh, he knew all right. He just wouldn't tell me."

"Why not?"

"Told me I was too young to appreciate it."

"And he never told you."

"Died in a car accident. Hell, with these crazy New Orleans drivers, it's a wonder we're not all dead."

"Ain't that the truth," Tony said.

"That's the story. All I know about where the horn came from."

"So you want me to find out who gave you the horn?"

"Yes."

"The case is cold, but I'll give it my best shot. What else?"

"You know how much that horn's worth today?"

"I'm sure it's priceless."

"Bingo. Problem is I don't have it anymore."

"What happened to it?"

"My papa, he took it from me. Said I needed to forget music and start concentrating on family business."

"You're the boss now. Have him return it to you."

"Not that simple. Papa's dead."

"I hadn't heard."

"We've kept it quiet for obvious reasons."

Tony stared at the old photograph, wondering what Frankie's obvious reasons were. When the scratchy recording ended, another quickly began.

"So your father took your horn and now you want me to find it for you. You also want me to prove it was King Oliver's horn, and find out who gave it to you, and why. Pretty tall order, Frankie."

"I didn't hire you to tell me it's impossible. You interested or not?"

86

The annoyance he heard in Frankie's voice told him he'd pressed a little too hard for information. He waited a beat before answering.

"Like I said, I'll give it my best shot."

Your retainer is in the folder. If you need more, call my personal number that's also in the folder."

He pushed the Manila folder, stuffed with documents and photos, across the table. Tony thumbed through it until he came to an envelope with his name on it.

"This is a lot of money," he said after taking a quick peek.

"I mean business, Tony, and I expect results. Don't let me down."

Chapter II

It was getting late when Tony returned home. Sitting at the kitchen table, he mulled the folder of information mob boss Frankie Castalano had given him. He had no idea where to begin or what to do with the ten grand in hundred dollar bills Castalano had paid him. Lil was looking over his shoulder when he glanced up.

"Where did you get all that money?"

"Could be a bonanza, or maybe a pile of dog crap I just stepped in. Don't know yet."

"Talk to me."

Tony held the wad of hundred dollar bills to show her.

"I got hired today to find a missing brass instrument for someone. They paid me lots of money, all in cash."

"Oh my!"

"That's what I said. Can we put it in our bank account like this?"

"Of course, you can, but why would someone pay you with so much cash?"

"That's my problem. Actually, our problem."

"You'd better explain."

"My new client is Frankie Castalano."

Lil's hand went to her mouth. "You mean Frankie Castalano the Mafia boss?"

"Yep."

"Oh, shit! Tony, you can't work for that monster. We don't need the money that badly."

"He's not really a monster."

"That's not what the papers and magazines say."

"He's just a man."

"A man that can have someone killed at the drop of a hat."

"You don't really know that," Tony said.

"Maybe not, but it's what everyone thinks."

"Then what do you want me to do?"

"Give him the money back. Tell him you're too busy to do the job."

"What if he takes offense?"

Lil glanced at the clock on the wall as if it might hold the answer to Tony's question.

"You're right. We do have a problem."

"Then maybe I should just do what he hired me to do."

"I won't let you do anything illegal, Tony."

"It's a legitimate job. Nothing illegal about it."

"You have no clue where that money came from."

"And neither does anyone else. It's just a retainer. The man could have made the money selling lemonade on the sidewalk for all I know."

"You know that's not where it came from," she said.

"How do you know? How do you ever know where the money your employer pays you actually comes from?"

Lil glared at Patch when he came through the doggy door from the backyard and jumped into Tony's lap.

"Don't know," she said. "I never thought of it like that."

"He just wants me to find a horn for him. What could be illegal about that?"

"You sure?"

Tony grabbed Lil's hand and squeezed it. "Would I lie to you?"

"Every time you open your mouth."

"No way. Far as I'm concerned, this money's legit. I just need a place to start looking for the horn because I don't have a clue."

"Let me see your folder," she said, sitting beside him.

Tires screeched on the street outside their home as Lil began thumbing through the stack of photos and documents.

"Crazy New Orleans' drivers," Tony said when they

heard a crash.

Lil ignored the car wreck. "What's this?"

"A picture of the old cornet he wants me to find. He thinks a local jazz legend named King Oliver once owned it. It's also a mystery how he got it."

"So what's the problem? Everyone knows you're the best detective in New Orleans."

"Then why don't I have a clue where to start?"

Lil ignored his question. "He lost it? How?"

"His old man took it from him when he decided his attention was more focused on music than the mob. He never gave it back."

"Then ask his father. He knows what he did with it."

"Not so simple," Tony said. "He's dead. Maybe I should just give him back the money."

"Don't you dare," Lil said, taking the cash from him. "You're absolutely right. If we had to know where every dollar we receive comes from before we spent it, this country would grind to a halt."

"What'll we do?"

Lil peeled off ten hundred dollar bills and handed them to him. "In case you need it. I'll hide the rest in the sock drawer. It'll be our rainy day fund."

Tony stuffed the hundreds in his wallet. "Now what?"

"Maybe you could start at the Hogan Jazz Archive at Tulane University?"

"Never heard of it."

"My book club visited it a year ago," she said. "Check it out. It's as good a place as any to start."

The following day found Tony walking across the campus of Tulane University, trying to locate the Hogan Jazz Archive. The name imparted visions of grandeur. Reality was quite different. Although nothing like Castalano's private museum, this one, he quickly learned, had many resources. He approached the woman behind the desk to see if he needed to sign in.

"Ma'am, I've never been here before."

"I see that," she said. "You'll have to leave your briefcase and pens with me."

"Then what'll I take notes with?"

"A pencil if you have one. If you don't, we have plenty to lend. There's a pencil sharpener on the shelf by the window."

"I don't need much. Maybe you can help me."

"Sir, this is a research facility. We provide the resources, you do the research."

"But I'm not sure what I'm looking for."

She stared at him as if he were the town idiot, and then apparently decided to try one more time.

"Much of the reference material we offer is on computer. You are welcome to check what we have. If you see something you'd like to examine closely, be it book, reference, video, or CD, I'll be happy to retrieve it for you, but whatever research you do is up to you."

Tony wished he still had his badge. A glance was usually all it took to obtain any information he needed. He wasn't used to poring through documents in a research facility. Intent on the woman behind the counter, he didn't hear the person approach him from behind.

"Is there a problem here?"

He turned to see a man in a white shirt, tie, and sleeveless, wool pullover. The dark frames of his glasses marked him as a professor, his frown as the archive administrator.

"Mr. Wall, this gentleman has never used the Archive before and seems a little confused about our policies."

"Sorry," Tony said. "I hoped I could get someone to look at a picture of an old horn and maybe tell me a few things about it."

"Mr..."

"Nicosia, Tony Nicosia."

"Look, Mr. Nicosia, this is a research facility. We have one of the largest archives of jazz and Louisiana folk music in the world. If you have a question about jazz, you can probably find the answer here. We aren't the *Antique Road Show*."

"Sorry," Tony said, seeing he was getting nowhere. "If you don't mind, I'll use your computer to see what you have."

"Fine," Wall said, smiling. "Call if you need me, Doris. I'm going down the hall for coffee."

Doris didn't bother looking up or responding as she thumbed through Tony's briefcase.

"Here's a pencil. I'll supply another if you break it. You may take the Manila folder and yellow tablet to the table with you."

He nodded and turned toward a table with a computer, noting that only one other person was working in the archive. Mumbling to himself, he took the computer beside him.

"They have a way of making you feel like an errant third grader sometimes," the man said.

"Hey, I thought she was going to slap my wrist with a ruler for a minute."

The man grinned and extended his hand. "I'm Jason Fasempaur. I heard your question. Maybe I can help."

"Glad to meet you, Jason. I'm Tony Nicosia."

"Gentlemen, please lower your voices," Doris said, interrupting their conversation.

"I've been here all morning and was about to take a break. If you join me, maybe I can answer your questions."

Jason Fasempaur was younger, six inches taller and twenty pounds lighter than Tony was. He had the mannerisms of a college professor, although his Italian loafers and expensive tweed sports coat pegged him as a person with a more rewarding career. He also had a warm smile.

"Best offer I've had all day, Jason. Lead the way. I'm right behind you."

"Are you familiar with the student union?" Jason asked.

"Can't say as I am."

"It's a wonder, three stories tall, all open, with passive heating and cooling. The abundance of windows invokes the unmistakable feeling of being outside. Add the tropical plants and rain walls and you'll forget New Orleans' summer heat and winter gloom."

"Sounds inviting. I have a friend that teaches here. She told me about it."

"Who? I know a few of the professors."

"Professor Mulate. She teaches English."

"You know Doctor Mulate?"

"We go way back. You know her?"

"No, but I'd like to. In addition to being intelligent, she's also one gorgeous babe."

Jason nodded when Tony said, "You noticed."

"Tell you what. You introduce us, and I'll help you any way I can with your research."

"You got a deal. I'll call and see if she's busy. Maybe she can join us."

"Great. Grab a table and I'll get our coffee while you call her."

The student union was all but deserted, and Tony had his pick of tables. He chose one beside a rain wall, so called because of the water trickling down its stone surface. The slow moving panel above him fanned the humid air. He took a deep breath, feeling as if he were in a forest glen as he punched in Mama Mulate's cell phone number.

"Tony," she said. "What a surprise."

"I'm at the student union and thought you might like to join me."

"I'd love to, but I'm on my way to a staff meeting. It'll probably take the rest of the day."

"Doesn't sound like fun. Sure you can't cut it short?"

"The Dean of our department will be there. I'd love to join you, but I'd better beg off. Come by the house and see me. It's been too long."

"I'll do it, Mama. You take care now."

"Bad news?" Jason said, handing him a cup of coffee.

"Afraid so. Mama's on her way to a staff meeting."

"It's okay. I'm not sure I could concentrate on your problem if she were with us."

"She has that effect on men."

"Show me what you have."

Tony pulled out the photos of King Oliver, and Castalano's missing horn. Fasempaur studied them intently.

"You want to know if the horn in Oliver's hands is the same one in the other picture."

"You're good," Tony said. "You'd probably make a great detective."

"That's what we researchers do. We call it research, but it's actually just detective work. I'm curious. What difference does it make?"

"It makes a humongous difference to my client. Someone gave him the horn in the second picture, and he thinks it was Oliver's horn."

"Let me have a look, and I'll tell you," Jason said.

"That would work if he still had it. It ain't that simple. His daddy took it because he didn't think he was paying enough attention to the family business. All he has left is this photo."

"Why doesn't he just have his father return it to him?"

"Because the old man is dead."

"He could buy another horn. They sell lots of vintage horns on eBay, and I'm sure he could get a replacement at one of the shops on Royal Street."

"My client is Frankie Castalano, and he wants his own horn, not a substitute."

"Frankie Castalano the mob boss?" When Tony nodded, he said, "Now I see your problem."

"Can you at least tell me if it's the same horn in both pictures?"

Jason placed the two photos on the table, crossed his long legs, and took a sip of his coffee. Tony was suddenly aware of recorded orchestral music playing softly in the background.

"They're not the same horn," he finally said.

"How can you be so sure?"

"There are dozens of cornet manufacturers, and many have several different models. You have Blackburn, Courtois, Schilke, Besson, and Getzen. The list goes on. Though they may all look similar to the untrained eye, I promise you, they are all different. Even the same models had differences through the years."

"And you can tell the difference?"

"This one I can. The horn King Oliver's holding is a King Silver Tone made by H.N. White. You can see the engraving on the bell."

"And how is it different from the horn in the other picture?"

"The bell of the Silver Tone was made of solid sterling silver. These photos are both black and white, but you can see the shading difference. The second horn has a brass bell."

Tony held the two photos together. "I thought it was just a color change because the photos were old."

"Nope, they're two different horns."

"But they are both stamped with the word King."

"The Silver Tone was a great horn, and maybe the name on the bell was part of the reason King Oliver owned one."

"But the horn in the other picture is also engraved with the name King."

"Yes, elaborate engraving. It's not a Silver Tone. I'd say it's an Artist horn."

"A what?"

"A one-of-a-kind made for a particular musician."

"Then it could have been King Oliver's horn," Tony said.

"That's right. An instrument specially designed for a particular artist's playing style. More coffee?"

"With whiskey in it after what you just told me. I have no clue where to start looking for Frankie's horn."

"I've done all I can at the lab today. I was going to take the streetcar back to the Quarter and browse some of the antique shops on Royal. I know a specific shop that specializes in vintage horns. Come with me, and we can get that whiskey along the way."

"If I was my boss, I'd fire me and hire you. We may have to split my retainer."

"Just buy the first round of drinks, and introduce me to Professor Mulate when you get a chance."

Chapter 12

Tony sensed the debonair man he'd met at the jazz archive was his best hope of achieving success in solving Castalano's mystery. Since he had no better idea on how to proceed, it didn't matter much. They were soon on their way down St. Charles Avenue heading for the French Quarter.

"You seem to know lots about jazz," Tony said.

"It's what I do. I'm a researcher."

"From N.O.?"

"Upstate New York, originally. Now I live in Paris."

"Texas?"

"France. I visit New Orleans once or twice a year to do research at the Archive, and engage in the local music culture. It's still quite vibrant, even after Katrina."

"We've dodged lots of bullets. Katrina almost got us."

"Yes she did. Back to the horn. Do you have a serial number for the one in the photo?"

"Why?"

"It might tell us what instrument company made it, and the year it was manufactured."

"Never thought of that. Doesn't matter because I don't have one unless Mr. Castalano wrote it down someplace. I'll ask him."

"If he did, we can put a tracer out to all the used instrument dealers," Jason said.

"You're making my day. When we reach the Quarter, I'm buying as many drinks as you can handle."

"You got a deal."

Tony found a parking spot close to Royal Street. Tourists, many dressed in the colors of Arkansas and Texas, crowded the sidewalks. Jason threw up his hands when a football fan bumped into him, almost bowling him off his feet. He never even noticed.

"What the hell's going on?" Jason asked. "Mardi Gras is still sixty days away."

"Sugar Bowl. Apparently you're not a college football fan."

Jason grinned. "I like cricket and squash."

"Bugs and vegetables? You're crazy," Tony said.

Jason grinned. "I've been called worse. The Brass Bell is up the block. You won't believe the instruments they have."

Many of the shops on Royal specialize in antiques such as Persian rugs, old books and original artwork. They all have something in common—even the postcards at the front door are expensive. It didn't matter because Lil liked to window shop on Royal Street. When she did, Tony usually got dragged along.

"I hate antiques," he said, producing a smile on Jason's face.

He'd still spent countless hours with his wife, looking and occasionally buying. He and Jason crossed the street to avoid football fans arguing about who would win the big game.

"Here it is," Jason said, a bell ringing as he opened the oak and cut glass door.

A little man was polishing a brass instrument, a smile appearing on his face when he saw Jason.

"Professor, I didn't expect you back in town until spring."

"I had a wild hair. Zeb, this is Tony Nicosia. He has more questions than I have answers, so I brought him to meet you. Tony, this is Zebudiah Zuckerman. People in town just call him Double Z."

"Nice meeting you, Double Z," Tony said, shaking his hand.

Zeb Zuckerman was probably in his eighties but had a smile and bounce in his step of a much younger man. He also had an enormous cigar in his mouth, unlit but well chewed.

97

"I'm running a special on flugelhorns today. Either of you in the market?"

"Zeb, you have specials every day. I'm going to browse while you speak with Tony. Maybe you can answer his questions."

"You got some beautiful horns, Zeb," Tony said. "How long you been in business?"

"Longer than you've been alive."

"Then maybe you can help me."

"You a cop?"

"Used to be. Now I'm just a private dick. A person hired me to find this cornet. Can you help me?"

Zeb gazed at the photo. "Frankie Castalano's horn. I'm the first person he asked when he started looking."

"Then I guess you're telling me you haven't seen it."

"I know every brass dealer in America. If it were on the market, believe me, I'd know about it."

"Mr. Castalano seems to think the horn belonged to King Oliver."

"What does Jason think?"

"He don't think so," Tony said.

"Then you better go along with his opinion. He's the only person in the world that knows more about horns than me."

Tony's mouth was agape when Jason returned and whacked him on the back.

"Did Zeb tell you what you need to know?"

"Tony still has a problem. I've been looking for that horn for more than ten years now. I'm convinced it's not in New Orleans," Zeb said.

"Well then there's your answer," Jason said.

"If it's not in New Orleans, where do you think it might be?" Tony asked.

"In a private collection somewhere. Frankie was a brilliant horn blower back in the day. You know how much a collector would pay for that horn?"

"No idea," Tony said.

"Who are we talking about?" Jason asked.

"Frankie Castalano."

"I didn't know he was a musician."

"A real talent when he was young. All the players knew about him."

"What happened?"

"Other things to pursue," Zeb said. "His papa took the horn from him."

"And his father is dead," Tony said.

"Where'd you hear that crap?" Zeb said.

"But Mr. Castalano told me..."

"He's not shooting straight with you. The old man is my age. I've lived in N.O. my entire life. Believe me when I tell you I know every influential person from here to Algiers. I'd have heard if he had died."

"Then where is he?" Tony asked.

"Don't know. He and Frankie had their issues. They got worse as time went on."

"You don't think..."

Zeb shook his head. "Frankie has probably whacked a lot of people. His papa isn't one of them."

"Sure about that?"

Zeb nodded. "Paco's still alive. Bet money on it."

Tony had already stuffed the photo of the horn back into his folder. Someone opened the front door, ringing the bell. After looking inside, they'd left without entering.

"Damn tourists," Zeb said. "No one wants to buy a quality vintage horn these days."

"Don't feel sorry for him," Jason said. "He sells ten a day on eBay. If I had Zeb's money, I'd burn my own."

"Don't listen to him, Tony."

"Not to worry, Double Z. I got other things on my mind."

"Such as?"

"Wondering why Frankie told me his dad was dead," Tony said.

Frankie didn't whack him and he ain't dead. Frankie's a musician at heart and has a soft spot. Believe me, his papa has no such soft spot."

Zeb nodded again when Tony said, "Sounds like you know that for a fact."

"Take it to the bank. Sure I can't interest you in a

flugelhorn?"

Jason pointed to a horn in a display cabinet. "How much for that old Conn?"

"Three hundred bucks for my regular customers, two hundred for you, Professor."

"Does it have a case?"

"You bet it does, still in excellent condition. I'll even throw in some sheet music."

"Great," Jason said, handing him two bills. "Give it to someone deserving."

"Thank you, Professor," Zeb said.

"We may as well find a bar and get that drink," Tony said.

"What?" Jason said as they exited the shop.

"That instrument you bought," Tony said.

"Zeb gives away more horns than he sells. That one will go to a budding talent, I promise you."

"Good for you, Professor," Tony said.

Giving him a fist bump, Jason said, "Now let's get that drink."

Chapter 13

It wasn't quite noon when Titia got out of bed. As we hadn't bothered closing the curtain over the balcony door, late morning sun radiated in through the hanging ferns. Kisses was locked outside and tapping on the door for us to let her in.

"What a beautiful kitty," she said, cradling the cat in her bare arms.

"Now I have two beautiful girls in my bed."

"What time is it?"

"From the sound of the people on the sidewalk, I'd say it's getting close to lunch time."

"I have to go," she said.

Our clothes, laid victim to our passion, were strewn across the floor. Titia gathered them in her arms, and then rushed into the bathroom.

"Please don't go," I said.

She was already using her cell phone to call a taxi. "I have to. Sorry."

Bertram was standing in the hall when she hurried out the door.

"Damn, Cowboy, that was one fine looking woman. You surprise even me sometimes."

"Throw me that robe," I said.

Grabbing the garment, I wrapped it around me and padded to the bathroom. Bertram was still in the doorway when I returned.

"I thought you was dead up here. I didn't see you come in

101

last night."

"Are you my mother now?"

"Dirty job, but somebody's gotta do it," he said.

"Bertram, you're worse than a little old lady. You don't have to snoop around. I always tell you everything anyway."

"Yeah, well I think you better come downstairs."

"And why is that?"

"There are three women sitting at the bar that just saw your pretty new girlfriend hurry down the stairs. I'm guessing none of them's gonna be happy with you right about now."

He nodded when I said, "They sent you to get me?"

"If I was you, I'd cover up that hickey on your neck."

When Bertram shut the door behind him, I returned to the bathroom to look in the mirror, the red spot on my neck glaring back at me. Having nothing to cover it up with, I decided to ignore it. When I approached the bar where Carla, Mama, and Lilly waited, I might as well have had the letter S branded on my forehead. They all gave me dirty looks, but Mama was the first to comment.

"Been swimming with a lamprey eel?"

All three women were sipping sugary drinks through colorful straws. To say they had the attention of every male would have been an understatement.

"Don't start," I said. "You were on your way someplace last time I saw you. I'll bet it wasn't a church social."

Mama grinned, and so did Carla and Lilly. Lilly motioned to an empty stool.

"Join us?"

"No more crass comments?"

"Peace," she said. "We want ask how you got the hickey, and you don't ask what we did since the last time we saw you."

"Deal," I said.

Lilly smiled, and Bertram winked at her when he brought me a glass of lemonade. The countdown to the Sugar Bowl had begun, fans from the two opposing schools doing cheers on the sidewalk outside the bar.

"Quit looking at me like that," Carla said.

"Like what?"

"Like I'm an axe murderer, or something. Mama was

released from the hospital, and her doctors say she'll make a full recovery. Aunt Beth is with her. They told me to stay away until they call because they need to catch up on sister talk."

"Great news about your mother."

I was sitting between Carla and Lilly, Mama Mulate feeling left out of the conversation. When a table opened behind us, she slid off her stool.

"Let's grab that table. It's too hard for four of us to communicate sitting at the bar."

We made it to the table just in time as a group of football nuts came in from the street, noise and craziness outside the door crashing in around them.

"What's up with all these people in football jerseys and college sweatshirts?" Lilly asked.

She shook her head when I said, "Not a college football fan?"

"Physical education is the only course I ever flunked."

"It's Sugar Bowl madness in the big N.O. Get on board."

"If you say so. At least Bertram likes it."

"I love the Sugar Bowl," Mama said. "I try to attend every year."

"Mama's a football nut. Don't insult the Saints or she'll smack you," I said.

Lilly just shook her head. "I don't even know what you're talking about."

"Good," Mama said. "We need to tell Wyatt what we're doing later tonight. You're coming, too."

"Oh?"

"Something exciting and we're not going without you," Lilly said.

"Where are we going?"

"Carla got us into Charity. We're meeting a guard at midnight. He's going to let us in the place," Lilly said.

"Why so late?"

"Really, Wyatt," Mama said. "You don't go ghost hunting in broad daylight."

"Could be dangerous. Transients living in the building."

Carla shook her head. "My friend on the medical board says the building is safe. A big fence around the place."

"I don't know," I said.

"Don't be a scaredy-cat," Lilly said. "Mama, Carla, and I will protect you."

"Yeah," Carla said. "You told me once you weren't afraid of anything."

"Okay," I said. "It's a long time till midnight. What are we doing until then?"

"The three of us are still in bar-hopping mode. A girl thing. You aren't invited," Mama said. "We'll meet you in front of Charity at twelve."

They waved at Bertram as they made their way through the crowded saloon to the front door. Lilly blew him a kiss. People were waiting for our table, so I returned to an empty stool next to Eddie, who had arrived without notice. Bertram pushed a glass of lemonade toward me, along with the girl's tab. I did a double take when I glanced at it.

"You kidding me! You padding tabs now?"

"You seen the way those three drink? I'm surprised they can walk out of here. I'll just add it to your running total," he said as he hurried off to wait on some noisy customers.

Eddie made a face when I finally glanced at him. "What are you doing here? It's a long way from your pad in Metairie."

"I had to take Jeneen to the airport. She almost missed her flight."

"Where is she going?"

"Latitia didn't tell you?"

"Hell no!"

"Europe for six weeks, along with the rest of the band."

"Titia also?"

"Yes."

"She never said a word to me about it."

"You sound like a whipped puppy. We just met them last night. We had a terrific time and now they're gone."

Eddie's words hit me like a slap in the face.

"But..."

"But what, Cowboy? They'll be back in six weeks. It isn't as if you're engaged."

"She could have at least said something."

"Get over it. You're single, and this is the Big Easy. You

104

were just sitting with three gorgeous women, for God's sake. Besides, there's something I have to tell you."

After downing half of my lemonade, I took a deep breath, trying to make sense of why I still felt hurt and confused.

"Tell me what?"

"Last night at the club I went in the kitchen and found Paco."

"You didn't."

"Yes I did. He was peeling potatoes, and you won't believe what he told me."

"Probably right, but tell me anyway."

"You know who Frankie Castalano is?"

"The Mafia kingpin in New Orleans. Who doesn't?"

"Paco is his father."

"No way."

"I'm not making this up."

"Then why was he peeling potatoes in one of the many clubs his father owns?"

"That was my question to him. He apparently has a loose tongue and a tendency to blurt things out when he shouldn't."

"An unwise trait, considering the scene Pancho Bergamo created when you asked him a simple question about the mob."

"Sounds to me as if they have issues. Frankie doesn't want to whack his own dad, so he's apparently spread it around the old man is a little crazy."

"And Paco goes along with it?"

"He's not exactly on positive mental footing. I'd say his condition is related more to old-age dementia or Alzheimer's than schizophrenia."

"Then how do you expect him to distinguish between fact and fantasy?"

"His long-term memory seems reasonable. He just has problems with what happened five minutes ago."

"Did you ask him about the lynching?"

"He claimed to know all about it. He was about to tell me the story when two goons interrupted us and directed me, in no uncertain terms, back to our table."

"What now?"

"Don't know," Eddie said. "I think Frankie's men keep a close eye on him. I was hoping you'd have a suggestion."

"Nothing that comes immediately to mind. I'll think about it."

"Me too," he said. "What's the deal with Carla, Mama, and their friend."

"Lilly's a writer working on a screenplay for a movie to be shot here in the city. The producer has hired Mama, Carla and me to help her add a little local color to the script."

"Sounds like a sweet gig," he said. "Pay well?"

"You wouldn't believe."

"How do I get onboard? We government men aren't exactly overpaid."

"First, you'd have to make amends with Mama and Carla."

"I'm working on the Carla thing. Mama is another matter altogether."

"What did you do to her? She's usually laid back and forgiving."

"Stood her up," he said.

"For another woman?"

"Long story."

"I've got no place to go until midnight. Let's hear it."

"Big case at headquarters. I forgot about our date and didn't remember to call until the next morning. Mama wasn't buying my story and hung up on me."

"You didn't remember until the next morning?"

"Don't look at me like that. Everyone has memory lapses. And I was working on the single most notable case of my career. Sorry, I'm not perfect."

"Watch it or you'll be peeling potatoes alongside Paco."

Eddie ignored my comment, waiting until the group cheer behind us had subsided to a minor roar before continuing his explanation.

"Mama's one of the greatest women I've ever known. We had lots of fun, and I don't just mean in bed. I'd at least like to continue being her friend, if nothing else."

"Mama doesn't usually hold a grudge. Too bad. It'd be fantastic if you went with us tonight."

"What's the deal?"

"Ghost hunting at the old Charity Hospital. Maybe Carla and Mama will forgive you if you promise to protect us."

"I'm game, even if it does sound crazy. What are we looking for?"

"Ghosts," I said.

"You're weird, Cowboy."

"Better talk about it a little later. Your old buddy just walked into the place."

Tony Nicosia smiled as he opened the door for a taller, though slimmer man.

"That prick," Eddie said.

"You're not still holding a grudge, are you?"

Eddie sipped his Scotch. "I don't like getting kneed in the nuts. Doesn't matter because I've been informed, in no uncertain terms, to let the matter rest."

"And?"

"As long as he stays on the other side of the bar, we'll be just fine."

Tony saw me, waved and walked in our direction.

"Didn't your mama tell you not to play with low lifes?" he said.

Eddie slid off the bar stool and gave Tony a shove. Seeing what was unfolding, I got between them.

"Get outa the way, Cowboy," Tony said. "I'm gonna kick a mudhole in the ass of this Yankee prick."

"No, you're not."

"Back off, Wyatt," Eddie said. "It's me that's going to kick this little rooster's ass."

Bertram, hearing the commotion, appeared with his weighted club.

"Ain't nobody fighting in my bar unless they want a little love tap from Billy, here."

"Fine," Tony said. "I'd just as soon whip your sorry ass out on the sidewalk."

"You got it, bro," Eddie said, pushing me aside and starting for the door.

"Now wait a minute," I said, grabbing their jackets. "Listen to me first. Then, if you still want to fight, more power to you. Bertram bring drinks for these two and put them on my tab."

They continued glaring at each other as I pulled up a barstool and directed Tony and Eddie to sit on either side of me. The stranger that had entered with Tony was grinning and had bellied up to the bar along with us. Bertram just frowned and shook his head, still tapping his palm with the club.

"What'll it be, mister?"

"Whiskey sour," Tony's friend said.

"I'm sick to death of this," I said. "You two have been feuding for almost a year now."

"I don't like being kneed in the balls," Eddie said.

"You had it coming, you prick," Tony said.

When Eddie reached across me, trying to grab Tony, I pushed him away.

"Stop it! You two were as close as brothers. Neither was right doing what you did. Now, both of you need to apologize to each other and forget this crazy incident."

"I'm not apologizing," Tony said.

"Yes you are," I said. "I helped you get your first job after the N.O.P.D. canned you. You owe me."

"I don't owe you," Eddie said. "I'm not apologizing to this sawed-off piece of shit."

It was Tony's time to try and get at Eddie. "I said stop it!"

"Eddie, you need to retract that comment. Tony may have kneed you in the balls, but I remember him saving them for you more than once. You didn't have a better friend on the N.O.P.D. Remember?"

"That was then, this is now."

Bertram arrived with the drinks, frowning as he placed them in front of us. For emphasis, he whacked the club on the bar, the sound momentarily silencing the noise. It didn't last long.

"Fine," Bertram said. "If you two wanta piss off a longtime friendship, then I think there's nothing I can do about it. You wanna go settle things outside, go ahead. At least have a drink first."

They both needed a drink after blowing off so much energy. They were both drinking Scotch and Bertram was ready with a bottle.

"Well, Eddie, what's your answer?"

"I guess I had a knee in the nuts coming, Lieutenant. Sometimes I have a hard time keeping my mouth shut. I apologize."

Tony took a deep breath and glanced at the ceiling. "Hell, I ain't no saint. I was having a lousy day. I shouldn't have taken it out on you. I'm sorry, Eddie."

"Fine," I said. "Can we seal this little love fest with a handshake?"

Though neither man was smiling, they reached across me and shook hands.

"That's better. Who's your friend?"

"Boy's, this is Jason Fasempaur. He knows more about bugling than any man alive."

"I'm Wyatt, and this hothead is Eddie Toledo."

"Sorry, Jason. I'm usually calm and collected. It wasn't jazz, but Wyatt and I saw one of the finest brass show bands last night over in Fat City."

"I love show bands. Who were they?"

"Brass & Sass. Believe me, they had plenty of both."

"You're kidding me. I've seen them several times. Latitia Boiset is the darling of Paris. I've been in lust for her for over a year now."

"You and every other red-bloodied man that's seen her perform. Talk to Wyatt. He just spent the night with her."

"Lucky you."

Fasempaur's words caught me by surprise. "You're from Paris?"

"Most of the time. At least when I'm not traveling around the world doing research."

"The band's on their way there now," Eddie said.

Tony was glancing at his watch. "This will have to be my last Scotch. Lil doesn't like it when I stay out too late."

"Since when?" Eddie asked.

"Since I almost got divorced. I'm trying, like hell, to make my marriage work. It's kinda hard since, like I said, I ain't a saint."

Eddie laughed. "Hell, Tony, the only Saints in New

Orleans are on the football team."

"Got that right," he said.

"You making it okay since you left the force?"

"Wyatt got me some private dick work. I been making a living at it."

"Tell him the truth," I said. "You're making more money now than you ever did on the force."

"Yeah, well..."

"Working on anything unusual?" Eddie asked.

"Trying to find a lost horn. Seems the only person that knows what happened to it is dead."

"Who are you talking about? Maybe I can help," Eddie said.

"Paco Castalano."

Eddie had his elbows on the bar as he worked on his Scotch. He turned and looked at Tony.

"Paco's not dead. I saw him last night."

Tony gave him a look. "You feeling okay, Eddie? You know Paco Castalano?"

"Believe me, I know Paco. He's alive, though not quite all there upstairs if you know what I mean."

Tony glanced at his watch again. "Can I call you later and talk about it?"

"You bet. It'll cost you a drink, though."

Tony smiled and tapped his shoulder. "Just like old times. Jason, you ready to blow this joint?"

"Heck, Tony, I'm not working tomorrow and I was just getting warmed up."

"Come with us," Eddie said. "We'll take you back to your hotel later."

"Where are we going?"

"To visit a haunted hospital," I said.

Chapter 14

Before midnight, we took a taxi to Charity Hospital on Tulane, leaving Eddie's car in a parking space near Bertram's. The area known as the Hospital District was alive with fluorescent light and physical activity. Charity was different, only the howl of a stray dog in the distance, and the melancholy whistle of a tanker passing on the river breaking the night's stillness. A uniformed security guard was waiting for us at the locked gate. We were the first to arrive.

"Are you part of the group going into the hospital?" he asked.

"Yes," I said.

"I don't know who arranged this for you, but they have some stroke with the State of Louisiana."

"How so?"

"We've had a crew in there all afternoon installing auxiliary lights. You'll still have plenty of shadows, but at least it won't be pitch black."

"That's great," Eddie said. "We didn't even bring a flashlight."

"Who says?" I asked, showing him the little flashlight I always carried. "I don't go anywhere without this."

The guard scratched his stubbly chin. "Wouldn't help you much in there. Except for light beaming through a few grates, it's dark inside even during daylight hours."

He laughed when Eddie said, "Are you one of the permanent guards?"

"There are no permanent guards. The hospital is locked up tight though homeless people sometimes find a way in and out. They don't stay long cause it's like an oven inside during summer months. You're lucky it's December."

"You think it's safe?" Jason asked.

"Like I said, there was a crew inside all day long. They didn't see anyone."

"You coming in with us?"

"My orders are to wait outside."

"Fine," Eddie said. "Let's exchange cell phone numbers in case we need you."

Another taxi arrived, Mama, Carla, and Lilly exiting the back door still dressed in their party clothes. They were all laughing, though Carla's smile turned to a frown, and then tears as she stared up at the dark building.

"What are you doing here?" Mama said, glaring at Eddie. "Carla and I don't want you anywhere near us."

"Mama, I'm sorry. I've tried to explain three times. You just keep hanging up on me."

"That's right, and your two-dozen roses mean nothing coming from a scoundrel like you."

Eddie had to smile at being called a scoundrel. It was contagious, and Mama's glare softened.

"Please forgive me," he said, getting down on one knee. "Even though I do my best, I'm not a perfect person."

"Okay. I can only speak for myself. I just hope it's not you that's making her cry, or I may change my mind," she said, turning her attention to a sobbing Carla.

She and Lilly were locked in an embrace. When Mama joined the show, Lilly looked at me and Eddie for introductions.

"Lilly Bliss meet Eddie 'the scoundrel' Toledo."

Lilly shook his hand. "Scoundrels are my favorite people. How did you get such a reputation?"

"Believe me, it wasn't easy. I've had to work at it my entire life."

Since Eddie hadn't acknowledged Jason's presence, and I had yet to have a chance to, Mama extended her hand to him.

"I guess no one is going to introduce us. I'm Mama

112

Mulate."

Jason's mouth opened. Taking her hand, he squeezed it, not letting go.

"The hell you say. I've been trying to meet you and almost succeeded earlier today. I'm Jason Fasempaur."

Mama's expression changed from stoic to looking slightly stunned.

"You don't mean the real Jason Fasempaur, do you?"

"The one and only."

"I love you and all the books you've written. I'm your biggest fan. Wyatt, how dare you fail to tell me you were bringing the world's greatest expert on jazz."

"At this point, you know more about Jason than I do. We just met. Tony brought him by Bertram's."

"Oh my God! You were with Tony when he invited me for coffee, weren't you?"

Jason nodded. "The offer still stands."

"I'd rather go with you on a visit to every jazz club in New Orleans."

"If you love jazz as much as I do, it would be a pleasure. Who are these other two lovely ladies?"

"I'm Lillie Bliss, and this is Carla Manetti."

"I know you. We met at a book signing a few years ago. I asked you for a drink. You had an appointment with another gentleman."

"That was then, this is now. I'm all in for a jazz club crawl."

Carla was still crying and barely looked up when she shook Jason's hand.

"Folks," the guard said. "The gate is open, the auxiliary lights turned on. If you need me, you have my number. I'll be in the car."

While Lilly and Eddie exchanged pleasantries, I joined Mama to find out why Carla was crying.

"Baby, what's the matter?" Mama asked.

Carla finally calmed down enough to speak. "This is the first time I've been here since Katrina."

"You were at Charity during Katrina?" Mama said.

Carla nodded. "I often do charitable work on my days off

113

from the library. I was here when Katrina hit."

"At this hospital, during Katrina?" Jason said. "Poor darling."

Carla nodded again. "When the water began rising, we prepared the patients for evacuation. You can't imagine how desperate we felt. We waited, but no one came. A day passed, then two, and then three. We were all in shock, not believing the world had forgotten us."

"Jesus!" I said. "You were at Charity for four days?

"We had no electricity, no food, and no water. Some patients were on ventilators. We had to take turns working the hand pumps. The hospital morgue flooded. Bodies were floating, forcing us to retrieve them. We had to stack them in the stairwells."

"Oh my God!" Lilly said.

Eddie, feeling slighted because of lack of attention, joined us.

Carla glanced up, acknowledging his presence without speaking to him. When Eddie took her hand and began massaging it, she didn't pull away.

"The patients had no one except us. We were their only hope."

"You never told me this," I said.

"I've managed to block it from my thoughts, at least until now."

"It's okay, baby," Mama said. "It's over now."

"You can't go back in there," Eddie said. "I'll call a cab."

For the first time, Carla pushed Eddie's hand away.

"I'm here, and this was my idea. You want to see ghosts. I've already seen them. I just want to make them go away."

Eddie started to say something, but Mama shushed him.

"Sometimes it's best for PTSD sufferers to face their demons."

When Lilly shot me a quizzical glance, I said, "There are probably more people in New Orleans suffering from PTSD than those that aren't."

"I'll second that," Jason said.

Carla's tears had finally dried, and she started for the unlocked gate to the tall fence encircling the hospital. The rest of us followed.

"I'll go first," she said. "I may want to forget this place, but I know it better than anyone here."

Eddie caught up with her, clutching her hand again. Something more painful than her fight with Eddie was drawing her toward the old hospital, and she wasn't protesting.

As the guard had said, dim lighting cast shadows on the walls as we entered the building, odor of mold and mildew accosting our senses. It reminded me the hospital's first floor was underwater during Katrina. Broken chairs, patient files, and medical equipment littered the floor. Nothing had moved since the flood.

"We'll have to walk up," Carla said. "The elevators won't work."

"I don't think I'd get on one even if they did," Eddie said.

"That's a fact," Mama said, following them into the dark stairwell.

The center part of the M-shaped building was twenty stories tall, once the second tallest building in New Orleans. The flanking floors reached thirteen stories.

"Where do we go?" Lilly said.

Eddie just shook his head. "Does it matter? This place gives me the creeps."

"Keep climbing," Mama said. "There's something up ahead. I feel it."

"What's that sound?" Lilly asked.

"I hear it," Eddie said.

"Me too," Mama said.

Carla halted, holding up a hand.

"Sounds like children singing," Mama said.

As we listened, the choir sang, "I need you, you need me..."

Carla began to weep. "I don't think I can take this."

"What are we hearing?" Lilly asked.

"One of the nurses taught the children a hymn to help them cope with the situation."

"But they didn't die here," Lilly said.

"Intense trauma often leaves a permanent imprint on the place where it occurred," Mama said. "It's okay. Let's keep going."

We started up the stairs, ignoring humidity, and the sad hymn. The choir had grown dimmer when Mama grabbed my arm and yanked.

"There's something on this floor."

"Charity was a teaching hospital. The amphitheater where interns watched surgeries is on this floor."

Carla led us through the door to the top tier of the surgery amphitheater. A single operating table occupied the center of the O.R. below us. Syringes, scalpels, and medical devices littered the floor, and dim light seemed to emanate upward from the circular room to the funnel-shaped tiers above it. As we looked down into the O.R., we saw vague shapes of nurses and surgeons working on a shadowy body sprawled on the operating table. Unable to speak, Lilly tapped my shoulder.

"Spirits," I said in a whisper.

Doctors and nurses weren't the only ghosts in the amphitheater. Shadows of spirits floated above us and around us, some of them in wheelchairs, or on crutches, flashes of color lighting their translucent bodies like pulsating bulbs on a Christmas tree. The chorus of children continued to grow ever louder.

"Is this real?" Eddie asked.

A flying apparition passed through his body, answering his question.

"Ectoplasm," Mama said, touching the gunk left on his shirt.

"Holy crap!" he said. "Let's get the hell out of here."

"Seen enough?" I asked, touching Lilly's arm.

"Not till I get some pictures," she said, snapping away with her cell phone camera.

When Carla, Eddie, Jason, and Mama started for the door, I had to grab her shoulders and shake her.

"We have to go," I said. "Now!"

Mama took her hand, tugging her forward, and I gently nudged her shoulders. The choir stopped when the door closed behind us. Our experience with ghosts had yet to finish, our exit blocked as we reached the bottom floor. Even Mama jumped when it raised its outstretched hands. It was Zacharie

Patenaude.

"Set me free, Courtmanche. Do not make me wander forever like the lost souls that inhabit this building. Set me free."

"How can I do that?"

"End your curse."

Patenaude's specter disappeared, and the door leading to the bottom floor opened. I was suddenly aware that moisture on the back of my arms and neck had chilled, as had the temperature in the stairwell. I wasn't the only one to notice, and we were all running when we passed through the high fence surrounding Charity Hospital.

We piled into a cab for the ride back to Bertram's. Already approaching three in the morning, the customers were gone, the place dim. Bertram was sitting at the bar, sipping a shot of Cuervo. I pulled up a stool beside him.

"Whatever you do, don't say you look like you just seen a ghost."

"Did you?" he asked as everyone crowded around him.

"We all did," Lilly said, rubbing his shoulders. "If you had been with us, I wouldn't have been so frightened."

Bertram was purring as he languished in Lilly's gentle massage.

"Eddie boy, I can't move right now. If you mix the drinks, they's on the house."

"I hear that."

Eddie didn't need Bertram to ask him twice. Vaulting the bar, he began pouring liquor.

Lilly continued rubbing Bertram's shoulders as Eddie dispensed drinks.

"Miss Lilly," Bertram said. "I'm giving you just twenty-four hours to stop rubbing my shoulders."

"Or what?" she asked.

"Or I'll have to give you another twenty-four."

With everyone still too upset to laugh, Bertram and Lilly's repartee earned them only a titter. Lilly put her arms around him and squeezed.

"I took pictures. Want to see?" Lilly pulled out her phone.

Bertram craned his neck to see the screen on Lilly's phone. Seeing no ghost pictures, she continued scrolling.

"Oh my God! There's nothing here but bare walls."

"They were there," Mama said. "We all saw them, and I don't think one drink will be enough."

"Then break out the shots," Bertram said. "Can you handle it, Eddie?"

"Still on you?"

"Pour 'em, big boy. You're drinking on Big Daddy tonight."

The fact that Lilly was nibbling Bertram's earlobe had lots to do with his suddenly mellow mood. It didn't matter. Eddie was up to the task, pouring tequila for everyone and a jigger of lemonade for me.

"Bottoms up!" he said.

No one needed any goading, killing their shots, and then slamming the glasses against the counter.

"Keep 'em coming, Eddie. I think I'm in love," Bertram said.

"I think you're just a horny Cajun," Lilly said. "It's all right. I don't want to sleep tonight alone either."

"Then don't get me too drunk," he said.

"That ain't possible," Eddie said.

Carla stopped staring at the floor and glanced up at Eddie. "I'm better," she said. "And I just remembered why I'm so mad at you."

"Uncle," he said, raising his arms. "Wasn't I there for you tonight?"

"Yes you were," she said, grabbing his hand across the counter. "A good thing too, because I was going to have Wyatt punch you in the nose."

"That weenie? Fat chance of that," Eddie said.

"Hey, I helped you and Tony work out your differences, didn't I?"

"Where the hell was you all, anyway?" Bertram asked.

"Charity Hospital," Lilly said. "Even though Carla suggested we might experience some ghosts, I wasn't prepared for what I saw."

"How'd you manage to get in the place?" Bertram asked.

"They got a twelve-foot fence around it."

"Carla has connections," I said.

"Good going, Miss Carla," Bertram said. "So you seen a ghost?"

"Why do you think we're all drinking like fishes?" Eddie said. "My poor Catholic mother would have had a heart attack. Hell, I almost did."

"Then pour us some more shots, Eddie boy," Bertram said. "Booze cures all ills. Except for Wyatt, that is."

There were still drunks on the sidewalk outside the bar, many still calling the hogs or yelling 'hook 'em Horns.' Old rivalries never die, and this one was far from dead. When someone rattled the front door, Bertram didn't bother turning around. Lilly continued rubbing his shoulders. Even with all the booze she'd consumed, she hadn't forgotten our encounter with the ghost of Zacharie Patenaude.

"I'm mystified by the apparition we encountered before leaving the stairwell. You were both speaking French."

"Impossible. I don't speak French, except for a little Cajun, maybe."

Jason edged closer to Mama. "Trust me. It was French."

"We all heard you," Eddie said.

"I told you, I'm haunted by a ghost from a past life. Mama, can you help me on this?"

"Maybe," she said. "First, I'll need a dirty martini and another tequila chaser."

"Coming right up," Eddie said, already mixing and pouring.

"You're pretty handy with those bottles," Bertram said. "Where'd you learn bartending?"

"How do you think I paid for law school?"

"Waiting bar?" Bertram asked.

"Can't you tell?"

"Well, now I know who to call when I need a day off," Bertram said, still wallowing in Lilly's attention.

"From the looks of things, it may be tomorrow," Eddie said. "I don't work cheap."

"How much we talking here?"

"No money, just free drinks for a month."

"You kidding me?" Bertram said. "You'd drink me out of house and home. We got to figure something else out."

"Suit yourself. My offer doesn't last forever," Eddie said.

Jason was still interested in what Mama had to say about my ghost.

"Seems I'm the only one that's not in on the story of Wyatt's ghost. What's the deal?"

"Wyatt's haunted," Mama said.

"Guess that accounts for what they said."

"I don't speak French," Lilly said. "Tell us."

"He called Wyatt Matthieu, and asked him to remove the curse he'd placed on him. Wyatt told him it was something he would do willingly if he only knew how."

"This is all too creepy for me," Lilly said. "No one will believe this if I put it in the screenplay. I was there, and I'm not sure I understand it myself."

"What we all saw was a glimpse into the spirit realm," Mama said. "They are all trapped in Charity Hospital because of some traumatic end to their lives."

"A rare glimpse," Lilly said.

Mama sipped her martini before speaking. "Maybe not so unusual. There are probably more displaced spirits in this city than there are living beings."

Chapter 15

It was almost nine when I finally got out of bed, Kisses none too happy having her breakfast served so late. Some faded dream lay heavily on my mind as I took a hot shower. When I started downstairs to Bertram's bar, the uproar of many football fans told me it was open for business again.

The first person to greet me was Lilly Bliss, smiling as she stood behind the bar, pouring pitchers of beer. Lady was with her, wagging her tail. Bertram was nowhere to be seen as I pulled up a stool.

"Happy New Year's Eve," she said.

"You're kidding me!"

"No, tomorrow's another year."

"Where's the Cajun?" I asked.

"Still in bed. I made him bacon and eggs. He ate it and then went back to sleep."

"Congratulations," I said. "In all the years I've known Bertram, you're the first person I've ever known to wear him out."

"Believe me, it wasn't easy. He's ravenous."

"And?"

"I think I like it. Maybe I'll marry him and move to New Orleans. We could buy a house and live forever and ever in the Garden District."

Her words made me smile. "I've heard those sentiments more than once."

"And?" she said.

"You don't see a woman around, do you? Bertram's so hard headed, his own mother couldn't live with him more than a week or two."

"It'll take more than one night in the sack for me to get serious with anyone. Still..."

"I can already tell how much he likes you."

"You can?"

"Except for me, you're the only person he's ever let tend bar for him. He doesn't trust anyone."

"I wish he'd wake up. I've already gone through a keg of beer. Care to help me connect another one?"

I crawled under the counter and helped her install a keg to one of the taps, the two of us waiting tables until Bertram finally came dragging out of his apartment in back. He quickly grabbed Lilly and twirled her around.

"Allons dancer!"

"I love it when you talk Cajun to me," she said with a kiss.

"You got a good one, Bertram. I can't claim as much for Lilly."

"Don't make me have to hurt you," he said.

"You do, and Lady will bite your big, Cajun butt," I said as I crawled under the bar.

"She probably would, too," he said, pouring me a glass of lemonade. "Don't matter though, cause I owe you big time for introducing me to this beautiful lady."

"And don't you forget it," I said. "What time did things finally break up?"

"Shortly after you left us and went to bed," Lilly said. "Bertram dragged me off to his apartment and swept me off my feet."

"And the others?" I asked.

"Don't know," Bertram said. "Miss Lilly and I were kind of preoccupied if you know what I mean. My Scotch stock looks a little depleted."

"Lilly saved your bacon this morning while you were sleeping in."

"I'll make it up to this beautiful woman. You like some breakfast?"

"Thanks, but I have business."

Grabbing Lilly, Bertram said, "So do we. I might just have to shut the bar early today."

"I'll believe it when I see it," I said as I headed for the door.

Late December, a breeze chilled my neck as I walked out to the sidewalk. Regretting I hadn't worn even a light jacket, I grabbed my collar and hurried toward Canal to catch a cab.

As I paid the cabbie in front of Mama Mulate's old house, a tugboat whistled a mournful dirge. I probably should have called first, but I needed to see her and gambled she'd be home. She met me at the door in her old cotton robe, smiling as she opened the screen door to let me into the house. She wasn't alone.

Standing beside her was Jason Fasempaur, his arm encircled around her waist. He was also dressed in an old robe, and he had a mile-wide grin on his face.

"I don't know about Eddie and Carla, but it looks like everyone got lucky last night except me," I said.

"Quit whining and come in this house," Mama said.

She led us down the hallway to the kitchen, the smell of eggs and beignets greeting us before we reached her table. The back door was cracked, and one of Mama's cats peeked in to see what was going on.

"It's a little late. Aren't you teaching today?"

"Semester break. Thought I told you. I don't work again until after the New Year. Yesterday was an organizational meeting."

"Lucky you," I said.

Jason patted my shoulder. "Lucky me."

"I'm making omelets. Eaten yet?"

"Even if I had, I wouldn't pass up one of your omelets."

"Or my peach beignets. Wyatt has quite a sweet tooth."

"So do I," Jason said. "I haven't had a homemade peach beignet since I was ten."

"I thought you were from New York."

"My favorite aunt lived in New Orleans. I spent lots of summers here."

"You won't have to wait much longer for a peach beignet." Mama's smile disappeared when she looked at me.

"What's the problem? You look so serious, and I know you're not here for one of Mama's beignets?"

"I'm jealous. Everybody went home with someone last night except me."

Jason glanced at Mama. "Don't feel sorry for him. He spent the night before last with Latitia Boiset."

"Is that the young woman we saw rushing down the stairs from your room? Who is she?"

I didn't have to answer because Jason did it for me. "Just about the hottest artist to come down the pike in the last decade. She has a voice and face of an angel, and a body built for sin."

Mama gazed at me with a look I couldn't decipher. "And you're jealous?"

Jason winked at me when I gave him a dirty look.

"I see I'm getting no sympathy here," I said. "Does the offer of omelets and beignets still stand?"

"Depends," Mama said. "Sounds like Jason and I need a blow-by-blow of your night with Miss Boiset."

"She's part of the reason I'm here."

"Sit. You can tell your story while I finish the omelets."

Jason seemed right at home, pouring me a cup of coffee while petting one of Mama's cats that had jumped into his lap. He looked even happier when Mama turned on her stereo and an older jazz favorite wafted softly through the kitchen.

"Latitia's the lead singer for a touring band called Brass & Sass. I've seen them several times in Paris. Wyatt caught their act at a nightclub in Fat City."

"What were you doing there?" she asked.

"Long story."

"It's semester break. We have all day."

"Eddie and I were looking for an old man that works in the kitchen. We were watching the stage show when I realized I'd graduated from high school with one of the horn players."

"Which one?" Jason asked.

"Jeneen Presley."

Mama stopped working on the omelets. "Elvis' daughter?"

"No. Born and raised right here in New Orleans."

"Janeen's one of the best sax players in the business," Jason said. "She could spend her life in a recording studio making tons of money if she wanted. Seems she likes touring better than staying in one place."

By now, Mama's eyebrows were raised. "How do you know her?"

"High school bandmates. We used to hold hands on bus trips."

"Jeneen's also a babe," Jason said. "Don't ever expect me to feel sorry for you."

"Or me," Mama said as she put our omelets on the table and joined us. "If you were with Miss Boiset, what happened to Jeneen?"

"Eddie," I said.

Mama frowned. "Figures. That man must have grown up in an alley from all the tom-catting he does."

Jason was enjoying the omelet. If he'd noticed a twinge of jealousy in Mama's voice, he didn't show it.

"Mama," he said. "It's not fair that a woman with your beauty and intelligence is also a world class cook."

"Go on," Mama said.

"You also know more about jazz than I do. I'll refrain from bragging about what else you're excellent at because it would make Wyatt blush."

"Baby, you just earned one of Mama's peach beignets. Wyatt, you also get one, though you've never complimented me like that."

"I second every word," I said. "Except the last part for which I have no idea what you're talking about."

Mama joined us at the table. "Jason's making me blush. "Maybe you'd better finish your story."

"Even though Titia and I only spent a few hours together, I'm experiencing strong separation anxiety. I can't get her off my mind."

"She's an extraordinarily attractive and talented young woman," Jason said.

"Wyatt's known more than his share of gorgeous women," Mama said.

"This whole deal with the ghost has me remembering things I haven't thought about in years."

125

"Such as?"

"The place I lived until I was ten."

"Which was?" Mama said.

"A cotton plantation on River Road."

"The Thomas Plantation?" Jason asked.

"My grandfather renamed it when he bought the place years ago."

"Your grandfather was Jess Thomas?"

"Yes."

"The governor of Louisiana?" Mama said. "You never told me that."

"More like the king," Jason said. "He had more money and power in this state than just about anyone in recent history."

"What happened to all the money?" Mama asked.

"Dad lost it trying to be like Grandpa. I've blocked most of it from my memory. At least until now."

"Matthieu Courtmanche owned a cotton plantation. Your spirit told me so," Mama said.

"The Willows," Jason said. "The Willows and the Thomas Plantation are one in the same. It's where you grew up."

"Wyatt, what's the matter?" Mama asked.

"My father killed himself at the Willows. Madam Toulouse Joubert informed me Matthieu Courtmanche's father also committed suicide there."

"Coincidence," Mama said.

"She also told me my alter ego may also have committed suicide. What does that say about my future?"

"You're moody sometimes, but I don't believe you would ever take your own life," Mama said.

When I didn't respond, she cast a worried look. I jumped when she touched my wrist.

"Let's go to the back porch. Get some fresh air."

"Who are Armand and Madam Toulouse Joubert?" Jason asked.

"Tell you later," Mama said.

The day had warmed a bit, but it was still December, a nip in the air. Mama's cats didn't seem to mind, playing keep away with a plastic ball. Her covered porch had a slow moving ceiling fan to help fight the heat of summer. Today, it wasn't needed.

The stockade fence surrounding the yard, along with shrubs and fruit trees, afforded her all the privacy she needed. The yard was landscaped with fountains, flower beds, and stone pathways. Wind chimes hung on the eaves of the porch, ringing in a slight breeze moving up from the river.

"I like your rocking chairs," Jason said. "My grandparents had them on their back porch. I feel young again."

"Wyatt, are you okay?" Mama asked.

I sat in one of the rocking chairs and drew a deep breath. "I'm fine now. Your backyard is a stress remover. I love it here and I'm fine now."

"Like being in the country," Jason said.

"My little piece of heaven. Now tell me, Jason, how is it you know Tony Nicosia?" she said, changing the subject.

"I was researching yesterday at the Jazz Archive. Tony came in, lost as a goose. I offered to help."

"What was he doing there?"

"He had a photo of a lost cornet. Someone hired him to find it. I took him to a shop on Royal called Brass Shoppe. Zeb Zuckerman, the person that owns it, knows more about musical instruments than any person alive."

"Even you?" Mama said.

"Even me."

"We just met," I said. "How do you know so much about jazz?"

"Let me answer," Mama said. "Jason has a Ph.D. in music history from Harvard. He teaches at La Sorbonne, the University of Paris, but he lectures all over the world. You've written how many books?"

"Fifteen, I think. I've lost count."

"I get the picture," I said. "I'm impressed. Was Zuckerman able to help Tony?"

"No, but he recognized the horn in the photo and knew something about it. Seems it belonged to a mobster."

"Oh?" Mama said.

"Frankie Castalano. According to Zeb, he was once one of

the best young cornetists in the country."

When a cold breeze blew across the porch, rattling the wind chimes, Mama's three cats ran through the open backdoor, into the house.

"Wyatt, what's the matter?" Mama asked.

"Another curious coincidence."

"Tell us."

"Eddie and I went to the Havana Club to speak with an old man named Paco. Eddie found him peeling potatoes in the kitchen."

"What's so unusual about that?" Mama asked.

"He told Eddie his name is Paco Castalano, and that he is Frankie Castalano's father."

"That is strange," Jason said. "Frankie told Tony his father is dead. The old man took the horn away from his son because he thought he needed to concentrate on the family business."

"It apparently worked. Frankie Castalano is into most everything, including gambling, prostitution, and drugs. He also owns restaurants, nightclubs, and lots of legitimate businesses."

"What's the deal with the horn?" Mama asked.

"Someone left it for Frankie at a recital. The bell was inscribed with the word 'King' which caused him to think it was a gift from Joe Oliver, the legendary trumpet player also known as King Oliver."

"Was it?" I asked.

"Impossible," Jason said. "King Oliver was dead. The horn was given to him by someone else."

By now, the cats were back on the porch, one of them sitting in Mama's lap.

"I have an old LP by King Oliver. He was quite the horn player."

"He took young Louis Armstrong under his wing. Even gave him his first professional instrument. Armstrong idolized him."

"Don't you wish we could go back in time and listen to some of those wonderful musicians?"

"If we could do that, it would be Nirvana," Jason said. "Armstrong wasn't just a wonderful musician, he was also a writer."

"Oh?" I said. "I've never heard that."

"He wrote, much as he played—freestyle. His words were lyrical and poetic."

"An extraordinary man," Mama said.

"But very real," Jason said. "He liked grass, which he called gage, and was apparently addicted to a laxative called Swiss Criss. His grandmother used to collect the herb along the railroad track, and got him started using it at an early age."

"Makes me wonder," I said.

Mama gave me an inquiring glance. "Wonder what?"

"How his grandmother knew one weed from the next?"

Mama laughed out loud. "Indians, living here before the white man, knew. It was the only remedy they had. Slaves from west Africa and the Caribbean, also knew about herbs and medicinal plants. What they didn't know locally, they picked up from the Indians."

It was Jason's turn to laugh. "We should patent whatever you gave me last night. We'd be multimillionaires."

"You needed it, but after all the alcohol we'd consumed, I wasn't taking any chances."

"You two are making me blush," I said. "This time, I'm not kidding."

Jason suddenly became thoughtful. "You know, there's just no logical explanation for what we saw at the hospital last night. All gallows humor aside, it scared the living hell out of me."

Mama patted his cheek. "If you spent time here, you'd know this is the City of Spirits. Most people never see what we saw last night because they don't subject themselves to places where spirits are likely to proliferate."

"If you don't turn over a rock, you're unlikely to find a snake," I said.

"What about your spirit?" Jason asked.

"I wish I knew."

"Maybe you do. I speak French. The spirit clearly said you know someone that can help you remove the curse."

"Madam Aja, perhaps," I said.

"Of course," Mama said. "And I haven't visited my

favorite herbalist lately to replenish my supplies."

"You mean Senora?"

"Who's Senora?" Jason asked.

"Daughter, or maybe granddaughter of Madam Aja, one of the city's most prominent voodoo women."

"Voodoo?" Jason said. "I thought you practiced Vodoun."

"Yes, but voodoo, or hoodoo is the local offshoot of the religion. Marie Laveau practiced voodoo. So does Madam Aja."

"It's New Year's Eve," I said. "Aren't you two celebrating tonight?"

"Celebrations can wait. I'm sensing we need to visit Madam Aja."

"When?" Jason asked.

"Now."

Chapter 16

Mama lowered the top of her Sprite so all three of us could fit inside. It was still cramped, my legs draped across the gear shift as we raced downtown. She finally screeched to a stop at a liquor store, my heart rate almost returning to normal.

When Mama came out of the package shop with a bag under her arm, I didn't get back in the car.

"Madam Aja's house isn't far from here. I'll walk the rest of the way."

"Complaining about my driving again?" she asked.

"Not complaining, walking."

"Then let's walk," she said. "Faubourg Marigny is so popular with tourists these days, we'd have a hard time finding a parking place anyway."

"You won't get an argument from me."

"You think I'm a bad driver?"

"Is the Pope Catholic?"

"Stop it, both of you," Jason said. "Mama is a very good driver."

"You weren't sitting on the trunk lid. There's no seatbelt there, you know."

"I can't help it if you're a wuss."

I rolled my eyes but knew when to shut up about Mama's driving ability, or lack thereof. They weren't waiting for me anyway. Dodging a bicyclist racing down the sidewalk, I hurried after them.

Long after sunset the last time I'd visited the old woman, I didn't remember much about the neighborhood. Now, it was daylight, scads of tourists on the sidewalk, and cyclists racing down the narrow streets. We found Madam Aja and her daughter on the front porch. Senora was in a rocking chair beside Madam Aja's ancient wheelchair. She greeted Mama with a crushing hug.

"Well, look who finally came to visit."

As if she'd known me forever, she also gave me a hug. When Mama broke away from Madam Aja, I took the old woman's hand.

"Back so soon?" she said.

"It's been a few months."

"More questions for me?"

My reply brought a smile to her wrinkled face. "Why not? You have more answers than anyone in New Orleans. This gentleman is Jason Fasempaur."

Madam Aja extended her hand. "Senora and I saw you on the History Channel not long ago. I was impressed with your knowledge of jazz, and Senora thinks you're a cutie."

Jason winked at Senora and squeezed Madam Aja's hand. "You wouldn't believe the calls I get every time they air that episode."

"Yes we would," Senora said. "Madam Aja and I are both jazz fans."

"Glad to hear it," Jason said.

Senora was a stocky woman with gray hair draping her shoulders. Her African-print dress matched the sunny day, as did the orange shawl draped carelessly around her shoulders.

Madam Aja shawl covered her shoulder, a homemade quilt her legs. She seemed the epitome of old age, with facial skin shrunken around prominent cheekbones. As my mother used to say, her hands were like ice. From the brown paper bag under her arm, Mama gave Senora a bottle of Weller's, Madam Aja her favorite, Old Crow. A couple strolled past on the sidewalk, arguing about their next adventure, not caring that we were listening.

"Senora, get some glasses. I haven't had a nip of whiskey in a month or more. The rest of you pull up a chair and sit a spell," Madam Aja said.

When Jason and Mama appropriated the porch swing, I plopped down on the edge of the porch, my feet on the steps.

"You look terrific, Madam Aja. Last time we were here you were sick, in bed."

"I'm doing good, but I'll feel even better after a nip of whiskey. You three can share Senora's. The Old Crow's all mine."

"We wouldn't have it any other way," Mama said.

Senora handed me a glass of ice tea, and empty glasses for everyone else.

"Sorry, I have no lemonade," she said.

"No problem. Thanks for remembering."

She opened both bottles of whiskey, filling Mama and Jason's glasses of ice with Weller's.

"I've never tasted Old Crow," Jason said. "May I have a sip of yours? I swear I won't drink much."

Madam Aja laughed. "Course you can, if you don't mind drinking after an old woman with no teeth."

"I have no problem whatsoever drinking after a beautiful woman," Jason said, kneeling beside her rocking chair.

"You are a cutie. Too bad I'm not fifty years younger."

"If you were," Jason said, "I'd have a hard choice to make between you and Mama."

"Mama, I think you have a keeper. I don't trust a word out of his mouth, but I sure like the way they sound."

"I'd keep him if he weren't going back to Paris in a few days."

"Senora pour this dashing gentleman some of my Old Crow. He needs to sit with Mama Mulate, and not share a glass with an old woman."

Senora complied. "Madam Aja likes you. She doesn't share her Old Crow with anyone."

"I heard that," Madam Aja said. "Don't be telling all my secrets."

Whistles of tugs and oilers on the nearby river echoed off the rows of wooden houses. When a flock of pigeons landed in the street, wrangling for peanuts some tourist had dropped, Mama explained why we were there.

"We have a problem. Wyatt is possessed with a spirit."

"Oh? Tell me."

"There was a curse placed on another man during the time of French leadership in New Orleans. When I channeled that person's spirit, he begged me to have Wyatt remove the curse and give his soul peace."

"And Wyatt has no idea how to accomplish that particular feat," Madam Aja said.

Mama nodded. "You read my mind."

"An ability I never possessed. Now that I'm old, those powers I still have are vastly diminished."

"I don't think so," Mama said.

"It's getting a little chilly out here. Let's go inside, and I'll put some thought into your problem."

We followed Senora as she wheeled Madam Aja into the French cottage. The front room had a wooden counter and shelves stocked with labeled jars. Jason released Mama's hand for a closer look.

Mama laughed when he said, "Eye of newt?"

"Don't make fun," she said. "Senora is the most proficient herbalist in New Orleans."

"Au contraire, I'm not making fun. I'm in awe," he said.

Senora pushed Madam Aja into a dark room, all light from the street blocked by black curtains. Only the soft glow of a few candles lighted the top of a round table and the voodoo altar behind it. That quickly changed as Senora began lighting the many votive candles on the altar.

Catholic icons and various African figurines populated the holy table. Mama added a dollar bill to a basket, making a ritual sign with her hand. I added another dollar. Not knowing the secret sign, I bowed my head a moment before backing away, Senora and Madam Aja nodding their approval. Jason quickly followed our lead.

"Join me at the table," the old woman said. "You may want to take a healthy slug of your whiskey before we begin."

After topping everyone's glass, Senora took a seat beside Mama Mulate. I started feeling pain, my neck burning as Madam Aja stared a stiletto through my soul.

"You can lift the curse, but you'll have to do some Traveling, and you can't go alone."

"Pardon me?" I said.

"You may have forgotten, but you know what I mean."

"I'll go with him," Mama said.

"Sorry, baby. You're not a Traveler. It's Jason that must help him."

When Mama glanced at Jason, he returned her puzzled gaze with one of his own.

"Jason's a Traveler?" Madam Aja nodded. "But he's due back in Paris in a few days."

"Plenty of time."

The room had grown deathly quiet, except for wax popping on an altar candle.

"What's a traveler?" Jason asked.

"Finish your whiskey before I tell you."

Jason licked his lips after downing the Old Crow. "This is good. I don't know why everyone's making faces."

"More Weller's for Mama and me," Senora said.

By now, Jason was feeling no pain, smiling as the reverberation of a brass band began oozing through the walls.

"It's Traveler," Madam Aja said. "With a capital tee. Most folks are fixed in time, and the place they were born. Travelers aren't. They can come and go, from place to place, and time to time."

Jason listened intently, holding the old woman's hand across the table as Senora poured him more whiskey.

"If that's true, why do I have no memory of living during another time?"

"When you travel to a place you've lived before, you become the person you once were. Unless you've never been there. Then you don't change at all, except maybe to get younger or older."

"Sounds complicated."

"That's why someone needs to go with Wyatt."

"I'm still confused," Jason said.

"Wyatt has to return to a place he once lived as another person. He'll become that person and won't remember why he's there. Since you didn't come from that place, you won't be affected."

"This whiskey is good," he said. "I'm a little tipsy, so let me be clear on this. Wyatt and I are going to travel back through time. He won't know it, but I will."

"Yes," Madam Aja said, giving his hand a reassuring squeeze.

"How do we get to this other time and place?" he asked.

Madam Aja flashed him a toothless grin. "Don't know. At least not yet. Senora bring my pipe, and the moonflower."

I didn't miss Senora's worried expression, and neither did Mama. Though apparent she didn't like what Madam Aja had asked her to do, she placed a corncob pipe and a small jar in front of the old woman, pushing the candle to within her reach.

"Perhaps the spirits can help me answer your question," she said.

Tapping a small portion of the herbal concoction from the jar into the pipe, she tamped it down. Holding it over the candle flame, she puffed until smoke swirled from the bowl. Within seconds, her eyes rolled to the back of her head, a silly grin replacing her venerable appearance. Jason's curiosity had caught up with him.

"Senora, what did you give her?"

"Datura tincture," she said. "I've only seen her use it once before. Please, ask your questions. I can't let her stay drugged for long."

Madam Aja's mouth was open, saliva dripping from her lips. Her eyes disjointed, she stared at a spot on the ceiling. Mama squeezed Senora's hand and nodded.

"Madam Aja, how can Wyatt and Jason travel to the past?"

The voice issuing from the old woman's lips sounded raspy and thick as if it were coming from another person.

"A portal. They must enter it tonight before the clock strikes twelve, and return before midnight on the eve of the New Year."

"But today is New Year's Eve. How can they possibly have the time to complete their task?"

"Time doesn't always walk a straight line," the voice issuing from Madam Aja said.

"And if they don't return before midnight?" Mama asked.

"Then they will remain forever trapped in time."

136

"Then there is little time remaining to accomplish their task."

Madam Aja's head bobbled on her scrawny neck. "Yes, time is fleeting."

"Where is this portal?" Mama said.

"Only Baron Samedi knows."

"No more," Senora said. "She's fading."

Hurrying around the table, she placed something under the old woman's tongue. Grasping her chin, she began trickling Old Crow into her mouth. When Madam Aja's eyes finally refocused, all the candles flickered and died. For a moment, we sat in the darkness as the pounding beat of the brass band grew stronger outside the walls.

After relighting the candle, Senora said, "I'll stay with Madam Aja until she recovers. Please wait for us on the porch."

I sprawled on the front steps, Mama and Jason returning to the swing. The marching band was louder now, as were the crowd sounds of a distant parade.

"I doubt if my colleagues at the Sorbonne would accept my story of what we just saw in there. What is datura?"

"Nightshade, sometimes known as moonflower or Jimson Weed. A powerful hallucinogen only a few knowledgeable herbalists can use. It's so dangerous even a tiny amount can kill you," Mama said.

A tourist bus passed on the narrow street, stench of burning diesel replacing the herbal scent of Senora's candles.

"Madam Aja told us what we have to do. She didn't tell us how to do it," I said.

"Unless you know whom this Baron Samedi character is," Jason said.

"A Haitian voodoo deity, keeper of the dead and guardian of the crossroads," Mama said.

"Guess it rules out using my cell phone," Jason said.

We all turned when Madam Aja said, "Baron Samedi is a powerful loa and doesn't tolerate mockery. I like you, but I'll not suffer a fool."

Jason jumped from the swing, grabbing the old woman's hand. "I'm so sorry, Madam Aja. I swear I wasn't making light of your religion. Forgive me?"

Madam Aja smiled as Senora wheeled her to the porch. Her confused look was gone, her words again sounding normal.

"Yes, and I'm sure Baron Samedi will as well. You're going to find out sooner than you think."

"But how?" I asked.

"When Marie Laveau was alive, she conducted rituals on St. John's Bayou during the winter solstice."

"Isn't it a little late? The winter solstice occurred before Christmas."

"Madam Marie will also forgive us. Senora and I will be there, and I'll summon Baron Samedi. He will provide the answers you seek."

"I look forward to meeting the Baron," Jason said.

Madam Aja grinned. "Most believers aren't so inclined. Doesn't matter because you are chosen to help Wyatt lift his curse. The only way he'll stop this possession."

"I'm possessed?" I said.

"Oh yes. Very much so. And you're lucky the spirit is benign and not demonic."

Chapter 17

We returned to the car, Jason carrying a grocery bag filled with potions Mama had bought from Senora. They were holding hands, jabbering like love-struck teenagers when she noticed my frown.

"What's the problem? You look as if you're on your way to the dentist."

"Sorry. Madam Aja just kicked my last ounce of confidence right out from under me."

"She told you how to solve your problem."

"Maybe."

"Don't be that way. She'll summon Baron Samedi tonight at the solstice ceremony. He'll tell us where to find the portal."

"If you don't mind me asking," Jason said, "What the hell is this solstice ceremony?"

"Madam Marie had a daughter, also named Marie Laveau. She continued her mother's work long after the first Madam Marie had died. Each year, she'd carry out ritual ceremonies near St. John's Bayou, on St. John's Eve and the winter solstice. Thousands of followers would come."

"There's been no Winter Solstice ceremony in my lifetime," I said. "We'll be the only ones there."

"Stop it! There will be believers, I promise you."

"How can you be so sure?" I said.

"It doesn't matter. Even if no one is there but us, Baron Samedi will give us the answers we need."

"I hope you're right."

"We have to trust Madam Aja. I practice Vodoun, and it's not the same as voodoo and hoodoo."

"I don't know about that," Jason said, giving her hand an extra squeeze. "You've managed to hoodoo me."

Mama pinched his cheek. "Yes, and I'm going to hoodoo you upside the head if you don't stop playing around. Wyatt has the blues, and I'm trying to cheer him up."

"Where is this winter solstice ceremony?" I asked.

"Don't worry your pretty little head about it. Mama will get us there."

Before reaching her car, I'd already decided to return to Bertram's on foot. Mama's nose was slightly out of shape that I had little faith in her driving prowess.

"It's a beautiful day, and I need the exercise," I said, hoping to appease her.

Mama frowned. "Whatever. We'll be at your room around eleven."

I watched them disappear in a screech of rubber before heading toward the French Quarter. With the Sugar Bowl approaching, Bertram's was packed. I found Eddie sitting alone at the bar.

"I was wondering where you were," he said. "I knocked on your door upstairs."

"Side trip," I said. "What's up?"

"I called Adele, and she's managed to calm Pancho. I thought you might want to come with me and have dinner there later on."

"Can't make it tonight. I'm going to a winter solstice voodoo ceremony."

Eddie stared at me with his mouth open. "You're a little late. The first day of winter was a week ago."

"We're starting a new tradition."

"Okay, weirdo. Guess I'll have to go by myself," he said.

"What about Carla. You two already on the outs?"

"Still thick as thieves. She has a charity bazaar tonight."

"And while she's away, you're going to try to fix yet another busted relationship."

"Amusing, Cowboy. You should try standup. Adele has Pancho primed for my apology. I'm taking him a bottle of the

140

best brandy the liquor store had. If I don't go tonight, I'll end up drinking it myself."

"Then say hi to them for me. Since I'm probably going to be up the rest of the night, I'm going upstairs for a nap."

Eddie watched as Wyatt disappeared through the crowd. He had a few hours to kill before leaving for Metairie, and during such times, Bertram usually kibitzed with him. Tonight, the Cajun bartender was busy with Lilly Bliss, who hadn't returned to her hotel since visiting Charity Hospital. The way she and Bertram were mooning behind the bar, it was obvious she had no plans to go there anytime soon.

A drunk banged into Eddie's stool on his way to the men's room. He didn't notice, and Eddie didn't bother saying anything. He was about to motion Bertram to bring him another drink when Tony Nicosia walked through the front door.

"You still mad?" Tony asked as he sidled up to the bar.

"Hell, you're the only person here that'll even speak to me. Pull up a stool. I'll buy you a drink."

Tony hesitated. "Looks like someone's sitting there."

"When he comes out of the bathroom he won't remember where he was. Grab his stool and slide his beer down the bar. I'll scoot over a little."

Eddie was correct. The man never returned to the bar, walking his tab. Bertram yelled at him, shaking his fist as he wobbled out the door.

"Damn drunks," he said. "How you doing, Lieutenant?"

"Passable. You, Bertram?"

"Couldn't be better," he said with a mile-wide grin.

"Bertram has a new squeeze," Eddie said.

Bertram nodded and tapped the counter. "And this one may be my last. I think I'm in love."

Eddie shook his head. "I've heard it all before. Better bring the Lieutenant a drink and put it on my tab."

"Comin' right up," Bertram said. "You?"

"Yeah, bring me another. What are you doing out alone on New Year's Eve?" Eddie asked.

"Trying to tie up a few loose ends on my new case before I

go to the house."

"Then you better hurry before midnight and all hell descends on the French Quarter."

"Tell me about it. Lil's waiting with a chilled bottle of champagne. If I don't get home soon, I'll be in trouble."

"Hell, Lieutenant, you stay in trouble. What's the problem with your new case?"

"I'm having trouble getting traction."

"If it were easy, everyone would do it," Eddie said. "Besides, that's why they pay you the big bucks."

"Yeah, well this client may just take the big bucks back if I can't get him some answers."

"I'm having dinner tonight at Via Vittorio Veneto, the best little Italian restaurant in town. I can't get anyone to go with me. Come with me and maybe I can help you with your case."

Tony shook his head. "Dipping kind of deep in the barrel, huh?"

"Don't get your panties in a wad," Eddie said. "If I had known you were going to be here I would have asked you first."

Tony didn't believe him but decided to keep it to himself. "Lil wouldn't like it."

"She will if I can help you break through. You been to Via Vittorio Veneto?"

"Lots of times. Lil and I love the place. It's even saved our marriage a time or two."

"Then come with me. Afterwards, you'll have a straight shot home."

"You said last night you saw Paco Castalano. Tell me where and I'll buy."

"What's the deal with Paco?"

"A client hired me to do a lost and found. Seems the only person who knows where I can find what I'm looking for is the old man. Problem is he sorta dropped out of sight. My client says he's dead."

"He's as alive as you and me. I wasn't lying when I told you I talked to him."

"What business do you have with the old man?"

"My new girlfriend. A mob hanged her grandfather for a murder he didn't commit. I'm trying to clear his name, and I think Paco Castalano may have the answers."

"I don't remember any hangings. Was it a while back?"

"Early forties. A mob broke him out of jail and strung him up. Over in Metairie."

"Yeah, now I remember hearing about it," Tony said. "You think Paco had something to do with the murder?"

"He was only a boy when it happened, but I'd almost lay money he knows the killer's name."

"Probably right about that," Tony said.

Almost dark, the place was already starting to rock. When another drunk banged against them, Eddie didn't bother turning around. Instead, he shook his head and downed his drink.

"After dinner, if you have time, we'll check out the Havana Club. If we can get by the goons watching him, we can both talk to Paco."

"Why don't we just go there now?" Tony said.

"Because I've got business at Via Vittorio Veneto."

"What kind of business?"

"Lieutenant, you're still the nosiest cop in town."

"The only way to get answers," Tony said.

"That's why I want you with me when I talk to Paco again."

"Then don't leave me in the dark. Tell me about it."

"I'm friends with the family that owns the restaurant, and got crosswise with the old man last time I was there. His daughter has arranged for him to be away from the restaurant. When he shows up and sees me, I'm going to apologize and give him a bottle of expensive brandy. Come go with me. We can help each other on this one."

Tony glanced at his watch. "Don't know. Lil's expecting me."

"Tell her it's business. Put me on the phone and I'll vouch for you. I promise you're not going to see Paco during the day."

"I'll have to get her to feed my dog," Tony said.

"So?"

"She don't like him."

Eddie shook his head again, but this time he was smiling. "Lil wouldn't let anything go hungry. You know that."

"Probably not," Tony said, punching in Lil's number on his phone.

Eddie listened to the conversation. When Tony hung up, he dialed another number. Eddie couldn't help but overhear.

"Problems?" he asked.

"Lil's not happy, but she'll feed the dog."

"Good. Who else were you talking to?"

"My client. He wants a rundown on where I'm at in the investigation."

"Who is this client?"

"Frankie Castalano."

After motioning Bertram to bring them another drink, Eddie crossed his arms tightly against his chest. On the street outside the bar, Arkansas football fans were calling the hogs, the sound echoing against Bertram's picture window.

"You kidding me, Lieutenant? You slipped over to the dark side?"

"This is legit. I told you, I'm only trying to find his lost horn. No funny business included."

"It still looks bad confabbing with New Orleans' most notorious mob boss," Eddie said.

"You're gonna find out," Tony said, slugging his drink.

"What's that supposed to mean?"

"He's meeting us at Via Vittorio Veneto."

The night had grown chilly, Tony and Eddie glad to be at a warm table inside the Italian restaurant. A flickering candle in the middle of the checkered tablecloth added to the warmth of the dimly lit room. When Adele went into the kitchen, Eddie started in on Tony.

"What kind of bone-headed idea were you thinking of, inviting Frankie Castalano to join us."

"I'm working, remember? You knew that when you asked me to join you."

"I just hope no one sees me. I could lose my job because of this."

"Yeah, and Frankie could get whacked for colluding with the authorities."

"No one's colluding here," Eddie said.

"Then just be cool and pretend you have no idea who he is. If he recognizes you, I'm sure he'll do the same."

"What if he's wired?" Eddie asked.

Tony's eyes rolled as he glanced at the ceiling. "Hell, dumbass, why would he be wearing a wire? He don't even know you're here. Probably wouldn't care if he did."

"I think I'm getting mad at you again, Lieutenant," Eddie said, his arms and legs crossed tightly.

"Sorry, Eddie. I only meant it in the nicest way."

Adele came out of the kitchen and joined them, ending their bickering for a moment. She gave them each a wine glass and began filling them.

"Eddie, you look angry. Did I do something wrong?"

"You could never do anything wrong to me," he said. "I didn't realize you knew Tony."

Adele patted Tony's shoulder. "We go way back. Lil and I shop together whenever we got the time. You not mad at Tony, are you?"

"I'll get over it."

"Good, cause it's New Year's Eve and everybody ought to be happy."

"And Pancho?"

"Papa's not back yet, but I have him primed for your apology."

"And it'll be a good one, even if I have to get down on my hands and knees."

Adele kissed his forehead and hurried back into the kitchen. Toni was getting the coats for a departing couple, the restaurant's only other customers. When she opened the door for their exit, Frankie Castalano and a handsome young man entered. Toni seemed all taken with the young man that towered over Castalano. After checking their coats, Frankie glanced around the room, saw Tony, and waved.

"Pull up a chair," Tony said. "Frankie, this is Eddie."

If Frankie recognized Eddie, he didn't admit it and left their introductions at first names only.

145

"This is my nephew Vincenso. Since I'm a little night blind, Vince drives me when I go out after dark."

Vince had a full head of dark hair with eyes to match. He was probably mid-twenties and dressed like a GQ runway model. Toni had noticed his chiseled looks and couldn't stop smiling in his direction. The attraction seemed mutual.

"Frankie, this is Adele. She and her dad Pancho own the restaurant. The lovely young woman at the front door is her daughter, Toni."

"Family business," Frankie said after standing and shaking her hand. "I love that. Vince is a senior at L.S.U. majoring in economics. He got my sister's looks and not mine, thank God."

"I think you're very handsome, Frankie," Adele said. "I hope you enjoy our hospitality tonight."

"I already am, and from the wonderful aroma coming from the kitchen, I'm sorry I didn't plan to stay for dinner."

"Maybe I can change your mind," she said.

Adele flashed him another smile before returning to the kitchen. Vince didn't notice his chair turned so he could see what Toni was doing.

"You've not eaten here?" Tony asked.

"Never had the pleasure," Frankie said. "I didn't know you were with somebody."

"Don't mind Eddie. He knows about the horn and doesn't care if we discuss business," Tony said.

"Good. You found it yet?"

"No, but I'm on it. I did find out your horn wasn't owned by King Oliver."

"Oh? How do you know that?"

"I ran into an expert at the Hogan Jazz Archive over at Tulane. He said the horn in your picture was a one-of-kind. He called it an artist's horn."

"Then what about the inscription?"

Eddie was listening to every word. "What inscription?" he asked.

"The bell was inscribed with the name King," Tony said. "Frankie and I both thought the horn was previously owned by jazz legend Joe 'King' Oliver. Turns out, it's a King Silver

146

Tone, one of thousands that were made."

"Who's this expert you consulted with?" Frankie asked.

"Jason Fasempaur. Heard of him?"

"You kidding me? The real Jason Fasempaur? He knows more about jazz than anyone alive."

"That's a fact," Tony said. "He's putting out some traps for us. Meantime, the trail's a little cold."

"What next?"

"Your recital made the papers. I have an appointment to look at the Picayune's files. See if they have any pictures, or names of those who attended. Maybe I'll get lucky and find someone who remembers seeing the person that brought in the horn."

"Good. Keep at it, Tony," Frankie said, slapping his shoulder. "Me and Vince better get going."

They were starting for the door when Adele appeared from the kitchen with a plate of appetizers.

"You're not leaving, are you? I made bagna cauda along with fresh veggies and crusty bread to dip it in."

"Oh my!" Frankie said. "I haven't had bagna cauda since I was a kid."

"Your wife doesn't make it for you?" Adele asked.

"She passed several years ago, may her wonderful soul rest in peace."

Adele hugged his arm. "I know how you feel. I lost my husband in a rig accident out in the Gulf."

"How can a pretty lady like you not be married?"

"Guess nobody appreciates my cooking."

Frankie closed his eyes after dipping a carrot into the bagna cauda and savoring it. "I can't understand that. This is wonderful."

"Please don't go," she said, squeezing his hand. "I promise this is just the beginning."

Frankie glanced at his nephew. "Got a hot date you need to get to?"

"I'm here for you, Uncle Frank," Vince said.

"Okay, then," Frankie said, returning to his chair. "We're in your hands, Miss Adele."

Vince was quick to follow. "I kind of like this place."

"That ain't all he likes," Frankie said, poking Tony. "Makes me wish I was young again."

"Seems like you're getting more than your share of attention," Tony said, poking a piece of cauliflower into the hot bagna cauda.

Adele locked the front door and flipped on the closed sign. Eddie's frown had finally disappeared as he probed the delicious dip with an asparagus spear. Jazz played in the background, Frankie tapping his fingers to the music.

"Too bad Sinatra never sang a song about New Orleans," he said.

"Good thing," Tony said. "We already got all the tourists we can handle. You get a load of the football crazies jamming the Quarter?"

"Same thing every year," Frankie said. "Good for the economy."

"Who you betting on to win?" Tony asked.

Eddie didn't miss Frankie's next statement, but tried not to be conspicuous.

"No business tonight," Frankie said. "I'm enjoying myself way too much."

Their attention quickly turned to the kitchen. Adele was bickering with Pancho as she pushed him through the door. His frown spoiled the lines of his usually smiling face, and he didn't see anyone else at the table until he glanced up at Eddie. He gasped when he saw Frankie Castalano, his eyes rolling as he slumped to the floor in a heap.

Chapter 18

I was waiting on the sidewalk when Mama stopped in front of Bertram's. The roof on her Sprite was still down, my perch on the back of the car just as insecure as it had been earlier in the day. Mama and Jason were laughing and having a grand old time, seemingly oblivious to my discomfort.

Cottony clouds blowing up from Pontchartrain cloaked moon and stars. There were no streetlights in the undeveloped part of St. John's Bayou where Mama parked on the side of a dirt road.

"Looks like rain," she said. "Help me raise the roof."

Mama watched as Jason and I struggled with the Sprite's stubborn canvas top, and then rolled up the windows. African drums, muted by the night's unrelenting humidity, sounded in the distance.

"Where to?"

"Follow the drumming," she said, pointing into the darkness.

When the moon emerged from the clouds, I got a glimpse of the bayou. Neighborhoods had grown up around much of it. Where we were, there were only bushes, drumbeats and shrouded moonlight.

"Slow down," I said. "This isn't a track meet."

Mama ignored my plea. "Just try to keep up with me," she said.

"We're not going to be eaten, are we?" Jason asked.

"This is a voodoo ceremony. No cannibals here."

149

"There might be one later on," he said, nibbling her neck.

"Promises promises," she said.

The dark path led to a clearing beside the bayou. Senora, dressed in white, stood behind Madam Aja's wheelchair. They weren't alone. A man pounded an ancient cadence on an African drum as a small audience crowded around a fire. Two men were digging a trench, others gathering brush and logs with which to fill it. It was soon ablaze, flames and smoke from the fire wisping skyward as more people, many also dressed in white, began arriving.

Soon, more drummers arrived, as hundreds of worshippers danced in the clearing. I stayed with Madam Aja as Mama and Senora pulled Jason into the fray.

"Did you send out a written invitation?"

My question evoked a chuckle from the old woman. "They know. Many more will arrive before the sun appears."

Believers continued to appear, joining the manic ceremony.

"Where are they coming from?"

"Everywhere. Madam Marie directed the dancing when she was alive. She never tired."

"You mean Marie Laveau's daughter?"

"The true Madam Marie was always present as she is now."

I didn't question her as the tempo of the drums intensified, the frenzy in the circle of dancing worshippers growing wilder. Everyone, including Mama and Jason, seemed caught in the frenzy. The clothes of many of the dancers were in disarray. Some were rolling on the ground, speaking in tongues. No one stopped dancing when the clouds opened, and cold rain began drenching the masses.

"The possessions have begun," Madam Aja said.

Jason was in the midst of the action. Someone had handed him a top hat, cigar, and flashy sunglasses. When Mama produced a bottle of rum, pouring it down her chest, Jason began lapping at it with his tongue. His aberrant behavior became even more so as he stalked through the dancers, exchanging overt sexual gestures, moves, and sensual touches.

"Is Jason..."

Madam Aja nodded. "The Baron has possessed him, and they are one."

Lightning flashed over the bayou, followed by a clap of thunder so close, it seemed to shake the ground. The storm's force caused some of the dancers to run for cover. Most continued dancing, oblivious to the rain pouring off their shoulders.

"The ceremony will continue through the night," Madam Aja said.

"Even in this storm?"

The old woman nodded. "They are believers. So am I, but I am old. Will you push me to the car?"

Grabbing the back of Madam Aja's wheelchair, I pushed her to the rows of cars parked on the nearby dirt road. Senora's four-door sedan was unlocked. After helping the old woman into the front seat, I crawled in back, shutting the door as thunder rocked the car.

"Can you pass me a towel?" she asked.

A basket of clean towels lay beside me on the back seat, Senora apparently cognizant of threatening weather before leaving their home. I gave her one and then used another to stem the water dripping down my face. Senora, Mama, and Jason soon joined us.

"My head's about to explode," Jason said.

Senora started the car and cranked the heater. As warm air blasted into the back seat, I wiggled my toes, realizing just how cold I'd been. Senora passed out pills and bottles of water. Jason swallowed his pills without asking what they were.

"Some voodoo potion to make me feel better, I hope."

"It'll make you feel better, but it's only aspirin," Senora said.

"My stomach is queasy," he said. "I feel as if I just drank a bottle of rum."

"That's because you did," Mama said. "Good thing you were possessed by the spirit of Baron Samedi, or you'd probably be dead."

"The way my head and gut feels, I wish I were," he said.

Madam Aja glanced at Mama and pointed to the glove box. "You have lots to accomplish before the night ends. You can't be sick."

She gave Mama a brown paper sack filled with white powder. Mama blew it up Jason's nose.

"What the hell!"

"Magic voodoo powder," Mama said.

"What is it?" Jason asked.

"Doesn't matter. You'll feel better in a minute."

"I already do. Something else," he said. "I know where Wyatt's portal is."

It was late, rain falling in bucket loads as we vacated the dirt road from Bayou St. John and headed toward the French Quarter. Jason was in the Sprite with Mama Mulate. I was grateful to stay in the backseat of Senora's sedan.

The tourist area of Bourbon Street had closed to vehicle traffic. It didn't matter because the rain had markedly diminished the enthusiasm of most of the all-night revelers. Only a few drunken souls stumbled down the wet street as I opened the door. Madam Aja grasped my arm.

"When you pass through the portal, you'll become the person you once were. Jason must alter the curse. And Wyatt, if you're not back before midnight on New Year's Eve, you will remain in the past forever."

"But that's only a few hours from now," I said.

"Have faith," she said when I stepped out into the rain.

Jason and Mama embraced as Senora and Madam Aja disappeared around a corner. I was hoping it wouldn't be their last. We stood in silence, getting dripping wet, but none of us moving.

"Wyatt, what Madam Aja told you isn't entirely correct," she said.

"What do you mean?"

"I have a drug that will transform your consciousness once you pass the portal. It'll force your return to reality."

"That's wonderful news," I said.

"It's powerful but also dangerous. Jason can only give you a small amount and then no more than twice. A third dose might kill you. I explained this to him on the way over here."

"Then why are you telling me?"

Mama grasped my hand, pulling me into a tight hug. "I don't know if I can live with myself if you die. Traveling, as you and Jason are about to do, is probably the most foolhardy thing you've ever done."

"Surely it's not that dangerous," I said.

"Even more so. That's why I'm giving Jason the drug. I don't know what else to do."

"Then tell me where to find the portal. I'll go alone."

"No way," Jason said. "I wouldn't miss this grand adventure for the world."

"There's something else we need to discuss," Mama said. "Wyatt will know you when you cross, but he won't know how or why. It'll be up to you to concoct a convincing story."

"I'll think of something," Jason said.

"I'm still worried," she said.

I gave her a kiss on the forehead. "We'll look out for each other."

Mama slipped something around Jason's neck.

"The drug is in the gris gris bag because it's the only way it'll pass through the portal."

Jason kissed her. "Stop worrying."

"I'll be waiting," she said. "Please don't stand me up."

Chapter 19

After blowing Mama a kiss, Jason pulled me into the rainy darkness. Though we didn't look back, both of us knew she was watching.

"Wyatt, I can't explain why I know where we're going, but I do."

"I'm okay," I said. How about you?"

"Scared shitless. I can't imagine spending the rest of my life in a world without jazz."

"Then when the time draws near, even if we haven't lifted the curse, just get us out of there," I said.

"Buddy, you don't have to say it twice. I'll do my best with the curse, but if it doesn't work out..."

I stopped him and shook his hand. "I've only known you less than two days. Doesn't matter because you feel like a brother to me."

He nodded. "Then let's do this, brother, before my better judgment kicks in."

We jogged down Bourbon Street, our clothes soaked and driving rain threatening to blind us. He quickly detoured down a narrow side street.

"I'm drowning," I said. "How much further?"

Without answering my question, he halted. The storm had caused a power outage in the Quarter, all lights, and neon having gone dark. Only an ephemeral glow from Canal Street marked the narrow gap between buildings where Jason waited.

"This alleyway is the portal," he said.

"You kidding? I wouldn't go in there during broad daylight."

"Sorry, pal, but it's now or never."

Jason tapped my shoulder, the last thing I remembered as I followed him into the blackened void.

Except for the gris gris bag around Jason's neck, he and Wyatt were both naked when they exited the alleyway. At least he and the person that accompanied him through the portal. For a moment, Jason could only stare at him. The man he saw was still Wyatt, but his hair was longer and tied in a pigtail. He also looked at least ten years younger.

Apparently just as surprised, he glanced at his naked body and then at Jason.

"Why are we standing naked in the rain?"

Surprised by the question, Jason had to think quickly. "We lost a drinking bet. After the rum we drank, I can see why."

"I know you, but cannot remember how or why," he said

"I'm your friend Jason Fasempaur. I just came today from Paris for a short visit. You were showing me the city."

"Did we meet during the year I spent in Paris?"

"Yes, don't you remember?"

"Vaguely," Matthieu said.

"I hope you haven't also forgotten where you live, or we may drown out here."

"The other side of the fence." Matthieu rattled the gate leading into the courtyard. "It is locked, everyone asleep. We will have to do some climbing."

"After you," Jason said, giving him a leg up.

Matthieu stuck his foot in Jason's hand and reached for the top of the wall. Moments later, they both tumbled into the courtyard. Cold rain continued trickling down their backs as an old, black man rushed out and grabbed the young man's hand.

"Monsieur Matthieu, your clothes."

"A drinking bet," he said. "Harve, this is a friend I met in Paris..."

"Jason Fasempaur," he said, shaking the old man's hand. "I got here today."

"Drinking bet?" the old man said.

"Matthieu's friends told us there was a wild woman that would do us both if we stripped down and ran into the rain."

When Matthieu smiled, Jason knew he had somehow bought into his wild tale.

"Harve, take Monsieur Jason to his room."

Harve was staring at the gris gris around Jason's neck. "Yassuh," he said. "Follow me, Monsieur Jason."

The old man's eyes rolled when he'd first seen them. Apparently used to such shenanigans, he led Jason to a room upstairs without commenting. The candle he lit caused shadows to dance on the walls.

"I'll need some clothes. I'm not sure what became of my bags."

"Yassuh. Young Master Matthieu has clothes in the armoire. If you are hungry, I can bring a plate of food from the kitchen."

"Fantastic. I'm starving."

"Bring it right up," he said, disappearing into the hallway outside the door.

Jason opened the armoire, searching until he found a pair of pants. Though a size too small, they at least cured his biggest problem.

Harve soon returned with a warm bowl of stew, a crusty slice of French bread, and a pitcher of water.

"Has this been boiled?"

"No Suh, it's straight from the cistern."

"That's what I thought," Jason said.

"Suh?"

"Just babbling. Wondering if I'm going to get out of here alive. Any Yellow Jack or other fevers going around town?"

"Not dangerous for this time of year. Come summer, though..."

"Hope my vaccinations are up to date," Jason said.

"Suh?"

"Nothing. Say, Harve, this stew is delicious. What's in it?"

"Wild game, Suh."

Jason smacked his lips. "More than good, it's fantastic."

"Can I get you something else?"

"You've helped me a lot already. Just tell me how many more days until New Year's Eve."

"Suh?"

"I lost track of time on my journey from France."

"The day after tomorrow."

"Doesn't give me much time."

"Suh?"

"Just mumbling to myself. Get some sleep. I'll see you in the morning."

"Yassuh," Harve said as he shut the door behind him.

Although the room wasn't cold, it was noticeably cooler than Jason liked it. After searching through the armoire again, he found a wool sweater that lessened the night's damp chill. A knock on the door disturbed his musings. He opened it, expecting to see Harve. Instead, it was Matthieu.

"Get your clothes on."

"Where are we going?"

"We have jokesters to repay, and the night is still young."

"You have to be kidding me," Jason said.

"New Year's approaches and we will soon have to journey up the river to the plantation to visit my parents. Tonight, we spend on the town."

Rain sprinkled their shoulders as beleaguered Harve opened the gate to let them out of the courtyard. Jason may just as well have arrived from France because he'd lost all track of time, his senses jet-lagged by the trip through the time portal.

"I do not want to wait up all night, worried sick, for your return, Master Matthieu," Harve said.

"And you won't. Give me the key."

Harve frowned as he dropped the brass key into his hand. "You know how dangerous the Quarter is after dark."

"I haven't flogged you in a while, but I will if you persist in treating me as a child."

"Yassuh," Harve said. "You just be careful."

"Do you flog him often?" Jason asked as the heavy door closed behind them.

Matthieu smiled. "Harve raised me. When I was a boy, we used to play master and slave. I would beat him with a strand of twine, and he would pretend to writhe in pain."

"You never really beat him?"

"No, but he whipped my butt plenty of times when I got into trouble. And that was quite often."

"What did your mother and father think about that?" Jason asked.

"Nothing at all. Harve and Shug, my black nanny, raised me. They are more like parents than my real ones. Is that not the way it is done in France?"

"Not exactly," Jason said. "It's dark out. Where are we going?"

"Up Rue Bourbon to a bar where sailors and wenches congregate. It is dangerous and exciting. It is also the place we will find the culprits that tricked us."

Jason didn't know whom Matthieu considered the culprits that had tricked them. He only hoped they wouldn't somehow contradict his falsehood.

"Are there more lights where we're going?"

"Though this is not Paris, we have streetlamps. You will see."

Soon, gas lamps began lighting the brick street. Lightning flashed over the French Quarter, reminding Jason at least the climate in New Orleans hadn't changed. As they reached the front door of the bar, a man came tumbling out, rolling past their feet.

"And do not come back," the burly man that had thrown him out said.

He bowed and opened the door for them when Matthieu and Jason smiled at him. In the courtyard outside the bar, someone was playing an accordion and violin, and they could barely make out the melody over the dissonance in the bar.

The noise that sailors, aristocrats, and wenches were making overshadowed the music in the courtyard. Some were singing bawdy sea ditties out of tune. From the smiles on the faces in the tavern, no one seemed to notice, or to care. Matthieu bellied up to the counter and motioned for a drink.

"What are you having, mate?" the bald bartender with a handlebar moustache asked.

"American whiskey," Matthieu said.

The bartender produced a bottle of whiskey, pouring two

shots, one for Matthieu and another for Jason. He nodded when Matthieu tossed him a coin.

"You like American whiskey?" Jason asked.

"Ever drink any French whiskey?"

"I get your point,"

"It is rumored that Jean Lafitte and his brother Pierre once owned this place. Give us the whole bottle," he said, handing cash to the bartender.

They grabbed their glasses and half-empty bottle of whiskey, moving to a large table. A young woman with wild hair and pretty face plopped herself in Matthieu's lap.

"Where have you been? I have not seen you in a while. I missed you."

"We were here earlier."

"Oh?"

Matthieu put his nose between her ample breasts. She just grinned, yanked down her already low-cut blouse, grinding against his face.

"The only thing you missed was my pocket book," he said, hugging her.

"You hurt my feelings. Who is your handsome friend?"

"Lucy, this is Jason. He is visiting from Paris."

"Oh my, then you must be very rich."

"If I hadn't lost all my bags, and all of my money on the ship coming over. Without Matthieu's kindness, I would be in trouble right now."

"Maybe Matthieu will lend you enough money to spend an hour upstairs with me."

"And how much would I need to borrow to make that happen?"

He smiled when she put her arms around him and whispered in his ear. Matthieu also laughed.

"Lucy, you are such a tart. What about me?"

"I will take you both upstairs for the same price."

Matthieu stuffed a note in her cleavage. "Maybe later. Right now, we have some drinking to do."

After kissing them both, she headed for the empty lap of another young Frenchman.

"Pretty girl," Jason said.

"The night is young, and there are lots of pretty girls in this town."

"I can see. Those men at the table beside us aren't speaking French."

"Italian sailors," Matthieu said. "Almost as rough and dangerous as the Greek sailors, though not quite."

"I hope they don't try to rob us."

"We are safe as long as we remain inside the bar. The owners are intolerant of ruffians. We do, however, want to leave with others, if at all possible."

"That's reassuring," Jason said. "Perhaps we should remain sober."

"That is not going to happen," Matthieu said, killing his shot and immediately pouring another for himself and Jason.

Music wafted through the open door leading to the courtyard, along with shouts and laughter.

"What's going on out there?" Jason asked.

"Frivolity. Shall we join the fun?"

A tall, stucco fence surrounded the courtyard, two men playing accordion and violin barely audible over the noise caused by a bunch of rowdies enjoying the mild night. Rain had ended for the moment, leaving only damp flagstones under their feet. Japanese lanterns, swaying in a gentle breeze, lighted the courtyard. Except for one, customers occupied all the benches around the plank tables. A black man, regally dressed in expensive clothes, was talking with a Greek sailor.

"I knew there were free men of color in New Orleans," Jason said. "I didn't realize they were allowed to fraternize with the white community."

"There are many things you do not know about New Orleans. That is John Montenet, the root doctor and practitioner of dark secrets. He comes often to dispense potions. For a price, of course."

"You're kidding me! The actual Doctor John?"

"Have you heard of him?"

"He's almost as famous as Marie Laveau. What's the story on his facial scars?"

"He was an African prince before Spaniards captured him and took him to Santo Domingo. The scars are tribal markings that indicate he was born into royalty."

"How did he get to New Orleans?"

"When his master freed him, he became a sailor. He possesses enormous power. When he landed in New Orleans, people began to notice. He now has quite a following."

A half dozen sailors and Frenchmen waited to talk to Doctor John, or to buy medicines and gris gris from him.

"I can see," Jason said.

"Shall we join them before he goes?"

"He'd talk to us?"

"For a price. He makes ten times more money catering to the wealthy than he does all the Greek and Italian sailors combined."

"Then why does he take so much of his time with them?"

"Word of mouth. Every time he cures or helps someone, his fame spreads even further. Let's join him."

Doctor John smiled and nodded when Jason and Matthieu sat beside him at the table. Instead of speaking, he handed a tiny tin to a tough Greek sailor with a patch over one eye. He stuck his index finger into the white salve, opened his mouth, and mimicked rubbing it on his gums.

The sailor smiled as he took the tin, handing Doctor John two coins. Before he left the table, he tried the ointment on his gums. After closing his eyes and breathing a sigh of relief, he smiled, nodded his thanks, and melted back into the crowd.

"His tooth will eventually have to come out. My ointment will reduce his pain until he gathers the courage to have it pulled," Doctor John said in broken French.

The magic man was so black it was difficult to see the features of his face. His waistcoat was expensive and decorated with medals and epaulets. Open to the waist, it revealed the man's brawny torso, bare beneath the fancy coat.

"I am Matthieu Courtmanche. This is Jason Fasempaur. We have no ailments. We just wanted to meet you."

"Pleased to meet you, young Monsieur Courtmanche and you Monsieur Fasempaur. You are not from New Orleans."

"Paris," Jason said. "I'm visiting Matthieu."

"Have you been here long?"

"Just arrived today, actually. The city is fascinating."

"And dangerous. Everyone wants a cure for Yellow Jack."

"Do you have one?"

Doctor John shook his head. "Only God can eliminate the fever once it strikes. I have amulets and gris gris that will ward off the sickness if you do not already have it. Even Doctor John has his limitations."

"I would like to purchase such an amulet, and one for Jason and my mother and father," Matthieu said.

"Then you must come to my house tomorrow night. I see Monsieur Jason already has a gris gris."

Matthieu glanced at Jason when he touched the bag beneath his shirt.

"You're good," he said. "How did you know I was wearing a gris gris?"

Doctor John smiled. "It gives out potent juju. Where did you get it?"

"From a powerful voodoo woman."

"Madam Laveau?"

Jason shook his head. "Someone I know from France."

Doctor John let the comment pass. "I will need something particular from your parents, and a lock of hair from you and Jason. You know where my house is?"

"On Bayou Road?"

Doctor John nodded and stood to leave. "Come after dark. That is when my spells work best."

"You will be awake?"

The tall man patted Matthieu's shoulder. "Doctor John never sleeps."

Matthieu and Jason watched him disappear into the crowd. As he did, three regally dressed young men approached the table.

"The three musketeers," Matthieu said. "Raynard, Jean, and Alain. This is my friend Jason, but apparently you have already met him."

The three men could have passed as brothers with their dark hair and eyes. From the style of their clothes, they were all as wealthy as Matthieu. Jason waited for them to deny having already met him, and for being guilty of tricking them. They had other things on their minds, the subject never broached.

"We are glad we found you," Jean said. "Zacharie Patenaude is dueling. Come with us?"

"But of course. I would not miss the chance to see Patenaude duel."

Hearing the name, Jason was quick to respond.

"You know Zacharie Patenaude?"

"Only by reputation, and it is a nasty one. He has fought more duels than any man in New Orleans."

"And he never loses," Raynard said.

"It is not how he wins the contests," Alain said. "It is what happens to the loser afterwards."

"Like what?" Jason asked.

Raynard moved closer. "He always maims the loser in a terrible manner. He once castrated one of his opponents."

"Oh my!" Jason said. "I don't want to see anything like that."

"Come," Matthieu said. "If a man fights a duel, he must be prepared for the consequences if he fails."

"Have you ever fought a duel?"

"Not in real life, although I spent a winter in France under the tutelage of a French master. I stayed with your parents. Don't you remember?"

"Oh yeah," Jason said. "How do you know about the Three Musketeers?"

"Alexandre Dumas was a fellow student of mine. We went drinking many times. He had already written the story and serialized it after I left France."

"Small world," Jason said.

"Are you coming with us?" Alain asked.

"We would not miss a Patenaude duel for the world," Matthieu said.

They followed the Musketeers out of the courtyard, back to Rue Bourbon. They soon reached the Place d'Armes. Jason didn't see the statue of Andy Jackson.

"Are there Americans here yet?" he asked.

"Oh yes. They usually work uptown, on the other side of Canal," Matthieu said.

An alleyway separated the Cabildo and the St. Louis Cathedral. Jason had visited it several times, though never like

163

this particular night. Torches lighted the far end of the alley, a crowd already gathered as they reached the place where the duel was to happen.

"There is Patenaude," Reynard said.

He pointed at a tall man, regal-looking, and with a prominent Gallic nose. As they watched, he removed his green, broadcloth coat, tossing it to his second. In exchange, the man tossed him a sword.

"Tonight, they are fighting with broadswords," Jean said. "They are rarely used anymore."

"Then why..."

Matthieu answered Jason's question. "Patenaude is the master of many weapons, including the broadsword. He used one to cut a competitor to pieces in a recent fight. The man died a horrible death."

"They fight to the death?" Jason asked.

"Rarely. Patenaude prefers to maim his opponents, but the man had particularly angered him."

"The same may happen tonight," Alain said. "The man he is dueling is Laval Chereve, a former officer in the French army. He runs a sword-fighting academy on Royal. Patenaude has never fought such a worthy opponent. The fight should be entertaining."

Unlike Patenaude's regal attire, Chereve's clothes marked him as a working merchant. His thinning hair had begun to gray around the edges. It didn't stop him from looking healthy and knowledgeable as he tested the blade with the palm of his hand.

Each fighter had seconds. After agreeing on the rules, they backed off, into the crowd. The two combatants approached and exchanged nods. Crossing swords, they clicked them together once, and then began to fight.

The broadswords were longer and heavier than the short swords most duelers had begun to favor. It didn't seem to matter, both men proficient with the weapons as they challenged each other with their blades. Jason watched as the battle grew ever more animated, the fighters lunging and parrying, neither seeming to enjoy an advantage.

Lunge and parry, retreat and advance. The fight continued,

Patenaude's shirt in shreds from his opponent's cuts. When he stepped back, tripping on someone's foot, Chereve gashed his arm with a vicious slash.

A murmur flowed through the crowd, everyone sensing an embarrassing upset and maybe even death. Though awash in flickering torch light, shadows still cloaked much of the surroundings. It didn't stop Jason from glimpsing the momentary flash of steel in Patenaude's left hand.

"He's got a dagger," he said, poking Matthieu. "Is that allowed?"

"If they agreed on it beforehand," Matthieu said, backing away as the two fighters bumped into them.

Glimmering torchlight mesmerized the onlookers as shuffling feet, and clink of cold steel began to dominate the fight. With a swipe of his sword, Chereve again ripped through the sleeve of Patenaude's frilled shirt.

"He is good," Reynard said in a whisper. "Patenaude is hurt, and in trouble."

When another stroke of Chereve's sword lifted a ruffle from Patenaude's shirt, a rush pulsated through the crowd. It was then the two men came together and met in a clinch.

Chereve's dark eyes opened wide as he slumped to his knees. Patenaude kicked him backwards with the heel of his polished boot, holding the tip of the long sword to his neck.

"You fought well. For that, I will spare your life." The group moved closer, gasping when Patenaude produced the dagger and slashed off one of the bleeding man's ears. "That is for ruining my shirt."

Patenaude's second took his sword and handed him his expensive jacket. Without another word, they walked away. Chereve's second attended to him, staunching the wound with a rag as the crowd of onlookers began to disperse.

"For a moment, I thought Patenaude was in trouble," Alain said.

Matthieu and the musketeers stared when Jason said, "He's the one that deserves to have something sliced off his body, and I'm not talking about his ear."

Chapter 20

Jason awoke in a strange bed, sun from a different era shining through his French Quarter curtains. Harve stood in the open door, hands filled with garments as he stared at Jason's bare chest. When he touched the gris gris bag around his neck, Harve quickly averted his eyes.

"Did you sleep well?" Harve asked.

"Like a top. I even managed to find the facilities," he said, nodding toward the porcelain pot situated behind a curtained room divider.

"You and the young monsieur got home late last night," he said.

"You didn't wait on us, I hope."

"I was worried and could not sleep. I had a feeling."

"Oh?"

"Something terrible is about to happen, and there is nothing any of us can do about it."

"Tell me."

Harve just shook his head. "I cannot because I do not know."

"What's that you're carrying?" Jason asked.

"You are bigger than Monsieur Matthieu, and his clothes do not fit you. Try these on."

Harve presented him with shirts, pants, broad coat, and accessories, all of which fit perfectly.

"These clothes are terrific. How did you know what size I wear?"

"Arlette saw you in the hallway. She has a keen eye."

"Arlette?"

"Monsieur Matthieu's adjoint."

"His assistant," Jason said. "How many people does Monsieur Matthieu employ?"

"There are six of us."

"Do Matthieu's parents also live here?"

"Only young Monsieur Matthieu resides in the townhouse. His parents live at the Courtmanche Plantation on River Road. We will all go there soon for the New Year's celebration."

"Tell me again how long until New Years Eve?"

"Tomorrow," Harve said. "Now that you are dressed, are you ready for breakfast?"

"I'm starved. Should I wait for Matthieu?"

"After his nights on the town, the young monsieur likes to sleep until noon. If you are hungry, then do not wait on him."

"I'm not sure my stomach would allow it even if I wanted to."

"Shall I bring the food to your room?"

"No way. I'll take my breakfast in the kitchen."

Harve nodded his approval. "Then I'll wait outside until you are dressed and ready.

The old man was waiting when Jason opened the door, leading him downstairs to a rustic kitchen. He pointed to a plank table.

"This is Sarah. She will fix whatever you want."

"Hi, Sarah. I'm Jason."

Dressed in a brown print dress, apron, and white cap, Sara was stirring a pot of dough. Something that smelled delicious simmered in a covered kettle over the fire beside a Dutch oven for the cornbread. The black woman didn't turn around, but Jason could tell she was smiling.

Shelves, stocked with jugs, flatirons, cooking tools, and other kitchen implements sat ready for use. Jason also spotted bottles of homemade vinegar and freshly dried herbs hanging from a cord stretched over the hearth. There were no faucets, only wooden buckets filled with water from the cistern. A large window opened out to the courtyard, assisting the candles in providing light to the room.

"Are you hungry?" she asked.

"Famished and whatever you are cooking smells wonderful."

"I sampled a bowl myself. It is winter okra soup," she said, placing a bowl in front of him.

Jason's eyes closed, and a smile enveloped his face when he tasted the soup.

"Extraordinary. What's in this bowl of heaven?"

"Thought you might like it. I make it with okra, tomatoes, oysters, rice, and red pepper pod without the seeds."

"Oh man! I may need another bowl. What do you call it?"

"Winter okra soup," Sarah said.

"Never had it, or even heard of it, but it's incredible. I could become attached."

"Would you like wine?"

"I know of nothing else that could make this soup more enjoyable."

His mouth opened in awe when she put a bottle of Alsace, vintage 1836, in front of him.

"I have died and gone to heaven," he said. "Are French wines easy to come by?"

"If you are as rich as the Courtmanche family," Sarah said.

She smiled when he said, "Guess I'm in trouble then. Who taught you how to cook?"

"Learned from my mama. She liked to improvise, and so do I. Sometimes my experiments work, and sometimes they do not."

"I can assure you, this time it did," he said.

A younger woman, dressed much the same as Sarah, entered the kitchen.

"I am Arlette," she said. "Is there anything I can do for you?"

Jason decided to ignore what appeared to be an unintended message. Instead, he pointed to the open window.

"I'm Jason. It was dark when I arrived last night, and I didn't see how beautiful the courtyard is."

Arlette nodded. The courtyard was alive with colorful

plant life, creeping vines and flowering shrubs. Flagstone pathways weaved around a central fountain where the mouth of a baroque cherub spouted water. A circular staircase led to the balcony of the second floor from which baskets of lush ferns hung.

Arlette was younger, but her skin no less black than Sarah's. Though she wasn't grossly overweight, her smallish frame carried a few extra pounds, likely due to the older woman's food. As Jason finished his soup, he could see why.

"Do the new clothes fit?"

"Arlette, you have more perspective than my mother. My shirts and pants were always a size too large."

"Better too large than small," she said. "You looked a sight yesterday. If you do not mind me asking, what do you and Monsieur Matthieu have planned today?"

"Harve tells me Matthieu likes to sleep until noon. We saw part of the Quarter last night, but it was dark. I'd like to do a little sightseeing."

"I am going to market for groceries. You are welcome to come along with me."

"When?"

"I am in no hurry. Whenever you are ready, we will leave."

Jason returned upstairs briefly to finish dressing and try on his new boots. Like clothes and broad coat, they fit perfectly. He noticed as he walked downstairs to meet the young woman. "I will summon Gaston to bring the carriage around to the front," she said.

"It's such a beautiful day, why don't we walk? It's not that far, is it?"

"We may have lots to carry when we are finished."

"Then have Gaston meet us there. It's too beautiful to travel by carriage when we could be walking."

"As you wish," she said.

Jason glanced at the oversized basket she had propped against her leg.

"If you have another basket for me, we can buy twice as much."

"Most Frenchmen do not like doing a woman's work,"

she said.

Jason put a finger to his lips. "Then don't tell anyone."

They were soon strolling down St. Ann, toward the French Market and the Mississippi River. Jason's eyes darted from building to building as if he were seeing the French Quarter for the first time.

"There are so many colors. Everything seems alive."

"The Spanish rebuilt after the Great Fire, using tile instead of wood. They placed the buildings closer together, and nearer the streets to provide fire brakes. The different colors help us distinguish the structures from one another."

"Paris would be envious."

It was as if the city had been painted by magical fairies. Azure, pastel pinks and off-yellows melded with red tile roofs and bright blue sky.

Horse-drawn shays and carriages tooled brick and cobblestone streets as pedestrian traffic moved at a leisurely pace along the sidewalks, or banquettes as the Creoles called them. Unlike the last time Jason had seen the Quarter in daylight, there were no cars, no streetlights, no noise at all, except for the occasional whinny of a coach horse, or bray of a donkey.

There was apparently no zoning as shops, sidewalk coffeeshops, and cozy cafes flourished beside schools, churches, and residences. No one seemed to care, everything melding together in a perfect motif.

"I've visited New Orleans many times, but I've never seen it quite like this. The different colors are stunning. It's absolutely incredible."

"There is no place like it on earth. At least that is what everyone tells me," Arlette said.

"You've never lived anyplace else?"

Arlette shook her head. "Just here and the Courtmanche Plantation."

"Everyone is right," Jason said. "New Orleans is one of a kind."

When they passed a coffeehouse, the aroma stopped Jason in his tracks.

"That smells wonderful. Let's get a cup."

"I will wait out here for you, Monsieur," she said.

Jason started to protest, and then realized slaves weren't allowed to fraternize with whites.

"I apologize for being so inconsiderate," he said. "Will you forgive me?"

"You do not need my forgiveness, Monsieur."

"Yes, I think I do," he said, touching her hand. "You are an excellent and knowledgeable tour guide."

Jason's words made Arlette smile. As they neared the French Market and the river, he saw the differences a hundred and fifty years had made. There was no Cafe du Monde, Jax Brewery, or large levee, or the Moonwalk fronting the Mississippi River. Riverboats of another era were lined up, unloading bales of cotton and other items, gathered from the hinterlands.

Sailing vessels, waiting to unload their merchandise from France and Spain lay anchored in the river. The whistle of a passing snag boat echoed all the way to Bourbon Street. Though still early, the river and docks were alive with activity. The Market was no different, wagons unloading produce, furs, fish, and oysters to supply the vendors occupying hundreds of colorful stalls.

"Oh, my word!" Jason said, eyeing the leather goods stacked in one vendor's stall. "Is there anything you can't buy?"

"Fresh okra and tomatoes," Arlette said. "For those vegetables, we will have to wait until spring. Right now, we can purchase kale, Swiss chard, mustard, collards, endive, and turnips."

"I had okra and tomato soup an hour ago. How do you explain that?"

"Ask Sarah when we return to the townhouse."

Jason pawed through a stack of cabbage. When he handed one to Arlette, she shook her head.

"This one is better," she said, placing it in her basket.

They continued shopping, slowly traversing dozens of noisy aisles. A tapestry embroidered with purple and gold fleur de lis hung from one of the stalls. Red, yellow, and blue banners flapped in a light breeze. Like a kid in a candy shop, Jason found several things he wanted to buy as souvenirs. At least until he remembered he was unable to breach the gap with anything other than his own body, and Mama Mulate's gris gris bag he wore around his neck.

"You are entrusted with money?" Jason said as Arlette paid.

"I am a slave, not a thief," she said.

"Arlette, I'm truly sorry. Forgive me?"

"There is nothing to apologize for. Most white folks call me a nigger, and not in a subtle way. Monsieur Matthieu and his mother do not call me that, and I have not heard it from you."

"And you never will," he said. "If I could change things for you, I would."

"Our baskets are full," she said. "Let's find Gaston and return to the townhouse."

Chapter 21

Matthieu was awake, in the kitchen when Jason and Arlette returned to the townhouse. He was smiling as he drank wine and ate some of Sarah's soup.

"Sightseeing," Jason said before he had a chance to ask where they'd been.

"How do you like New Orleans?" Matthieu asked.

"Love it. Gaston had the top down on the carriage on the way back. It was a little nippy, though most enjoyable. I've always wondered what it would be like with no streetlights."

"Streetlights?" Matthieu said.

"Not important," Jason said, pulling up a chair beside him.

"Would you like a bowl of soup, Monsieur Jason?" Sarah asked.

"Love one," he said. "Sarah, there were no tomatoes or okra at the market today. What did you use to make your soup with."

Sarah pointed to the rows of jars on the shelves lining the brick and mortar wall.

"We can fruits and vegetables during the growing season. There is plenty of everything all year long."

"I wasn't sure when people started canning."

"Monsieur?"

"Just thinking out loud."

Sarah shook her head as if he were at a mental disadvantage, and then went about her work.

Jason poured a glass of wine, sipped it, savoring the taste. "I could grow used to this," he said. "Hope it doesn't spoil me for the future."

"You have a strange sense of humor," Matthieu said.

"Acquired at a different place in time. The duel last night was riveting. The first I've ever witnessed. I thought Patenaude was beaten until he pulled the dagger."

"He has a reputation as a very dangerous man," Matthieu said.

"No doubt about that. Do you know him? I mean personally?"

"We have never met."

"Do you have a reason to dislike him?"

Matthieu pushed his bowl of soup aside, giving Jason a quizzical glance.

"I know little about him and have no reason to either like or loathe him. Why do you have that look like you just swallowed a caterpillar?"

"Matthieu, I have to tell you something in private."

"Upstairs?"

"That'll work. Bring the wine. We may need it."

They went outside, into the courtyard, a cold wind blowing up from the north rustling ferns hanging from the upper deck. Wooden stairs creaked as they jogged up to Jason's room overlooking the patio.

"Let me top up your wine," he said, taking Matthieu's glass.

Turning away, he tapped some of Mama Mulate's powder from the gris gris into the glass. Swirling it, he waited a moment for the powder to dissolve, and then handed it to Matthieu. He obliged by taking a deep drink.

"I wish I had my wristwatch," Jason said.

"Your what?" Matthieu asked.

"Nothing. How do you feel?"

"I am fine. Why?"

"Just wondering. Thought you might be a little dizzy from all the wine"

"Did you put something into it?"

Jason didn't have to answer the question. Matthieu sat on

the bed, closed his eyes, rubbing his forehead. When he opened them, he looked first at his clothes, and then glanced around in amazement."

"What the hell?"

"Wyatt?" Jason asked.

"Oh my God! My skull's about to split. Where are we?"

"First tell me your name, and then I'll tell you where we are," Jason said.

"I'm Wyatt. You know me."

Jason smiled and gave his shoulder an enthusiastic pat. "Hooray for Mama Mulate. She didn't let us down."

"What the hell are you talking about?"

"I don't have much time to explain. Mama's potion lasts less than an hour. We have traveled back in time, circa 1840, I suspect. You are Matthieu Courtmanche."

Wyatt stroked his long hair. "Do I look different? I mean other than my hair."

"Yes, and fifteen years younger. There's nothing I need to tell you, but I wanted to check out Mama's potion."

"How's it going?"

"Like an exotic vacation for me, though I don't have a clue yet how to solve your problem. Your alter ego just told me he has never met Zacherie Patenaude."

"What else?"

"We had a little break coming through the time warp. New Year's Eve isn't until tomorrow. Doesn't give us much time."

"Any leads as yet?"

"We met Doctor John, the hoodoo man, last night in a bar. He's invited us to his house. We also watched a duel between Patenaude and another man. I can see why lots of people might want to curse him."

"That bad, huh?"

"If you weren't involved in the curse, I'd say let him suffer," Jason said. "We may have no choice."

Wyatt nodded. "It's in your hands, buddy."

Someone knocked on the door, and Jason opened it to see Arlette in the hallway.

"Monsieur Matthieu has a business appointment in an

hour. Gaston will be waiting with the carriage."

"Merci, Arlette," Matthieu said. "We will be down directly."

Wyatt was rubbing his forehead when Arlette shut the door. "I'm so dizzy," he said.

"Lie down and close your eyes until the drug runs its course."

Jason stared out the window, watching water drip from the cherub's mouth as Wyatt's heavy breathing indicated he'd fallen asleep. When his boots hit the ground, he wheeled around to see he was once again awake, and no longer Wyatt.

"I have something I must do that is distasteful. You do not have to accompany me and can stay here if you wish," he said.

"What could be so distasteful?"

"I am meeting my father at a slave pen on Baronne. He is intent on selling and acquiring some new slaves, and my services are requested."

"Maybe you need to explain."

Matthieu paced to the window, staring out at the courtyard below. "I own no slaves. My father does."

He blinked when Jason said, "You oppose slavery?"

"No one speaks of such things here in New Orleans."

"But I detect a certain tone in your voice."

"As I said, I have an unpleasant task to perform. You are welcome to accompany me. Just know that what you are about to see will haunt you forever."

"Though visiting a slave market isn't something I want to do, I think I need to see it. I'm going with you."

Gaston met them on the street outside the courtyard, hobbling to help them into the carriage. Dressed in top hat and tailored jacket, the old man tried to act as regal as his young master. His belabored limp and scuffed boots belied his attempt.

"Baker's slave market on Baronne," Matthieu said.

Gaston cracked his whip and started away. Many people strolled the sidewalks, window shopping and enjoying the mild weather. A yellow cur ran in front of the phaeton, causing the horse to buck and thrust his head sideways. When a boy threw a rock at the dog, he slunk away into a narrow alleyway. Jason did a double take when they reached Canal Street.

The distance of a hundred yards separated the sides of the two roads traversing the extremely wide median. Matthieu smiled when he saw him gawking.

"The widest street on earth," he said. "The city planned to build a canal here, though I now imagine it will never happen. Canal is neutral ground between French and Spanish in the Vieux Carre, and the Americans that inhabit its other side."

"You don't like Americans?" Jason asked.

"They are corrupt and vulgar, but they have lots of money. You will soon see."

"Monsieur Baker?"

Matthieu nodded. "My father is a silent partner in his slave market. Though Baker is actually his employee, everyone thinks he is the owner. My father owns it."

"Why keep it secret?"

"So people in New Orleans will not know the extent of his wealth."

"I don't think you approve."

"The market is inhumane. You will see."

"But your father..."

"We are family, but he is a beast. He has a mulatto mistress here in the city, and he takes liberties with the female negroes on the plantation. He does not even care that my poor mother, and everyone else knows about it."

"Matthieu, I am so sorry."

"It is okay. Someday I will inherit the plantation. The day my father dies, I will liberate all the slaves."

"I hope you get that chance," Jason said.

Gaston drove up St. Charles Avenue, cutting across to Baronne. He pulled the phaeton to a stop in front of a two-storied brick building.

"Thank you, Gaston," Matthieu said. "Please return for us in three hours."

"Yassuh, Monsieur Courtmanche," the old man said as he cracked his horse whip and started down Baronne.

The entrance to the building led to a large room. There were no chairs or other furniture, only a raised platform for parading the slaves. Windows set high above the floor level provided light but seemed incongruous with the architecture. Matthieu noticed Jason looking.

"The windows are high enough off the ground to prevent escape. When the slaves are paraded in, there'll be a guard at the front door and one at the back."

"That's all?"

"There are many ways to prevent escape, mind control the most powerful. If a slave escapes, his family is severely punished. Many slaves are permanently scarred from the whips of their masters."

"Brutal," Jason said.

"If a runaway is captured, he is often beaten to death, or beheaded, the head sometimes displayed on the iron fence at Place d'Armes."

"Where are the slaves kept before they are sold?" Jason asked.

"In a pen behind this building. Baker usually keeps a hundred to two hundred slaves there."

"Can I see them?"

"It is not a pretty sight."

"I'm up for it."

Jason followed Matthieu through the single entry in back, a horrible stench, along with shouts and moans, instantly accosting his senses.

"My God!" Jason said when he saw the enclosure.

A pen measuring no more than twenty by twenty held a hundred slaves. At least a third of the people were children. Some were crying. Some had the glazed stare of individuals facing total loss of hope. Women were hugging their children, men beating their heads against the cage. The single odor overpowering the stench of human excrement was the smell of bacon.

"They keep them in the pen for a week or so before each sale, trying to fatten them up. Bacon is what they use to accomplish that purpose."

"Some of those people look like walking skeletons," Jason said.

Two white men, one fat and balding, the other young and missing all his front teeth, exited from the pen before Matthieu could respond to Jason's comment. They were carrying the body of an old man. Slinging it to the ground, they reentered the pen for another, finally tossing both corpses into a wheelbarrow.

"Where are you taking the bodies?" Jason asked.

"To the river," the fat man drawled.

"You bury them in the river?"

Jason's question brought grins to both men. "I wouldn't call it burying. They're going to the dead boat. Bodies sink fast in the Mississip, and don't come up till they reach the Gulf of Mexico."

Jason wanted to beat the man. Instead, he looked at Matthieu.

The wail of a woman prevented him from commenting. The two men entered the pen, returning with a child's body, his mother crying behind them.

"No-o-o-o! Don't take him. Please don't take my baby."

"Shut the hell up, or we'll be back with the whip," the fat man said.

The woman sank to her knees, unable to stop her tears and wails as she clasped the cage and shook it. A toothless old man knelt beside her, trying to offer comfort.

Mr. Baker, the purveyor of the slave market appeared behind them. Since he bore such a striking resemblance to the fat man with the wheelbarrow, Jason quickly concluded he was his father.

"Monsieur Matthieu. Your daddy will be here any minute. Right now I gotta get these niggers some better clothes to wear."

Baker entered the enclosure. "You, you, you, and you. Come with me."

Three men and a woman followed him out of the pen. He led them to a bench and tossed them some clothes, cheap suits for men, and a calico dress for the woman.

"This is barbaric," Jason said. "Can't the clergy intervene?"

"Why would they?" Matthieu said. "They own slaves as well."

Neither heard the man behind them. Matthieu jumped

when he touched his shoulder.

"Jason, this is my father, Boone Courtmanche."

"Pleased," Jason said with a frown.

Boone Courtmanche's hair, dark like Matthieu's, but with shades of gray, draped his shoulders. Though four inches shorter than his son, he shared his same blue eyes. Dressed in a suit of solid white embroidered with gold, he came across as an aging dilettante. His spit-polished boots did nothing to change Jason's first impression.

"I hear you are from Paris," he said.

"Just here for a short visit," Jason said. "At least I hope. Matthieu tells me you own this establishment."

"A profitable venture and I have first choice of the slaves. The crowd is starting to gather outside. Please deal with this for me, Matthieu. I have other business to conduct."

Boone Courtmanche touched his son's shoulder and then disappeared around the slave pen.

"My father suspects Monsieur Baker is stealing from him. I have to count the slaves sold to make sure he is not cheated. I understand if you do not want to watch the sale."

Jason shook his head. "I'd not miss this for the world."

They found the open room crowded with potential customers. Baker had donned coat and top hat and was standing on a raised dais. With a wooden staff in his hand, he tapped three times to quiet the crowd.

"Welcome. We got healthy niggers like you never seen before—field hands, kitchen wenches, carriage drivers. You name it. First up is a powerful nigger man. He can work the fields or drive your wagon. He's guaranteed of gentle temperament and free of disease. Who'll start the bidding?"

"Let's see his back," a man shouted from the crowd.

The black man beside Baker was a head taller and at least fifty pounds heavier than his captor, his upper body heavily muscled. Baker didn't seem to mind, turning the man with his whip, and then pulling out his shirttails, raising it to reveal his bare back.

"This man has never experienced the whip," Baker said. "He is as reliable as a big brown dog. Let's start the bidding at a thousand dollars."

The man was sold to someone in the audience. Matthieu and Jason watched as human cattle were paraded before the growing crowd. Prospective buyers gathered on stage, checking teeth, eyes, and other parts of the slaves. A handler, followed by two customers, led a woman to a room and closed the door.

"They will strip her and check her body," Matthieu said.

"And other things, I'm sure," Jason said.

As they watched, a woman and two boys were herded onto the stage. She looked no older than thirty, the two boys probably in their teens.

"Gentlemen, we got a strong nigger woman, and her two sons. The boys are old enough to work in the fields. What am I bid?"

A man from Baton Rouge bought one of the boys, a cotton farmer from up the river the other. The woman had become hysterical.

"Please don't take my boys. They all I got."

"Hold your tears, woman, or I'll take you out back and flog you."

Not listening, she ran and grabbed her son being herded out of the room.

"Oh baby, I love you so much. Don't ever forget me." She hugged him and then ran to her other son. "My baby, I'm so sorry."

Both the mother and son were crying when the boy's buyer grabbed his arm and pulled him away through the crowd.

"I love you, Mama," he called as the door closed behind him.

"I can take no more of this," Jason said. "I'll wait for you outside."

Chapter 22

When Pancho Bergamo walked out of the kitchen and saw Eddie sitting with Frankie Castalano, he'd swooned and collapsed to the floor. Eddie knelt beside him, making sure he hadn't injured himself in the fall. Adele stood over them, a look of utter shock on her face.

"He fainted, but he's okay," Eddie said. "Adele, get me a damp washcloth."

Vince joined Eddie on the floor. Together, they lifted Pancho into a sitting position, supporting him until Adele returned with a washcloth. Eddie pressed it against his forehead, holding it until his eyes popped open. When they did, Vince grabbed a glass of water from the table, holding it to his lips. Frankie helped raise him to his feet.

"You okay, Pancho?" he said. "You scared me half to death."

"I didn't expect to see you here, Mr. Castalano."

"Don't call me that. I'm Frankie, just like when you were running with Papa. That's good enough for me."

Pancho drew a breath and smiled. "Happy to see you again, Frankie. How you doing?"

"Good. You?"

"Top of the world. I got a lovely daughter, beautiful granddaughter, and the best little Italian restaurant in Metairie."

"That you have. We just had some of Adele's bagna cauda."

"Wait till you try her lasagna," Pancho said.

"I'm in heaven," Frankie said. "Sit and eat with us. We got lots of catching up to do."

"I'm an old man," Pancho said. "I eat at four thirty, but I'll drink some wine with you."

Frankie slapped him on the back. "Good. I think Eddie has something special for you."

At the mention of Eddie's name, Pancho's smile disappeared.

"Sorry about the other night," Eddie said. "Forgive me?"

Pancho glanced at Frankie. When he nodded, he turned back to Eddie. "I didn't like what you said, but you a good customer, and I forgive you."

Eddie didn't wait for Pancho to change his mind, bear hugging him. When they finished shaking hands, Adele broke out the hard liquor—whiskey, vodka, and Scotch. With the other diners already gone, Toni joined them at the table. Adele began serving entree after entree from the kitchen.

"Adele," Frankie finally said. "You gotta stop bringing so much food.

By now, Pancho was sitting next to Frankie, smiling and drinking wine.

"She don't listen to nobody," he said. "She got a strong head, just like her mama, God rest her soul."

With so much food already on the table, Adele pulled up a chair, just behind Frankie. Scooting his chair sideways, he made room for her to join them.

"You're not sitting back there all alone, pretty lady," he said. "Pancho and Papa used to play dominoes and pool on Sundays. I visited your house lots of times. You were just a pretty little girl, but I still remember you."

"I'll never forget. You used to bring your horn, and you could play like Al Hirt. I loved listening."

"You remember?"

"You were terrific."

"You like jazz?"

"You kidding me? The background music is from my personal collection. There's no bigger fan in N'awlin's than me," she said.

"And you really remember me playing the horn?"

"I was sure you'd be a star."

"Now you're really giving me a big head," he said, scooting his chair closer.

Adele touched his hand. "You had a real talent, Frankie. Do you still play?"

"Every now and then," he said, putting his hand on hers.

Tony was sitting beside Pancho, the old man well into his cups.

"You okay, Pancho?" he asked.

"Fine. Paco, Frankie's papa, and me had a little falling out a while back. He ain't nobody to mess around with. I was a little nervous when I saw Frankie."

"Falling out? About what?" Tony asked.

Pancho dismissed the question with a wave of his hand. "Been so long ago, I can't remember."

"I don't think Frankie knows about it. Looks like he only has eyes for Adele," Tony said.

"Good. I haven't seen her smile like this in a long time. Looks like Toni got herself a new friend, too."

Toni was doing more than just smiling at Vince. She was sitting in his lap, her arm draped around his neck. Eddie sipped his Scotch, taking in everything as Adele changed the background music to an album by Louis Armstrong.

"Satchmo might not have been the best trumpet player of all time, but he had a style like no one else ever did," Frankie said. "When he played, it was magic."

"I have music from all the classic cornet and trumpet players," Adele said.

"Gramps has a horn," Toni said.

"Oh?" Frankie said. "I didn't know you play, Pancho."

Pancho gulped his wine and quickly poured another glass.

"You dreaming, little girl. I never owned a horn in my life, and I sure don't know how to play."

"I'm not dreaming," Toni said. "I remember seeing you with it. Right here in the restaurant. Don't you, Mama?"

Adele shook her head. "Gramps is right, Baby. He never owned a horn. Ever hear him sing? He got a tin ear, him. He couldn't carry a tune in a bucket with both hands on the handle."

Everyone except Toni laughed. She just stared at her mother and then at Pancho.

"I'm sure I saw it," she said.

"How old were you?" Adele asked.

"I don't know, three or four, maybe."

"Baby, we weren't even living with Gramps back then. Your papa and me had moved into our own place by then. You must be dreaming because you were way too young to remember that far back."

"Maybe so," Toni said, her arms crossed tightly across her chest, her smile gone.

"I love the ambiance of your restaurant. So sixties," Frankie said, changing the subject.

"That's what Papa said a few years ago when I tried to get him to take a mortgage on the place and use the money to remodel," Adele said.

"You don't tamper with perfection," Pancho said.

When a medley of songs by New Orleans' crooner Harry Connick, Jr. began playing, Frankie stood and took Adele's hand.

"He's singing my song, pretty lady. Would you honor me with a dance?"

"I love to dance," Adele said. "Nobody has asked me in a while."

Before long, Tony, Pancho, and Eddie were alone at the table, Frankie and Adele waltzing to flickering candlelight.

"It's been lovely, Pancho, but Eddie and me got places to go and people to see," Tony said.

Seeing Tony reach for his credit card, Frankie waved to get Pancho's attention.

"Don't let him pay, Pancho. Tonight's on me."

"Thanks Frankie," Tony said as they walked for the door. "I'll give you an update soon as I have something. Sorry I wasted your time tonight."

"You kidding me? I reconnected with old friends and can't remember when I've had this much fun."

Adele blew a kiss as they walked out the door, into the December night that had turned suddenly cold.

Chapter 23

Tony followed Eddie to Metairie, accompanying him into the parking lot of his gated apartment to leave his car. From there, they continued in Tony's Mustang.

"Nice car," Eddie said. "You gumshoes must make more money than I thought."

"Wouldn't take much. I wasn't exactly getting rich working for the force," Tony said. "And I don't have to drag myself out of bed at three in the morning to investigate a homicide. Lil's happy, I'm happy, and my bank account is happy for the first time in twenty years."

"Glad to hear it. It's only a few more hours until midnight. If you want to forget about it tonight, we can check on Paco later."

"I'm probably already in trouble and may as well make it count."

"Then drive on, brother. I'll show you where to park. We can sneak in through the backdoor."

"Eddie, you may be a Fed, but you think like a flatfoot," Tony said. "Or criminal."

"Why should I let you guys have all the fun? I get tired of sitting behind a desk all day, digging through piles of bureaucratic bullshit."

Tony slowed as he passed the entrance to the Havana Club. Like the last time Eddie had visited, floodlights and flashing neon lighted the front parking lot, a half-dozen uniformed valets welcoming party-goers exiting limos, Porches and

Cadillacs.

"Too many goons hanging out in front," Eddie said. "Go around the block and find a dark place to hide this puppy."

A single fluorescent bulb on a tall pole lighted the rear of the nightclub. Tony parked in the shadows behind a trash dumpster.

"Hope my car's still here when we get back."

"My bet is there's less crime around the Havana Club than any place in the city."

Tony turned the key, waiting for the lights to dissolve into darkness. "Probably right about that, though I doubt they have a surveillance camera for the trash dump."

"Never know. We can drive to my apartment and walk from there if you're that worried about it."

"We're here. Let's just do it."

"Then lead the way, Lieutenant."

When a stray cat screeched, and then scurried between Tony's legs, he grabbed his heart. "Jesus! I'm getting too old for this."

"At least it wasn't a rattlesnake."

"Or alligator," Tony said.

Two old black men sat on the back steps, shucking oysters in the swath of light spilling out from the opened backdoor. They neither acknowledged Tony and Eddie's presence nor ceased talking as the two stepped past them and entered the building. Whenever a waiter took an order from the kitchen, trumpet and saxophone music blared through the swinging doors down the hall.

"Last time I saw Paco he was in a room by himself," Eddie said.

They started down the hall but pressed against the walls, trying to hide in the shadows when two men dressed in gaudy sports coats walked in from the nightclub. Tony and Eddie waited a moment before proceeding down the hallway, opening the door cautiously when they reached it.

The room was dark, except for the grimy glow of a small utility light over the sink. A mouse scurried across Eddie's foot before disappearing into the gloom.

"He's not here," Eddie said.

"What now?" Tony asked.

"From the commotion, I'd say the kitchen's around the corner. I'll ask someone."

"Sure about that?"

"If we don't, we're dead in the water anyway."

Tony peeked out the door. "Coast is clear."

"Wait for me. No use both of us attracting attention."

"Don't worry, big boy. I ain't going no place."

Eddie walked around the corner, into the kitchen, his senses immediately accosted by the clatter of clanging pots and pans, pouring water, and angry shouts. No one seemed to notice him, or to care. A pretty waitress in a skimpy French maid's outfit smiled when he tapped her shoulder.

"Hey gorgeous, I'm looking for my uncle Paco. Seen him lately?"

"Up in his room, too sick to come down," she said.

"Where's that?"

"Upstairs," she said. "Hey, haven't I seen you before?"

"I'm the big tipper. Remember?" he said, stuffing a twenty into her low-cut blouse.

She grinned and gave him a kiss. "No, but I will next time."

Eddie hurried down the hall to a steep stairway behind them. The narrow stairs led to another story of the building. The first door Eddie opened was a broom closet. Tony sneezed when another mouse ran between his legs.

"God bless you," Eddie said.

"From the dust, I'd guess no one comes up here much."

"Just rats and roaches. I'll bet the health department has never been on this floor."

The dark hall dead-ended at a doorway. Eddie turned the knob. It was unlocked and he entered without knocking, the stench of a dirty bathroom accosting their nostrils.

The bathroom was little more than a closet, but the door was open, a bulb over the mirror casting a pallor throughout the room. There were no windows, the only furnishings a chair and cot-sized bed. Lying on the bed, Paco lay still dressed in his clothes and shoes. A white cat lying beside him bounded to the floor and disappeared under the bed. Paco opened his eyes when Eddie touched his arm.

"Paco, remember me?"

"Who are you?"

"Eddie. I talked to you last week."

"You that reporter that got me in so much trouble?"

"What are you talking about?" Eddie said.

"Reporter from back east. Wrote something the boys didn't like. Guess I opened my mouth a little too much."

"We're not reporters," Eddie said.

"You bring me some food? I ain't ate all day."

Ignoring the old man's request, Eddie paused only long enough to sneeze and wipe his nose with a tissue.

"I was about to ask some questions when we were interrupted the other night."

"You look like my son. Is that you Frankie?"

"I'm Eddie, and this is Tony."

"That your pet?" Tony asked, glancing at the white cat that had jumped back on the bed.

"She thinks she is," Paco said. "I don't like cats."

"She don't know it," Tony said as the cat rubbed heads with the old man. "From the smell in here, I'd say she don't have a cat box either."

Paco stroked the cat's head. "She about a dumb one. Don't get no food except when they bring me some. Then she has to drink outa the toilet. Good company, though. If I liked cats, she'd be the one."

"Bet she keeps the mice in check," Tony said.

"She's a mouser all right. Brought me one yesterday. Dropped it at the foot of the bed."

"You remember what we talked about when I saw you?" Eddie asked.

"Why hell no! Who are you, anyway? Did you bring me something to eat?"

"You think you could go downstairs and get him something?" Tony asked.

"Sure," Eddie said. "They're so busy no one is worried about anything. Unless those two goons see me."

"Then get him a sandwich. And something for the cat."

"Yes sir, Lieutenant," Eddie said, saluting before exiting

189

the room.

Tony waited until he was gone. When he stroked the white cat, the skinny animal bounded into his lap and began to purr.

"You a cat person?" Paco said.

"Never owned one."

"You don't own cats," Paco said. "It's the other way around."

"What's her name?"

"I call her Silky cause that's how her fur feels when she cuddles up against my neck."

Tony chuckled. "Thought you don't like cats."

"Hell, I don't like my own family, but it didn't stop me from having one. Who the hell you are, anyway?"

"Tony. I'm looking for the horn you took from your son. Remember what you did with it?"

Someone flushed a toilet on the floor below, the noise rumbling out of Paco's tiny bathroom. When a cockroach crawled up the wall, Tony tried not to notice.

"Course I do. Think I'm crazy? Did Frankie send you to ask about the horn?"

"He told me you were dead. What's the story?"

Paco snickered. "Last time he asked me about the horn, I slapped the hell out of him. He's afraid of me."

"How can that be?"

"I'm still his Papa and some things never change."

Before Tony could question Paco further, Eddie returned with a sandwich, and a bowl of tuna. Paco didn't touch the sandwich, dumping it off the paper plate, onto the bed beside him. He didn't seem to notice. The cat did, hopping out of Tony's lap, licking every scrap of tuna from the plate Eddie had placed on the floor.

"Any problems downstairs?" Tony asked.

Eddie shook his head. "Like I said, it's so busy no one paid any attention to me. Got anything yet?"

"Paco was about to tell me what he did with Frankie's horn."

"You sure Frankie didn't send you?" Paco asked.

"He don't even know we're here," Tony said.

"Don't matter. I ain't telling nobody nothing."

"Come on, Paco. We brought you a sandwich and tuna for your cat."

"Give me a smoke and glass of whiskey and maybe it'll loosen my tongue."

Tony reached into his jacket and produced a pack of cigarettes. Tapping one out, he put it between Paco's lips and lit it with a match.

"Didn't know you smoked, Lieutenant," Eddie said.

"Don't, but I always keep a pack with me. Just in case. Sorry about the whiskey, Paco. A smoke is the best I can do."

Eddie reached in his jacket. "I still have that bottle of brandy I forgot to give Pancho." He twisted the cap off the bottle and handed it to Paco. "I don't have a glass."

Paco grabbed the bottle, gulped, and then swallowed loudly, wiping his mouth with his sleeve.

"That was good."

"Now can you tell us about Frankie's horn?" Tony asked.

Paco took a drag from the cigarette and another swig of brandy before answering.

"He's been after me for years to give that horn back to him. I think it's the only reason he don't just kill me."

"Why did you take it in the first place?" Eddie asked.

"I was getting older. Frankie needed to take over the family business from me, just like I did from my papa."

"But he was too involved in something else?" Eddie said.

"That damn music of his. I told him I'd give it back after he started acting like a grownup. I had to find a suitable hiding place because I knew Frankie would find it if I didn't."

"So what did you do with it?" Tony asked.

"Do I know you?" Paco asked.

"Tony. You were telling me what you did with Frankie's horn."

"Yeah, the horn. I give it to Pancho to keep."

"Pancho Bergamo?"

Paco nodded. "He didn't want to do it, but I bribed him."

"How is that?" Eddie asked.

"I had a small restaurant he wanted. I give it to him, and he agreed to keep the horn for me."

191

"Via Vittorio Veneto?" Tony asked.

Paco nodded. "Never transferred the deed. It's still in my name and always will be since the sorry S.O.B. lost the horn. I coulda killed him."

How did he lose it?"

"Don't know. Me and the boys tore his house apart looking for it. He swore to me he didn't pawn it."

Tony glanced at Eddie. "Sounds like Adele's daughter knew what she was talking about when she said Pancho had a horn. Maybe it's still at the restaurant."

"Could be. You got what you were after, Lieutenant. Mind if I ask a few questions?"

"Shoot, Luke," Tony said.

The old man's eyes opened when Eddie touched his shoulder. "Last time I saw you, a couple of goons interrupted us. You were going to tell me about a hanging."

The cat had returned to the bed and was licking Paco's neck. The old man grabbed it, hugging it to his chest.

"I was there, watching from the crowd. People were pissed because the Hand had smacked a local banker. A mob stormed the jailhouse and pulled out a bunch of prisoners. One was a wop, fresh off the boat from Italy. They strung him up outside. Took him nearly an hour to stop kicking."

"Vincento Pedretti?" Eddie asked. Paco nodded again. "Was he guilty?"

"Why hell no!"

"How do you know that?" Tony said.

"Cause it was me that did the murdering. I was probably twelve. Wasn't the first time I'd helped papa with company business. Vince's papa worked for us and got him a job when he came over from Italy."

"You're talking about the Black Hand," Eddie said.

Paco stroked the cat, nodded, and began recanting the story in dreamy tones.

"Papa wasn't like most. Instead of teaching me how to play baseball, he took me with him every time he killed someone.

"I was in a wagon between Papa and Vincento. He was young, just come over from the old country. His papa worked

192

for us and got him a job." A wry smile spread across Paco's withered face. "He didn't know what he was going into.

"Cold wind was blowing up from the Gulf that night, rain and mud kicked up from the horse's hooves splattering our faces. Didn't matter much cause my shirt and pants was wringing wet. We had a prisoner hogtied in back, and it was worrying Vincento.

"Non si è preoccupato di serpenti e gator?" he asked. His question pissed Papa off and he popped the reins, hurrying the old horse along the rutted path.

"Snakes, gators, and all that's dark are our friends tonight, Vincento. You in America now, not Italy anymore. You want to make it here, you speak English. Understand?"

"Mi dispiace."

"No, you ain't. Say it in English."

"I am sorry."

"Vincento was scared. He was sitting so close to me I could smell his fear, even in the rain."

"Please tell me again what we are going to do to him," he asked.

"Just rough him up a little. That's all," Papa said.

"What did he do?"

"Don't matter what he did. Our job is to teach him a lesson, so he don't do it again."

"You scared?" I asked him.

"Hell, I'd been on these trips with Papa before and already knew how he felt.

"We were on a dirt road beside the bayou. It was dark, our only light a coal oil lantern swaying from a hook in front. When a bobcat ran across the road in front of us, the horse reared up on its hind legs. Papa reined it to a stop cause our prisoner spit out his gag and had started screaming.

"That's okay, damn you!" Papa said. "Right here's as good a place as any."

"Papa's hands were rough as leather. Didn't stop him from cutting his finger on a broken tooth when he reached back and slapped the prisoner."

"Vincento, Paco, pull the dead man outa the wagon."

"Vincento didn't move. When Papa frowned, he jumped

off the wagon. Papa patted the horse, grabbed the lantern to where Vincento was trying to ease the man to the ground without injuring him.

"What the hell you doing?"

"Papa pushed Vincento away, grabbed the man's collar and pulled him over the side of the wagon. Papa didn't even bother wiping away the mud splattered on his shirt and pants. The fall knocked the wind out of the man, Vincento staring like a stump when Papa kicked him for good measure.

"Here's your hammer, I said.

"Papa rubbed his hand through my hair."

"Help me," he said. "This bastard's heavy."

"What are you going to do with that hammer?" Vincento asked.

"Just scare him with it. Now help me."

"They dragged him to the bank of the bayou, ground fog floating up around Vincento's ankles."

"I never beat a defenseless man before," he said.

"Papa was pissed."

"I'll do the beating," he said.

"By this time, Vincento was scared out of his mind."

"You said we were only going to scare him and rough him up."

"Plans change. He gonna die, and you gonna be the one that cuts his throat. First, though, I'm gonna bust up his knees and elbows. Once he's dead, we'll gut him, so he don't float."

"Vincento backed up a step, rain dripping down his face."

"I cannot," he said.

"Vincento's shoulders were shaking when Papa put a hand on him."

"There's a first time for everybody. Right, Paco?"

"Yes, Papa."

"You can do this. I'll hold your hand and help you. First time is always the hardest."

"Vincento couldn't speak, by now his whole body trembling. We both jumped when thunder rumbled behind us.

Let me do it, Papa.

"He didn't say yes or no. Our prisoner was crying like an old woman, and Papa stuck a finger in his face."

"You scream and I'll rip your tongue out," he said.

"Why are you doing this?" the man asked. "I have done nothing to you."

"But you have. You bankers are all alike. Got no time for little people like me. You made a powerful enemy when you refused to do business."

"You didn't need a loan. You wanted me to break the law."

"And you snitched to the police. Now, shut the hell up!" Papa said, smacking him again. "You crossed the wrong person. Now you gonna pay."

"The banker was crying."

"Don't kill me. I'll do anything you ask."

"Paco, bring me the hammer."

"Yes, Papa."

"He held the hammer in his hands, smiling as he hefted it. Grabbing the banker by his hair, he yanked him to his feet and whacked a kneecap with the hammer. I can still hear his screams."

"You ain't near done yet," Papa said. "Paco, get me some water."

"I ran to the bayou, filling a ladle with water. When I handed it to Papa, he lifted him off the ground as he threw water in his face. When the banker opened his eyes, Papa gave another knee a whack with the hammer.

"He was crying so pitifully, Papa was afraid he wouldn't survive the rest of the abuse he'd intended to inflict before cutting his throat. Vincento watched, scared shitless and afraid to speak."

"Stop it!" he finally said. "You are a monster."

"Yeah, and what you gonna do about it?"

"When Vincento reached for the hammer, Papa caught him across the side of the head with it. His blood splattered in my face as he fell backwards into a puddle. He scooted away, careful not to let Papa get too close."

"You are crazy!" he said.

"Vincento put up his hands when Papa charged him. Vincento was too young and fast. He caught Papa's ankle with his shoe and tripped him to the ground. Papa was dazed and

Vincento sprang to his feet, kicking him in the chest.

"Papa was dazed when Vincento ran away, into the underbrush. When his eyes open, I give him the hammer."

"I'm gonna kill that bastard," he said. "First things first, though, Paco. We got more pain to dispense. You want to do it?"

Paco chuckled.

"What's so funny?" Eddie asked.

"I was only twelve, and that banker was the first person I ever killed. Papa let me slice his throat and gut him so he'd sink. Got his stinking blood all over me. First time I realized how dirty you can get cutting someone up." He chuckled again. "Papa had to wash me down with a water hose, or Mama woulda killed him."

"Jesus!" Eddie said.

"Didn't even really need to worry about gutting him since the gators take care of spoiled meat plenty fast."

"Your papa was responsible for the hanging?" Tony asked.

"A matter of pride," Paco said. "Papa couldn't let that crazy wop get away with doing what he did."

"You and your papa sound like mean ones. You never told any of this to Frankie?" Tony said.

"You believe me and Papa were mean? Frankie puts both of us to shame. Who you think keeps me in this stinking room? He'd kill me with his bare hands if he knew what I just told you."

"He won't get it from us," Eddie said. "I promise you that."

Paco laughed. When it drew into a dry cough, he clutched his chest. Spittle rolled out of his thin lips as his eyes popped open in a stare of death. Not done, he grabbed Tony's wrist, squeezing it.

"Take care of my cat."

Paco's neck went limp and his bowels loosened, a foul stench permeating the room.

"Good God almighty!" Eddie said. "Is he dead?"

Tony put his ear close to the old man's nose, listening for a response. Hearing none, he put his finger to his neck. After crossing himself, he shook his head.

"I think we better get the hell out of here."

As Tony began to rise, the cat jumped into his arms.

"You're not taking that damn cat," Eddie said.

"We can't leave her here," Tony said, following Eddie into the hallway.

They hurried down the stairs and out the backdoor, the two old men still on the porch, shucking oysters. Tony's Mustang was where they'd left it. After tossing the cat into the backseat, Tony cranked the engine and started to pull out of the parking lot. He screeched to a halt when someone tapped the window with the butt of a .38.

Staring at them was one of the men they'd seen before going upstairs to Paco's room. Eddie recognized him as the person he and Wyatt had encountered on their visit to the Havana Club. He remembered the missing tooth when he grinned and motioned Tony to roll down his window.

"Going somewhere, bud?" he said.

"Sorry about that," Tony said. "We couldn't afford to pay the valet, so we parked back here."

"Oh?"

"We didn't think anyone would mind."

The man stuck a gun in Tony's face. "Well, you're wrong about that. Get out of the car, and don't make no funny moves or I'll blow your damn head off. You too, pretty boy."

Tony and Eddie got out of the car, arms raised, confronted by three goons, their guns pointing at them.

Chapter 24

A December chill had fallen on the French Quarter, vapor blowing from the horse's nostrils as he pulled the carriage onto the cobblestone path leading to Esplanade Avenue. Matthieu and Jason were no happier to be out on a blustery night than the horse, or the driver of the carriage. It didn't matter. Matthieu was set on visiting New Orleans' most famous hoodoo man, and Jason bent on finding out why. At least Gaston had raised the roof on the phaeton.

They turned on Bayou Road, the oldest thoroughfare in New Orleans. The Indian path leading from the Mississippi River to Lake Pontchartrain had been there long before the city existed. The reason Jean-Baptiste Le Moyne de Bienville had chosen the area that would become the city of New Orleans. Gaston slowed the carriage when he reached a house occupying much of a large tract of land.

Gaston was old, squat, and walked with a noticeable limp from where a horse had kicked him, shattering his leg. After hitching this horse to the cast iron railing, he helped his two passengers out of the carriage.

Unlike Gaston, Matthieu looked regal with no effort. His polished boots, silk pants, top hat, and greatcoat custom tailored in France marked him as one of the city's elite.

"Will you be long, Monsieur Courtmanche?" Gaston asked.

"I hope not, but please wait for us if we are."

Matthieu's comment brought a smile to the old man,

knowing he was going nowhere until his young master returned no matter how long it took.

The house they approached was much larger than Matthieu's townhouse, a replica of a Haitian plantation, complete with an encircling porch and slanting roof to protect it from spring rains and summer heat. A woman of color answered the cypress and cut glass door.

"Monsieur Courtmanche. Doctor John waits."

The turban topping the young woman's head failed to hide the curly locks protruding from the edges. She looked almost white in the room's faint light, her indigo dress only heightening the illusion. Lips and dark eyes required no makeup. Golden ear hoops draped almost to her graceful shoulders. Jason couldn't stop staring at her, but her own smiling eyes were only for Matthieu as he clutched her hand.

"Latitia, is that you?" Jason finally asked, breaking their momentary trance.

"Sorry, Monsieur. My name is Elise. Please come with me."

They followed her through the entryway, into a large, living area, burning logs popping in the brick fireplace. Matthieu blinked, his eyes adjusting to the dimness, the room lighted only by flaming logs, and the smoky radiance of a single coal oil lantern.

The temperature in the room was comfortable following their unheated carriage ride. Children were playing jacks on the polished floor in front of the fire. At least five women of various ages lounged on chairs and divans. Some were knitting and one shelling peas. They were talking, seemingly unmindful of the two men's appearance.

Doctor John reportedly had many wives and more than fifty children. The women and children in the living room did little to contradict what most citizens probably thought was only rumor. Elise stopped outside a closed door unlike either of them had ever seen. Voodoo symbols decorated its thick glass. An ephemeral glow emanated from within.

"Wait here," she said. "I will see if Doctor John is ready to receive you."

When the door closed behind her, Matthieu cupped his

hand, whispering something to Jason.

"Did you and Elise already met?"

"Why?"

"Your expression when she shook your hand."

"Maybe in another lifetime."

"I know the feeling. I am wracking my brain trying to remember if I ever met her. Though I think I have, I cannot remember where or when."

Jason already knew where. Elise was the mirror image of Latitia Boiset. Telling Matthieu would serve no purpose, even if he believed him.

"Maybe you went to school with her," he said.

"Not possible. She is a free woman of color, or would not be living in this house. From the lightness of her skin, she has more than a fair amount of French and Spanish blood. Most likely a quadroon."

"A what?" Jason asked.

"Someone no more than a quarter black. Beautiful enough to be a rich man's wife."

"Is that allowed?"

Matthieu shook his head. "Racially diverse women are forbidden from marrying white men."

"We need to talk about racial diversity when we return to the real world," Jason said beneath his breath.

"What did you say?"

"Nothing."

Matthieu ignored Jason's comment. "I wonder if Elise is one of Doctor John's wives."

Elise opened the door before Jason could answer. "You may enter," she said.

As she held the door to Doctor John's office for them, she glanced one last time at Matthieu **before shutting the door behind her. The room was dimmer than the rest of the house. The hoodoo man waiting for them.**

"You like Elise. I can tell," he said.

"She is dazzling," Matthieu said. "Your wife?"

"Daughter."

New Orleans' most powerful hoodoo priest, sat on the floor in front of them. Ceremonial scars on his forehead, neck and shoulders seemed to guarantee he was telling the truth about being a Senegalese prince.

"When my Cuban master set me free, I came to New Orleans on a ship," he said, answering their unasked question. "I worked as a longshoreman until people began noticing my other skills. Now, the wealthy citizens of New Orleans pay serious money for my services."

"We can tell as much from the size of your house and all your valuable possessions," Jason said.

The room was like a voodoo museum, animal and human skulls occupying space on the walls, bottles of unlabeled herbs and pickled scorpions populating shelves and tables. A live scorpion caught Jason's eye as it crawled up the wall. Doctor John didn't seem to notice. Several black candles burned on the voodoo altar dominating the far wall. A giant boa constrictor coiled around his master's arms, its tail draping the floor.

"Don't be afraid. This is my baby."

"I've never seen a snake quite so big," Matthieu said.

The voodoo man grinned. "She won't eat you."

"I hope I never have to find out," Matthieu said.

"You are from New Orleans. Your friend is not."

"I told you, I'm visiting from Paris," Jason said.

Doctor John gazed into his eyes. "I suspect you are from someplace other than Paris. Monsieur Matthieu, you want gris gris to protect you and your family from Yellow John. I think there are other reasons."

Wondering if the voodoo man could read minds, Matthieu said, "Such as?"

"You are curious about your future."

"Aren't we all?" Jason asked.

"Sometimes the future is best untold."

Doctor John stroked his pet snake when Matthieu said, "Then maybe you can just tell us the good news."

"The future often holds good news. Knowing what is about to happen in your life does not come without consequences, sometimes dire. You have something for Doctor John?" he said, holding out his hand.

Matthieu took a leather pouch from his greatcoat, handing it to the hoodoo man. When Doctor John loosened the leather strap and dumped the contents into his hand, coins flashed in the light of the ceremonial flame.

"For my services, I require only one gold coin," he said, returning the rest to the pouch. "But I need something else from you. Bend down."

With a knife, he sliced a snippet from Matthieu's hair. A colorful African rug lay in front of the altar, and he motioned them to join him on it. Taking Matthieu's hair, he attached it to a straw doll with a piece of twine. Adding aromatic wood to the pyre, he placed the figure in a cup carved from ebony. After pouring a secret concoction over the hair, he voiced a magical incantation, and then lighted it with sparks radiating from the tips of his fingers.

Fire and smoke snaked toward the ceiling. From a pouch retrieved from the altar, he poured a handful of small bones into his hand, topping them with ashes from the charred voodoo doll. After shuffling the bones and ashes in his palms, he tossed them on the rug. He didn't speak as he stared intently at the bones.

"What do you see?" Jason asked.

"Tell us," Matthieu said.

Doctor John rested his head on the snake before answering. "The threat of death lurks in your shadows. By tomorrow, your family will be cursed."

"How can you be so sure?" Matthieu asked.

"The bones never lie."

"Then what can I do?"

"Nothing. Your destiny is sealed. Forget the gris gris. You won't need it now."

"Has Matthieu been cursed?" Jason asked.

"I know nothing of a curse," the hoodoo man replied.

Doctor John extinguished the black candle on the altar, and then returned the bones to their pouch. The python slithered off his shoulders, disappearing into a dark corner. Seeing their meeting was ended, Jason pulled Matthieu to his feet and pointed him to the door.

"Should I be frightened?" Matthieu asked.

"I think he's full of hot air," Jason said as the voodoo door closed behind them.

Elise was waiting for them, taking Matthieu's hand.

"Are you coming to the ball tonight?" she asked.

"I know nothing about it."

"The Quadroon Ball," she said. "Mother wants to find a suitable gentleman for me to enter into a plaçage agreement with. It would please me immensely if you attended."

"What time and where?"

"A large building near Rue Bourbon and Orleans. The ball has started. I am late."

Matthieu kissed her hand. "Then look for me. I will be there."

Gaston was asleep in front of the carriage, jumping when they awakened him. After unhitching the horse, he headed towards Esplanade Avenue.

"We must return to the townhouse and change clothes so we can attend the ball," Matthieu said.

"But what about Doctor John's prophesy?"

"What about it?"

"Aren't you even the least bit worried?"

Seeing the unease in Jason's eyes, Matthieu tapped his shoulder.

"I am not a superstitious person. It does not matter because Elise is the most beautiful woman I have ever met in my life. I am going to the ball, and you are coming with me."

Jason gripped his hand as the city's gaslights loomed ahead. "Pal, I'm with you all the way."

Gaston drove them to the townhouse where they changed into tight pants, ruffled silk shirts, and tailored waistcoats. Jason's boots were new and stiff, and he groaned as he pulled them on his feet.

"Hope we don't have to do any dancing," he said.

"Stop complaining. Those boots are of the finest leather. Within an hour, they will fit your feet perfectly."

"Promises," Jason said. "You're looking forward to this."

Matthieu smiled and stared at the ceiling. "I feel I have known Elise all my life."

"What exactly is plaçage?"

"White men cannot marry a woman that has as much as a

taint of Negro blood. It does not, however, prevent them from taking a free woman of color as a mistress."

"This is condoned?"

"Plaçage is the contractual agreement between parents of the woman and the person taking her as his mistress."

"But you don't need a mistress. You're not married," Jason said.

"No, but most of the men attending these balls are."

"What's in it for the women?"

"Home, money, a place in the community, and their children often prosper in the local society."

"So plaçage is a contract?"

"A written agreement stating what each party will provide in the relationship."

Jason straightened his silk shirt. "Sounds like marriage to me. Bet the men's wives aren't enamored with the arrangement."

"I do not have a wife and perhaps never will. If I had one, I would never take a mistress."

"Are you thinking of taking Elise as a mistress?" Jason asked.

Matthieu finished straightening his own tie. "Who knows? The ball sounds like fun, and there is at least one beautiful woman waiting to see me. Can we not just go and enjoy ourselves?"

"I'm with you, pal," Jason said. "And I hope you're right about these boots because right now they feel like hell."

By the time they reached the ball, Jason had forgotten he was wearing boots. The street was jammed with carriages, picking up people and letting them off.

"I will park as close as I can, Master Matthieu."

"Thanks, Gaston. I have no idea how late we will be."

"I will be waiting."

A man at the front door smiled when Matthieu handed him the fee charged to enter the ballroom. Music from a string quartet wafted out the door. Young men dressed in their finest, many brandishing swords, filled the lobby, smoking, drinking, and laughing as they took a break from the festivities. Matthieu and Jason walked past them. The spectacle inside the ballroom was more than Jason had anticipated.

Dozens of eloquently dressed men and women occupied the high-ceilinged ballroom illuminated by crystal chandeliers. Every man in the room, with the exception of the waiters dispensing drinks, was white. Skin coloration of the young women ranged from cafe au lait to pearly white. Each was vying as the belle of the ball, their fancy coifs decorated with plumes, tiaras, and jewels. Matthieu glanced at Jason with a smile.

"What's so funny?" Jason asked.

"Every female here is breaking the law. Women of color are prohibited from wearing anything in their hair except a tignon."

"Tignon?"

"Headscarf. Arlette and Sarah were both wearing one."

"So much for the law," Jason said. "Do you see Elise?"

"Not yet."

"Let's hit the refreshment table. We can look for her on the way."

As they waded through the crowd, a young woman in a burgundy dress winked at Jason and then hid her smiling face with a decorative fan. Jason nodded as they continued through the noisy crowd. Matthieu paid no attention.

"I see her," he said.

Elise also saw them. Pulling away from the young man she was talking to, she hurried through the crowd toward them. Dressed in a baby blue gown, her dark curls draped to her bare shoulders as she kissed Matthieu.

"I was afraid you would not come," she said.

"No chance of that happening. We would have been here sooner, but Jason was complaining about his boots."

Elise turned and curtsied. "I'm thankful you brought Matthieu, despite your tight boots."

"Actually, they feel fantastic. I've never worn such a comfortable pair."

"For that I am happy. Would you like to dance, Monsieur Matthieu?"

"Of course," he said.

Jason watched the enamored couple move through the

crowded throng toward a group of couples dancing in front of the ensemble. Taking a glass of wine from a passing waiter, he tried to keep from making eye contact with the many flirtatious women. He wheeled around when someone behind him spoke.

"Afraid you will see something you like?"

It was Raynard, one of the musketeers. Like Jason, he was dressed to the nines.

"Good to see you, Raynard. Where are your two comrades?"

"They prefer the looseness of tavern wenches rather than committing to an arrangement with a woman of color, no matter how beautiful and beguiling."

"Maybe I should join them," Jason said. "I'm only here for a short stay and can't afford to get too attached."

"Then you came to the right place," Raynard said. "You will have to sign a contract before you bed any of these fine ladies."

"Is that your intention?"

Raynard smiled. "I have had my eye on a particular damsel for quite some time now. I think I am ready for a commitment."

"You and Matthieu both. He's dancing with the most beautiful woman at the ball and looks as if he is already committed."

"When did he meet her?"

"About an hour ago."

"Time spirals when you are in love," Raynard said.

When the song ended, Matthieu pulled Elise to him, venturing a kiss to her forehead. She didn't protest, pressing even closer to him. Matthieu's smile disappeared when he saw a man staring at them across the crowded room. He thought he recognized the frowning man but couldn't put a name to his face. When he returned his gaze to Elise, he saw she was crying.

"What is the matter?"

"My mother just informed me that a gentleman has inquired about me and that they have entered into a plaçage agreement."

Matthieu continued holding her hands, staring into her dark eyes.

"Tell her no. We need time to explore our feelings for each other."

"I have no control over the matter."

"Of course you do. It is your life."

"In that respect, Monsieur Matthieu, I am afraid you are wrong. I have no choice except to enter into the relationship. Unless..."

"Unless what?" Matthieu asked.

Elise drew closer to him. "Unless I have already lost my virginity."

"Have you?"

"Not yet, but you could help me accomplish that task."

She nodded when he said, "You mean right now?"

"There is an empty room upstairs. If we hurry, no one will pay any attention to us."

"The quartet is taking a break, everyone going out to the lobby to smoke and talk," Raynard said. "Join me?"

Jason glanced at the crowd on the dance floor, not seeing Matthieu and Elise.

"I better wait for Matthieu."

"He will be along shortly," Raynard said. "These breaks offer suitors time to talk with mothers and decide on their plaçage terms.

Jason didn't seem convinced.

"You sure?" he said.

The two sexes had begun separating, young men heading toward the lobby to the rustle of the departing women's flowing gowns.

"Trust me," Raynard said. "He will join us soon."

Chapter 25

Dozens of young men crowded the lobby, smoking and talking as waiters continued dispensing drinks. Jason was already on his third glass of wine when Raynard offered him a puff from his pipe.

"Home grown?"

"Imported," Raynard said. "Like most everything else in New Orleans."

"Though you may be right about the wine and tobacco, the food here is like none other in the world."

"And the women," Raynard said.

The lobby had become crowded with young men, Jason barely able to see over their heads

"I'm starting to worry about Matthieu," he said.

"Do not be," Raynard said, standing on his tiptoes and waving. "He sees us and is working his way through the crowd."

Matthieu had a giant smile on his face when he joined them. Jason shook his hand.

"I was starting to get worried," he said.

Raynard intercepted a passing waiter, handing wine to Matthieu.

"The woman you were with is the most beautiful female at the ball, and that is saying something. Are you planning to talk to her mother?"

"I do not know what I am going to do," Matthieu said. "I just met her tonight."

They both looked at Jason when he said, "I think you should be cautious."

"Sounds ominous," Raynard said.

"It's just wise to proceed with caution."

"What do you know about relationships?" Matthieu asked. "You are no older than I am."

"How old do you think I am?" Jason asked.

"Twenty-two, maybe," Raynard said.

"I'm close to twice that old," Jason said.

Raynard and Matthieu both laughed. "In your dreams," Raynard said.

Suddenly immersed by a strange sensation, Jason glanced at his hands, looking signs of age. There weren't any.

"Hey, maybe I am twenty-two," he said.

"You need whiskey instead of wine," Matthieu said.

"Is there any around here?"

Waiters working the crowd were dispensing only brandy and wine, and no whiskey. Deciding to move up from the wine they'd been drinking, they grabbed brandy from a passing waiter. As the music began in the ballroom, they headed through the double doors, along with everyone else in the lobby. Matthieu immediately began looking for Elise.

"I think I see her," he said.

A group of older women congregated in a group near the back of the ballroom. Elise was propped against the wall, arguing with an older woman. Her frown became a pleasant smile when she saw Matthieu. The other woman's expression never changed.

"Matthieu, this is my mother Cherise."

Elise's mother was probably no older than late thirties or early forties, and fetching in her own right. She continued frowning when Matthieu tried to shake her hand.

"So you are the vile person that deflowered my daughter," she said.

Matthieu quickly drew his hand away, glancing at Elise as he did. She was staring at the floor.

"I am sorry," he said.

Cherise's dark eyes continued glaring at him. "I would love to beat you, monsieur. Since I cannot, Elise must bear the brunt of my ire."

She slapped Elise hard across the face, snapping the young woman's head. Matthieu started to say something, thought better of it and stepped away from the older woman as a man inserted himself into the argument. He stood directly in front of Elise, frowning. It was Zacharie Patenaude.

"You cannot imagine the dishonor you have caused me. What do you have to say for yourself?"

Elise's frown was the only answer Patenaude got, and he slapped her for her defiance. Falling to the floor, she rubbed her jaw, her spirit still defiant. It was more than Matthieu could take.

Grabbing Patenaude's shoulders and then wheeling him around, he delivered a crushing right cross to his jaw. Like Elise, Patenaude slumped to the floor. Not yet done, Matthieu kneed his chin and knocked him on his back. Diving on top of him, he grabbed his throat and squeezed. Before he could break Patenaude's neck, the hands of a dozen men restrained him.

The music had ceased, the ball having gone deathly quiet, everyone crowding closer to witness the altercation. Patenaude wobbled as someone helped him to his feet. After feeling his jaw, he removed his white gloves from his jacket. Matthieu was in front of him, straining to detach himself from many sets of hands, and then recoiling when Patenaude used the gloves to slap his face.

"No one strikes Zacharie Patenaude. You may choose the weapons. It does not matter. You are a despicable coward, and I am going to kill you this very night."

Raynard tossed him the rapier he was carrying as a side arm.

"There is no time like the present," Matthieu said. "Draw your weapon."

Someone in the crowd tossed Patenaude a rapier, and they crossed swords. A woman screamed as their blades came together in a clang of steel.

Before either man could make a move, armed guards carrying muskets surrounded the two men. The chief officer was little, the top of his head barely reaching Patenaude's chin. Dressed in uniform, complete with epaulets and medals, he was also carrying a handgun that gave him all the height he needed.

"I cannot allow you to disrupt the ball. If you must fight then do it somewhere else."

"As you wish," Patenaude said. "We will finish this in Dueler's Alley."

"I will meet you there," Matthieu said, tossing the rapier back to Raynard.

Despite the rebuke, disrupt the ball Patenaude and Matthieu had. As they started for the door, every man, and some of the women followed them.

Jason felt the chill air the moment he followed the crowd out the door. He was searching for someone he knew as the mob gathered in the alley beside St. Louis Cathedral, their burning torches casting dancing shadows. He soon found Raynard. The battle began immediately, both men thrusting and parrying, masses backing away as metal clanged against metal. Raynard glanced at Jason when he began cursing in English.

"We have to do something," he said.

Raynard handed him two dueling pistols. "Then shoot them," he said. "They are mad dogs, and only death will stop their struggle."

"Are these loaded?"

"Of course they are loaded. What are you going to do with them?"

"I have a bad feeling."

"I never knew Matthieu was such a skilled swordsman," Raynard said.

He and Jason turned when a voice behind them said, "He told us he learned to fence in Paris, along with Dumas."

It was Alain and Jean, Raynard's other two musketeers.

"I thought you were drinking at the tavern."

"The place cleared out when we heard Patenaude was dueling. We had no idea it was with Matthieu. I hope he does not get maimed." Alain said.

"Or killed," Jean said.

It felt as though half of New Orleans was present. Both men seemed evenly matched. Whenever one of them gained an advantage, a deft move by the other thwarted it. The crowd had gone silent, anticipating a misstep that would result in a victory for one of the combatants.

Patenaude powered Matthieu backwards into an oak tree with a round of hard thrusts. When he took a swipe at Matthieu's head, he ducked, Patenaude's blade slicing a swath across the giant trunk. The ensuing crowd roar caused Patenaude to redouble his efforts, almost piercing Matthieu's chest with a violent thrust.

Matthieu parried, knocking Patenaude's weapon from his hand. He wasn't done, putting a bloody gash across Patenaude's face. Bowing to his opponent, he tossed his weapon to Raynard. With all eyes on the victor, the crowd roared their approval as he started to walk away.

As Patenaude wiped blood from his face, a dagger appeared in his hand. When he stepped toward Matthieu, Jason nailed him with the barrel of one of the pistols. Not seeing the dagger, the crowd quickly turned on Jason. Pointing a pistol skyward, he pulled the trigger. The resultant explosion echoed against masonry walls, causing the crowd to step aside.

"He has a dagger. He was going to stab Matthieu in the back."

"There is no dagger," Patenaude's trusted aide said.

Jason quickly glanced around, seeing the man had spirited the knife. The mob began advancing toward him.

"Stop right there," he said.

"He only has one bullet," someone yelled.

"Then who wants to die?" he said.

Raynard threw the rapier to Matthieu as he, Alain, and Jean all drew their weapons, forming a semicircle.

"Come and get us," he said. "I guarantee more than one of you will die."

The crowd roared its displeasure as the five men backed out of the alley. Trusty old Gaston was waiting, holding the door of the phaeton for them. He tapped the horse with his whip, angry men chasing after them as flying hooves clattered against midnight cobblestone.

Chapter 26

Neon flashed from the front of the Havana Club as Eddie and Tony stood outside the Mustang, their arms raised, waiting for the other shoe to drop. Tony finally got a chance to talk.

"Boys, this is a little drastic for getting caught parking in the wrong spot."

"Shut the hell up! You know what you did."

"What did we do?" Eddie asked.

"Last time you were here, you told us you were the D.A. You ain't the D.A. He was here the next night."

"Then who do you think I am?"

He didn't immediately respond, raking five fingers across his gelled hair as he glanced at the person next to him.

"Who do you think he is, Ray?"

"I don't have to think, Johnny Boy. I know. You're the reporter that flamed us with that crazy story you wrote."

Ray was six inches taller than Johnny Boy and looked like a pro linebacker for the Saints. His canted nose did little to disparage that assessment.

"I promise you, I'm not a reporter," Eddie said.

"Oh yeah?" Johnny Boy said. "Where you from?"

"Right here in N.O."

"What do you think, Petey?"

Petey was a slightly smaller version of Ray, but looked enough like him to be his brother. The earring dangling from his earlobe didn't cause him to appear friendly. His response was disturbing.

"He's got a New Jersey accent if I ever heard one."

"Now wait a minute. I grew up in New Jersey, but I live here now."

"Like hell you do!" Johnny Boy said. "You caused us a shitload of trouble with that article you wrote. You shoulda left well enough alone and stayed in New Jersey. Now you got hell to pay."

"You have the wrong man," Eddie said. "I may not be your D.A., but I am a D.A., and I work for the Feds."

Eddie could see the missing tooth when Johnny Boy smiled, glanced at Ray, and then back at him again.

"Yeah? Then let's see some I.D."

Eddie reached in his jacket. "I must have left my wallet in my car."

"Coincidence, huh?" Ray said.

"Exactly what it is."

When Eddie took a step forward, Petey smacked him in the face with a pistol grip. Tony reached to grab him but sank to his knees when Ray tapped him on the back of the neck with a leather-wrapped club. Johnny Boy fished inside Tony's pockets until he found his car keys, tossing them to the other man.

"Tie him up and throw him in the trunk. We need to get rid of the car."

A black sedan pulled up behind them, the driver, another bruiser, motioning Eddie to get in the back seat.

"Where are you taking us?"

Johnny Boy snickered. "Someplace you never been before, and you're never gonna leave once you get there."

"You intend to kill us?"

He flipped a cigarette from a pack and lit it before answering. "Your friend's just gonna die. You gonna die too, but not before you beg us to kill you."

"Look..."

"Save your breath. You gonna need it for screaming, and believe me, you gonna do lots of that."

After strapping Tony's hands behind his back with a cable tie, they threw him in the trunk of the Mustang. The black sedan pulled out of the parking lot, followed by Petey driving Tony's auto. Johnny Boy was riding shotgun in the front seat of the black sedan, the bruiser Ray in the back seat with Eddie. Eddie had little chance of overpowering his captors. Neither man was taking a chance, both pointing their pistols at his head.

"You can lower those popguns," Eddie said. "I'm not going anyplace."

He cracked a smile when Johnny Boy said, "Shut up, and enjoy the ride."

They were soon out of town, heading west on a back road, the glow of streetlights in their rearview mirror, a Bob Seegar ballad wafting into the backseat from a tinny speaker. Ten minutes later, the car turned on a dirt road. From the way the car was bumping and rocking, the Parish hadn't graded it lately, if ever. When the car stopped, Ray opened the back door. He didn't bother walking around the car. Instead, he grabbed the collar of Eddie's shirt and dragged him across the backseat.

"Joy ride's over," he said after kneeing Eddie in the groin.

Petey pulled up in Tony's Mustang as the three men were leading Eddie toward the bayou. Hearing the commotion, a night bird issued a shrill cry and flew away from one of the cypress trees growing in shallow water. As they disappeared down the trail, Petey turned off the headlights. The dirt pathway led to the bayou, and Johnny Boy held up a hand when they reached it. A stiff breeze blew off the water, cooling sweat dripping down Eddie's forehead.

"Right here's good enough," Johnny Boy said.

The driver of the black sedan was even bigger than Ray. When Johnny Boy stepped out of the way, he and Ray began working Eddie over with their fists and knees.

"Watch it, Kenny. Don't knock him out," Johnny Boy said. "He needs to suffer a little before we crack his kneecaps."

Kenny and Ray needed no instructions. Soon, Eddie's groans ceased, every other night creature becoming quiet as the beating continued.

"Enough," Johnny Boy finally said. "I forgot the hammer. Can you get it for me, Kenny?"

Eddie was on his knees, his head hanging as droplets of

blood dripped on the sand. He fell backwards when Kenny kicked him.

"Back off! Now!" Johnny Boy said.

"What difference does it make?" Ray asked.

Johnny Boy didn't bother answering. "Get me some water. I want him wide awake when we bust his kneecaps."

A wooden ladle, apparently used many times for the same purpose, lay in the sand near Eddie. Ray grabbed it and headed for the bayou. When he returned, he tossed water on Eddie until his eyes opened. When they did, he rotated his head as if trying to see if it were still connected. Something splashed in the bayou, the noise disturbing nearby birds roosting in a tree.

"I think we woke the gators," Johnny Boy said, prodding Eddie with the toe of his Italian loafer.

"The really nasty gators come out of their winter holes when they smell rotten meat." Johnny Boy grinned and winked at Ray. "And before long that's what you're gonna be."

"It's cold out here," Ray said. "Let's finish him off and get the hell outa here."

"Get your dick back in your pants. "We ain't going no place till Kenny brings the hammer."

❦

Tony rubbed his head when his eyes popped open. Once he realized where he was, he tugged at the cable tie binding his wrists. The sturdy strip of plastic had already cut into his flesh as he began feeling around the dark trunk for a sharp surface. Finding a metal ridge, he sawed at the plastic tie until it broke.

The car's trunk was dark, except for the red glow of taillights, flashing when the person driving his Mustang hit the brakes. The car slowed as it traversed a bumpy road, rattling down an uneven stretch. His head throbbed, and he could hear Paco's cat meowing.

Tony poked against the backseat of the Mustang, finding it wouldn't budge. Probably not a good idea as the man behind the wheel had a loaded pistol. There was a trunk release, but he decided to wait until someone appeared to let him out.

The car finally stopped, taillights fading into darkness when the driver turned off the keys. The car rocked when a door opened, and the man exited. Tony waited for him to

216

open the trunk. Instead, he heard doors of the other car opening and closing, and the sound of feet shuffling in loose sand. After waiting five minutes, he decided they intended to keep him there until they'd finished with Eddie. Grabbing the release latch, he popped the trunk.

Sparkling stars, unfettered by the glow of city lights, filled a clear winter sky. From the fetid odor, Tony guessed he was near a body of water. Dragging out of the trunk, he crept around the car to its passenger-side door, searching for the police-issue club he kept under the seat. When the cat's nose met him in the darkness, he gave her a long stroke.

"Hey, Silky. Kinda creepy, huh?"

The cat purred and rubbed against Tony. Before he found the club, someone behind him spoke. It was Petey.

"Don't know what you're looking for in there, but I got a gun pointed at your back."

"I got a thousand bucks in my wallet. I thought I'd left it back at the club. I found it, though. It's yours if you let me go."

"Back outa the car real slow. I didn't just fall off the turnip truck."

Tony grabbed the cat and turned around. "Sure thing," he said, tossing the hapless creature directly into the man's face.

Petey shrieked. "Oh, shit!" he said as he raked at sharp claws digging into his face.

Tony sprang from the front seat, kneeing him in the groin. When the cat ran under the car, Tony head butted the man. Petey sank into moist sand, his gold earring glinting in muted starlight.

"Good going, girl," Tony said, petting the cat when she ventured out from under the car.

After frisking Petey, he confiscated his gun, then stopped and listened. Somewhere in the distance, something splashed, followed by the hoot of an owl. Now he was sure they were on a lonely dirt road, probably near a swamp or bayou. He also heard the thuds of fists against flesh.

Already armed with Petey's pistol, he fished under the seat for the club. When the cat jumped back into the car, Tony stroked her arched back.

"Better stay here, Silky girl. That old bird might swoop

217

down and snatch you if you wander around outside. I got some business to take care of, but I'll be back."

The cat seemed to understand as Tony shut the door behind him. He found more electrical ties in Petey's jacket and used them to secure the man's wrists and ankles. Before leaving him, he stuffed his mouth with a rag he kept in the trunk.

"Dammit!" he said when a branch snapped beneath his foot.

The sound he'd created apparently didn't matter, the other men too engaged with their primary task of working over Eddie. His surroundings illuminated only by slight starlight, he was barely able to see the path. He kept moving until the glow of a lantern coming through the trees and brush caused him to stop. When he bumped into Kenny, returning to the car for the hammer, he thumped his head with the club.

Something cracked, maybe the club, or perhaps Kenny's skull. He slumped into a heap in the damp sand. Tony nudged him with his toe as he heard Eddie mumbling something about alligators. Pressing through thick brush, he saw the clearing illuminated by a flickering lantern. Eddie was on the ground, in the dirt, the two men standing over him taking turns kicking him. Neither noticed Tony approaching through the darkness. At least until he fired a shot into the air.

"I'm a cop, and I'll kill the first one that reaches for a weapon."

"I don't think you got the balls," Ray said.

When the gun sounded again, the man dropped to the ground, grabbing his thigh.

"Anybody else worried about my balls?" he said. "Now walk away from Eddie. Over by that tree."

"You gonna kill us?" Johnny boy asked.

Tony tossed him a handful of electrical ties.

"Hook him up. You know how to do it. And make it quick before my trigger finger gets itchy again."

"You kiddin' me? You shot him. He'll bleed to death."

"Shut up and do what I say before I put a bullet through your leg," Tony said.

"What you gonna do with me?" the man asked after he'd completed his mission.

"Let you live, but only because we both work for the same man."

"Who you think I work for?" Johnny Boy asked.

"Frankie Castalano, unless I miss my guess."

"You work for Mr. Castalano?"

"You got it," Tony said. "And you just came real close to making a career ending mistake. If Mr. Castalano knew what you and your boys tried to do, you'd be the gator bait. Now come here and turn around."

"What are you gonna do?" Johnny Boy asked.

"I ask the questions, not you. Do what I tell you, or I'll drop you where you stand."

Johnny Boy moved closer, facing the bayou. Tapping his head with the club, Tony gave him no time to think about what was about to happen.

Chapter 27

After returning to the townhouse from the duel, Jason had fallen into fitful sleep. He awoke early the next morning, Harve standing in the doorway, staring at him.

"Something the matter?" he asked.

"Yassuh," he said. "Will you wake young master Matthieu for me?"

Harve tapped his toe in a nervous cadence.

"What's the matter?" Jason asked.

"I do not know, Suh. I will remain outside."

Jason dragged himself out of bed, went to the porcelain basin, and washed his face. After dressing, he found Harve waiting in the hallway.

"Please bring the young master downstairs to the kitchen."

Jason could smell Creole coffee and chicory as it wafted up the stairway. His growling stomach caused him to remember he'd missed dinner the previous night. He wondered how Harve, supposedly the servant, always managed to give orders. He just smiled and shook his head as the old man limped down the stairs.

Jason entered Matthieu's room without knocking and found him, under the covers, a smile on his face as if he were in the throes of a pleasant dream. Though Harve's request had sounded ominous, Jason hated to wake him.

"Matthieu," he said. When he didn't respond, he patted his face with the palm of his hand. "Matthieu, you have to wake up."

Matthieu's eyes opened, and he looked first at Jason, and then at the curtain on his window before turning over and covering his head with a pillow.

"What is the problem? I just got to sleep," he said.

"Something's come up."

Matthieu turned over and stared at Jason.

"Like what?"

"Either Harve doesn't know, or else he wouldn't tell me. Whichever, he was quite adamant that something is wrong."

Matthieu rolled out of bed. "The duel last night. Patenaude has retaliated."

"How could he have done that?"

"He is cunning and had all night to think of a plan."

Seeing that Matthieu was up, Jason went outside to the hall.

"I'll be downstairs," he said. "Last night's duel has left me famished."

Matthieu was dressing as the door slammed with a resounding thud. Five minutes later, he joined Jason in the kitchen. No one was smiling, a circumstance that didn't go unnoticed.

"Harve, what has happened?"

The old man shook his head. "Eat your breakfast, Master Matthieu, and then I will tell you all I know."

Jason didn't stop eating when Matthieu appeared. A lemon yellow tignon covered most of Sarah's hair, a frilled apron strapped around her guinea blue dress. She handed Matthieu a cup of coffee, steam still wafting from its brim.

"Sit, Master Matthieu. I have calas and sausage for your breakfast."

Realizing no one was going to tell him anything until he'd eaten, Matthieu dug into Sarah's tasty cuisine. Jason didn't have to ask for seconds, more food appearing on his plate almost as soon as he'd finished his first helping. Harve stood behind them through the entire meal, not speaking until they'd finished.

"Gaston has the carriage ready, Master Matthieu. After you and Master Jason get dressed, you are summoned back to the plantation."

"But I was not planning to leave New Orleans until New Year's Day," Matthieu said. "Why must we go today?"

Harve glanced at the ceiling. "I do not know, only that it is urgent that you go immediately."

After breakfast, Matthieu met Jason in the hallway outside their rooms.

"What's going on?" Jason asked. "You think it has something to do with last night?"

"I do not know although there is one thing I am sure of. Harve and everyone else here do."

Gaston was waiting for them in the phaeton on the street outside the townhouse, Harve, dressed in a winter coat and hat, by his side.

"I have also been summoned to the plantation," he said.

Although the weather wasn't cold, there was an extra nip in the air because of rampant humidity. Gray clouds draped the sky, geese, flying to a barrier island where they spent the winter, raising the noise level above them. Matthieu didn't bother glancing skyward.

When a light mist began to fall, Gaston stopped by the side of the road, lifting the lid on the carriage. The horse's hooves clattered on cobblestone as they reached the outskirts of New Orleans and headed south on the unpaved road following the river.

Jason glanced out the window, marveling at the sailing sloops, sternwheelers, and trading vessels of another era. He also noticed the lack of levees existing in modern-day New Orleans. When the river flooded, it left nutrient rich soil and made the banks of the river an ideal place to grow cotton and other crops. The fields and stately plantation homes they passed were witnesses to the importance of the giant waterway. The horse was moving the light carriage along at a spritely clip, a cold gust blowing through the open windows.

"Don't you have a heater in this thing?" Jason asked.

"I beg your pardon," Matthieu said.

"Never mind," Jason said, pulling the collar up around his neck. "How far is it to the plantation?"

"Not far. Less than an hour by carriage."

"What's it like?"

"Big, pretentious expensive trappings imported from Paris. Objects of art."

"Your words are a bit facetious. Surely you love something about the plantation."

Matthieu smiled as he glanced at the ceiling. "My mother's garden of roses. When the weather is hot, and roses are blooming, the fragrance sends you to another place and time."

"You must really love your mother," Jason said.

"She is a kind, caring, and beautiful individual."

"And your father?"

"You glimpsed him at the slave market. He is an uncaring pig. My mother does not deserve his constant abuse."

"If she had not married him, you wouldn't be here."

Matthieu closed his eyes before answering. "She loves him in a way I cannot understand."

"He must have some good qualities," Jason said.

"He has no regard for human suffering. He cares only for himself."

"Did he hurt you?"

"Only by his lack of attention. I once craved it. It never came, and I learned to live without it."

When the carriage slowed to negotiate a low-water bridge, a snowy egret lifted out of the water, rising in a billowing of wings. Matthieu grew silent as he stared out the window.

"You're worried, aren't you?" Jason said.

"Something is wrong."

"How can you be so sure?"

"Harve, Sarah, Arlette, and Gaston. I could see it in their eyes, and Harve has never traveled to the plantation on my carriage. He and Arlette always come later,"

"If they know something, then why didn't they tell you?"

Matthieu turned away from the window, his long hair blowing in a sudden draft of chilled air.

"It is cold," he said. "Good thing we are nearing the plantation."

"I apologize for asking so many personal questions. I sincerely hope there's nothing wrong."

Matthieu patted Jason's hand. "You are a loyal friend. I did not thank you for saving my life last night. I would not be here if it were not for you."

"We are both lucky Raynard had the dueling pistols. I was impressed with your fencing skills."

"I told you I studied in Paris," Matthieu said. "Last night was the first real duel I ever fought."

Jason nodded. "And almost your last."

A riverboat, loaded with cotton, passed on the river, blowing its horn when Gaston and Harve waved. Its wake disturbed a flock of geese swimming near shore.

"I know it rarely gets cold in south Louisiana. Is cotton still growing?"

Matthieu shook his head. "Texas cotton, stored in warehouses until riverboats arrive to purchase it."

"Riverboats can travel to Texas from the Mississippi?"

"Up the Red River to the Port of Jefferson, in eastern Texas. Some say Texas cotton is better than ours."

"That must not make you very happy."

"I am not involved in the family business, though it has my father worried. He spends money as if he were the richest person in New Orleans."

"And he isn't?"

"Not anymore."

Their dialogue finally drew into silence, Jason dozing, opening his eyes when he sensed the carriage was no longer moving. A man opened the gate for them to pass. The path wound through giant oaks, their bare branches draping to the top of the carriage. At the slave shanties, people gathered on the front porches. When they rounded a bend in the road, a two-storied mansion appeared before them. Gaston stopped the carriage in front of a large house.

"Welcome to the Willows, the largest and most opulent plantation on the Mississippi River," Matthieu said.

"Magnificent!" Jason said.

It seemed as if the whole plantation had showed for Matthieu's homecoming. Kitchen staff, butlers, maids, and field hands alike, all dressed in their Sunday best, occupied the covered veranda and the yard around it. The arrival quickly became a hug fest, Matthieu embracing almost everyone in the crowd.

Jason noticed that more than a few people had tears in their eyes. A well-dressed black man finally grabbed Matthieu's arm, leading him across the veranda to the front door. When they reached it, he turned to the crowd, speaking in a booming voice.

"Thank you for welcoming young master Matthieu back home."

Before the ornate doors shut behind them, Jason heard the hymn they had begun to sing. Matthieu embraced the man.

"Royce, this is my good friend Jason Fasempaur."

Royce's hand gripped Jason. "It is a pleasure to meet you, Monsieur Fasempaur," he said.

"The pleasure is mine. But please, it's just Jason."

Once beyond the ornate entrance to the house, Jason saw how vast and magnificent it was. Two beautiful crystal chandeliers hung from the tall ceiling. Oriental rugs topped polished mahogany floors, and French art hung from frocked wallpapered walls.

A winding staircase led to the second story. Fully a dozen wait staff of both sexes greeted them with tears. Matthieu was in his own little world, apparently looking for his mother or father. Neither was present, and his concern was palpable. Harve had joined Royce, and they exchanged a passing glance when the young man spoke.

"Royce, where are my parents?"

"Your mother waits upstairs."

"Then take me to her."

The slave hymn continued as they climbed the stairs, the group entering a large bedroom. A woman was lying in the four-poster, canopy bed, three women positioned around her.

"Royce, what are these women doing?"

"Watching your mother, Master Matthieu."

"For what reason?"

"To prevent her from harming herself," he said.

"Why would she do that?"

Harve backed out of the room. "I am sorry, Master Matthieu. You must ask her that question yourself."

"Jason, this is my mother Mathilde."

225

Seeing her red eyes, Jason only nodded. Mathilde was a woman of about fifty years of age, not fat but big-boned. Beneath her knitted sleep cap, she had her son's dark hair. She also had his blue eyes. Jason could see the resemblance and realized why Matthieu was six inches taller than his father was. When Matthieu clutched her hand, she began to weep, and it was several minutes before she could speak.

"Mother, what has happened?" Matthieu asked.

"Your father," she said. "He has killed himself."

Seeing his mother was too distraught to explain, Matthieu glanced at Royce for answers.

"Please, you must tell me what happened. Did my father commit suicide?"

Royce nodded. "Yes sir, he did."

"Where?"

Royce glanced at the far wall of the bedroom. Seeing his eyes, Matthieu touched a smear of blood.

"The wallpaper will have to be changed," Royce said.

"Was my mother here when he did this?"

Royce nodded again. "She will not tell us what he said to her."

Matthieu returned to his mother's bed and took her hand.

"Why would he do such a thing, and why do it in front of you."

Her tears began flowing again. "I did not know your father was so deeply in debt. The bank in New Orleans had a mortgage on the plantation. This morning, they informed him they had called the note. We have only thirty days to vacate the property."

"What about the money in the bank? Was that not enough to cover the debt?"

Matthieu's mother hung her head, mother and son embracing for what seemed like an eternity.

"I will talk with the banker," he said. "There must be a reason for them to call the loan. This plantation has always been profitable."

Mathilde stared at the bed. "That is not all."

"Tell me."

"He said he had never loved me, and had only married me

226

because of your grandfather's name and fortune. He said he hated the sight of me, and the idea of touching me made him sick. He blamed all his untimely luck on me, and then put the gun to his head and pulled the trigger."

Matthieu embraced her until her tears subsided.

"The man was a pig," he said. "If he had not done the job already, after hearing what he said to you, I would have killed him myself."

"Please, Matthieu," she said. "Do not say such things about your father."

"My father no longer. From this point in time, I condemn him. Will you be all right?"

"I will never again be all right."

Matthieu pulled away from her grasp. "I must return to the city and put our affairs in order. Prissy will stay with you until I return."

"No!" she said, grabbing his hand. "I have something I must show you and everyone else must leave the room."

Matthieu turned to Royce. "Can you give us a moment alone?"

"Of course, Master Matthieu," he said, nodding for everyone to follow him.

"Jason can stay," Mathilde said.

When everyone left the room, Mathilde got out of bed, proceeding to the far wall to the picture of a man. Matthieu touched the frame.

"It is nailed to the wall," he said.

"No, it isn't," Jason said. Grabbing the portrait, he gave it a push, and a counter-clockwise twist. The painting came loose in his hands, revealing a small safe. "A French wall safe. The combination?"

"10 right, 30 left, and 21 right," Mathilde said. "Your birthday."

When Matthieu nodded, Jason turned the dial, watching as the door opened effortlessly. Mathilde reached into the safe, withdrawing a large stack of money.

"Prissy and Royce helped me hide this from your father. Now it is up to you to save the plantation, and all those that love you."

227

"I will do my best."

Royce opened the door as if anticipating the exact moment to do so.

"Are you okay, Madam Mathilde?"

Mathilde returned to her bed. "I am now, Royce. Son, travel with God."

They exchanged a wordless embrace. Jason and Royce followed Matthieu to the door, Harve waiting for them on the other side.

"I am sorry we could not tell you what had happened, Master Matthieu," he said. "Gaston awaits with the carriage and fresh horse."

Matthieu patted his wrist. "Saddle two fast horses. Jason and I have no time for the carriage."

Harve grabbed his wrist and squeezed. "Master Matthieu. Please do not forsake us."

"Only if my heart ceases to beat before I succeed. Take care of my mother until I return."

Chapter 28

It was late afternoon when Matthieu and Jason hitched their horses near the Cotton Exchange Bank. Jason had to hurry to keep up with Matthieu as he sprinted through the front door. A bevy of well-dressed customers turned to see who was causing all the fuss. He continued down the hallway to the center of operations.

"Monsieur," a female employee said. "You cannot enter Monsieur Rousseau's office without first being announced.

"The hell if I cannot," Matthieu said, pushing through the heavy oak door.

Jason and the secretary followed him into a large room with polished wood floors, and shelves filled with leather-bound books. An ornate desk dominated the room with original paintings, French pastoral scenes, draping the walls. The rotund man behind the desk didn't seem surprised by Matthieu's sudden appearance. An ink pen and blotter, the only two objects on the desk, bounced when Matthieu banged his fist against it.

"I demand to know why you called my father's note," he said. "We have never been anything but good customers to this bank."

When Rousseau stood, Jason could see he was short and overweight, with thinning hair. Reading glasses toppled off his nose, prevented from hitting the floor by their attachment to the silver chain around his neck. His smile seemed as phony as his show of concern.

"Your father was in default, Monsieur Courtmanche. He did not play by the rules, and the bank had no other choice but to foreclose its interest."

"What about our accounts? What did you do with all the money?"

Monsieur nodded to his troubled secretary. "You may go, Angela. There is no problem here."

The young woman with a prominent chin and dark hair worn in a bun returned his nod.

"As you wish, Monsieur Rousseau. I will be outside if you need me."

Jason reacted to her unspoken message. Grabbing Matthieu's arm, he tried to pull him toward the door.

"Maybe we better go," he said.

"Not until this cretin tells me where my father's money is."

The man's face and neck turned bright red. "I will not be called names in my own office. Now, you had better leave before I call the policier."

"Tell me what you did with my father's accounts."

"You called me a cretin. Well, I was trying to spare your sensibilities. Your father was an unabashed gambler. The bank did its best to cover his losses, but he finally went through everything with his gambling and whoring."

"I have money to cover the losses," Matthieu said. "I cannot let you take the plantation."

"Too little, too late," Rousseau said. "Someone has already acquired the note."

"Who?" Matthieu said, grabbing the banker's jacket and lifting him off the polished wood floor.

Hearing the commotion, Rousseau's secretary poked her head through the door.

"Monsieur, shall I call the policier?"

Rousseau held up a hand and shook his head. "Release me, Monsieur Courtmanche.

Matthieu let go of his coat. "Then tell me who bought the note."

Rousseau straightened his jacket, fingering his reading glasses.

"You may as well know. He will notify you soon enough."

"Who?" Matthieu demanded.

Rousseau took a step backward. "Monsieur Zacharie Patenaude."

Matthieu took his own step backward. "And all of my father's accounts?"

"Nothing left," Rousseau said. "All gone."

Jason grabbed Matthieu's arm again, this time succeeding in pulling him out the door of the banker's office. A crowd had gathered behind Rousseau's secretary, and they stared at the two men as they pushed their way through to the front doors. The police were arriving as they rode away down St. Charles Avenue.

"I need a drink," Matthieu said.

"And so do I," Jason said.

"Let's take the horses to the townhouse. Gaston will be there soon and he can take us in the carriage."

They weren't at the townhouse long when Gaston arrived. After seeing to the horses, Matthieu said, "Gaston, hitch up a fresh horse on the carriage and drop us in front of Lafitte's bar."

"Yassuh," Gaston said.

"What am I going to do?" Matthieu asked as the carriage pulled into the street.

"I don't know much about law, but I'd guess the bank has no right to foreclose on your property without proper notice. I suspect a good New Orleans lawyer can put a kink in Monsieur Rousseau's devious maneuvering."

"You think so?"

"I'd bet money on it, and it looked to me as if there's plenty of money in your mother's safe to hire the best lawyer in town."

"Thank you, Jason. I think you may be right. At least you have suggested a place to begin."

Twilight embraced the French Quarter as Gaston dropped Matthieu and Jason in front of the eclectic bar. As during their last visit, the place was humming. They waded through the crowd, purchasing a bottle of American whiskey from the bald bartender with a handlebar mustache.

"Be careful, Monsieur Courtmanche," he said as he handed the bottle to Matthieu. "The Quarter is dangerous tonight."

"Wonder what he meant by that?" Jason asked as they walked through the crowd.

Matthieu didn't have a chance to respond as the wench Lucy spotted them, smiled and intersected their path.

"Where have you been?" she asked. "Word on the street is you bested Zacharie Patenaude in a duel. Is it true?"

Matthieu picked her up, twirled her around, and then stuffed a note into her cleavage.

"I love you, Lucy, but tonight I have other things on my mind."

"Other than making love in my room upstairs?" she asked with a sly grin.

"Something far more important," he said.

"What could be more important than making love?" she asked, grabbing his shirt.

"Killing Zacharie Patenaude with my bare hands."

Seeing fire in his eyes and hearing anger in his words, she backed away into the crowd, smiling and blowing him a kiss as she did.

"Then happy hunting, Matthieu Courtmanche. I will keep my bed warm for you."

Matthieu grinned blew his own kiss. "If I know you, it will be blazing."

"Hot chick," Jason said as they passed through the crowded bar, toward the open patio.

Matthieu gave him a quizzical look and shook his head. They exited the bar, into an enclosed courtyard. The weather had turned chilly, accordion and fiddle player performing somewhere else. Only a few people were outside in the courtyard—a handful of Greek and Italian sailors, along with the hoodoo man Doctor John.

When someone tapped Matthieu's shoulder, he wheeled around to see a smiling Raynard. Jean and Alain were by his side.

"Sharing your whiskey?" Raynard said.

Matthieu's glass shattered when he threw it against the

232

wall surrounding the courtyard. After taking a swig from the open bottle, he handed it to Raynard.

"We wondered if you were still alive," he said, handing the bottle to Alain.

"And why wouldn't I be?" Matthieu asked.

"I think you know what I mean. Are you okay?"

Matthieu glanced at a shooting star, streaking slowly across the clear December sky.

"My father committed suicide, and the bank has foreclosed on the plantation."

"How is that possible?" Alain asked.

"Patenaude," Matthieu said.

The bottle was half-empty when it reached Jason. Emulating Matthieu's lead, he crashed his empty glass against the wall and then took a swig from the bottle.

"There is a rumor going around that he also had a curse placed on you," Jean said.

"Where did you hear that?" Jason asked.

"All over town," Raynard said. "Supposedly, Patenaude gave Doctor John twenty gold coins to lay the curse."

"The hoodoo man is sitting over there," Matthieu said. "Maybe we should ask him."

Raynard grabbed his arm. "I do not think he is very happy with you."

Matthieu glanced at the young man. "And why is that?"

"We heard he would have put a curse on you for no money."

"Then I need to talk to him," Matthieu said, wrenching loose from Raynard's grip.

The accordion and fiddle players had finally arrived, more people wandering out to the patio. Doctor John, his tattooed arms clasped tightly around his chest, frowned as Jason and Matthieu approached.

"We need to talk," Matthieu said.

"You are no longer welcome at my table," the hoodoo man said.

"What have I done?" Matthieu asked.

"If you do not know, then you are a fool."

"I have done many stupid things in my lifetime, and I am

sure I will do many more. All I can do is to try and atone."

Doctor John spat on the cobblestones. "You have no intention of atoning. Why are you here?"

"A curse on my soul. Is it true? If so, then how much must I pay you to remove it?"

"Your gold is worthless with me. Someone paid dearly for the curse, and a curse paid is a curse laid."

"Zacharie Patenaude. Is his curse the reason my father killed himself?"

"I think you already have the answers to all your questions. You knew them the moment you deflowered my daughter. Now, your troubles have only just begun, and you have eternity to rue the day you brought the curse upon yourself."

The music had grown louder; one of Lucy's breasts exposed as she danced a reel with a Greek sailor. Most of the crowd gathered on the patio was watching her twirling performance, though not the two men talking to Doctor John.

"We have twenty gold coins," Jason said. "They are yours if you lift the curse."

Doctor John's smile seemed evil in the wavering light of the Japanese lantern.

"You truly are a fool. You took my daughter's virginity, and now you think you can lift the curse with money? Trust me; the curse is eternal. Now leave me and tolerate your unholy fate like a man."

When Matthieu clenched his fists, Jason clutched his arm, pulling him away from the hoodoo man and into the crowd.

"Let's get the hell out of here," he said.

"Not yet. There is whiskey to drink and wenches to bed."

"Your father is dead, your plantation in foreclosure, and your mother in a horrible state of anxiety. Time is short. We must act."

Matthieu's silly grin informed Jason that he was drunk and numb to their situation.

"There is lots of time, and I need more whiskey."

Jason glanced over his shoulder. What's that?" he said.

When Matthieu turned his attention from his stare, Jason cold-cocked him with a hard right hand, then grabbed him as his eyes closed, and knees buckled. Like everyone else in the crowd, the Musketeers were fixated on Lucy, now naked to the waist with droplets of sweat dripping between her breasts. Jason pulled Matthieu toward the patio door.

"Help me," he called to Alain.

Alain broke away from the scene, joining him. "What happened?" he asked.

"Fainted. We need to get him to the townhouse," Jason said.

"I'll get the others."

Alain waded into the crowd, thumping Raynard to get his attention. The young aristocrat wheeled around, ready to fight.

"Matthieu has passed out and needs our help," Alain said.

Raynard grabbed Jean, pulling him from the scene that was growing ever wilder. Music and lights faded as the four men carried Matthieu away from Lafitte's bar.

"What happened?" Raynard asked as they approached the darkened entrance to Matthieu's townhouse.

"Too much whiskey," Jason said. "He was drunk when you arrived. He needs a warm bed to sleep it off."

"But it is the eve of the New Year," Raynard said.

"Maybe he'll come around before midnight," Jason said.

Harve met them at the courtyard entrance, giving the young men dirty looks.

"He'll be fine," Jason said. "We'll take it from here."

"Are you sure?" Raynard asked.

"Thanks for your help. I don't know what we would have done without you the last two nights."

Raynard shook his hand. "Then go. The Musketeers have a long night of festivity to enjoy."

Jason just shook his head. "You said last night you were looking for a permanent relationship."

"That was then, and this is now. Adieu, brother. Call us again if we can help."

Harve and Jason dragged Matthieu into the kitchen, quickly lighting some candles. Hearing the commotion, Sarah appeared from her room.

"Oh my!" she said. "Is Monsieur Matthieu all right?"

"A little drunk, I'm afraid," Jason said. "You wouldn't happen to have something to help sober him up, would you?"

Black Magic Woman

Sarah gave him a dirty look but reached for a jar in her supplies and potions. After using a wooden spoon to remove a lump from the jar, she dumped some brown powder into a glass of water and stirred it. Matthieu drank it when she held it to his lips.

Chapter 29

Matthieu opened his eyes in the kitchen of his townhouse, Arlette holding a wet cloth to his forehead. His eyes slowly focused.

"What happened?"

"You slipped and fell," Jason said. "Alain, Raynard, and Jean helped me carry you home."

"I must have fallen on my face," he said, rubbing his chin.

"Must have," Jason said. "I tried to catch you, but missed. Have a headache?"

"And a chipped tooth."

"Maybe you should go to your room and lie down," Arlette said.

"Not yet," Jason said, raising a hand. "We need some answers, and there's not much time left."

"Answers?" she said.

"The hoodoo man Doctor John told us he put a curse on Matthieu, and that is the reason Monsieur Courtmanche committed suicide. We offered him money to remove it. He refused."

A fire was burning in the oven, Sarah humming as she stirred a large pot with a wooden spoon. Matthieu, Jason, and Arlette turned their attention to her.

"You know something, don't you Sarah?" Jason said.

"Doctor John ain't nobody to mess around with, him."

"Did you hear something on the street?"

"Maybe," she said.

"Don't keep us in suspense."

"They say Monsieur Patenaude put a curse on Master Matthieu. And there is something else."

"What else?" Jason asked.

"Miss Elise, Doctor John's daughter."

"What about her?" Matthieu said.

"Even after what happened at the Quadroon Ball, Monsieur Patenaude signed an agreement of plaçage with Elise's mother. Elise refused to honor the agreement."

"Tell me more," Matthieu said.

She loves another, and is no longer in a place where her mother and Monsieur Patenaude can compel her into complying with the agreement."

"Oh? You know where she is?"

"The Ursuline Convent."

Jason could tell she also knew something she wasn't sharing. "Arlette, do you know something about this?"

"Monsieur Patenaude is furious, though not as mad as Elise's mother, and Doctor John."

"And that explains part of Doctor John's anger," Jason said.

"I must go to the convent," Matthieu said.

Jason grabbed his arm to stop him. "The problem with Elise will work itself out. I promise. There is something we must do."

"Like what?"

"Like finding a way to lift the curse before it becomes permanent. If we don't break it in the next couple of hours, it'll be too late. Arlette, can you help us?"

"You are making no sense."

Jason popped his forehead with his hand. "Wine. May I have a glass?"

Sarah produced a bottle of wine, pouring some into a crystal goblet for him. He'd almost finished it when he began to smile.

"Arlette, do you know Marie Laveau?"

His question raised Arlette and Sarah's eyebrows.

"No, Suh," Sarah said.

Something about the sound of her voice told Jason she was

lying

"Yes you do. Tell me."

"No, Suh, I don't know nothing."

"Sarah," he said in his sternest tone.

 "People in the Quarter talk about her a lot."

"What day is this?" Jason asked, looking at Arlette.

"Saturday," she said.

"No, I mean the date."

"December 31," she said. "New Year's Eve."

Jason glanced at his wrist for a watch, not seeing one. "Arlette, we must see Madam Laveau, and I don't mean tomorrow."

Arlette shook her head. "Sarah knows where she lives."

"Tell us."

"It is late, Monsieur Jason. She will be sleeping."

"Not on the eve of the new year. Even if she is asleep, we must wake her. This is crucial. Tell us where to find her"

"Surely it can wait until we eat," Matthieu said. "We have had no food all day, and whatever Sarah is cooking smells wonderful."

Sarah smiled. "Filé gumbo."

"Okay," Jason said. "But eat fast."

Arlette, Matthieu, and Jason were soon savoring Sarah's gumbo.

"What is the matter?" Matthieu asked.

Jason added a dollop of boiled rice to his steaming bowl. "Sarah's gumbo is excellent, but I can't help feeling it's our last meal."

"Do not be foolish. Why must we see Marie Laveau tonight? Did you see the way Lucy was dancing? Lafitte's awaits. Can your emergency not wait until tomorrow?"

"Trust me, it can't wait. We may already be too late."

"Too late for what?" Matthieu asked.

"Salvation."

"You are melodramatic."

"Sarah, tell us how to find Marie Laveau," Jason said.

"I does what Master Matthieu tell me to do," she said, suddenly imitating the vernacular of a field hand.

Jason put down his spoon, grasping both of Matthieu's

wrists and staring into his blue eyes.

"Your father is dead, your plantation at stake. We must see Marie Laveau. Are you with me on this?"

"You saved my life. Of course, I am with you."

❦

Gaston was not happy as he guided the phaeton down Rampart Street to an unlighted neighborhood he and the horse had never visited after dark. When Matthieu signaled, he reined the steed to a halt and hitched it.

"Thank you, Gaston. Sorry for getting you out of bed."

"Yassuh," Gaston said. "If somebody don't kill me first, I will be waiting."

Matthieu patted the old man's shoulder. "We will soon return," he said.

Matthieu's black coat made him almost invisible on the dark street. As the night had turned chillier, Jason pulled his own collar up around his neck.

"This is the address of Madam Marie's house," Matthieu said, stopping in front of a French cottage.

Jason knocked on the door. He waited, then knocked again, harder this time. Matthieu had already turned for the carriage when someone behind the closed door spoke.

A woman's voice said, "Who is it?"

"Someone that needs your help," Jason said. "Are you Marie Laveau?"

"Yes I am, and everyone desires my help. I asked your name."

"Jason Fasempaur."

"Who sent you?"

"Madam Aja," he said.

A deadbolt turned, and the door opened a crack, an eye peeking out.

"Madam Aja is dead," the woman said.

"She's very much alive, I assure you," Jason said.

"Then you must be a Traveler?"

"Yes," he said. "And so is Matthieu Courtmanche, though he doesn't realize it. Can you help us?"

A whoosh of warm air rushed past his cold cheeks as the woman opened the door to receive them.

"Come into my house, and follow me," she said.

The yellow shawl draping Marie Laveau's shoulders matched her green turban and African-print dress that draped to the old wood floor. The house was comfortably warm, heat wafting from some unseen fireplace. She led them to a closed door that reminded Jason of the one they'd seen at Doctor John's.

"This is where I do most of my work," she said, opening the door to reveal dozens of flickering candles. She pointed to a table with three chairs. "Please sit and tell me why it was so important to disturb Madam Laveau's sleep."

Jason glanced away from the candles glowing around the voodoo altar, and stared into the woman's dark eyes. Glowing candles at the altar weren't the only thing moving. A light fixture, fitted with candles dripping red wax on the table, rotated in a warm draft. The effect was mesmerizing. Matthieu's chin rested against his chest, apparently already under Madam Laveau's spell.

Jason's eyes blinked, trying to resist the heaviness in his eyelids. When something slithered around his ankle, his fingers touched a thick, reptilian body. A giant snake crawled up his leg, its mouth open and tongue probing, its lidless eyes staring straight into his soul. He was too spellbound to scream.

"Do not move," Madam Laveau said. "Zombi can sense evil. If you are genuine, she will not hurt you."

The snake was now fully extended, its head just inches from Jason's nose. It didn't matter. Lights dancing above him, the snake's eyes and swaying head had him locked in a state of paralyzed anesthesia. It didn't stop his heart from attempting to beat its way out of his chest.

Zombi kissed Jason's lips, and then slithered down his legs to the floor. His eyes slowly refocused on Madam Marie's steely gaze and aquiline nose. Matthieu's head continued to sag against his chest, and Jason realized the voodoo woman wanted it that way.

"You hypnotized us," he said.

"You are no longer under my spell. Tell me where you are from?"

"I live in Paris."

"That is not what I mean."

"New Orleans, one-hundred-fifty years from now. Madam Aja sent us, and Baron Samedi told me how to get here."

Madam Marie smiled. "And how is Madam Aja?"

"Very old and ready to die, but she has the mind of a twenty-year old," Jason said.

"You are a good person, or else Zombi would have swallowed your head."

Jason's heart rate had slowed, and he grinned. "I thought she was going to for a moment. Doctor John also has a pet snake."

"Zombi's sister," she said.

"You know Doctor John?"

"Of course I do."

"Then maybe you can tell me why he is so upset with Matthieu that he would curse him for eternity."

"The answer to your question is obvious."

"Elise? It's not Matthieu's fault that she went to the convent."

"Oh, but it is."

"He didn't intend the outcome that ensued."

"None of us ever intends anything. It is our destinies."

"Doctor John said Matthieu's was sealed with twenty coins of gold, and that his fate is sealed." Madam Marie continued to stare at him, but her stoic expression became a grin. "Or is it?" he asked.

"No matter how much Doctor John would like to believe it, almost nothing is written in stone," Madam Marie said. "I can intercede, but not easily."

"How, then?" Jason asked.

"A little black magic. Monsieur Courtmanche is not the only person cursed. Zacherie Patenaude inadvertently blighted himself. Doctor John allowed it to happen because it supported his vendetta against Matthieu. The two are now intertwined for eternity."

She nodded when he said, "There's something you can do?"

"Zacherie Patenaude is a bastard, and I mean that in the

worst sense of the word. Still, he has the ability to make a fundamental change in his life, and that of young Matthieu. Bring him to me. Perhaps I can convince him to atone his sins and reverse the curse."

"You can do that?" Jason asked.

"Not I, but he can. Will he? That I do not know. But he must do it quickly. It is New Year's Eve. You are not from this place. I am sure Madam Aja informed you that you must accomplish your mission and depart before midnight, or be doomed to stay here forever."

Chapter 30

Tony ducked his shoulder under Eddie's arm, lifting him to his feet. The cat met them when they opened the Mustang door, Tony taking Eddie's reaction as a positive sign.

"You still got that damn cat?" Eddie said.

"And a good thing for you. She saved my life, and you'd be dead right now if I hadn't come when I did."

Tony helped Eddie into the passenger seat and buckled him up. When the cat jumped into his lap, he was too weak to care. Tony put her into the backseat.

"Sorry about that. Hope you aren't allergic."

"Wouldn't make much difference right about now."

"They'll fix you up at the emergency room," Tony said.

"No."

"What do you mean, no? You're beat all to hell."

"I'm okay. Maybe a concussion and some bruises. I'm not gonna get fired over this. Besides, it's New Year's Eve. The Quarter will be rocking."

"I promise you one thing, bad as you look, you won't be out there with the crazies this year. Hell, you probably got broken bones."

"A couple of cracked ribs, maybe. Had one when I played high school football. Nothing much you can do about it."

"What about pain medication?" Tony asked.

"A double Scotch would do me a world of good right about now."

Tony reached in his jacket and pulled out the brandy he'd

taken from Paco. Twisting off the lid, he handed to Eddie.

"There's still plenty left if you're not afraid of getting lockjaw from Paco."

Eddie slugged straight from the bottle. "Tastes like shit," he said. "No wonder Paco died. You think Frankie's boys will come after us?"

"They're stupid, but not crazy. They'll be lucky if Frankie don't kill them first. You gonna press charges?"

"Hell no! If this got back to the wrong people, my job would be on the line."

"Well, you can't go home by yourself. I'm taking you to my place, and Lil will look after you. She was a nurse until she got pregnant."

"Appreciate it, Tony, but I'd rather you drop me at Bertram's."

"You are crazy!" Tony said.

"I need Scotch, or I'm not gonna make it to next year."

Tony glanced at his watch. "I'm already in so much trouble, I may as well go with you."

"I get it. You were just using me to save yourself from Lil"

"She might have bought my story if you had. It's okay, though. She won't kill me."

"Give her a call," Eddie said. "I'll explain things to her."

"You sure?"

"I owe you one."

Tony dialed the phone, handing it to Eddie when it started ringing.

"Tony?"

"Lil, it's Eddie Toledo."

"Where's Tony? Why are you calling from his phone? Is he okay?"

"Sorry I'm mumbling. I took a beating, and my lips are busted up. Tony saved my life. I asked him to take me to Bertram's. He won't do it unless you join us."

"It's late, and I already have my nightgown on."

"I didn't wake you, did I?"

"I'm watching Times Square on television."

"You and a billion other people."

"I opened a bottle of champagne waiting for Tony. Now

it's almost gone."

"I'll buy you another bottle if you'll join us. Please?"

Eddie started coughing before Lil could answer, blood dribbling on the phone. Tony grabbed it from him.

"Lil, Eddie's in rough shape. I'm taking him to the emergency room whether he likes it or not."

Eddie yanked the phone out of Tony's hand. "Lil, I'm okay. Join us at Bertram's, and I'll think about going to the E.R. later. Otherwise, I'm jumping out of this car."

When Tony tried to turn toward the hospital district, Eddie grabbed the wheel, almost causing them to career into a row of cars. Tony slammed on the brakes, screeching to a halt.

"You're acting Looney Tunes and probably have a concussion. Now cut the horseshit and let me take you to the emergency room."

Eddie opened the door and stumbled out. "You'll have to carry me, Lieutenant. I'm going to Bertram's, even if I have to walk."

Tony hurried around the car and grabbed his arm before he fell on his face. He still had the phone, and Lil was screaming at him when he took it.

"Sorry, Babe. Eddie's flipped out, and I gotta take care of him. I apologize about our date. I'll see you when I get home." He helped Eddie back into the car. "Okay, one Scotch, and then I'm taking you to the emergency room."

Eddie slumped against the passenger door during the trip to Bertram's, not worrying about the cat that had returned to the front seat and fallen asleep in his lap. When Tony pulled to a stop, the animal bounded into the back.

"Thanks, Lieutenant," Eddie said. "I owe you one."

"You owe me more than that. Don't matter though, cause Bertram's probably already closed."

"Not tonight, he's not! It's New Year's."

Eddie was correct. Hundreds, maybe thousands of people cruised the streets, most carrying alcoholic beverages. Like every other spot in the Quarter, Bertram's was jamming. He was pulling double duty—taking care of his customers and trying to spend time with Lilly and Carla Manetti. They occupied Wyatt's usual booth as a blues guitar riff echoed from

Eric Wilder

Bertram's aging jukebox. When they saw Tony and Eddie coming through the door, they slid out of the booth.

"Oh my God! Eddie, what happened to you?" Carla asked.

She and Tony helped him into the booth. Lilly ran to the lady's room, returning with a handful of damp paper towels. She began wiping dirt and blood off of his face, handing the towels to Carla to finish the job. Eddie winced when she touched his ribcage.

"Bring him in back," Bertram said, giving Eddie a double Scotch. "He too messed up to work on him out here. I don't want him to scare none of my customers."

Except for Lilly no one at the table had ever seen Bertram's quarters. The compact suite of rooms opened up to a tiny courtyard, complete with hanging ferns, bromeliads, and water dripping from a cherub's mouth. The Oriental rug covering much of the wooden floor looked classy and went with the rest of the furniture, sparse but expensive. A vase of multi-colored flowers topped a table, obviously part of Lilly's work. Tony helped Eddie to the table.

"Get his shirt off," Bertram said. "Theys washrags and hot water in the sink. I'll get some tape to bind them busted ribs up."

Eddie was soon stripped to his boxer shorts with two women and two men administering to him. Lilly dabbed his bruises and contusions. Bertram taped his chest.

"Be right back. If I leave those hungry piranhas unattended too long, they'll start pilfering my whiskey and beer."

"Another Scotch would be much appreciated on your way back," Eddie said, his voice reduced to a hoarse whisper.

Bertram returned with a tray of drinks. Lil was with him, carrying a black bag.

"Lil..." Tony said.

"You didn't think I would stay home after the commotion I heard on the phone, did you?"

"This is Lil, my better half," he said, introducing her.

"I brought my nurse's kit," she said.

"He has wounds on his arms and hands that probably need

stitching," Carla said.

"I can butterfly them, and give him a shot of something to ease the pain," Lil said after examining the cuts. "What happened, Tony? Eddie looks as though he went through a meat grinder."

"You ought to see the other guys," Eddie said in a mumble as Lil stuck his arm with a needle.

"Easy on the hooch," she said. "I just gave you a shot of morphine. When it wears off, you'll need to be in a hospital bed."

"He can't be hurt too bad if he's still got a sense of humor," Bertram said.

Eddie sipped the Scotch through his cracked lips. "Thanks everybody. You saved my life. And thanks for the hooch, Bertram."

Bertram grinned. "Don't worry. You paying for it. And here's a straw. I think you gonna need it."

"Just what I needed," Eddie said. Bring me another when you get a chance, and a bottle of champagne for Lil."

Everyone except Carla was smiling. "I can't believe you, Eddie Toledo. You're the most selfish person in New Orleans."

Eddie already had problems communicating through busted lips. Pain killers and alcohol only made it worse.

"Why are you attacking me?" he asked.

"Just look at yourself, surrounded by compassionate and concerned friends, you just sit in your underwear, drinking whiskey and not caring what anyone thinks about it."

Lilly touched her arm. "We know you are harboring ill feelings for Eddie, but he's injured. Perhaps this discussion could be saved for another time."

Her words brought tears to Carla's eyes. "I'm sorry. I had such strong feelings for Eddie, and he..."

"Ground them into the dirt?" Lilly said.

Eddie quickly became the recipient of glares and frowns from everyone except Tony.

"Now wait a minute," he said. "I'm the first to admit Eddie's far from being a perfect person."

"Go ahead," Eddie said. "Kick me while I'm down."

Tony held up a hand. "Let me finish. Eddie can be a real prick sometimes, but he took this beating because of you."

"For me?" she said, touching her chest. "Surely, you're not serious."

By now, everyone had focused on Tony. "Carla's grandfather was an Italian immigrant and got involved with the Black Hand after moving to Metairie."

"He wasn't a gangster," Carla said.

"I'm not done. Carla's grandfather got a job, not realizing it was with the Black Hand. He quit when he found out, but not before pissing off the local mob boss. That little mistake got him arrested, and then lynched by an angry mob."

"Hung?" Lilly said. "When did this happen?"

"Back in the forties," Tony said.

"So how is Eddie involved?" Mama asked.

"He was trying to clear Carla's grandad's name. Tonight, we found out what actually happened, and it almost cost him his life. Bottom line is Eddie was doing this for you, Carla."

"Oh shit!" she said, hugging Eddie. "Now I feel like a heel. Eddie, will you ever forgive me?"

"If you'll stop squeezing so hard," he said.

"The old year is almost over, and I think we all need some champagne," Lilly said. "Let's go outside before Bertram has an anxiety attack."

"I'm taking Eddie home with me," Carla said. "He doesn't need more alcohol."

"Scotch and morphine are a powerful combination. I love you, Miss Carla, but since I'm feeling better, I have unfinished business."

"What business?"

"Yeah," Tony said. "What business?"

"Shaking down Pancho Bergamo."

"You got what you wanted. Pancho's my problem."

"We're partners on this, and we're on a roll. Let's keep pushing until we find Frankie's horn."

"Eddie, no," Carla said.

"You're a strong woman, Miss Carla. I know I'll need you tomorrow. Tonight let me do this thing."

"You can't even make it out the door without help."

"You kidding? With Lil's Cloud Nine, I can fly out of this place. Trust me, I'm okay."

Tony glanced at Lil. "Go with him," she said. "We can celebrate tomorrow."

Kisses were exchanged all around. Then, with the help of Bertram, Tony walked Eddie to his car.

"Nice cat," Bertram said. "Thought you was a dog man, Lieutenant."

"Whatever you do, don't say nothing to Lil about it."

"She don't like cats?"

"Other people's cats. I'll need to break the news to her gently."

"Good luck with that one."

Before their taillights disappeared around the corner, Bertram returned to a crowd that had only grown larger. He briefly joined the three women in the booth, Lilly smiling and handing him a tall Scotch as he scooted in beside her.

"I'm so proud of Tony," Lil said. "For once in his life, he wasn't lying to me."

"Then maybe I shouldn't break the news to you," Bertram said.

"What news?" she asked.

"Tony's got another pet. This time, a cat."

Lil's smile quickly faded. "You're kidding me!"

"Nope, he told me to tell you."

"Has he totally lost his mind? He knows I'm allergic to cats."

"Have some more champagne and worry about it tomorrow," Bertram said.

Lil closed her eyes. "I think I liked him better when he was running around with loose women."

Bertram laughed. "It's a cute cat. I'll bet you gonna like her."

"Jeez!" she said with a glance at Mama and Lilly. "Tony's chased pussy his whole life. Now he's caught one, and he expects me to like it."

Carla grinned, and Lilly laughed out loud when Bertram said, "Forget about it till next year."

"Sorry I'm such a drama queen. Maybe I will have more

champagne. I can get a taxi home."

"That's the spirit," Lilly said.

Bertram's lull didn't last, and he was working the customers when Mama came through the door.

"Where is Wyatt, and that new beau of yours?" Lilly asked as she slid into the booth.

"On a journey."

"On New Year's Eve?" Carla said.

"I'm beat, wandering up and down Bourbon Street."

"What in the world for?" Lilly asked. "Does it have something to do with Wyatt and Jason?"

"Yes," Mama said, draining the glass Lilly had given her, and then pouring herself another.

"Tell us about it," Carla said. "We have another hour, or so before this place goes completely crazy."

"I need to be on Bourbon Street when Wyatt and Jason return."

"You haven't told us where they are," Lilly said.

"Because you wouldn't believe me."

"I've known Wyatt long as you," Carla said. "Trust me, I'd believe almost anything."

"Especially after what we witnessed last night at the hospital," Lilly said. "Please tell us."

Fireworks began popping on the street as Mama sipped her champagne.

"Wyatt is a Traveler, and apparently so is Jason."

"A what?" Bertram said, bringing more drinks and another bottle of champagne.

"Someone who has lived many lives and has the power to travel between them."

"Time traveler?" Lilly said.

"Yes. Wyatt didn't know it until recently. He's had no reason to travel until recently when something came up."

Bertram rubbed his chin. "Like what?"

"A ghost from his past. The same spirit that confronted us when we visited Charity Hospital."

"I remember. He called Wyatt Matthieu and begged him to remove the curse he'd placed on him," Lilly said.

"We consulted an old voodoo woman. She conducted a

ceremony near St. John's Bayou and summoned Baron Samedi, a voodoo deity."

Lilly's smile disappeared. "And you didn't invite me?"

"It was on short notice. Baron Samedi possessed Jason. When the ceremony ended, he knew where to find the portal to return to old New Orleans."

"You two sound batty to me," Bertram said. "I'm gonna go load a fresh keg of beer."

Lilly, Lil, Carla, and Mama ignored his departure. "So the portal is near here?" Lilly said.

"A few blocks away. I must be there when they return."

"But why?"

"If they have a problem, maybe I can help. Also, they'll need clothes to wear."

"They'll be naked?"

"As the day they were born."

Lilly grinned. "From what I understand, there'll be lots of naked people in the Quarter on New Year's Eve."

"Though it sounds foolish, I assure you it is deadly serious. They have to complete their mission before midnight tonight."

"Or what?"

"They'll be trapped in the past forever."

Chapter 31

Tony drove out of the French Quarter, careful not to hit any of the drunken revelers that had only increased in numbers.

"Where to?" he said.

"Via Vittorio Veneto."

"What's on your mind?"

"We gotta shake Pancho down. You were a cop for twenty-five years, Lieutenant. You know what I'm talking about."

"I've never had to shake down a friend before."

"There's a first time for everything."

A car's horn blared, and Tony slammed on the brakes. "Easy," Eddie said."Lil's morphine is making me feel better, but my ribs are still cracked."

Tony ignored his rant. "Maybe Pancho forgot what he did with the horn."

"He hasn't forgotten. When Wyatt and I asked him a simple question about the mob, he almost came unglued."

"Then it's too bad we aren't part of the mob," Tony said.

"Hell, Lieutenant, that's a great idea."

"He'd know who we are right away."

"Not if we blindfold him and disguise our voices. With my busted lips, I can do a pretty good Paco impersonation."

"Paco's dead."

"Pancho doesn't know that."

"How do you intend to pull this little caper off without Adele and Toni knowing?"

"It's close to midnight. They shut down and went home hours ago; at least Adele. Toni's probably getting wild on Bourbon Street."

"Then what makes you think Pancho will be there?"

"Because Adele told me he has an old recliner in the stock room and that he takes a nap there almost every night. Sometimes, he's still there in the morning."

"How will we get in the door?"

"Shouldn't be hard for an old cop like you, Lieutenant."

"And if they have a burglar alarm?"

"Then we run like hell!"

The cat awoke from her nap in the backseat, jumping into Tony's lap. Tony didn't have to turn to know Eddie was shaking his head.

Eddie was right about the restaurant, all the lights off, including the neon sign over the front door. Tony stopped the car in the shadows behind the restaurant.

"Pancho's old beater is parked at the backdoor. You may be right about him being asleep in there."

"Only one way to find out," Eddie said.

Tony's collection of entry keys rattled as he tried the door. With a screech of swelled wood and rusty hinges, it finally opened. Listening before entering, they heard no sound of movement. Eddie found an empty rice sack in the room's muted light, along with several strands of cord.

"You right, Eddie boy. He's asleep in the chair."

"Then let's do it."

Pancho shrieked when Eddie pulled the sack over his head. Tony gave him little time to react, pulling his arms behind his back and then using cord to tie them.

"What the hell!" Pancho said. "Who is it?"

"Paco," Eddie said.

"Let me go, Paco. I ain't done nothing."

"You still got my horn. I want it back."

"I ain't got it no more."

"Then you better tell me where to find it."

"I'm not sure I know where it is."

"What kinda crap talk is that? What did you do with it? Tell me now or we're gonna have to get nasty with you."

"Paco, it's been forty years."

"Time don't matter none when you break a solemn vow. Now tell me what you did with it."

Tony gave him a shake, and it sent the old man's shoulder's into a shiver.

"You gonna kill me, Paco?"

"Tell me where the horn is and everything will be copacetic again."

"I left it on a Mardi Gras float. About fifteen years ago."

"You did what?"

"The theme of our krewe that year was New Orleans jazz. I was in the parade and used the horn as a prop. I got a little too drunk. When the parade ended, I forgot and left the horn on the float. I still got the case, though."

"Where?" Eddie asked.

"In the bottom of the potato bin."

Chapter 32

When Jason reached the sidewalk, he broke into a trot, Matthieu chasing after him.

"Jason, slow down. What is the hurry?"

"I can't explain right now. You have to trust me."

"We have all night."

"Two hours, maybe. Where do you think Patenaude is?"

"I am sure he is in the Quarter, along with every young Frenchman."

"Lafitte's, maybe?"

"I would not be surprised," Matthieu said.

"Then we'll take a chance that he is."

Gaston was asleep when Jason entered the phaeton, Matthieu right behind him. Jason didn't bother waiting for the old man to unhitch the horse, doing it himself.

"Where to, Suh?" he asked as the two young men piled into the carriage.

"Lafitte's, and hurry."

The sound of hooves clattering against cobblestones echoed through the Quarter as Gaston hurried to Lafitte's. As Matthieu had predicted, the streets were filled with young men, roaming from bar to bar. Gaston almost ran over one of them when he wandered aimlessly into the street.

"There is a place to hitch a horse, Monsieur Jason," Gaston said.

"Let me out in front then drive around the block and wait at the back gate. Don't bother hitching the horse. I won't be long."

When Matthieu started to step from the carriage, Jason raised a palm.

"Stay with Gaston."

"I am coming with you."

"No, you're not. If Patenaude is in there, your appearance will spoil my surprise, and we'll never get him to Madam Laveau's."

"And how do you intend to accomplish that particular task on your own?"

"I won't be alone. The Musketeers are here someplace. I'll find them. They'll help me."

Hooves clattered as Jason pushed through the crowded barroom. Fiddle and accordion music poured from the open door leading to the courtyard. When Alain spotted him in the mass of revelers, he abandoned the bar wench he was with, wading through the crowd to join him.

"Did you return to enjoy the fun?"

"Just business," Jason said. "Is Zacherie Patenaude around someplace?"

"With his entourage," Alain said, pointing.

"Where are Jean and Raynard?"

"I do not know. Can I get you a drink?"

"Though I need one badly, there's something we have to do first."

"Like what?"

"Kidnap Patenaude and take him out the backdoor of the courtyard."

"You must already be drunk."

"Can you round up Jean and Raynard? Perhaps between us, we can devise a plan. And Alain, please hurry. We haven't much time."

Alain had barely disappeared when Lucy appeared through the throng, honing in on Jason like a heat-seeking missile.

"Monsieur, you're back. I thought you had left for the night. Did you return for me?"

Jason shook his head as she put her arms around his neck. "You are beautiful, Miss Lucy. As much as I'd like to change my fate, I'm afraid you are not in my future."

"You hurt my feelings, but you are wrong about that," she said, putting her hand between his legs and squeezing.

"Baby, you're getting me horny, and I can't afford to let that happen."

"And why not?"

"You're going to think this is just a line, but I've traveled here from a different time and space. I have little more than an hour to return, or be trapped here for eternity."

"You are a liar, Monsieur," she said. "You have no money to bed me and are making excuses. No matter. I like you. It is late and I will take you to my bed without charge."

Jason grabbed her, pulled her close, and then kissed her full on the mouth.

"There's nothing I would like better than savor the salty taste of your breasts, or caress the delicate curve of your gorgeous back for the night, but I'm not lying when I tell you our next kiss must truly be our very last."

Lucy's smile disappeared as she stared into his eyes. "Men lie to me every night. Something in my heart tells me your words are true."

"Then listen to your heart."

Alain, Jean, and Raynard appeared as Jason squeezed Lucy's hand.

"You have a problem?" Raynard said.

"An understatement. I'm in a great deal of trouble and need your help."

"We are here for you," Alain said.

"Can you start a fight?"

"A duel?" Jean said.

"An old-fashioned knock down, drag out, fisticuff's brawl. Something that will divert everyone's attention for ten minutes, or so."

Jean grinned and poked Alain. "Sounds like fun. For what reason do you need this diversion."

"To give me cover when I kidnap Monsieur Patenaude."

The three glanced at each other, all with amused expressions

"Alone?"

"I require the assistance of Miss Lucy, if she will help me."

258

"What is it that you want me to do?"

"Entice Monsieur Patenaude to join you by the back gate of the courtyard. Once the fight starts, I'll take care of the rest."

"Patenaude is a dangerous man," Raynard said.

"So am I. Wait until Lucy and I are ready. When I give you the high sign, start a brawl."

The Musketeers watched as Jason and Lucy melded into the crowded courtyard in search of Zacherie Patenaude. T noise level had reached a crescendo, accordion and fiddle music barely audible over the bar's cacophony.

"There he is," Jason finally said. "You think you can get him to the back entrance?"

"I will have him melting like warm butter on a hot summer's day."

"That, I know is true. I think you melted my socks."

Lucy quickly made contact with Patenaude. After letting her whisper something in his ear, he followed her to a palm tree growing near the courtyard's rear gate. Jason followed them, little worried that Patenaude would turn and recognize him.

Seeing Raynard through the crowd, he shook his head and mouthed the words, "Not yet."

Lucy's dark eyes flashed in flickering lantern light as Jason approached Zacherie Patenaude from behind. He turned abruptly when Jason tapped his shoulder.

"You!" he said.

"You dropped something," Jason said, pointing at the flagstone floor.

When Patenaude glanced at the ground, Jason popped him with a quick uppercut to the chin, grabbing him as his knees buckled.

"The old Paris sucker punch," he said. "Works every time.

Seeing Raynard through the crowd, he raised his fist, pumping it. Within seconds, a fight started in the courtyard amid grunts, shouts, and multilingual cursing. Jason dragged the unconscious Patenaude toward the heavy wooden door at the courtyard's rear entrance.

"It is locked, Monsieur," Lucy said, rattling the doorknob.

"Shit!" Jason said. "Wouldn't you know it? Matthieu, can you hear me?"

"We are here, Jason," Matthieu called from the other side of the wall.

"I have Patenaude but the door's locked."

An eight-foot stucco wall encircled the courtyard, Matthieu's upper torso appearing from the other side. The ongoing skirmish in the courtyard had only intensified, a man bouncing against Jason as he supported the unconscious body of Zacherie Patenaude.

"If you boost him up to me, I will drag him over the wall," Matthieu said.

With Lucy's help, Jason lifted Patenaude high enough such that Matthieu could grasp beneath his arms. After a concerted effort, Patenaude disappeared over the wall, Jason and Lucy trying to stay out of the melee behind them.

"Come with me," he said. "You'll get hurt if you stay here."

"I will be fine, Monsieur, and there will be many men in need of loving care when the fight ends."

"Then adieu," he said.

"Will you ever return?"

"Only in my dreams," he said. "But I will never forget you."

Lucy wrapped her arms around him. "Nor I you, Monsieur. If this is our last kiss, then let us make it a good one."

Their kiss continued until Jason shouted at them. "What are you waiting for?"

When a fallen fighter fell against it, Jason used it to catapult himself to the top of the barrier. Before dropping to the other side, he waved to Lucy. Matthieu, Gaston, and the unconscious Patenaude were waiting for him on the stoop.

"Do you have some rope, Gaston? Monsieur Patenaude will not be happy when he comes to."

"Yassuh!" Gaston said, immediately returning from the carriage with rope and a large tow sack.

After stuffing a rag in Patenaude's mouth, and then pulling the sack over his head, Gaston tied him securely.

"Quickly, let's get him into the carriage."

They were soon racing across brick and cobblestone, Gaston avoiding groups of young men prowling the French Quarter. He didn't slow until they reached Marie Laveau's.

Warmth exuded from the pot-bellied stove in Madam Laveau's cottage as Jason, Matthieu, and Gaston dragged Zacherie Patenaude into her hoodoo room. Gaston lowered his head when she spoke to him.

"Back for more love potion, Gaston?"

Gaston averted her gaze and didn't answer. Marie apparently didn't expect one.

"What now?" Jason asked.

"Remove the ropes and put him in a chair. We have no time to waste."

Zacherie Patenaude, moaning as he rubbed his head, was soon sitting across from Marie Laveau. She quickly produced a polished wooden box marked with intricate carvings. As candlelight flickered in Patenaude's dull eyes, she wound it with a brass key, and then open its ornate lid. The old music box soon began playing a delicate melody. Marie bent across the table, slipping a necklace with a polished stone around the man's neck.

When the song began filling the room, Matthieu, Jason, and Gaston grabbed their ears. Patenaude's eyes popped open and he stared at the hoodoo woman.

"Breathe in," she said. "Breathe out. Close your eyes and become one with the tones. Focus only on the melody."

Patenaude's eyes rolled back in his head as the music box's metallic pegs picked out a timeless theme. In pain from the noise, Jason, Matthieu, and Gaston were forced to leave the room and wait on the other side of Madam Marie's magic door.

The music was earsplitting and Marie's own eyes rolled to the back of her head as she tried to muffle the sound with her hands. Patenaude's head was spinning as they entered another state of consciousness. Transported in time and reality, Marie held Zacherie's hand, both enraptured as they floated through the roof, into the night sky above the flickering gas lights of old New Orleans.

"Am I dead?" Patenaude asked.

"You are very much alive."

"Then I must be dreaming."

"This is no dream. Observe carefully because your actions will impact the rest of your life, and beyond."

They were soon observing a funeral procession—horses pulling a wagon piled high with corpses. The one on top stared at them with cold dead eyes.

"Blessed Mother Mary!" Patenaude said. "Is that my body?"

"You die of yellow fever, like so many others. They are transporting the bodies to the funeral pyre."

"They burn my body? Do I receive absolution?"

"You received no absolution because of the curse you placed."

"What difference could that make?"

"You delved into black magic and conspired with the devil. No priest will ever absolve you."

"It is Matthieu Courtmanche that is cursed."

"When you incurred the ire of Doctor John, he added a postscript to the curse. He tricked you into cursing yourself and now the two of you are united forever. Unless..."

"I did nothing to Doctor John."

"Oh, but you did. Elise is his daughter."

"I am not to blame for what happened to her."

"Doctor John thinks you are. Now, it is you that suffers because Courtmanche has mostly avoided the curse."

"How is that possible?"

"He is a Traveler and you are not. You are doomed to wander forever in the realm of ghosts and spirits."

"I do not believe you," he said.

"You soon will."

Flickering gaslights from the city below suddenly went black. When there was light again, Marie and Zacherie Patenaude were inside a building, floating weightlessly near the ceiling. There were no lights, illumination provided only by an ephemeral glow that danced from wall to wall.

"Where are we?"

"Charity Hospital," Marie said. "It is where you die."

Below them, hundreds of sick and dying people lay almost

262

shoulder to shoulder, draping the floor in a writhing carpet of agony.

"What has caused such a scene?"

"Yellow Jack," she said. "The plague."

"Where are the doctors and nurses? Who is tending those wretches?"

"Others that are also sick. No one else will come near. Not even their own families."

Marie and Patenaude weren't the only entities floating above the sickened mass of humanity. Headless wraiths and disembodied specters had joined them. Patenaude recoiled when a wispy spirit passed through them.

"This is not real!"

"Not yet," Marie said, "But it will soon be your eternity unless you invalidate the curse."

"But Doctor John said a curse laid with twenty gold coins can never be reversed."

"Doctor John is a powerful hoodoo man. He is wrong. You alone have the power."

"Tell me how."

"You must make an apology to Matthieu Courtmanche, and then you must atone to everyone in the city you have wronged. Moreover, you must do so this very night before the clocks toll midnight."

When the music inside Madam Marie's voodoo room ceased, Jason, Matthieu, and Gaston opened the door a crack. Patenaude and Marie were rubbing their heads, trying to refocus their eyes. Marie's snake crawled from behind the altar, slithering toward the table.

"Madam Marie," Jason asked. "Are you okay?"

"Trancing is never easy though there was no other way. Zacherie, do you have something to say to Monsieur Courtmanche?"

Patenaude's legs wobbled when he attempted to stand. Using the table to regain his balance, he faced Matthieu. Jason waited, holding his breath.

"My apologies for everything, Courtmanche. I was angry when you ruined my plaçage agreement, and then bested me in a duel. I am also sorry about what happened to your father. That, I cannot change, but I will see to it you have your plantation, and your birthright restored." Patenaude turned to Madam Marie. "What now?"

"Midnight Mass at St. Louis Cathedral. The witching hour draws near and we must hurry."

A crowd milled around outside the magnificent cathedral as Gaston slowed the carriage. Opening the door, he waited for the exit of Zacherie Patenaude and Marie Laveau. Madam Marie handed a small bottle to Jason.

"It is almost midnight. The curse will soon be lifted and you must return to the time and place from where you came. Adieu."

Jason kissed the voodoo woman's hand before she had stepped from the carriage.

"Thank you, Madam Marie. You are everything I expected, and much more."

Marie Laveau smiled and nodded as she and Patenaude made their way into the entrance of St. Louis Cathedral.

"I must return to your own world," Jason said. "And you must remain here, though the person you become in the future must return with me." Jason gave Matthieu the potion. "Good luck in restoring your affairs. I wish there were some way to know if you succeed."

"Is the Courtmanche Plantation still present in the future?"

"Very much so," Jason said. "And just as regal as ever."

Matthieu shook Jason's hand and then hugged him. "You were like a brother to me and I will miss you. I will leave you a message in my mother's wall safe."

"I look forward to reading it, now drink this," Jason said, handing him a vial from inside his gris gris bag.

Matthieu's eyes closed briefly after draining the vial. When they opened again, he shook his head to clear the cobwebs.

"Jason, where are we?"

"About to be stuck in the past forever, unless we get a move on. Gaston, take us to Bourbon Street, and hurry as if our lives depend upon it."

Gaston started away from the square, moving slowly as he navigated through the crowd mobbing the streets of the French Quarter. Seeing they were making no progress, Jason vaulted from the carriage.

"We have to run, Wyatt. We'll never make it in this traffic jam. Happy New Year, Gaston!" he said with a wave. "Take care, old man."

"God bless, Suh!" the old man called after them.

Wyatt followed Jason out of the carriage, dodging bodies as he chased him down the street. When they encountered a wagon blocking their path, Jason leaped onto the back, bounding across to the other side. Wyatt wasn't far behind. Cathedral bells from St. Louis Cathedral began sounding.

"There's an alleyway and we have about ten more seconds to run through it."

Sprinting for their lives, Jason and Wyatt bowled over a young man standing in their path, the church bell pealing for the tenth time.

"We're not going to make it," Wyatt said.

The twelfth clang of the bell sounded as the two men dived for the entrance to the alleyway.

Jason and Wyatt emerged from the darkness onto a frenetic Bourbon Street crowded with shoulder-to-shoulder revelers. Fireworks exploded, arching fiery pathways through the sky. Music issued from open doors, along with the combined dissonance of thousands of celebrants cheering the beginning of the New Year. None of them seemed to notice, or to care that the two men alongside them were entirely naked.

"Oh hell! Now what?"

Wyatt raised his hand in a high five. "You did it, buddy. You got me in and out in one piece. I owe you a big one."

"Wyatt, Jason," someone called through the crowd.

It was Lilly and Mama Mulate, yelling at them through the mob of people. When Jason and Wyatt reached them, they wrapped them in bathrobes. Mama handed Jason a Hurricane in a tall box with a straw, and faux Hurricane for Wyatt.

"Don't keep me in suspense," Mama said. "Did you lift

the curse?"

"Was there ever any doubt?" he said, giving her a thumbs up, and then lifting her off the pavement, spinning her around until they were both dizzy.

Chapter 33

Jason, deep in the sleep of the dead, lay cradled in the arms of Morpheus. Sand on the beach beneath him warmed the bare skin of his back as he watched a bikini babe wade through the surf toward him. Their hands never touched because something kept jostling his shoulder.

"Jason, wake up. Someone's banging on the door downstairs."

Jason's eyes popped open as one of Mama's cats walked across him on the bed. He didn't immediately remember where he was.

"What time is it?" he managed to mumble.

"Six," Mama said. "Can you go downstairs and see who it is?"

"Burglars or maybe an angry ex-boyfriend?"

Jason's blurted comment miffed Mama Mulate. "Fine, then I'll go."

"Wait," Jason said, grabbing her arm. "I'm awake. I'll go."

Muted light from the bedroom window silhouetted Mama's naked body.

"No problem. It's your first rational response since we got here. I wanted to have wild sex to celebrate your return from the past. You just wanted to sleep."

Feeling the warmth of her body, he said, "Maybe we can remedy the situation. At least if the person at the front door will go away."

"Doesn't sound like it," she said.

Mama got out of bed, gliding across the room to the closet, quickly returning with robes for both of them.

"Party pooper," he said as he pulled the frayed cotton robe over his shoulders and started downstairs.

"I'll be in the kitchen making coffee. Perhaps we can give the New Year a better start once you get rid of whoever it is trying to knock down the door."

Jason padded into the hall, wishing he had slippers for his cold feet.

"Who is it?" Jason said.

"Eddie and Tony."

"Starting early, or up all night?"

"Let us in and we'll explain," Tony said.

"And hurry," Eddie said. "There's a cop car cruising the neighborhood, and I don't feel like spending New Year's Day in the Parish poky."

Jason slipped the deadbolt and let them in, a gust of cool air flooding across his bare legs.

"Nice robe," Tony said.

"A little short, but the polka dots become you," Eddie said.

Jason just grinned, not bothering to respond. "Mama's got a pot of coffee on in the kitchen. I think you boys could use a cup."

"You don't know the half of it," Tony said.

Once in the light of the hallway, Jason noticed Eddie's bruised and swollen face.

"What the hell happened to you?"

"Train wreck," Eddie said.

"I hope you got the license number. You okay? You look as if you should see a doctor."

"Feeling a little punk, but I'll live."

"What's that under your arm, Tony?"

"Instrument case. It's why we're here."

Tony nodded when Jason said, "Frankie's lost cornet?"

Mama glanced up from the coffee pot on the stove as they entered the kitchen.

"Oh my God, Eddie!" she said, grabbing his arm. "What happened to you?"

She gave him no chance to answer, dragging him to a kitchen chair, and then stripping off his coat and shirt. A hand went to her mouth when she saw the bruising, and swollen marks on his chest and arms. She grabbed the jar from her stash of herbal potions, ointments, and medicines.

"You must be in pain," she said.

"Lil gave me a shot of morphine before we left Bertram's. It's pretty much worn off."

"I don't have morphine but I have some pills that will help."

"Prescription?" Eddie asked as he popped two with a glass of water.

"Juju," Mama said.

Still hours before rush hour traffic, tires screeched on the main street near her house. Tony waited for the sounds of a crash that never came as Jason poured him a cup of coffee. Pulling up a chair, he put the instrument case on the table and opened it.

"Where's the horn?"

"Long story."

"I have all day."

"We think it's in a warehouse in Algiers where old Mardi Gras floats are stored."

"What makes you think that?" Jason asked.

"Like I said, long story. If we can't locate it, can you tell us anything about the horn from the case?"

Jason touched the purple felt lining. "It's hand crafted. Probably means it housed an artist horn."

"A what?"

"A one-of-a-kind created for a particular musician."

"Which musician?"

"Can't tell you without doing some research."

"Frankie wants answers now."

"Hey, the sun's barely up."

"Tell me about it. I'm so tired I can hardly think straight, and Lil's gonna knock a knot on it when I get to the house."

Mama's three cats, Bushy, Cliffy, and Ninja came wandering through the kitchen, soon creating a commotion as they scratched on the front door.

269

"What's the matter with those cats?" Mama asked. "You didn't leave a mouse on my front porch, did you Lieutenant?"

"No ma'am. They probably hear the cat in my car."

Mama stopped dabbing lotion on Eddie's wounds and gave Tony a look.

"Why do you have a cat in your car?"

"Long story."

"Is that all you have to say this morning? Whose cat is it, anyway?"

Eddie snickered. "Tony's, now. At least until Lil gets a load of it. She's gonna kill him."

"No, she ain't. You want another cat, Mama?"

"Trying to give away your cat? What kind of man are you? Give me your car keys," she said.

She headed toward the front door when Tony tossed her the keys. Her three cats followed her into the kitchen when she returned, cradling Paco's cat in her arms.

"The poor little thing's eaten up with fleas," she said, glaring at Tony.

"Don't look at me like that," he said. "This time yesterday, she wasn't my responsibility."

"Well, she is now," Mama said.

Finding some flea medication, she applied it to the back of the cat's neck. When she released her grip, the frightened creature bounded into Tony's arms.

"I don't know who Paco is, but it looks like she's your cat now."

Eddie snickered again. "I'll refrain from making a crude comment."

"Shut up, Eddie," Tony said.

Mama wagged her finger in Eddie's face. "If you want more of Mama's loving care, you'd better take the Lieutenant's advice. I'm still mad at you, you know."

"I'm sorry," Eddie said. "I'll be good."

"Are the pills working?" Mama asked.

Eddie gave her a thumb up. "Don't know what's in your juju pills, but the pain has gone numb."

Jason had continued to examine the cornet case, and ex-homicide detective Tony Nicosia noticed something in his expression.

"What? You see something?"

"Maybe. There's an emblem engraved on one of the brass snaps."

"Show me," Tony said, squinting to see the tiny engraving. "What is it?"

"A crescent moon."

"What's it mean?"

"It's the symbol of the craftsman that made the instrument."

"Do you know who?"

"Ordinarily I wouldn't. This one I recognize."

"Well, don't keep us in suspense," Tony said.

The sun peeked over the horizon as Tony and Eddie left the house. Mama and Jason stayed behind, nursing their hangovers and Tony's new cat. Mama's balm had worked wonders on Eddie's face and body, the bruises and swelling already starting to heal. Tony didn't notice as he barreled across the Crescent City Connection to Algiers, the New Orleans' ward on the other side of the muddy Mississippi River.

"Slow down. I don't want to be in another train wreck," Eddie said.

"I've never had an accident."

"Then stop pressing your luck. You barely missed the back fender of that pickup we just flew by."

"Knock it off, Eddie. I'm the only one in the car capable of driving right now so live with it."

A hint of anger in Tony's voice caused Eddie to stop nagging. As they neared Algiers, New Orleans' skyscrapers and the city's hustle and bustle disappeared in their rearview mirror, replaced by quiet streets and frame houses with gingerbread exteriors. Tony slowed the Mustang to a crawl.

"We made it. You happy now?"

"Good. Now what?"

"Find Pancho's Mardi Gras float."

"Easier said than done. There are dozens of warehouses on this side of the river that store Mardi Gras floats. How will you know where to start?"

"No idea, but I know someone that does."

Tony rounded a corner of one of the ward's narrow streets and pulled to a stop in front of a ramshackle apartment building. An open door led into the apartment, a man, and a woman sitting outside on the sidewalk in cheap lawn chairs.

"How you doing, Lieutenant?" the man said when Tony stepped out of the car.

"Passable, Bruno. You?"

"Like a fat hog in warm slop."

The man was probably mid-forties, black hair draping the shoulders of his faded Hawaiian shirt. It failed to cover the bald spot that widened his brow, seemingly even more offset by his dark eyebrows and bushy moustache.

"Bruno Steegle, this is Eddie Toledo."

"Glad to meet you, Eddie," Bruno said, pumping his hand. "This is Jan. We been married eighteen years."

"How you doing, Jan?" Tony said. "Should I congratulate you, or give you my condolences."

Bruno and Jan both laughed. "He can Cajun two-step better than any man alive. Guess I'll keep him."

She grinned when he elbowed her and said, "That ain't all I can do better than any man alive. You boys want a beer?"

"Love one," Eddie said. "And I'll take Tony's if he's not thirsty."

Jan and Bruno were both laughing as he disappeared into the dark hallway, quickly returning with two cans of Pabst.

"Were you in a car wreck, Eddie?" he asked.

Eddie smiled as he popped the top on the beer. "Bar fight. Believe it or not, I won."

Jan and Bruno's laughter turned into a belly roll. "And I bet you got a bridge in Brooklyn you want to sell me," Bruno said.

"Hey, it's an excellent bridge," Eddie said.

"You're up early for New Year's Day," Tony said.

"What makes you think we've been to bed yet?" Bruno said. "We been partying since dark last night."

"Good for you. Wish we could say the same."

"What's up, Lieutenant? You didn't come to Algiers to talk about bridges, bar fights and all night parties with old

Bruno."

"You right about that. We got a float we need to find."

"Then you came to the right place. What krewe you looking for, and what year?"

"Don't know the krewe, or year, but it was about forty years back."

Bruno slugged the rest of his beer, crushed the can, and threw it into the flowerbed.

"Tall order, Lieutenant. We got warehouses filled with Mardi Gras floats here in Algiers."

"How many krewes are there?" Eddie asked.

"Hell, thousands—Pegasus, Venus, Iris, Rex, Hermes... A good many have come and gone. It would help to know the krewe you're looking for."

"The old man that set us on the trail was only a member for a year. He was half drunk and don't remember much about it."

"You could say that about ninety-nine percent of the krewe members that ride them floats."

"That's a fact," Jan said. "You boys want another beer?"

"I'd love another," Eddie said. "And morphine, if you have a shot. That and Mama's juju pills are my new favorite drugs."

"Don't have any of that, but we could smoke a little pot."

Eddie grinned and shook his head. "Better pass. My boss would frown on that."

"Make you take Monday piss tests, huh?" she said.

"Not quite that bad, but almost. I'll have that beer, though."

Jan returned with a beat-up old ice chest and bag of pot. After handing Eddie a beer, she proceeded to roll a joint, taking a long drag and then passing it to Bruno.

"You're not afraid your neighbors will turn you in?" Eddie said.

Bruno and Jan both laughed. "Hell, man," Bruno said. "Where do you think we got it in the first place?"

"In that case, toke away."

"You know the parade route, or anything, Lieutenant?"

"Pancho has lived in Metairie all his life."

"Hell, then it was probably Thor. It started in '74."

"Could be," Tony said. "You know where the warehouse is?"

"Hell, Lieutenant, does an alligator shit in the swamp?"

Tony and Eddie were soon driving down the road paralleling the river, Bruno in the backseat giving them directions. Metal warehouses lined the street, most seemingly inactive.

"That one, Lieutenant," Bruno said, pointing to an empty parking lot.

"You know I ain't with the force anymore," Tony said as Bruno began sorting through keys on his giant keychain.

"I heard what happened. No matter. You the best cop I ever known. You'll always be Lieutenant Nicosia to me."

"Thanks, Bruno. Can you find the key?"

"It's here someplace. No one has been in this warehouse in a while. It's full of old floats and Mardi Gras bits and pieces."

The door finally opened with a metallic screech, expelling years of must and mildew in a dampened wave. Though Bruno seemed unaffected, it sent Eddie and Tony into coughing jags.

"Smells like hell in here," Tony said.

"Sweat, puke, and rat shit."

"Sorry I asked."

With no light fixtures in the old warehouse, Bruno left the front bay open. It didn't help much as they began wading through littered debris of carnivals past—Egyptian pharaohs, faded dragons, giant jester's heads with mouths locked in perpetual smiles, a plaster pig no longer quite pink. Eddie ducked when something swooped over his head.

"What the hell!"

"Bats. We must have kicked up some bugs. Don't let 'em get in your hair."

"Peachy," Tony said. "Are these all Thor floats?"

"Yes sir, Lieutenant. What you looking for?"

"The theme that year was jazz in the Big Easy."

"Don't remember that one. Must have been a while back. Maybe these will help."

Bruno tossed flashlights to Eddie and Tony. Once lighted,

their swaths reflected years of dust stirred up by the three intruders. Eddie continued cursing beneath his breath.

"There must be a hundred floats in here," Tony said.

"What exactly are we looking for, Lieutenant?"

"Brass horn."

"You mean like a bugle?"

"More like a trumpet."

"And you think it's in one of these floats?"

"If not, we're back to square one."

"The only way we're gonna find it is to crawl inside each one and give them a look see," Bruno said.

"Then let's get started," Tony said.

After divvying up the territory, they began searching through rubble piled in the old floats.

"Jesus," Eddie shouted. "Check out what I found in this one—two used condoms, a pair of panties, and a set of false teeth."

"No telling what you're liable to come up with. We uncovered a dead body once," Bruno shouted, his words echoing against metal walls. "And it wasn't no homeless person. Oh and hey, better watch out for copperheads and rattlesnakes."

"I hope you're kidding," Eddie shouted.

Bruno's sly laugh told him he probably was. Tony tried to ignore the banter as the batteries in his flashlight began to grow dim.

"I never seen so many empty beer cans and liquor bottles," he said.

"Six hours or more on a slow float to Chalmette can become kinda tiring," Bruno said.

"I'm surprised they could still throw their beads and doubloons."

Bruno laughed again. "Some of them can't. Every year we find one or two still passed out when we drag the floats into the warehouses."

He laughed again, when Tony said, "Bruno, you're so full of shit!"

"Speaking of shit, I've found a petrified pile or two," Eddie said.

"Some of the older floats didn't have portable toilets, and lots of hours in a parade make for a long day."

"You're a hell of a tour guide, Bruno, and you've already given me too much information," Eddie said.

Tony coughed. "My flashlight just died. Got any more batteries, Bruno?"

"I didn't think we'd take this long. Mine's about gone, too."

"Then let's call it a day and try some other time," Tony said.

"Not yet, Lieutenant. I may have found it. You boys come help me."

The three men were soon scratching through the litter strewn everywhere in the old float decorated with giant horns and floating musical notes. Eddie had launched into a fit of sneezing caused by dust blown up by their search. He'd even stopped swatting at bats that continued to zoom past his head. Their search ended with an abrupt war whoop that rattled Tony's eardrums.

"I found it, Lieutenant."

"Hope you ain't kidding," Tony said.

Bruno put his lips to the mouthpiece and blew a sour note to show he wasn't.

"Good work, Bruno," Tony said. "Damn bats are getting a little too close for comfort. Hang on to the horn and let's get the hell outa here."

Chapter 34

Wind frothed white caps atop the muddy Mississippi River as a paddle wheeler thudded against the dock fronting the Willows Plantation. Jason Fasempaur and Mama Mulate watched from the upper deck as ducks lifted from the water, flying farther south.

"It's beautiful, and I'm freezing," Mama said, pulling a shawl around her neck.

"I told you to bring a warmer coat."

"I'd feel lots better if you'd tell me why you insisted we visit so soon after the holiday. You still haven't shared your story."

"Maybe because it's too fresh on my mind, and I have a few unresolved questions. That's why we're here."

"At least tell me what Wyatt looked like."

Jason squeezed her hand. "He was at least ten years younger and tied his long hair in a ponytail. I wanted him to come with us; he would have no part of it."

"This place has dark and foreboding memories for him."

"And I think I know why."

"Then tell me."

"Before we leave, you'll know everything I know."

Mama had to shake her head. "There are New Year's festivities all over town, and we're missing the Sugar Bowl."

"We can play catch-up when I get some answers."

"Visiting the Willows is going to give you those answers?"

"I sincerely hope so."

"How?"

"Patience."

"Hard to do with cold wind frosting my eyelids," she said.

A gusty breeze tousled Jason's hair as he started toward the ramp with Mama in tow. Now, most football fans were trying to sober up enough to attend the big game. The small group following Jason down the gangplank had ventured south for other reasons. Exploring a historic cotton plantation was one of them.

A blue tram sat parked at the foot of the ramp, a young woman dressed in antebellum attire waiting until everyone had secured a seat.

"Welcome to the Willows. My name is Sarah, and I'll be leading your tour."

Jason," Mama said. "You look as though you've seen a ghost."

"Our tour guide looks exactly like someone I met in old New Orleans. Her name was also Sarah."

The electric-powered tram snaked through towering oaks and manicured hedges bordering the path, replete with Greek statuary, leading to the Willows. The tram unloaded in front of a veranda encircling the front of a large house.

"There was no air conditioning when this plantation was operational," Sarah said. "During hot summer nights, the occupants of the house would sit in these rocking chairs on the veranda, sipping something cold."

The group followed her up the steps and through the oak and cut glass doors of the house, into the foyer. Warmth radiated from a large fireplace when she opened the doors to the main living area.

"The house is decorated much as it was in 1840, the chandeliers and mirrors imported from France."

Mama gazed at Jason when he nodded his head. "You visited this plantation?"

"Matthieu's father killed himself. We were in New Orleans when they summoned us."

"One of the former owners, Boone Courtmanche, committed suicide in his wife's bedroom, and she was present when he died," Sarah said. "His spirit still haunts the plantation.

Some visitors occasionally catch a glimpse of him in the mirror behind us."

The group turned to see the mirror on the wall. A gray-haired woman's hand went to her mouth.

"I saw him!"

The group began murmuring, though no one else professed to seeing anything in the mirror other than their own reflection. Having seen it all before, Sarah was grinning.

"It's quite common that some can see Monsieur Courtmanche and others can't."

Leaving the hallway, Sarah led the small group into the rustic kitchen.

"One of my ancestors was a cook for the family that once owned this plantation."

Sarah gave him a quizzical glance when Jason asked, "Was she also named Sarah?"

"Why yes," she said. "How did you know?"

"Wild guess."

The tour continued to the rear veranda, landscaped backyard, overseer's quarters, and finally, upstairs to the bedroom of Matthieu's mother. It was mostly unchanged since the last time Jason had last seen it. He saw a reflection in the gilded mirror on the wall opposite the bed. No one else seemed to notice.

"This was the bedroom of Mathilde Courtmanche," Sarah said. "She died in that bed."

"Did she kill herself, like her husband?" a visitor asked.

The question brought a smile to Sarah's pretty face. "She died at the ripe old age of nearly a hundred. Why do you ask?"

"I thought the Courtmanche family had lost the plantation."

"That almost happened. It didn't because Mathilde's son Matthieu regained control of it, some say with the help of the voodoo woman Marie Laveau."

"Is this where her husband killed himself?" a young woman with a New York accent asked.

"Yes. There is a stain on the flocked wallpaper behind you. It's the exact spot where Boone Courtmanche shot himself."

Everyone turned to look at the reddish blemish on the

lime green wallpaper where Sarah was pointing.

"Is it a blood spot?" an older man in a corduroy sports coat asked.

"Yes," Sarah said. "And something even stranger happened in this very room."

"Tell us," a woman said.

"Boone Courtmanche wasn't the only person to commit suicide here. Another owner did as well. Believe it or not, both of their bullets ended in exactly the same place."

The man in corduroy was shaking his head. "No way."

"Oh, yes," Sarah said. "The spot you see is the commingled blood of the two dead men."

"Why do you leave it there?" the person's bespectacled wife asked.

"Former owners have removed it several times. It always reappears."

"Surely you're pulling our legs," a woman asked.

"No ma'am, I'm not. You may touch it if you wish. I promise it will remain unchanged."

"What was the name of the second man that committed suicide in this room?" Jason asked.

"Jeb Thomas, son of a former governor of Louisiana. The Governor owned this property, briefly changing the name to the Thomas Plantation. He left it to his son Jeb in his will. It was in the process of being repossessed when he killed himself."

"Wyatt's father," Jason said in a whisper.

"When Matthieu Courtmanche regained possession of the Willows he freed the slaves, and it was never again a cotton plantation."

"Did Matthieu ever marry?" Mama asked.

"His wife died of consumption at an early age. He never remarried though it is rumored he was quite the lady's man. He had no heirs."

"How did he and his mother survive?"

"They somehow managed. Matthieu sold the plantation when his mother died."

Jason grabbed Mama's elbow when Sarah left the room, along with the sightseers, to continue the tour.

"Guard the door while I do something," he said.

"What?"

"Bear with me," he said as he maneuvered a French pastoral picture on the wall.

Mama watched him swing the hinged picture away from the wall to reveal a hidden safe. He twirled the tumblers, opening the safe and removing an envelope yellowed with age and sealed with red wax.

"What is it?"

"I'll explain later. Let's get out of here before someone realizes we've left the group."

Jason had already closed the safe, pivoted the picture back into place, and stuffed the envelope into his coat pocket. The mirror glowed as he followed Mama to the door.

"Au revoir, Mathilde," he said before exiting into the hallway. "Rest in peace."

The group had finished its tour of the house, most of them crowded into a room converted to a gift shop, buying postcards and souvenir key chains. Sarah was chatting with a couple in the foyer. No one seemed to notice Mama and Jason bounding down the stairs.

Within an hour, they were back on the paddle wheeler moving slowly up the river to New Orleans. Mama and Jason were finally alone at the rail near the rear of the boat, the rest of the group opting for the warmth of the visitor's deck. The winter sky grew dark, the sun close to sinking into the depths of the mighty river. Lost in thought, Jason smiled when Mama elbowed him.

"Are you ready to tell me what you took from the safe?"

"Nothing that wasn't mine," he said. "The letter is addressed to me."

She glanced at the signature on the envelope when he pulled it from his jacket and handed it to her.

"Oh my, it's like a message from the dead."

"On the contrary. Matthieu was alive when he wrote the letter."

"What does it say?"

"Wyatt and I departed before the curse could be lifted. Even though history reveals what happened to Matthieu and his family, it tells us nothing of the curse. This letter does."

"Don't keep me in suspense."

Jason returned the letter to his jacket. "Though I've known you less than a week, I have seen your Vodoun powers in action. Madam Aja has so much knowledge she should be a national treasure. I met Doctor John, the most powerful hoodoo man the Big Easy has ever known. He placed a curse on Matthieu and Zacharie Patenaude. A curse made with twenty coins of gold."

Mama turned her gaze to the rapidly setting sun. "Then it is unbreakable and Wyatt still cursed."

"Nope. New Orleans had someone even more powerful than Doctor John."

Madam Marie Laveau," Mama said. "How did she do it?"

"By convincing Patenaude to confess his mortal sins before the whole congregation attending midnight mass at St. Louis Cathedral. Matthieu's letter confirms he did exactly that."

"Don't stop now. I'm dying to hear the rest of your story."

"And a long one it is, my dear, best saved for a dreamy night on your back porch, along with a bottle or two of the best Bordeaux France can provide."

Chapter 35

Days had passed since the first day of January, most resolutions long since broken. The doors to Via Vittorio Veneto were locked, the Bergamos playing host to a private party. Eddie Toledo and Carla Manetti smiled as they held hands beneath the table.

Frankie Castalano occupied the place of honor, Adele Bergamo by his side. Beside them were Tony and Lil, Pancho Bergamo, Toni Bergamo and her new boyfriend Vince. Frankie lifted his glass.

"A toast to all my friends, and especially Tony. Even though you didn't find my cornet, you introduced me to my new love Miss Adele. I'm grateful." Tony grinned and his expression caused Frankie to do a double take. "Am I missing something here?"

"When someone gives Tony a job to do, he doesn't quit until he completes it," Lil said.

"There's two Tony's at the table," Tony said. "It's Miss Toni that has something for you."

When Vince released Toni's hand, she ran into the kitchen, returning with something behind her back. It was Frankie's cornet. He hugged both her and her mother when she handed it to him.

"Oh my God! How did you find it?"

"Your papa told us it was here in the restaurant," Tony said. "Pancho was a little nervous about telling us he'd misplaced it about a decade back."

"I'm so sorry, Frankie, I..."

Frankie cut him off with a wave of the hand. "No matter. You're forgiven. No one at this table can do any wrong. Where was it?"

"The case was in the bottom of the potato bin," Pancho said. "I borrowed the horn as a prop for a Mardi Gras parade. I thought it was gone forever, but Tony and Eddie found it."

"Where did you find it?"

"Long story," Tony said. "I had lots of help, but Jason Fasempaur solved the mystery of who gave it to you in the first place."

"Oh my God! I've been waiting my whole life for the answer to that one. Who was it?"

"They can tell you all about it later," Adele said. "Let me hear if you can still play like you used to."

Frankie smiled as he put the instrument to his lips and began to blow, mellow notes issuing from the antique horn. When he finished the slow riff, everyone applauded.

"You still got it," Adele said, hugging him.

Frankie's tears flowed, and he had to dab his eyes with a handkerchief before he was able to speak.

"This is the best day of my life," he said. "I got my horn back, and Adele has consented to marry me. Tony, I don't know how to thank you."

"Jason Fasempaur gave me some answers I needed, but I'd have never found the horn without Eddie's help. He's a birddog when he's on the trail."

"Thank you, Eddie. You know who I am and I know who you are. Though we got our differences, I'm beholding to you now. Is there anything I can do for you?"

Eddie nodded. "Well, there is one little thing."

Chapter 36

For the first time in nearly a month, not a single tourist occupied a table or barstool in Bertram's bar. The unhappy Cajun was wandering around with a rag in his hand, cleaning imaginary dust off the empty tables as Lilly, Carla, and Eddie watched him from Wyatt's favorite booth.

"Honey, take a break, and come sit with us," Lilly said.

"I'm going broke in this place!"

"Relax, Bert. You made so much money in the last two weeks, you could take the rest of the year off and not worry about it."

"You never know about those things," he said. "We could have another recession anytime now."

"Or maybe an earthquake," Eddie said.

Bertram cracked a smile. "At least I got you in here drinking. That right there would keep most bars in bidness."

"Got that right," Eddie said. "Now, if you don't stop whining and bring us another round I'm gonna move my bidness down the street."

Bertram rubbed his palms and hurried behind the bar, Eddie and Carla holding hands.

"You two look so happy," Lilly said.

"Eddie is my knight in shining armor," Carla said. "I'll never be able to repay him."

"Oh, I'll think of something," Eddie said.

Since Bertram was bringing fresh drinks, Lilly quickly finished the one she had. "What did he do that's so wonderful?"

"Something I didn't think possible. He persuaded the Godfather of New Orleans to clear my grandfather's name."

"Frankie Castalano hired Tony to find the horn an unknown man had given him when he was a teenager. His father Paco, the local head of the mob at the time, took it from him thinking it would cause him to concentrate more on family business."

"Now I remember. Maybe I can use this in my next book," Lilly said. "Tell me more."

"A mob hung Carla's grandfather for a crime he didn't commit. Frankie's dad and granddad were behind the murder leading to the hanging. I helped Tony find the horn, and he persuaded Frankie to act in Carla's behalf."

"What did he do?"

"Leaked the story to a Picayune reporter. It didn't matter anymore because his father, the last person involved in the crime is dead."

"And the horn?"

"Lost for forty years. Thanks to Jason Fasempaur, Frankie now knows the name of the person who gave him the horn."

"You wouldn't be talking about me, now would you?"

It was Jason and Mama coming through the front door. "Where have you two been?" Eddie said.

"Like Bertram says, we had a little bidness to attend to. Now, my whistle needs wetting in the worst way."

Mama hugged Lilly and Carla after scooting into the booth. A horse drawn carriage passed on the street outside the window, its hooves echoing against Bertram's picture window.

"Bert," Lilly yelled. "You have customers."

Bertram's grin had returned when he peeked out the kitchen door.

"Well, look what the cat drug in," he said, bringing drinks for Jason and Mama Mulate. "Not you, Mama. That no good with you."

Mama grabbed Jason's arm, cuddling against him. "I love this no good, I'll have you know."

"Yeah, yeah! We heard that before."

"This time it's true," she said. "At least until Jason returns

286

to Paris."

"If I still have a job left," he said. "I'm ten days overdue already."

"Hell!" Bertram said. "They can't eat you."

Jason grinned. "Literally, no, but figuratively, I'm a pork chop."

"Then do like my old pappy used to say. If you ain't got no control over the situation, start drinking and don't sweat it no more."

Jason hoisted his glass. "Sounds like a plan. Call us a taxi when we reach that point."

"You got it, bro," Bertram said.

Lilly gazed at Jason. "Now, you have my curiosity piqued. Who gave the horn to Frankie Castalano?"

Jason smiled and sipped the whiskey before answering. "Frankie thought the horn had belonged to King Oliver because of the name King engraved on the bell of the horn."

"Who is King Oliver?" Lilly asked.

"Joseph Oliver, a New Orleans cornet player that started out in Storyville. His peers nicknamed him King because when it came to playing the cornet, there was no one better."

"How do you know it wasn't him that gave Frankie the horn?"

"Not possible. Oliver died in 1938. Frankie didn't receive the horn until '59. I recognized Frankie's horn the first time I saw the photo."

"A horn is a horn. They all look pretty much the same to me," Bertram said.

"This one doesn't. It's a King Silver Tone, the bell made of solid sterling silver and engraved with the name King."

"But not for King Oliver," Lilly said.

"That's right. King is the model name of the horn. As it turns out, King Oliver in a manner of speaking did give it to Frankie."

"Now I am confused," Lilly said.

"H.N. White manufactured lots of King Silver Tones over the years. Frankie's is unique."

"How so?"

"It's an artist horn, made by an independent craftsperson

specifically to suit the individual style of the artist intended to play it. It was stamped by H.N. White, but it's unquestionably one-of-a-kind."

Bertram left to mix more drinks, Lilly continuing to look confused.

"How do you know all this?" she asked.

"Because I knew the craftsperson's symbol stamped on the case. The man is dead, but his son still lives here in New Orleans. I've known him forever and gave him a call."

"He told you who his dad made the horn for?"

"Yes, but there's more to the story."

"I'm listening," Lilly said.

"King was a talented musician but not much of a businessman. He lost everything during the Great Depression and spent his last days working as a janitor in a recreation hall in Savannah, Georgia."

"That's horrible!" Lilly said.

"Someone he had mentored eventually became world famous. King had given him his first professional horn when he was just starting out. That person had a horn specially made for him by my friend's father."

"Who?"

"Louis Armstrong."

"You're kidding me."

"King Oliver was already dead before Satchmo could deliver the horn. He kept it, finally deciding to give it to a promising New Orleans' cornet player."

"Frankie?"

Jason nodded. "According to the newspaper, he was performing in town at the time. Tony verified it. He apparently knew about Frankie's recital and decided to deliver the horn in person."

"I'm surprised someone didn't recognize him," Mama said.

"Someone did; Frankie's music teacher. The recital had started, Frankie playing his solo when Satchmo walked down the aisle. He apparently knew Frankie's teacher. After giving him the horn, he swore him to secrecy and then left the building without causing a fuss. Frankie's teacher kept the secret to his grave."

"The instrument must be worth a fortune for historical value alone," Lilly said.

"Frankie doesn't need the money, or the exposure. He was just happy to get it back."

Mama squeezed Carla's hand. "I'm so glad to see you two back together."

"Mom will never stop cooking spaghetti dinners for him, even if I end up hating his guts."

Eddie's eyes rolled. "I haven't given you any reason to hate me."

"Not yet," Carla said. "But the first blue-eyed bombshell you flirt with will get me quite upset."

"She would have to be flirting with me, and I'd just turn the other way," Eddie said.

Carla grinned. "That's like asking a bulldog not to slobber when he sees a bone."

"You're the only bone I'm looking at," Eddie said.

"I love you, Eddie Toledo, though my expectations aren't high."

Eddie bit her earlobe. "You're hurting my feelings. We're a team now. Carla is an expert on the history of this city. After solving her grandfather's mystery, we're working on another puzzle together."

"Such as," Mama said.

"The Metairie Cemetery mystery," Carla said.

Before Mama could quiz them further, Wyatt descended the stairs.

"Hey, Buddy," Jason said. "Come sit with us. We have terrific news for you. Matthieu Courtmanche didn't commit suicide."

"That's good to know," Wyatt said.

"Well, don't you feel a bit of relief?"

"Thanks, Jason. Of course, I do," Wyatt said. "I have other things on my mind right now."

He wasn't smiling and Mama noticed.

"Something wrong, baby?"

"I'll be okay."

"One of your moods?"

"Too bad I don't do well with alcohol."

"Tell Mama what's wrong."

"A woman."

"Latitia Boiset?"

When Wyatt glanced at Eddie and Carla, Eddie averted his gaze to the floor.

"Who is she?" Lilly asked.

"New Orleans' own Creole Angel," Jason said. "The lead singer for a group called Brass & Sass."

"What happened to her?" Lilly said.

"She left for Paris without telling me she was going. Though we just met, I feel as if I've known her forever."

"You have," Jason said.

Bertram came out of the kitchen before Jason could explain.

"Cowboy, something came while you was gone," he said, handing Wyatt an envelope.

"What is it?" Lilly asked.

"A letter from France," Bertram said.

Wyatt took the letter and slid out of the booth. "Thanks. I have to go."

They watched as he disappeared out the door of Bertram's bar without a word of explanation.

"That boy has a moody streak," Eddie said.

"I been dealing with it for years now," Bertram said.

"Who sent the letter?" Lilly asked.

"Miss Latitia, one of the prettiest women I ever seen," he said. "It almost made me blush."

"You read Wyatt's mail?" Mama said.

"Dirty job, but someone has to do it."

"That is just wrong," Mama said.

"You better tell us now," Carla said.

"Or what?"

"Or we're going to kick your Cajun ass," Lilly said, putting him into a headlock.

"Okay, okay," he said. "She and her band is coming back to N'awlin's next month, and she wants to spend some time with Cowboy."

When another carriage passed on the street, Mama scooted

closer to Jason.

"You didn't tell Wyatt about Elise."

"One of these days he'll need to hear the story. Right now, I think he has other things on his mind."

On the Twelfth Day, Mardi Gras would begin. Until then, the Quarter was almost deserted. Wyatt sat alone on a levee overlooking the Mississippi, a full moon illuminating river traffic that never slowed. After smelling the perfume on Latitia's envelope one more time, he stuffed it in his pocket.

A jazz band had cranked up on Bourbon Street, dulcet notes of a cornet solo piercing the silence of the night. The wail of a distant siren, along with the mournful horn of a passing tug, joined the city's serenade.

Fog moved up from the river as Wyatt pulled the jacket around his neck. He desperately needed a sugary beignet and cup of hot coffee, and Cafe du Monde wasn't far away.

End

About the Author

ERIC WILDER is the author of *Big Easy*, *City of Spirits*, *Primal Creatures*, *Ghost of a Chance*, *A Gathering of Diamonds*, *Murder Etouffee*, *Bones of Skeleton Creek*, and *Of Love and Magic*, among other books and novels. He lives in Oklahoma, about a mile from historic Route 66, with his wife Marilyn, five dogs, and one great cat.

CPSIA information can be obtained at www.ICGtesting.com
Printed in the USA
LVOW07s0135300714

396594LV00002B/84/P

9 780979 116575